Doctor *in* Petticoats

SOPHIE'S DAUGHTERS

Doctor *in* Petticoats

MARY CONNEALY

BARBOUR
PUBLISHING

© 2010 by Mary Connealy

ISBN 978-1-60260-146-8

All scripture quotations are taken from the King James Version of the Bible.

This book is a work of fiction. Names, characters, places, and incidents are either products of the author's imagination or used fictitiously. Any similarity to actual people, organizations, and/or events is purely coincidental.

For more information about Mary Connealy, please access the author's Web site at the following Internet address: www.maryconnealy.com

Cover design: Lookout Design, Inc.

Published by Barbour Publishing, Inc., P.O. Box 719, Uhrichsville, OH 44683, www.barbourbooks.com

Our mission is to publish and distribute inspirational products offering exceptional value and biblical encouragement to the masses.

ecpa Member of the
Evangelical Christian
Publishers Association

Printed in the United States of America.

Dedication

I like to include tough women in my books, in case you haven't noticed. I like to think I've raised four tough women. Not so tough in the ways of gun slinging and buck skinning but tough in ways that really count: good hearts, intelligence, and faith. This book is dedicated to them—my daughters Joslyn, Wendy, Shelly, and Katy.

★ One ★

Beth McClellen would die before she missed Mandy's wedding.

That wasn't some cute expression. It was a plain, bald fact.

She would probably be pounded to death any minute now.

The stagecoach, in its four-day-long quest to hit every bump and rock in northwest Texas, lurched into the air then slammed back onto its wheels. She'd planned to take the train all the way to Mosqueros, but a cyclone had ripped out a bridge somewhere and the trains weren't running. So Beth had no choice but to take the much slower stagecoach.

She'd still hoped to make the wedding. But it was cutting things really close. Even with the irritating delay, the stage had appealed to her. Horses, fresh air, Texas scenery—after four years in the teeming city of Boston, she thought the stage was brilliant.

She was an idiot.

The coach tilted up sharply as the trail rose. Beth fell against the seat back. "How can this thing stay in one piece?"

She didn't expect an answer from the drunk across from her and she didn't get one.

He did slide farther down on the seat, slumping sideways, growling in his—well, Beth wasn't about to call it sleep. Stupor was more like it. She braced herself to shove him to the floor if he fell forward onto her. She'd use him as a footrest, and for the first

7

time in days the man would serve some use on this earth.

*Give me strength to keep from knocking him to the floor on purpose,
Lord.*

They reached the hilltop and the ascent switched to descent.
The stage picked up speed and the hooves of the horses rose from
plodding walks to fast clips.

Beth knew it by sound and feel, not sight. She'd closed the
curtains to block out the sun, hoping to also block some of the
billowing dust that seeped through the windows. And if it lessened
the stifling heat of an August Texas a few degrees, it might also
lessen the stench of her fellow rider.

Darkness might keep him asleep, too. She could only pray to
the good Lord it would. The few times he'd been semi-lucid, he
tended to break into rants about the dreadful state of the world.
He'd start with generalities then launch into particulars, muttering
to himself as if she wasn't there and he was a lunatic.

Well, if he thought he was alone, then he was wrong, wrong,
wrong. But he was right on one count—he was definitely a lunatic.

More than once in the last four days, she'd been tempted to
shut him up with the butt end of the pistol she had strapped to
her ankle.

The driver shouted over the thundering hooves of his four
horses. He'd been shouting at the poor horses for days.

Beth was tempted to swing out the door, clamber onto the top
of the stage, and beat the man to within an inch of his life for the
way he pushed his horses. And it didn't pass unnoticed that Beth
was contemplating violence against every man within her reach.

It had been a long trip home.

The driver wasn't completely heartless. They'd stopped several
times and gotten a new team, but the relentless pace, the shouting
of the driver—they wore the poor horses down long before they
finished their run.

Another shout had Beth sitting straighter. It was a new shout,
laced with fear—nothing she'd heard from the driver before.
She pushed aside the curtain on the window and saw the same

desolate, broken range she'd been seeing all day. West Texas, a brutal, barren place.

Her family had found a fertile valley in this desolation, but almost the only one. A rugged, man-eating, soul-crushing country that either hardened people into gleaming white diamonds or pulverized them into useless coal dust.

Beth liked to think she was a diamond. And she'd crushed her share of men into dust right along with Texas.

The trail was narrow. They were rolling quickly down one of the thousand dips in the mountainous area.

The driver shouted again. "Whoa."

That *really* caught her attention. The man never said whoa. Not outside of town. He stopped for *nothing*.

She leaned forward, holding her breath because she was a little too close to the snoring, reeking passenger. She'd been on this stage for four days in the sweltering heat and roiling dust and she was no fresh posy herself, but this guy was ridiculous.

The stagecoach slowed, slid sideways, and picked up speed. The driver shouted and cursed and Beth could see, if she angled her head, the man battling with the brake.

Had the brake given out? Was the stagecoach a runaway? No, not a runaway. She could feel the brakes dragging on the wheels, hear the scrape of the brake as it tried to slow the heavy stage.

"Keep your head. Keep your head." Muttering, Beth knew the side she'd just looked out of rode too close to a rock face that rose high on her left. She slid to the other side of the coach. Before, she'd been too close to the man's feet. Now she could smell his breath.

Inhaling the dusty air and stench through her mouth to make it bearable, she pushed back the curtain on this side and her stomach twisted.

The whole world fell away from this side of the coach.

She stood, holding on to the rocking, jouncing stagecoach. Letting go with one hand, she shoved the door open. Poking her head out she saw. . .disaster. Dead ahead.

Emphasis on dead.

No way was she getting home for that wedding.

A stagecoach lay on its side not a hundred yards down the trail. Bodies everywhere. A quick glance told Beth that five people were unconscious or dead on the ground. If they hit that wreckage, they'd kill any passengers left alive then plunge over the side of the mountain.

Beth saw a horse racing away far down the trail, dragging harness leather behind him. No sign of the three other horses that had pulled the ruined stage. A sudden twist in the trail concealed the accident, but it was still coming.

Beth started praying with every breath. And she asked for the thing this country demanded most.

Lord, give me strength.

The driver shouted again, throwing his whole body on the brake while he sawed on the reins. His horses leaned back until they were nearly sitting on their haunches, fighting the forward motion of the heavy stagecoach. He didn't have the strength to hold the brake *and* the horses on this steep incline.

Beth's ma hadn't raised her to spend a lot of time fretting and wringing her hands. If there was a bronc to bust, Beth busted it. If there was a wagon to pull, Beth hopped out and started pulling before anyone had to ask.

That was the McClellen way.

So helping was a given, and it didn't take but a second to know she wasn't going out on the side that might crush her between the mountain and a racing stage. So the cliff side was her only choice.

One horse whinnied, a terrible, frightened sound. Beth could have wept for the scared animal if she was inclined toward tears— which she wasn't.

The shout and the frightened horse jerked the nasty scourge of a man who was Beth's traveling companion upright in the seat, as if he'd been poked by a pin. "Wha'waz'at?"

Ignoring the idiot, Beth swung herself onto the roof, grateful she'd changed into her riding skirt for the journey home. Just as she heaved herself upward, the stage rounded a bend in this poisonous sidewinder of a trail.

Beth's feet had just hooked over the top of the stage and they slipped. For a terrible second, Beth was thrown out. Her legs dangled over nothingness. Her fingers clawed at the railing atop the stage. Her wrists creaked as the weight of her body fought her slender hands. One hand lost its grip. She clawed frantically for a hold. Her fingers ached; the palms of her hands were scraped raw.

Give me strength.

After heart-pounding seconds of doubt that she had the strength, she regained her hold.

Then the trail straightened and Beth's legs swung back with nearly as much force as they'd flown out. Her boots, with their pointed leather toes, smacked into her fellow passenger.

"Hey!"

It felt like she hit him in the head. That cheered her somewhat and helped her ignore her now-bleeding hands.

Give me strength, Lord. Give me strength.

Scowling at the mess ahead of them on the trail, Beth assumed—if they figured out a way not to die in the next five minutes—they'd be held up for a good long time. She was definitely going to miss the wedding, and that made her mad clean through.

Rage gave her the burst of energy she needed to drag herself onto the roof. She landed on her side on top of her wretched home for the last few days with an *oomph* of pain. She didn't know if God gave strength in the form of rage, but she took it as a gift anyway.

Rolling to her hands and knees, she scooted forward. "Get over!"

The stage driver shouted in surprise and practically jumped off the seat. A stage driver ought to have steadier nerves.

"I can drive a team. Get over and hand me the reins. You concentrate on the brakes."

The man didn't move, staring at her like he was a half-wit.

Beth dropped down beside him and wrenched the reins out of his hands.

"You can't drive this thing." But before he was done yelling, the lout must have noted her experienced grip on the handful of reins. He left her to the horses, turned to the brake, and threw every ounce of his considerable weight against it.

The wheels scratched on the rocky trail, skidding, slowing, shoving the horses along in front of it.

"Whoa!" Beth shouted, rising to her feet, hauling with all her strength—and some strength besides that must have been supplied by the Almighty because the horses responded.

With the stage slowing from the brake, the horses weren't being pushed as hard. They slowed.

It was taking too long.

They came around the next curve. Death and destruction loomed only yards ahead.

Beth leaned harder, bracing her feet, calling to the team in a voice she'd learned years ago got an uncommon response from animals. Her family being the exception, she'd rather be with animals than most people she'd met.

Give me strength. Give me strength. Give me strength.

Suddenly, a weight hit her from behind and almost tossed her headfirst onto the horses' hooves. A viselike arm snaked around her waist to stop her fall. Then, the second she was steady, two hands gripped the reins. And she had the strength of ten.

And the stench told her who was helping her.

High time the drunk got involved in saving his own worthless hide.

The stage driver shouted with exertion. The stage slowed. The wheels locked, sliding now, scratching on the coarse, rocky trail.

They skidded straight for the wreckage. The trail narrowed. No getting around it.

Just ahead the stage lay on its side. It looked like it had rolled at least once, judging by the damage. Doors were broken off, wheels shattered.

Only a miracle had kept the coach from plunging off the edge.

One woman lay closest to Beth's stage. Her four horses would trample the injured woman. Then the stage would roll over what was left of her.

She shouted to the team, but the horses were nearly sitting on their haunches now. The lead horse on the left, a dark red chestnut with black mane and tail, screamed in terror at what lay straight in their path.

Give me strength. Give me strength. Give me strength.

The man's arms flexed. Muscle like corded steel flexed as he pulled and added his voice to the shouts of "Whoa!"

The woman on the ground lying facedown stirred. She raised her chest up with her arms and turned to the noise. Blood soaked her hair and face. Her blue gingham dress had one arm ripped off and the woman's bare shoulder looked raw. Her eyes widened at the oncoming stage. Her mouth gaped in horror as the stage skidded nearer, nearer, nearer.

Twenty feet, then ten, then five.

Give me strength, Lord.

The man behind found more strength and pulled until his muscles bulged.

The stage passed over the woman.

The skidding stopped.

Too late.

★ **T W O** ★

Dust swallowed the stage. Beth was blinded.

The horses had trampled the poor woman.

Give me strength. Give me strength. Give me strength.

Practically throwing herself to the ground in the choking dirt, one battered, bleeding hand slipped on the stage seat and Beth nearly fell. Ignoring her own pain, she hung on grimly, scrambled to the ground, and rushed to the horses' heads.

The woman had rolled off to the side or they'd have crushed her to death. She'd saved herself.

Beth wanted to shout in triumph and give the woman a big hug. Instead, Beth dropped to the rocky, dusty trail beside the bleeding woman. "Lie still. Please." She guided the woman to her back. "Let me make sure you don't have any broken bones."

Beth had trained four years for this. But this was her first real chance to use her medical skills—more doctor than nurse thanks to the generosity of the doctor she'd apprenticed with.

Out of the corner of her eye, Beth saw the stage driver lead the horses to the side, tie them to a scrub pine on the uphill slope, and then rush to the closest victim.

The woman stared sightlessly upward as if the horror had taken a firm hold of her mind and wouldn't release her.

"Don't be afraid." Beth used her horse-soothing voice. People responded well to it, too. Finally she slipped past the lady's terror.

"My husband. Is my husband all right?" The injured lady's face was coated in drying blood. She grabbed the front of Beth's dress with one hand. Her other, more battered arm moved weakly, nearly useless. Beth let the woman drag her forward until their noses almost touched.

Smoothing back the woman's hair, Beth tried to soothe her. "I'll go check your husband."

Beth didn't waste time prying the overwrought woman's hands loose. Instead, she murmured comfort and, even with her head held tight, managed to check the woman's arms and legs, her ribs and head, searching for injuries.

There was obvious swelling along her ribs and the woman winced with pain when Beth pressed, but the bones held. Cracked, not broken—Beth hoped. The bleeding arm was cut to shreds, but the bone was intact. The woman gritted her teeth and dragged in a painful breath when Beth touched too close to the shoulder.

Beth noted the bleeding head wound was more dried than wet. That told its own story of how long these folks had been here—hours most likely, but not days. There was a chance the wounded could still be helped. "Please, let me go so I can check on your husband."

No response.

Give me strength. Give me strength.

This time Beth's strength might be required to tear loose from the death grip.

Suddenly the woman released Beth's collar. "Go." The woman's pain-filled eyes seemed rational. "I—I can tell my arms and legs work. I'll be fine. Go check the others."

Beth gasped for breath then nodded, satisfied the woman didn't need anything right now. God willing, this one would survive. Beth patted the woman's hand. "I'll see to your husband."

Beth stood and raced toward the next victim. She noticed the drunk climbing down from the stage at last, unsteady, more of a danger to the injured than a help. He might trip over them, and if

15

that didn't kill them, his breath would finish them off.

Beth scolded herself. They'd have never gotten the stage stopped without his help.

Fine, she'd stop thinking of him as a waste of human flesh. Now if only the bum would stay downwind.

The stage driver rushed to another victim.

Beth headed for a man pinned under the wrecked coach. His body was crushed. The man was beyond help, and Beth prayed for his soul and any loved ones he'd left behind as she raced on. Another man lay dead beneath the wheels of the stage, his neck bent at a horrible angle, his eyes gaping and empty.

There were six in all. Four alive. Only the woman was conscious.

The woman finally got to her feet and assisted. She found her husband, unconscious but among the living, and turned her attention to him.

The stage driver got a canteen of water and the three of them washed wounds.

Two more of the victims began rousing. One had a badly broken leg.

The woman's husband had a dislocated shoulder. As he awakened, he was maddened with pain. Still only partly conscious, he couldn't lie still, yet every move caused cries of anguish, awful to hear from anyone but somehow worse from a man.

Beth had read of dislocated joints in her studies, but she'd never had the opportunity to try and repair one.

His wife struggled to calm him. Every time he lashed out he'd bump her somehow and she'd gasp with pain.

"What's your name?" Beth asked, trying to get the situation under control. Maybe if they all just took a minute to calm down. . .

"It's Camilla. Camilla Armitage. My husband's name is Leo."

"Mrs. Armitage, you've got to stay away from him," Beth urged the woman. "Leo doesn't know you're here so you're not helping. Your arm has started bleeding again. We don't want that to get worse. And I'm sure you have cracked ribs. A blow landed just right could break them. Your husband will be sick to think he did such a thing to you. Please just move back."

"He needs me. I'll be fine." The woman's chin firmed stubbornly and Beth didn't waste more time trying to get her to move away.

Beth couldn't restrain the poor man. With one furious glance at the drunk who sat, staring away from the carnage, turning his back to the whole mess, Beth said to the driver, "We've got to pop his shoulder back into its socket. It takes a lot of strength. And someone needs to hold him down bodily. That will anchor him and give me something to pull against."

The driver gave her a long, quiet look. "I should be the one pulling. I've never done it before, but I can try."

"You should, but I don't have the weight to anchor him." She reached for Leo's arm. "It has to be held out straight, jerked hard—"

Before Beth could do more than lift the arm, the man screamed in pain and struck out. He caught her in the face and knocked her flat on her backside.

Beth felt her temper rise.

The woman must have noticed and been afraid of what Beth might do. "Please, my Leo is a good man. A gentle man. He'd never do such a thing if he was awake."

It was the absolute truth that the man was beyond rational thought.

The stage driver knelt beside the flailing man. These struggles deepened Leo's agony.

Beth knew it would take three people. One to hold his shoulders down—the man's wife was already trying to do that, through her tears, and failing. One to restrain his feet so he was motionless. One to jerk on the arm and hopefully to reset the joint.

Shuddering to think of the pain they'd soon cause the man, Beth was suddenly furious at the bum who sat there, not helping. True, he'd come through and helped pull the stage to a stop, but that was to save his own pathetic, drunken life. Wasn't it? When it came to helping others, he was worthless.

She hadn't actually seen him take a single drink on the whole trip. She suspected he'd drained his flask quite a while ago. In fact, she'd never seen the flask, assuming he was sneaking nips on the sly at the beginning of the trip then sleeping it off the rest of the way.

Beth surged to her feet. "We need help over here!"

The man didn't even look up. He stared as if asleep with his eyes open.

Well, Beth wasn't one to let a good temper tantrum go to waste, and seriously, this afternoon had worn her out right to her last bit of restraint. . .and beyond. Who better to punish?

She looked down at the stage driver and the woman, struggling to hold the man in place. "I'm going to get us some help."

The stage driver looked with distaste at the other passenger. "Good luck."

Beth whirled and used the hundred-foot downhill march to get her knees to stop shaking. Not because she was afraid of this man—she still had her gun butt—but because the afternoon had just been more than too much.

She stomped to the man's side, and carefully considering her approach—or maybe not so carefully—she grabbed the man's filthy, flattened, black Stetson off his head and swatted him with it.

"Hey!" He turned as if surprised to see her.

"I didn't exactly sneak up on you, now did I?" She whaled on him again.

He shielded his face. His once-white shirt tore up one side at his sudden movement. "Will you stop that?"

The sound of the ripping fabric—good grief, it looked like silk—gave Beth a sense of doing the Lord's work. She wondered how long he'd been wearing it. The cloth must be rotten to tear so easily.

"Do I have your attention, you miserable worm?" Beth threw the hat at his head.

He held his arms over his face, the bedraggled white sleeves rolled up nearly to his elbows, and glared through his wrists at her. His eyes narrowed.

It occurred to Beth that the man might be dangerous. Well, she could be dangerous, too. If he was, she'd make him sorry he showed that side of himself.

Doing her very best to set his skin on fire with her eyes, she leaned down, hoping to find a balance where she could rage at him without Mrs. Armitage hearing her. The poor woman had been through enough. "You get up off the ground and help us, you worthless skunk!"

And wasn't *skunk* just exactly the right word for the filthy pig?

"Get away from me." The wormy, skunky pig's eyes flashed like he had rabies.

Gritting her teeth so she could look fierce and still breathe through her mouth, she leaned closer. "You stand up right now." She hissed at him like a rattlesnake, so she had a few animal attributes of her own. "I need *help*. I don't care how drunk you are, how lazy you are, or how *stupid* you are. Right now I need some muscle, and I know you've got it. Get on your feet and get over there and help us, or so help me I will rip your arm off and beat you to *death* with the bloody stump."

The man's eyes seemed to clear. Maybe she'd pierced the alcoholic fog. "I'm not drunk."

Interesting that he hadn't protested being called stupid or worthless or a skunk. . .what else had she called him? She'd lost track of her insults somewhere along the line.

"Oh, *puh-leeze*, you expect me to believe you're this worthless without the help of whiskey?" Beth jammed her fists on her hips and straightened away from him. She had to get some air. "If that's true then I might as well shoot you here and now. Do the whole world a favor."

The drunk's eyes slid from her to the writhing man.

Beth had always been sensitive to others. Her ma had told her many times that was her finest gift. Right now it felt like a curse.

Beth saw something so vulnerable and fragile in the man's

eyes that she almost regretted asking for help. It wasn't fear or laziness or stupidity or drunkenness. It was as if Leo's suffering ate into this man's soul.

"What's your name?" Beth asked quietly, very much afraid the man was on the verge of running.

"Alexander." He rubbed one hand over his grizzled, unshaven cheeks, his eyes imprisoned by the sight of the man's agony. "Alex Buchanan."

What horror had Alex seen to put such a look in his eyes? Beth couldn't give him the break he so desperately needed. "I can't do it without help. Please, Alex. Please. We can end Leo's suffering."

"He'll still hurt. Dislocated shoulders take a long time to heal."

Beth realized what the man had just admitted. He knew something about healing.

"Yes, it'll take time to heal, but the second that joint is back in place the pain will lessen. Please." She stiffened her compassionate spine. "You've got one more chance to say yes then I'm taking your hat to you again."

Alex didn't look at her. Instead, riveted on Leo, he pushed himself to his feet. His eyes filled with tears. His lips moved silently.

She wondered if it was a prayer. He didn't strike her as the praying kind.

He swiped his sleeve across his forehead, in a way meant to disguise wiping his eyes. "I...I can't. I can't help him." He wheeled away from the blood and pain.

Beth caught his forearm with a hard slap of flesh on flesh. "You don't have a choice."

"I do."

Beth was afraid she might have to tackle him. "I'm not giving you one."

Alex turned, stared at her. Their eyes locked.

Seconds stretched to a minute, maybe longer. Growing slowly, a sensation Beth had never felt before almost made her let go, back away. Those eyes, it was as if he was looking all the way into her soul. She felt strength drain from her as if he was drawing on reserves within her, soaking up courage like desert ground in a rainstorm.

Her hand was on his wrist, and out of habit, she slid her fingers a bit to feel his pulse slamming at double the rate it should have. To Beth's sensitive touch it was as if his very blood cried out to be delivered from what he had to do.

God, give me strength. Strength enough for us both.

Still Alex watched her, drew from her. Leo fell silent, or maybe Beth was drawn so deeply into Alex's eyes that she couldn't connect with the world anymore.

Finally, Alex's eyes fell shut. Beth saw tears again, along the rims of his lashes, thick dark lashes to match hair, hanging long, nearly in ringlets around his neck.

His lips kept moving. She held on to his wrist, to lend support now rather than to restrain him. Then he started nodding. He physically changed—he seemed to grow taller, his shoulders squared, his chin came up. When he opened his eyes, a new man was there. Or maybe an old man, the man Alex Buchanan used to be before he crawled inside a bottle.

Beth could see what this was costing him. As if he paid for this courage by stripping off his skin with a razor.

He'd awakened something in her while their eyes were locked, something brand new.

"Let's do it," he said.

She'd never been so proud of anyone in her life.

Three

Alex had never been so ashamed.

He turned away from the little spitfire who had more guts in one arched, white-blond eyebrow than he had in his whole body.

The blood. No, never again. . .Shut up. Do it and forget it.

Alex had played this game the whole time he'd been in the army. Talking to himself, beating himself up, goading himself until he could do what needed to be done. He'd gotten out, and after four years he was still haunted by the things he'd seen.

Ignoring what it did to him. Ignoring the agony in his soul. Turning away from *this* feeling and *that* feeling, until he'd turned away from so much of himself he was barely human.

By the time he'd stopped, it had been far too late to regain his humanity.

He stumbled. The pretty blond steadied him.

A weakling, held up by a slender girl.

Why did he let this tear him apart?

He moved closer to the man.

Do it. Forget it. Don't feel it. . . . The blood. The pain.

Alex was going to make it so much worse.

But then he'll get better. Hurt him to heal him.

Alex knew all the reasons behind inflicting agony on patients. He detached himself from his feelings to the extent possible.

She thought he was a drunk. If only it were that simple. If only drink helped. He lived like a drunk—slept most of the time, was haunted the rest. Always moving, worthless, broke—or as good as because the money he had was like poison to him, dollars earned in blood and pain.

Digging deep into his scarred soul, Alex crouched by the man's side. He began speaking. He had a knack, he knew it. But there was a terrible cost to remaining calm in the midst of mayhem.

The spitfire had said his name. Alex wished he didn't remember. "Leo?"

The man wasn't lucid. His eyes opened, maybe in response to his name but more likely just in response to a voice. His pupils were dilated. There was no focus, no reason.

Alex ran his hands over the man's skull while he studied the wife. "What's your name, ma'am?"

He wasn't used to women. There'd been a few he'd had to work with but not many. Women were the worst. This one was so battered, covered in her own blood; Alex wondered if he might start crying like a girl child. The final shame—or no, who was he kidding? There was no end to the shame.

"Camilla Armitage."

"I had a creek that ran by my home in upstate New York when I was a child. We call it Camy Creek. I wonder if it was named after a woman named Camilla. You've had a terrible day, haven't you, Camilla?"

She nodded. "My Leo calls me Camy sometimes." Her hand moved on her husband's arm, caressing, comforting, strong enough to stick even when it was so hard. Stronger than Alex.

"Your husband is going to be fine. He's in terrible pain and this is going to hurt for a while. He's got torn tendons and muscle damage but it will all heal. He'll favor the arm for a few weeks, maybe a month, but even at that, with a sling, he'll be able to be up and walking. He'll be fine."

Some of the fear eased from Mrs. Armitage's eyes. Alex thought the man calmed a bit, too, still not clearheaded, but Alex's voice was reaching past the confusion. There was a terrible goose egg on the crown of the man's head that explained his incoherence.

Alex continued speaking softly, practically singing as he moved from Leo's head, down his unaffected arm, trying to get the man to just be calm, relax, trust.

My touch doesn't hurt you. My hands are healing hands.

Duping him to relax so Alex could turn to the ugly dislocated shoulder and betray his patient, inflict horrible pain on him. "No injury to this arm. No fractures anywhere. No stitches needed. Your shoulder will be tender for a few days, but the humerus isn't compromised. The clavicle and scapula are intact."

He heard the little spitfire who'd slapped him around gasp. That might well mean she knew some of these words. Well, she thought she knew everything, so why not this?

She knelt beside him, by Leo's knees, across from the driver. Poor Leo was surrounded.

Alex reminded himself that there were other wounded and he'd soon be called upon to help them. Controlling a deep inner shaking, he kept talking. "The deltoideus muscle is the one on top of the shoulder." Information meant little to the suffering couple, but any words were comforting. "And pectoralis muscles are on the chest. They're bruised and they'll be sore like any strained muscle, but they'll heal."

Leo had a wild look—the whites showing around his pupils like a terrified horse. But that eased. He still wasn't fully conscious, and he'd probably be addled for the next twenty-four hours and, in the end, not remember a thing Alex did to him.

But in the next few seconds, the man was going to hate Alex enough to kill.

The stage driver was holding the man's feet so securely that Leo had quit trying to fight the driver's firm grip.

As Alex slid one hand over Leo's chest, testing for cracked ribs, he reached sideways for the spitfire's hand and guided her to touch Leo's chest, flattening her hands. He flicked a glance at her, telling her with his eyes that it was time—never letting that warning sound in his voice as he soothed Leo.

She nodded. She knew what lay ahead. Good.

"Now." In one smooth motion, Alex grabbed Leo's wrist and upper arm, straightened it, and jerked.

An audible pop sounded a split second before the man's scream. His shoulder snapped back into its socket.

Leo's wife held his other hand, but she didn't have a good enough grip. The man flailed, shouted with agony, wrenched his hand free, and slugged Alex in the face so hard he fell over backward.

Alex kept going, scrambling backward like a frightened bug.

After the first eruption, Leo subsided. All his screaming cut off. The pain was manageable now. The madness was over.

And Alex felt the blood pouring from his nose and turned. Crawling on his hands and knees like a baby, he made it to the cliff alongside the trail, hung his head over the edge, and vomited.

The spitfire came up beside him and steadied him with a hand on his shoulders. Whispering gracious words, thanks, encouragement, Alex thought she'd have done the world a favor if she just shoved him over the edge.

Then, maybe, his nightmares would finally stop. The accumulated screams of agony would be quieted in his brain, the flashes of blood and gore, severed limbs, the dead and dying.

When it was over, he sank to his belly on the ground, his head still extended in midair as all the memories flooded back.

A cloth wiped his face. Damp. The spitfire had found water. Well, of course there'd have been a canteen or two on the stage.

He lay there, looking down, down, down.

The spitfire had her own soothing voice. He recognized it.

Then his eyes sharpened on the broken crags beneath him, and he saw that they hadn't counted all the dead. A young woman lay down there, way off to his right. Her eyes, wide, locked right on him, looked into him as if she hated him for not saving her.

He had to get down there, help her somehow. Alex launched himself to his feet. His legs went out from under him.

The spitfire knocked him away from the ledge, flipped him on his back, and wrapped his hands in something that immobilized them. "Give me strength," the woman muttered under her breath.

Why would she want even more strength than she already had? Near as Alex could make out, the woman could have subdued the entire unsettled West with one hand tied behind her back.

"What are you doing?" He found himself hog-tied as tightly as a calf set for branding.

She knelt beside him and glared down into his eyes. But her voice was sweet as sugar. "I still need you, so you're not going down there."

"I've got to save her."

"She's dead," the spitfire hissed as if someone had splattered water on her red-hot temper. She took a quick look behind her, and Alex realized Mrs. Armitage, now cradling her husband's head in her lap and cooing to him, was listening to every word they said.

Was that young woman at the bottom of the cliff the Armitages' daughter? He couldn't know, but a shouting match over the poor thing wouldn't help anyone.

He quit struggling. "Untie me."

"No."

"No?" He wanted to launch his body at her, tackle her, but he didn't.

"That's right. No. You understand short words. That's a good sign, but even half-wits understand that, so I'm still leaving you tied up."

"You can't just say no."

"Can and did. You're staying right here until I believe you've got yourself under control."

Alex saw the stage driver kneeling beside someone else. Another victim. Alex hadn't even gone to take a look at this one. Yet.

He looked back at Miss Spitfire. He was on real thin ice. . .as if there'd ever be anything so cool as ice in this brutal, arid stretch of Texas. He decided to try and act sane. . .for a change.

"I—I know she's—" He couldn't say it.

"Dead." The fire faded from her eyes, replaced by worry. "I'm sorry but the word you're looking for is—*dead*."

Alex flinched. "I'm not looking for that word."

"You say you need to go down and help her, but it seemed to me like you were getting ready to throw yourself off a cliff. Considering the semi-lunatic behavior you've exhibited up until now, I suppose it's possible you thought you could help her. But since there's no path, nothing but a sheer drop, it amounted to killing yourself. I decided to act first and ask questions later. Not much good asking questions once you'd pitched yourself over the edge, now was there?"

He tasted the panic over seeing that girl down there, obviously another victim of this stagecoach accident. It was a terrible fall. Of course she was beyond help. He *was* looking for the word dead.

"You're right. I wasn't thinking clearly. All I could hear was her—" No sense removing all doubt from her mind that she was dealing with a crazy man. Alex had gotten lost in the gaping eyes and the woman's hate for him because he failed her.

"She seemed to be begging for help. I heard it, too."

He snapped back into the present and looked into the spitfire's eyes. Blue eyes. Blue. So blue. His were as dark as his broken soul. Her voice, too. She had the gift of soothing with her voice. A caretaker's voice. He shared that with her. Except he hadn't shared his soothing voice with anyone for a long time. And he hoped to never share it again.

Now she was soothing him. He wanted so desperately to believe that was possible, to calm the madness of his memories.

She'd called it right. He *was* a crazy man.

"I'd like for you to untie me. I need to check the other victims and make a sling for Leo's arm."

She studied him, weighing his demeanor, thinking, he knew, about that moment when he'd almost gone over that ledge. Then she produced a knife that gleamed in the late afternoon sun and slashed the leather straps on his arms. "I can use the help. We're going to have to get that other stagecoach out of the way so we can drive on. It's going to take all the strength we have. And then some."

Alex sat up. The spitfire stood and extended her hand. He took it but did his best to stand on his own and not tax her strength, though she had so much.

When he was upright, he found himself far too close to those blue eyes and a craving was in him to hear her voice again, soothing him. "Thank you."

"You're a doctor." She wound the strips of leather around her waist. She'd tied him up with her belt?

He hadn't noticed it there before, but he didn't notice much anymore. "No, I'm not."

"Yes, you are. I don't know anyone else who would use the terms you did. *Humerus, clavicle, deltoideus*—those are words only doctors and nurses know. And you handled that dislocated shoulder with too much skill to have picked up some tricks on the trail. You've had training. You're a doctor."

"If you can call four years sucked into the carnage of war training. If hacking off limbs with little more than a butcher knife, digging bullets out of the arms and legs of screaming men, and using a branding iron to cauterize a wound is training, then yes, I guess I'm a doctor."

"It counted today. You helped that man." Such kindness, such a beautiful tone.

He felt like he dared to admit some of what boiled inside. "I had to hurt him to help him."

The spitfire used her eyes on him, as if she was hunting around inside his head, looking for—what? Some sign of intelligence probably.

"It figures you'd look at the help you gave that man and find a reason to hate yourself for healing him. It just figures."

Alex knew he shouldn't ask. He'd lived too long to ask. But she was so lovely, and her eyes were so blue, and she was talking and he wanted her to keep on. "Why does it figure?"

"Because, Alexander Buchanan"—

He saw it in her eyes and he'd asked, so he had it coming.

—"you are measuring up to be a complete idiot."

And that was nothing less than the truth, his high grades in medical school notwithstanding.

"Now don't make me tie you up again, because the next time, I swear, when I'm done with you, you'll be taking a nap all the way to the next town."

Alex turned to Leo, hoping for a bit more kindness from the man he'd put through torture a few minutes ago.

Four

Beth thought it was fair to say she had a God-given gift for compassion mixed with toughness.

But it'd been a long day.

Right now, she was within a hair's breadth of showing her toughness with the back of her hand on her brand-new friend, Alex "The Skunk" Buchanan—guaranteed mental patient. She was slap out of compassion.

This wasn't the first time Beth had noticed that in Texas they let mental patients roam free. Texans figured living in Texas cleared their heads or killed them, either one solving the problem.

Beth fetched her doctor's bag out of the stagecoach and set to work on the wounded. The rest of the troop of injured were finally seen to. Alex seemed capable enough, but there was a mild thread of panic running under every word he spoke and every move he made. Alex expertly splinted one older man's leg. Beth put Leo's arm in a sling and bandaged Mrs. Armitage's head. Camilla was working as hard as Beth and the stage driver.

The third victim, a youngish man dressed like he lived in the city, came around and, though battered, seemed to have no major injuries. He was addled enough to be no help though. And Beth could have used more help.

"What about the young woman?" Beth asked Mrs. Armitage

after a final adjustment to the older man's broken leg.

Mrs. Armitage's jaw clenched and her eyes went to the ledge as if she felt guilty for not looking. "The one who fell to her death?"

Beth caught her arm. "You don't need to see her. Did you know her name?"

"It was Celeste. Celeste Gray."

Gray. Beth recognized the name of the man Mandy had just married. Not a common name but not that rare either. Was this young woman on her way to Mandy's wedding? She could very well be. The cyclone that had torn out the bridge had come through several days ago.

Suddenly it was far more personal. That young woman down there might well be Mandy's sister-in-law or perhaps a cousin. That made her Beth's family, too. Beth had no idea what to do about it. No one could go down there to get her, but leaving her in the open was obscene. They'd dragged the bodies of the two dead men off to the side of the trail with plans to come back later for them. There'd be no burial on this stony ground. Maybe whoever came back could bring enough rope to go down for poor Celeste.

With a sharp shake of her head, Beth turned back to Mrs. Armitage. "We've got everyone as patched as we're going to get them. We need to move."

The stage driver, who called himself Whip, heard Beth and turned to study the wreckage and his own restless team.

"Can we get turned around and go back?" Beth asked.

"Nope, too narrow."

"Then we either walk out of here or shove the wrecked coach off the ledge. It's beyond repair, so setting it on its wheels would do no good." Beth studied the terrain, her available help, and the weight of that broken-down stage.

"There's a nice length of rope on the back of your stage, Whip. Go fetch it and unharness your team." Beth went to the damaged stage and took every inch of rope and leather off it she could find.

"What'a'ya got in mind?" the driver asked.

"We'll rig a pulley to that overhanging tree up there"—Beth pointed—"and use the horses' strength to knock that stage the rest of the way off the trail."

"No, wait!" Mrs. Armitage cried out.

Beth turned. The distraught woman was still bloody. They didn't have enough water to spare to wash her clean. Under the blood her skin had gone deathly pale.

"What is it?"

"My husband's satchel—it has money in it. I don't know what we'll do if we lose it. I have to get it out."

"No." Alex had moved away from the group once the doctoring was done and had been studiously looking down the trail with longing eyes as if tempted nearly beyond control to desert them all. "That stage is too close to the edge. No one's going in there to get anything."

"It's wedged tight, Alex." Beth regretted overruling him the first time he'd shown any spunk, but there was no reason they couldn't give poor Camilla this bit of comfort. "I'll get it."

"No!" Alex strode toward Beth. "You won't! No amount of money is worth your life." He came close enough that his voice, dropping to a barely audible whisper, only reached her. "You only get one life, you understand? Don't kid yourself that you'll get lucky or be fast enough or smart enough to get in and out. It's too big a risk."

Beth tried to help him. She understood, at least somewhat, that he was traumatized, and she felt sympathy for him. But the stage wasn't going to slide anywhere. "It's going to take every ounce of strength every one of us *and* the horses have to pull it off those rocks and get it off the trail." She rested her hand on his forearm and tried to soothe him. "I know life is precious, Alex. I would never put myself in danger for money. But there's no danger. You're overreacting."

"I'm not." His arm jerked away from her touch and he grabbed her wrist. "And you're not doing it."

Beth—short on compassion—was tempted to hog-tie him again. In fact, she was looking forward to it. In fact, she found herself looking forward to it so much she decided she couldn't trust herself and held up. Rather than jerk away from him—and honesty forced her to admit she wasn't all that sure she could break his iron hold—she leaned closer. "Get your hands off of me. I don't know if you're sane enough to know you're about half-crazy, but your judgment is pathetic. I can't trust a single thing you say. There is no risk, and if getting that woman's things will put her mind at ease then I'm doing it. Now let go of me *right now* or I will make you regret you were ever born."

Alex's fingers tightened. Their eyes held. It wasn't like before when Beth felt him sucking the energy from her. He was trying to dominate her with his will, his fierceness, his grip.

She almost smiled. It was kind of sweet, his trying that when he had to know he didn't stand a chance. Crazy or not, he did have her best interests at heart. Still, she knew she'd slug him if he didn't let go and do it fast. "I'm gonna count to three."

Alex's hand almost had a spasm, but at last he let go. "Fine!" He practically threw her arm away from him. "Risk your life, maybe die for a few dollars. That's what most people would do. I expected better of you though. You seem like a woman with a shred or two of sense."

Well, that hurt.

She glared at him then turned to the stage. "It's wedged in that narrow part of the trail like a rock. It couldn't begin to fall."

Alex's response was a noise so rude Beth barely kept her back to him. Averting her eyes from the two men pinned and dead beneath the coach, she called out, "I'm going to throw everything out. Gather what needs to be taken."

Beth tried her very best to give Alex credit for worrying about her. But she'd already learned the poor guy worried about everything, so this was no great surprise.

Grimly, she climbed up the stage, which lay on its side. It was a shame it wasn't teetering on the cliff's edge. Then one good shove might have solved their problems. Instead it had slammed into a rocky outcropping on the downhill side and was wedged tight.

Gaining the top, which was in fact the side, she found the door ripped off and gone. Inside, a few satchels and bags were jumbled around. Any larger parcels and crates would have been strapped on the roof, and she'd noticed a few scattered here and there.

She lightly swung her body down into the tipped-over box. It was disorienting to be in the stage while it was on its side. She didn't like the feeling of the whole world being tipped on its axis, so she quickly began tossing things out the door, making sure they went onto the trail rather than over the cliff.

Wedged under the seat lay a heavy reticule of black velvet. Maybe Mrs. Armitage's purse?

Beth grabbed it just as an awful crack sounded from outside the stage. A crash of tumbling stones scared her as if she'd heard a gunshot.

The stage rolled toward the cliff.

★ **Five** ★

"Sophie, I'm worried about Beth." Clay McClellen clamped his hat on his head and stared down the trail out of town to the east.

"She's late. And she's going to want to see you, Mandy." Sophie didn't grab Mandy's arm, but Mandy could tell her ma wanted to, badly. And it was all Mandy could do to not grab right back.

"Ma, we've gotta go." Mandy hated it, but Sidney was right, they needed to hit the trail. They were already getting a late start. Yes, it was still blazing hot. But winter came early in the mountains. Pa knew it and admitted that every day lessened their chances of settling in well before winter came to the Colorado Rockies.

Mandy adjusted her Winchester 73 on her shoulder, so the rifle hung at an angle on her back, the muzzle pointing down by her right hip, the butt end of the gun pointing up by her left shoulder. She was barely aware of touching the rifle, and yet she never forgot it was there. She felt vulnerable without it and had rearmed herself immediately following her wedding ceremony.

Sidney didn't like her rifle much. But apparently he liked her enough to put up with the ever-present firearm.

The Wild West was a lot tamer when a body had a steady hand and was a dead eye with a Winchester. And Mandy had both and she liked tame, even if she had to do the taming herself.

And now it looked like she was going somewhere even wilder than West Texas, if there was such a thing.

"Beth was hoping to be here on the afternoon stage. She'll want to see you. Surely you can wait until tomorrow morning."

Mandy threw her arms around her mother's neck, mostly so Ma couldn't see her face and know how scared she was of setting off across half the country in search of a new, better home. The home she had right now was as nice as any Mandy had ever dreamed of, so the idea didn't hold much appeal. When she'd accepted Sidney's proposal, she'd never reckoned on moving halfway across the country.

Sidney came close and slid his arm around Mandy's waist and pulled her close. "We've got to go, Mrs. Gray." He was on her left. Sidney had learned fast she didn't like her shooting arm impeded. It gave her an itch between her shoulder blades.

Letting loose of her ma almost felt like tearing her own skin, but Mandy needed to leave her mother and her home and cleave unto her husband. The Bible was clear.

Settling against his side, Mandy's heart raced. This happened every time Sidney got close. Love had hit her so hard it left her breathless, and when Sidney had proposed after they'd only known each other a month, she'd felt such joy she could have sprouted wings and flown straight to heaven.

"I'm sorry," he whispered in her ear and made her shiver. "If we don't catch this stage, we'll miss the train. It'll be another week before there's a stage heading north out of Mosqueros. I really am sorry." His hand caressed her side, up and down. His voice settled somewhere deep in Mandy's heart.

She couldn't believe her good luck in snaring such a fine man. Handsome and strong and sweet. Rich, too, and he looked so nice in his store-bought suit. He had studied the possibilities of opening a law office in Mosqueros. But he decided a week before their wedding—after a month and three weeks of almost no lawyer business—that he had to go elsewhere. He had a line on a law office that needed a partner near bustling Denver, Colorado.

The jingle of iron in the traces made Mandy glance over her shoulder. The stage driver was almost finished getting his fresh team harnessed.

Not seeing Beth was unthinkable. Her little sister hadn't been home for four long years. But Sidney was her husband now. He was head of the house. Mandy had promised to obey and she intended to keep that promise.

She looked at the trail, praying for Beth's stage to round the corner of Mosqueros's rutted Main Street, bringing her little sister home. Just a hug, just ten seconds to tell Beth how much she'd missed her.

Mandy knew how far away this journey would take her. It was very possible—probable in fact—that she would never see her family again. She fought the tears by thinking of sweet Sidney. Mandy couldn't let Ma sway her into cajoling Sidney to wait yet again. "Ma, she was supposed to be here three days ago on the train. We held the wedding off until this morning for her because her telegram said she'd be coming on the stage yesterday."

Sidney had been irritated. He'd made no secret of not wanting to spend his wedding night sitting up on a bouncing stage. He'd complied with her wishes finally, but it had been their first fight, the first time she'd really gotten a glimpse of Sidney's hot temper, and it was all Mandy's fault. She was going to do her best to be a perfect wife and never make him unhappy again. She didn't dare ask him to delay their departure.

"You know they've broken down or something, Ma. She's not going to get here."

"I'm going to ride out and meet the stage." Pa glared at the street as if he blamed the very ground for preventing Beth's homecoming. "If there's trouble, I'll help 'em clear it up. I'm taking an extra horse, and even if they're broke down, Beth could ride hard for home and get here by morning."

Leaving Pa was almost harder than leaving Ma, but Mandy had found a man just as brave and true. That made it bearable.

"I don't think you gave the law office in Mosqueros a fair try,

Sid. Taking off for the mountains this time of year, with winter only a couple of months away, is reckless. Winter comes early in the Rockies. I know. I grew up there."

A quick, almost painful spasm of Sidney's fingers on her side reminded her how annoyed he got when someone called him Sid. "We'll be fine if we go now, sir." His fingers relaxed and he caressed her side again.

Mandy loved the respectful way Sidney talked to her pa. Even if he was irritated, he remained a real gentleman.

Pa didn't approve of this marriage, just because it had happened so fast. Mandy got half a dozen stern lectures since she'd announced her engagement, but she knew her heart and she wanted Sidney.

She was too old to still be single, an old maid of twenty-two. And the truth was, she'd run off her share of men waiting for a prince. He'd finally come. Just an hour ago they'd said their vows and she was now Mrs. Sidney Gray.

And anyway, Mandy'd never had a boyfriend that Clay McClellen thought was good enough, so Pa's disapproval didn't mean a whole lot.

"Denver is a fast-growing town." Sidney's hand moved steadily on her side, so comforting. "I've got work lined up."

"I thought you just had a line on a job." Pa adjusted his hat, pulling the front brim low. "It didn't sound like a sure thing to me."

"We'll be fine, sir. We'll be settled and safe before the first snow flies."

"You should spend the winter here. There's room in our house if you don't find the right place in Mosqueros. Then you could start out in the spring if the lawyer business hasn't picked up here." Pa held Sidney's eyes for too long.

Mandy looked at her ma and glared, hoping for once Sophie could control her husband.

With a little shrug, Ma just stayed out of it. Ma never stayed out of anything unless she wanted to, which meant she wanted Mandy to stay, too. It was understandable. Her parents loved her and she loved them. But it was time to grow up.

"Load up!" the stage driver hollered. There were two other people waiting on the wooden sidewalk by the stage station.

Mandy threw her arms around first Ma, then Pa. Then she went down the line, hugging her two little sisters.

Sally, a reckless tomboy of seventeen, was dressed—under protest—in a riding skirt. She wore buckskin pants on the range. Ma had given up trying to make her behave like a proper lady, except in town, and Sally almost never came to town except for church, so the girl nearly lived in disgraceful men's pants. But despite her boyish behavior, Sally hugged her fiercely with all the love in her unconventional little heart.

Eleven-year-old Laurie was next. She was overly proper, as if her whole life was a reaction against Sally's refusal to be ladylike. Laurie's eyes filled with tears as she hugged Mandy tight. "I don't want you to go." Laurie's voice broke and Mandy remembered the hand she'd had in raising her littlest sister.

Four little brothers needed a hug, then Adam, a longtime friend of the McClellen family who owned a ranch near them, and his wife, Tillie, a former slave who'd been kept in chains long after the War Between the States had ended. Mandy considered them and their brood family. She didn't bother trying to hug Buff— she knew it'd embarrass him to death—but she said good-bye. "Where's Luther?" How could he have missed seeing her off?

Buff stood, clutching his coonskin cap in both hands, dressed in heavy leather that had to be smothering in the heat. He turned his head toward the end of the street and nodded.

Mandy turned and saw Luther coming, riding his horse and pulling a second horse behind him.

"I had Luther pack some things for you to set up housekeeping," Ma said.

"We're burnin' daylight!" the stage driver shouted and gave Mandy and Sidney a surly look. The other passengers were aboard.

Mandy glanced frantically at Luther. She had to tell him good-bye. She had to.

39

Luther helped load a big box on the stage, giving Mandy a chance to hug everyone one more time. When she threw her arms around Luther, his cheeks turned pink under his full beard. He and Buff had been like kindly uncles to the McClellen brood for years.

With a smile that she kept locked on her face to keep the tears at bay, Mandy let Sidney pull her toward the stage. Amid waves and shouts of good-bye, she climbed aboard the crowded stage, heartbroken to leave her family, devastated to miss Beth, and thrilled to be with the man she adored.

She slid the strap of her Winchester off over her head and settled her rifle between her and the stagecoach wall, the trigger close to her right hand. She rubbed on the little callus that had formed on her trigger finger and fought down the flicker of fury toward her new husband who couldn't wait another week to take her halfway across the country. When she had her anger under control, she looked out the window to wave one last time. They all waved back almost frantically. Then Pa tipped his hat to the family, swung up onto his horse, and rode off in the direction of Beth.

Sidney's arm slipped around her waist.

She smiled at him but tried, with her eyes, to warn him to behave with the two men sitting across from them.

Sidney leaned down and kissed her on the neck.

Mandy was embarrassed to death and slid as far from him as possible in the cramped space.

Sidney just followed. "We'll be in town late tonight." When he had her cornered, he dropped his voice to a whisper. "We'll have ourselves a wedding night, Mandy."

She shivered, but it wasn't with pleasure. The two passengers were watching every move. One had his eyes fixed on them. The other was pretending not to stare, but Mandy caught him peeking.

"We should have been married days ago. . .weeks ago. We would have if we hadn't put the wedding off for so long for your sister."

Mandy pushed on Sidney's chest forcefully and spoke sharply. "Now behave." She smiled at him when she realized how harsh she'd sounded.

He frowned. She'd seen him frown before, but never quite like this and never at her. She'd annoyed him. Her heart trembled to know she'd made him unhappy. How could she fix it? Certainly not by letting him kiss her in front of others.

"Tell me when the train we're meeting is coming in." Distract him. That might do it.

"Early tomorrow morning."

With a sigh, Mandy said, "We had to take this stage, I know, to get there, but I would have loved to see Beth." Tears burned at her eyes.

"I'm your family now, Mandy." He straightened away from her. The annoyance in his eyes flashed to true anger. "Your loyalty is supposed to be to me."

Mandy noticed both men straighten subtly as if. . . But no, they couldn't think she would need protection from her husband. Rushing to calm Sidney down, she smiled. "It is to you. I just love my sister and miss her, but I'm here with you now, aren't I? I love you, and I'm excited about our new life in Colorado."

She was stunned by her new life in Colorado. She'd had no notion that Sidney wasn't settled in Mosqueros when she'd accepted his proposal. But she loved him and would follow him anywhere.

His mouth was a tense line and he watched her, as if judging her words. Finally, he turned and put the length of the seat between them and pushed the curtain aside to look out the window.

Mandy felt awful. Married two hours and she'd already done something wrong. She had no way to fix it now though, not with an audience, so she settled into the corner of the stage and did her best to rest her head, wishing sleep would come and this uncomfortable part of their journey was over so they could settle in and be happy.

★ S i x ★

It's rolling!" Alex's shout only told her what she already knew.

Beth took one look up at the tilting doorway that was right about head high. It was going the wrong way for her to climb up there to get out. Both doors had been torn off and Beth now stood on the ground, but the stage wouldn't clear her head when it went over.

She dropped. Shouts grew louder. The stage tipped. When the opening on which she now stood rose, she looked under it and saw dangling feet—

The stage stopped.

—Alex's battered cowboy boots. He must have his hands on the top of the stage, using his weight to stop it from rolling.

Then, instead of rolling, the stage slid.

If it rolled, she had a chance of getting out. If it slid, it'd scrape her right off the cliff with it.

"Let go!" She snaked her hands out the door opening and caught his feet and yanked. "Let go and get down here."

The lunatic either didn't hear her or didn't think she was making sense because he hung on and the stage slid again. Alex's feet rose higher, risking his fool neck.

Another few inches and Beth could slide out of the stage on her belly. "Alex, let go and get down here." Then she thought of what the crazy man might respond to. "I need help. Catch my hand. Please."

Alex dropped to the ground, all the way down to look at her. The stage, without his weight, began rolling again. Alex thrust his hand forward.

Beth grabbed him. She needed another five inches, a space wider than she was, and she could get her body through. It rose three, then four.

The stage slid suddenly, instead of rolling.

"No!" Alex's free hand grabbed the door frame and lifted. Beth's grabbed right beside his hand. While keeping a firm grip on each other, they lifted with such strength a groan ripped out of Beth's throat. The stage canted just enough. Beth dropped flat on her belly in the dirt.

The stage slid again with her between the ground and the heavy vehicle. Alex pulled until she thought her own shoulder might be dislocated. Her head was under the stage now. If it dropped she'd be crushed.

Another pair of hands appeared, lifting on the stage door frame, rugged hands—the stage driver. A third single, feminine hand caught hold—Camilla Armitage. Then another pair of man's hands, smooth—the young man in the dark suit, fit for city life.

The stage lifted, lifted. Alex pulled and Beth shoved off whatever purchase she could find inside the stage and propelled herself forward. Alex dragged her.

With a roar of tumbling stone and scraping wood on rock and dirt, the stage was gone, rolling down the cliff, cracking and slamming into granite and stunted brush that clung to the rugged cliffs.

Beth's feet dangled over the ledge for only a split second. Alex used that amazing strength of his to pull her all the way to safety. She flew forward and knocked her rescuer over backward. With a grunt of pain, she sprawled full length on top of him.

Their eyes met.

"Thank you." She only had a moment to say it because the

others were easing her onto her back, talking. Mrs. Armitage was crying. Beth saw that they'd all come rushing to help her—Whip, the stage driver; Mrs. Armitage; and the young man. Only Leo and the man with the broken leg hadn't rushed to help. Beth suspected Leo was still somewhat addle-headed or he'd have chipped in, too.

It was all Beth could do to keep tears from coming to her eyes. But tears were nonsense for the most part, a waste of salt and water, Pa liked to say. So she didn't take the time to break down and cry. Instead, she stood, noticed she still had Camilla's reticule looped over her wrist, and offered it to her.

Camilla shook her head. "That's not mine. You threw out the satchel we needed almost first thing."

"I noticed the young woman carrying it," Whip said. "I wonder if she had family we should notify?"

"Well, we got the stage off the trail then. Let's be on our way." Beth smiled at the driver and hung on to the reticule with no idea what to do with it.

The driver didn't react. He seemed dazed, as if the scare had gone to his head as much as the blow had to Leo's.

Beth could sympathize. It'd been a long day. She decided to give him just a few more minutes to settle down.

She looked at Alex, still lying on his back. Reaching down, she offered him a hand.

"Thanks, Alex." Beth didn't think he heard her. And he'd really been through a lot, considering whatever trauma still pounded inside the man's head. "You were right about the stage being dangerous. Thank you for saving me."

His eyes flashed. He reached up and caught hold of Beth's hand with a slap of flesh on flesh and a death grip.

Beth felt a little thrill of fear race up her spine—well, more thrill than fear, honestly. She knew the feeling of fear well. No one grew up in West Texas without learning to have a healthy fear of the rugged land. Thrill though, oh yes.

"Let's get loaded." The driver seemed to come out of his daze, and the group straggled toward the waiting stage.

Beth tugged on Alex. He came to his feet in a move so graceful he could have been a mountain lion. . .a pouncing mountain lion. . .a pouncing mountain lion who smelled really bad.

"I told you not to go in there." He didn't yell. Beth wished he would because the stage driver might come and save her. Alex looked for all the world like, after all the trouble he'd gone to saving her, he was now considering tossing her over the cliff.

But since when had Beth ever needed someone else to save her? She'd save herself, thanks very much. "I had no idea those rocks might crumble. They looked as solid as. . .well, as solid as a rock."

"I told you it was dangerous." He ignored her explanation and, his hand like a vise on her wrist, took a step toward her, using his height to loom over her.

Give me strength. Strength not to clobber Alex.

Beth wanted to sympathize with the poor, half-crazy man, but honestly, she'd had a hard day, too. "You were right." If she couldn't say that with complete humility, she blamed it on stress.

"I told you the stage might roll."

"I was wrong." The words were good, but Beth knew the tone didn't sound a bit contrite. In fact, it sounded like a child's chant, something a body might hear on a schoolyard at recess. "Neener, neener, neener."

She jerked but he didn't let go. Chanting again, she said, "You were right. I was wrong. You're smart. I'm stupid. Is that what you need to hear?"

His eyes narrowed at her mocking tone. His grip tightened. "I tried to make you use your head."

Well fine. He wanted her close, she'd get close. She took a step forward. "Can we go now?"

"No amount of money is worth dying for. Not even *risking* death." He shook her arm hard.

Oh, dear God, give me strength not to pound this guy. And if I do pound him, give me plenty of strength for that.

"But you wouldn't listen." His fingers were starting to hurt. He was insane, so she decided to give him one more chance.

"You don't know me well." There, that sounded rational and calm and adult. No schoolyard taunt.

"You almost killed yourself for a *purse*." He was so mad his hair might have been standing up a bit straighter, not that easy with his battered hat.

"So you couldn't possibly know how much I hate, 'I told you so.'" It was only fair to warn him. . .before.

"I almost *died* saving you." He dragged her forward until her forearm was pressed against his chest.

She tried to sound reasonable. "So you couldn't know that you are within about ten words—"

"We *all* almost died saving you." His nose almost touched hers.

The man seriously, profoundly reeked. "Of losing your ability to—"

"Life is *precious*." His eyes shot out blue flames until she thought they singed her lashes.

"Stand upright if you don't—" Beth wasn't counting, but she figured he had about one word to go.

"You risked your life for *nothing*!" His burning eyes connected and Beth felt that tug again, like they saw inside her, in her mind, in her heart, drawing from her. Compassion, understanding, hope, strength.

Terror—it made her feel terror. Because she didn't want to feel any of that for a crazy man. Which made her react in the way any good McClellen girl would. "Get your hand off of me. Last chance."

He didn't.

She quit relying on words.

He dropped over backward with a cry of pain.

She hated to hurt him. Not because she hated his *being* hurt—shameful to admit, but she kind of liked that. But it was going to make more work for her, and she was worn clean out.

The man stank. He was heavy. Now someone had to toss him into the stage—which picked that moment to roll up beside her. Everyone loaded.

It had to be her to load him. No one else but the driver was up to it. And he'd be slow climbing down from his perch.

She reached down and, hurt though he was, Alex seemed to learn it was best to work with her and not against her. She hoisted him in.

There was really no room for him. Three people on one side—the Armitages and the young man. On the other side, the man with the broken leg took up the whole seat. His leg was neatly bound.

Beth was relieved. She'd have had to tend him once they got to town if he'd needed more help. Beth shoved Alex inside onto the floor, still curled up with pain. She stuffed his legs in and slammed the door and swung up beside Whip on the high seat.

There was barely room. Whip had stowed everything saved from the wrecked stage up here, including on the seat beside him.

She lifted a box onto her lap and smiled at the crusty old driver. "Let's head for Mosqueros."

He slapped the reins so quickly and obediently, she suspected he'd witnessed her encounter with Alex.

★

The stage pulled to a stop about the same time Alex's blood started circulating again.

He had recovered enough that he'd grown sick of the floor and decided he'd use this opportunity to sit on the roof for the rest of the ride.

Even if it did mean being within striking distance of the spitfire. Beth, she'd said her name was Beth. It was a peaceful, gentle name.

Inaccurate as all get-out.

He swung the door open, still on the floor, and scooted out. A tall stranger riding a gray mare and pulling two black mustangs behind him rode to a stop, smiling up at the driver. "Beth, honey, we've been wondering what kept you."

He wasn't looking at the driver at all. He was obviously riding out to meet the spitfire. The cowboy looked to be around forty. He rode with a steady hand. His eyes wrinkled in the corners as if he'd seen a lot of Texas summers. He had a cool, competent gaze, a revolver on his hip and a rifle in a boot on his saddle. A man who'd seen his share of trouble in his life and expected more.

"Is Mandy gone, Pa?" The spitfire could handle herself, but now, just in case she needed more firepower, she had a well-armed, cool-eyed Pa on the scene.

Alex did his best not to groan out load. The cowboy didn't look as Alex stood and swung the stage door shut, but Alex had a good suspicion that the man didn't miss much.

"She had to go, honey." The cowboy swung down from his horse just as the spitfire hopped off the driver's seat. "It's so good to see you again," the man murmured as he drew her into a bear hug. There was more warmth and love in that one hug than Alex had seen since his own pa died.

"I wanted to see her so bad, Pa." The spitfire started crying.

"Now, Beth, don't start that." The cowboy set her away from him, his eyes wide as if she scared him.

Alex sensed that the man could handle most anything. But apparently not tears.

Alex could relate.

The spitfire shook her head and dashed the back of her hand across her eyes. "Sorry, Pa. I just wanted to see her so bad. I wanted to meet her husband."

The cowboy grunted as if the spitfire hadn't missed much.

"We've gotta get on to Mosqueros, folks."

"I'll ride in with you, Pa."

The driver nodded and lifted the reins.

"Hey, wait a minute!"

The spitfire, her pa, and the driver all looked at Alex. He regretted earning their attention, but the driver was going to drive off without him. "I'll ride up top with you. It's too crowded in there."

"Pa, this is Alex Buchanan. Alex, my pa, Clay McClellen." She said it as if she wanted her pa to know exactly who he was going to shoot.

Alex felt a little shiver of fear. He then thought of her strong, slender arm in his grip and how he'd dragged her against him. And he remembered how intelligent and compassionate and strong she was, and what had passed between them when their eyes had locked.

He might deserve to be shot. Although the spitfire had punished him pretty well on her own, Alex would just as soon that didn't come up.

"Can you give him a lift, McClellen?" the stage driver asked. "There wasn't really room for your girl up here, and the stage is full. We picked up passengers and stowed some luggage from a wreck we found back up the trail."

Clay McClellen's eyes were assessing, cool. Alex wondered what the man saw. Filth, tattered cloths, a bad attitude. Whatever he saw must not have worried him much. "Sure, grab a horse." Most likely because McClellen figured it'd be no problem to shoot him down like a mangy coyote, should the necessity arise.

"Make sure the injured are helped to a good room in town. Tell them I'll check on them tomorrow after Sunday services." The spitfire gave orders in a polite tone, but Alex never doubted she was in charge.

"Sure enough, Miss McClellen. I'll see to 'em."

Riding along with these two was way down on the list of things Alex wanted to do right now. But even lower was crouching on the floor of that stage for the rest of the trip or sitting squashed up against the driver. "Obliged for the use of the horse, McClellen," Alex said.

The spitfire took a few minutes to check on everyone in the stage while McClellen got the particulars on the accident from the stage driver.

Alex moved toward his horse, not wanting to get pulled into the doctor exams but listening to the spitfire's quiet questions and her patients' answers. He heard her promise to check on them all again.

Then she swung up onto horseback. "We left three dead behind, Pa."

Alex noticed the way she moved, as if she was part of the horse, completely at home.

Reins slapped into Alex's hands and caught him lightly across the face. Alex looked up and saw McClellen watching him, scowling. Alex wondered just exactly what expression had been on his face as he watched the heavily armed man's daughter.

From now on, keep your eyes strictly on the horse, idiot.

"Pa, I'll just ride on for home. I don't want to go all the way into Mosqueros now."

"No, I'm not letting you ride the range alone. You know better'n that."

"Mosqueros is an hour out of our way. If you want to ride in with Alex—"

"I'll stay with the stage." Alex cut her off and handed the reins back to McClellen.

"You got a destination in mind, Buchanan? A job or family in town waiting, or are you just passing through?"

"I thought to stay in Mosqueros a while. Maybe for the winter." Alex had no idea how he'd live through the winter, but he couldn't stand the thought of going back East to his father's home, even if it was well heated and there was plenty of money for food and comfort. That inheritance was never going to be his. If his father would've lived, he'd've disinherited Alex for the things he'd done—so Alex disinherited himself.

"You huntin' work?"

Alex shrugged.

"Ride with us to the ranch. You can sleep in the bunkhouse, eat with the men, clean up."

Alex looked closer at McClellen when he said "clean up" to see if the man was sneering, but the man's expression was contained, unreadable.

"We always go to town for Sunday services. You can ride along then to Mosqueros, and we'll be handy to lead the horse home."

From the cool look in McClellen's eyes, Alex suspected this was a test. He just wasn't sure what to say to pass or fail. Was it about attending church? Coming to McClellen's ranch? Accepting a handout? Probably not knowing was the *real* test and just hesitating proved he was flunking. Well, that was something McClellen had probably figured out just by looking, so what difference did it make?

Since Alex couldn't figure right and wrong out, he decided to just do as he wished, and the meal and a bed were too tempting to pass up. "Thanks. I'll accept." Maybe he ought to ask for a job while he was at the ranch. He'd done a bit of cattle wrangling in the last four years as he'd drifted. He'd done just enough to know he was pathetic at it. He'd be found out as incompetent and fired within days. But in the meantime, he'd eat. Eating was good.

Not wanting to ask for work in front of the spitfire, he decided to wait until later.

"Pa, we've got to send someone back to bring in the dead from that stage wreck."

"I'll handle it." McClellen kicked his horse to pick up the pace.

The three of them set off at about five times the speed of the stage, which creaked along in their wake and was soon left far behind.

"Pa, Alex is a doctor." She smiled as if she'd done him a favor with her announcement.

"He is?" The look the rancher gave him was as close to shocked as someone so contained could muster.

"No, I'm not!"

"You're not?" McClellen asked as he and the spitfire turned off the trail and struck out to the south while the well-traveled trail headed on west. Alex had to hustle to keep up. It was all he could do to ignore the lingering ache left behind by Beth's. . . annoyance.

"Yes, he is."

McClellen looked between them. "Well, which is it?"

"I'm not."

"He's a doctor, but he's not doctoring these days."

"Mosqueros could use a doctor."

"Pa"—she gave him a disgruntled look—"Alex can't be the *Mosqueros* doctor. *I'm* going to—"

"You can't be a doctor!" Alex cut her off.

"Do it." She glared at him.

"No, you're not." McClellen talked over her this time. "Doctoring's not a proper job for a female."

Alex looked at the spitfire's father and found a kindred spirit.

The spitfire, however, wasn't having it. "I spent the last four year training to be a doctor."

"A nurse, you mean," her pa said.

"No, a doctor. It's true I went to nursing school."

"Then you're a nurse." Alex flinched a bit when she turned her fiery eyes on him.

"But I apprenticed with a doctor. He knew I'd be the only person in the area with doctoring skills. He taught me everything. He let me do surgery."

"With a knife?" Alex gasped.

"No, I cut my patients open with a carrot, idiot," Beth snapped. "Of course with a knife."

"That's awful. That guy oughta be reported." McClellen's jaw stiffened with anger.

He ought to be arrested and shot and maybe hanged, too, Alex thought. "What all'd he let you do? A woman can't be examining a man."

"None of your business, Alex."

"You're not gonna be a doctor and that's that." Her pa rode right up close so he could tower over her whilst he laid down the law.

"You can do some midwifin' if your ma says it's okay and she goes along, and maybe a few other little things with women and young children, but you'll be living at the ranch, and you aren't going off alone in the night to care for sick people. That's just asking for trouble."

"Amen!" Alex slapped his pommel and McClellen looked at him. They jerked their chins in agreement.

"He can be the doctor." McClellen jabbed his thumb at Alex.

Beth glared at Alex. "He's not a doctor."

"I'm not a doctor." Alex and the spitfire had spoken at the same time.

"You just said he was a doctor." McClellen looked between the two of them.

"I'm not." Alex knew that even if the spitfire didn't.

"He's not." Now she was just being stubborn because she wanted the job herself.

McClellen shook his head in disgust and kicked his horse into a faster gait, which took him out from between them.

They glared at each other for too long.

Then Alex got his own horse moving faster. He liked it better when he couldn't see her pretty blue eyes anyway.

★ Seven ★

A loud whistle jerked Mandy awake. Her hand slapped down and found her rifle and she felt better. Sleep had been a wish, but she'd never expected to really get any.

It was pitch-dark.

Truly, it made sense that even in the rattling stagecoach she'd nodded off. It had been a stressful week. She hadn't slept much since Sidney had announced they were moving to Colorado and Mandy realized she would have to leave her family.

The stage pulled to a stop. Mandy heard the nervous snorting of the horses, most likely unhappy with the roaring train.

"What's that?" Sidney asked.

"A train." One of their fellow passengers said in a voice that seemed to call Sidney stupid.

Her door swung open and the stage driver stuck his head in. "We don't have much time to move your bags from the stage to the train. Let's get moving."

"We aren't going yet?" Sidney sounded outraged. "Our train leaves in the morning."

Mandy knew he was overly anxious for the wedding night. He'd made it abundantly clear. Mandy admitted to relief on several occasions that her pa and ma had been fierce about chaperoning them because Mandy had been nearly alarmed with Sidney's

54

forward behavior when the two of them were alone. He'd acted like delaying the wedding in hopes Beth would arrive was done strictly to thwart him.

The driver shook his head. "Someone was waiting with the news when I pulled up. This is tomorrow's train. It's early. This is the one you folks have to take if you're goin' north. Let's get you loaded."

The stage driver vanished from the door, and Mandy felt the coach sway as he climbed to the top. A valise flew off the top, followed by a trunk.

The two men in the stage hesitated. Mandy assumed it was to let her and Sidney go first. She moved toward the door away from the flying luggage.

Sidney caught Mandy's arm and looked at the men. "Go ahead."

They exchanged glances then left.

Sidney turned her around to face him. "Now we're getting on a train? Our tickets go straight through to Colorado. We won't be alone together for days." He whispered, but it sounded like anger rather than discretion. "Let's wait and take a later train."

"We've got our whole lives, Sidney. You're the one who said we don't dare miss the train."

"Yeah, but that was mainly to get away from your family. Colorado will still be there in a week."

With a pang of sorrow, Mandy asked, "You mean we could have waited longer for Beth?"

"I wanted to get you alone."

"But I might never see my sister again, Sidney. It breaks my heart to think of it. If we can wait a week, let's go back to Mosqueros and—"

"You need to grow up, little girl."

Devastated to think Sidney would make such a choice for so frivolous a reason, Mandy ignored his insulting tone, turned, and moved to leave the stage.

Sidney caught her upper arm and jerked her back. "You're my

wife now." He leaned over her. Sidney wasn't very tall—an inch or so taller than Mandy's own five foot five. And he was going soft like so many city men, so his strength surprised her. "You're not Clay McClellen's daughter anymore."

Even in the dim starlight, Mandy saw Sidney's face redden with anger, and she felt that cold, that strange cold that came over her when there was trouble. Her thumb slid over that callus on her index finger once before she could stop herself.

Protect me, Lord.

What she felt wasn't new bride nerves. It was real, solid fear that she might be in danger. Fear was something Mandy had experienced many times in her life. And she knew to face it head-on, usually with a rifle. Her hand slid to her trusty Winchester as she glared at Sidney. "I'm *both*. I'll *always* be both. And more importantly, I'm *Sophie McClellen's* daughter."

"What's that supposed to mean?" The grip on her forearm began to hurt until she knew she'd have a bruise tomorrow.

Her parents could fight like a house afire. Mandy had seen them squabble many times, though not so much after the first year or so. But her pa had never put his hands on her ma, and Ma had never, ever backed down. Well, maybe she did just for peace and quiet, but *never* out of fear.

Fearing a man she loved was ridiculous, and Mandy refused to do it. "It means that if you know what's good for you, you'll get your hand off of me right this minute."

"I'll let you go when—"

A grunt drew Mandy's head around. The stage coach driver stood there, his eyes narrow. They went from Mandy to her arm to Sidney's florid face.

Sidney released her arm so quickly there was no doubt he'd gotten the driver's message.

She had a message or two of her own. But now wasn't the time. "Let's get loaded onto the train." She grabbed her rifle, swung out of the stage, and dropped to the ground, not caring if Sidney came along or not. As she settled the gun into place and gathered up her things, she wondered just how much trouble marriage was going to be.

A vague, troubling memory flirted around inside her head. Her pa—but not Clay McClellen, her first pa. Mandy had only shadowy memories of him, and those were muddled because, of course, being twin brothers, her first pa, Cliff, looked exactly like her second pa, Clay. It was hard to separate memories.

But she had one that was crystal clear. The day her first pa died.

Pa had only been back from the war for a little while. He was a quiet man. Her second pa was quiet, too, but a pleasant, good-natured kind of quiet. Her first pa was sullen quiet. Moody. Mandy remembered how they all tried hard to placate the man. . . . The dinner table. On the day he died.

Ma told Pa there was a baby on the way. Mandy had started laughing, and she and her sisters, Beth and Sally, had giggled and talked about the new baby.

"It better be a boy. I'm sick of nothing but girl children." Pa slapped his hand on the table and made the plates and silverware jump and clatter. Then he jabbed a finger at Ma. "Try not to kill my son this time."

All of them fell silent.

Mandy had no idea what he meant, though later she'd learned Ma had lost a baby boy between Beth and Sally. She'd been thrown from a horse, doing man's work Pa wouldn't do.

Tears brimmed in Sally's eyes, and for one second Mandy hated her pa. Mandy was eight, a big girl, and she'd gotten used to him. He didn't hurt her feelings hardly at all anymore. Beth was pretty good at ignoring him, too. They'd learned to protect their hearts. But Sally was only three and she adored him. She took all his hard little digs and stuck by him, defended him, loved him. She tried so hard to be good enough to earn Pa's love. But no one could be good enough to earn something that didn't exist.

Ma had looked around the table on that long-ago day, with

her eyes wide, sad, full of love—apologizing wordlessly for Pa's cruelty. Mandy knew her ma was glad she'd given birth to girl children.

Ma's gaze settled on Sally's hurt little face for a second then Ma's eyes lit with fire. Absolute rage ignited.

Mandy felt a chill of fear.

"These *girls* are the best children any man could have." Ma spent her life trying to keep the ornery man she'd married happy. She almost never lost her temper—a fearsome thing when she did. "The *only* one in this family who doesn't measure up is *you*." Ma glared from her end of the table.

Pa glared back.

They looked as if they hated each other.

Mandy could remember the slashing pain of the first moment in her life when she'd realized finally, fully, that her pa didn't love her, never would. That heartbreaking truth hurt nearly as much as if she'd been stabbed. But even then she knew it wasn't her. There was something broken in her pa. He didn't know how to love.

Even at eight years old, Mandy wanted to beg Ma not to fight. Ma was decent and strong. Pa was selfish and weak. The decent, strong person had to do decent, strong things like love unlovable people and keep peace even when it wasn't easy.

Pa had shoved his chair back hard enough that it tipped over with a loud crash. Without another word—silence was so often his way—he left, slamming the cabin door behind him.

Ma stormed after him.

As she swung the door open, a crowd of men rode into the yard, yelling, guns drawn, surrounding Pa.

Someone shouted, "Horse thief."

Shouting threats and accusations, the crowd grabbed Pa and rode off.

Ma screamed and ran out of the house. But they left her behind in a cloud of cruel laughter and dust. Within the hour, Pa was dead and Ma was digging him a hole in the ground.

I've married a man just like my pa. Oh, God, protect me. Protect me. Protect me.

There would be children of course, and Mandy would spend her life praying this prayer for herself and her young'uns.

Mandy felt sick. Then she remembered that Sidney had a charming side, too. He wasn't all sullen and angry like Pa. There would be good times, plenty of them if Mandy could just be good enough, cheerful enough, obedient enough to keep him happy.

And on the days she couldn't do enough, she'd find a more painful way—painful for Sidney—to calm him down. No man was *ever* going to put his hands on her in anger. And she'd shoot any man who did such a thing to her children. Being her husband wouldn't save him. She'd make sure Sidney knew that for a fact.

She lifted all the luggage she could carry, squared her gun-toting shoulders, and headed for the *chuffing* train now pulling to a stop in the darkened town. She suspected this load of work was her lot from now on.

The driver came alongside her, carrying the heavy box Pa had sent along, leaving behind the single large trunk for Sidney. "You don't have to go with him if you don't want." The driver spoke quietly to her so his voice didn't carry past the screeching brakes and steaming locomotive engine.

Mandy exchanged a look with the man. She didn't know him, but she knew his kind. Gruff, taciturn Western men didn't talk much. They minded their own business except when it came to protecting women. The grizzled driver would take care of Mandy if she asked him to.

But he was wrong. Mandy had said her vows before man and God. She had to go.

Oh, Lord, protect me.

"Thank you, but he's my husband. I do have to go."

With a shrug, the man fell silent as he helped her load her things onto the train. Then he left to tend his own horses.

She still hadn't spoken to Sidney when the train pulled out on a journey that left her precious family behind forever.

★

"I've brought in three more. They all resisted. They're dead."

The colonel's blue eyes narrowed.

"I'm here to collect my reward." Cletus Slaughter knew what the man was thinking. He'd have let all these cowards roam free if it was up to him.

They'd had this fight before. But the colonel always paid.

"What poor men did you catch this time, Slaughter?" Lifting the papers up, the colonel read the three names, his fussy, trimmed white beard quivering a bit with anger.

Cletus enjoyed watching the man hate him while having to fork over the money because it was the law. "They're deserters and cowards. I hate a coward."

"So you shoot them in the back?" The colonel slammed a fist on his heavy desk. "I'd say a back shooter is the worst kind of coward."

Everything about this office was polished, uppity. But no amount of fancy furniture and slick uniform could make Cletus answer to anyone. He'd had his time in the cavalry. Now he savored shoving the rules and regulations down this pompous officer's throat.

"They're wanted men. I'm claimin' the reward." Cletus crossed his arms, enjoying the feel of his new shirt. He'd been livin' high since he'd found out the army paid for the return of deserters. Most of them begged and crawled, and a few of them tried to run. Yes, he'd put a few bullets in a coward's back. Glad to do it.

"This is the end, Slaughter. I've sent a wire back East asking the War Department to drop this business of hunting down deserters. This dead-or-alive rule for deserters is left from the War Between the States. They don't intend to enforce it now. Most of the time, if deserters are caught the only punishment is asking the men to serve out their times. Sometimes pay is even negotiated for them."

"Long as it's the law, I'm gonna keep huntin'. Now where's my money?"

"The purser has it." The colonel grudgingly wrote up the order to pay the bounty. "What poor fool are you going after this time?"

Cletus didn't trust the colonel not to interfere if he knew. "None'a your business, Colonel. You'll find out when I bring him in." Cletus snatched the note and smirked at the colonel, using the writ to give him a sloppy salute. Officers hated that.

He collected his bounty and rode out. When he was settled into a ground-eating walk on his thoroughbred—a grand horse, paid for on the backs of cowards—he pulled out his list and saw that it wasn't that far of a ride to a place one of the cowards had been sighted. Cletus had informers everywhere.

A deserter on a stagecoach riding along, enjoying the fat of the land—a land he'd betrayed. A doctor. Most likely left men to die. Now somewhere putting his filthy hands on unsuspecting citizens and living rich.

Cletus couldn't hold back a smile as he imagined this one making a run for it. He caressed his brand new Colt single-action army revolver. Best gun made. Cletus had the best of everything now. And he would for as long as the cowards remained.

Spinning the gun's cylinder to check that it was fully loaded, Cletus thought about the cowardly doctor. He hoped Alex Buchanan would run.

★ **Eight** ★

Alex finally felt good enough to concentrate on hating himself.

He preferred to starve wallowing in filth. It kept his mind occupied. But tonight he ate well, then bathed and went to bed. He could concentrate on self-loathing.

Clay McClellen had tossed him a change of clothes, even a worn but decent pair of boots and a battered hat, shoved a bar of soap in his hands, and directed him to a farm pond to bathe. There'd be no supper until Alex got back.

Alex had refused the clothes, but McClellen got gruff and said they had a mountain of old clothes left behind by former hands. Alex wondered about that. He was about McClellen's height. The clothes were probably his. But Alex was so hungry his belly button was rubbing against his backbone, so he took the clothes and scrubbed himself clean. It took a while because the filth was worked deep into his skin.

The beef stew in the bunkhouse was so delicious Alex almost made himself sick gobbling it down. The rest of the hands went for the chow with just as much enthusiasm, so Alex wasn't even embarrassed to be seen eating with the manners of a wolf.

Then Alex rolled into a hard bunk that felt like he'd floated into heaven compared to a lot of the places he'd slept. And the nightmares came.

Alex jerked awake to find a grizzled cowhand named Whitey shaking his shoulder. Alex looked around in the dim light of dawn to see every man in the building awake and staring at him.

As soon as he'd come fully awake, Whitey slapped him on the arm. "Been to war myself, son. A lot of the hands have. And had my share of bad dreams. We have a light day on Sunday. See if you can get another hour of sleep."

Whitey handled the cooking in the bunkhouse, and he'd done a fine job last night. He was gray-haired and had knowing eyes. He walked away with a slight limp. The men flopped back on their beds, minding their own business the way only cowpokes could. Alex was too afraid to let himself sleep again.

His dreams were so real he seemed to be reliving the horror. The blood.

Alex closed his eyes, as if that could stop it, but it only made it worse. His dreams felt like his leg was being amputated. They tore a hole in Alex's soul as surely as a hacksaw tore through muscle and bone. Something he'd done and done and done. Now he was left with that hole, big enough to let the devil in. Because Alex felt the devil inside him, felt the rage and hate and evil.

He was lost.

God, I'm so lost.

He threw the blanket off and stood, grabbed his boots, and slipped out, even though he knew every man there heard him. They were a salty lot, plenty of soldiers in the bunch. McClellen knew how to hire hands. . . . That meant he'd know enough not to hire Alex.

Outside, in the dim light of early morning, Alex pulled on his boots and strode toward the pond where he'd bathed yesterday. Maybe if he soaked his head in cold water the nightmares would fade.

He neared the crest of a low hill, covered with scrub pines that blocked his view of the pond. Clay McClellen stood from an old tree stump and started toward him, carrying his rifle.

That's when Alex heard the distant sound of laughter, women's laughter.

He stopped and let McClellen come the rest of the way. The man was guarding his women. So many women. Alex had heard all about the beautiful McClellen women from the cowhands last night.

Clay had daughters, one married and gone to a man who wasn't good enough for her, although it sounded like no man could ever be good enough for her. Beth, the spitfire—they'd asked about her as if their own long lost daughter had returned. Some grumbling had erupted about her going off to school when she'd been way too young. But she'd been headstrong and gotten her way. Harum-scarum Sally, she sounded like their favorite. And Laurie, still young but so obviously adored. Which left Sophie, the prettiest and toughest wife any man ever had. Plus McClellen had himself a passel of sons.

The cowhands talked in absolutely respectful terms. In fact their tone was more in the way of a warning of stark and horrible pain should Alex ever dare to say a wrong word or give a wrong look to one of the McClellen women. They'd put it nicely—for brusque, Western men. He'd gotten the message.

And now here he was, most likely intruding on the women bathing.

Alex noticed that McClellen had stationed himself so he couldn't see the pond either, mindful of his daughters' modesty. Alex envied the man until he could hardly breathe.

"Sorry, McClellen. I didn't know there'd be anyone out here." Alex said it quick before McClellen could start shooting.

"Call me Clay. Don't worry about it. That's why I came out, so as to warn men away. The girls come out lotsa mornings for a little while, but only if I've got time to guard 'em."

"So, Clay, you looking for any more cowhands?"

McClellen's eyes narrowed, not with anger but with thinking, considering. "You're a doctor. Why do you want to be a cowhand?"

"I don't want to be a doctor anymore."

Clay shook his head. "Try to make some sense."

Alex almost smiled. Almost. He didn't do much smiling. He didn't exactly keep his past a secret. He just didn't talk to anyone about anything.

"I doctored on the frontier for the cavalry." Alex couldn't hold Clay's eyes anymore so he looked at the ground and saw his nightmares again. "It was bad is all. I got a belly full of sick and hurting people. I can't do it anymore."

"Beth told us last night you really helped that man on the stage. She said you were pretty good."

"She said that?" Alex looked up, startled. He'd just flunked another test judging from the scowl on Clay's face.

"You stay away from my girls." Clay took a step forward and Alex backed up quick. "No cowhand on this ranch gets two chances, you understand. And my girls' word is *law*. If one of 'em doesn't like you for any reason at *all*, you're gone. I don't listen to two sides of a story when one of my girls is telling one side of it. Understand?"

"Sure. That's the way it oughta be."

"There's a man in the federal penitentiary right now who was schoolmaster here and made the mistake of slapping Sally's hand with a ruler."

"They put him in prison for that?" Alex knew women were treated with respect in the West. But that seemed a little extreme.

"He did a couple of other things, too. But none of it mattered a lick to me 'cept what he did to my girl. She was five years old and her teacher convinced her I'd be on *his* side. So she didn't tell me he was thrashing her. Now they know I'll take their side. Always."

"Good. That's the way it ought to be." Alex had half a notion to ride to the federal penitentiary himself and take a piece of the man's hide. "Before you say I'm hired, I might as well tell you I'm not a hand on the range. I'll work hard for you but I'm...I haven't been at it very long."

"So go back to doctorin'."

Alex ignored the advice. "I just don't want you hiring me based on lies. I admit I've got a lot to learn."

Clay shook his head as if he were already tired and it was just past sunup. "Fine. I'll expect you to be worthless for a while. But Alex?" The tone of Clay's voice was frightening.

"What?"

"If one of my cowhands breaks an arm or needs a cut sewn up, you'll help us out." It wasn't a request. It was an order.

"I'm not a doctor anymore. I told you."

"And I don't expect you to be one. You'll be busting broncos and branding cattle with everyone else. But I'm trying to keep Beth under control, and I don't want her doctoring a bunch of beat-up cowpokes. It ain't proper. She's been a hand at healing all her life. I swear they used to *pretend* to be hurt so she'd come and make a fuss over them. That was part of the reason I finally gave in and let her go back East to study."

"Part of the reason? What's the other part?"

"She cried."

Alex flinched. He'd have let her go, too.

"I. . .I've seen some things. . .ugly things." Alex held Clay's eyes for too long. He didn't want to make that promise about doctoring. He didn't know if he *could* make that promise. And Clay McClellen didn't look like the kind of man who had much patience for weaklings. "It's a hard promise you're asking me to make. And I don't make promises I can't keep. All I can say is. . .I. . .I'll try. I'll do my best."

Clay stared as if a hard enough look could go all the way into Alex's brain. Finally Clay relaxed.

Alex didn't know if that meant Clay had managed to read his mind or he'd realized Alex had no mind to read so he'd given up.

"That's all any man can do, I reckon."

Alex nodded and turned back to the bunkhouse.

"Oh, Alex?"

"Yeah?" Alex wondered what other promises McClellen was going to wring out of him.

"The ranch hands all ride along with us to church."

His shoulders slumped. "I'm not a churchgoing man, not anymore."

"The only other job I've got this morning is to send some hands out to fetch back the dead bodies from the stage wreck. You're welcome to ride along with them."

Alex would rather go to church. He'd also rather take a beating. That must have shown on his face.

"Ride in with us then. I don't make attending church a requirement of the job. That's between you and God, but I like a big enough group that no one will consider messing with my girls. It's still a dangerous country. So you'll be expected to come."

"I'll be ready." One set of clothes. A borrowed horse. Alex was ready now.

N i n e

I missed Texas something fierce." Beth turned to Sally, marveling at how her little sister had grown up. "You're as tall as me. And Laurie! I can't believe how she's changed. She's almost my height. And the twins are nine now."

"It's been so long, Beth. It figured we'd do some growing." Sally had her hair tied back and her Sunday best dress and bonnet on. But no female finery could mask the fire in her eyes and the restlessness that marked every move and word from Beth's hoyden sister.

Sally liked to ride the range. Pa encouraged it and Ma had given up fighting it. Sally worked as hard as any cowhand on the place.

The twins, Cliff and Jarrod, nine, did their best to keep up with her. Seven-year-old Edward was dying to be allowed to ride herd and he did go out, but only with Pa or Sally riding beside him. Little Jeffrey, five, whom they all called Buck, could throw a screaming tantrum, but even so, he wasn't allowed to help yet. He could throw a loop over a standing calf and ride horseback, but he wasn't allowed to herd cattle. Pa didn't give him that much freedom.

Sally had already done cowhand work at age five, but that was out of necessity. Now when Beth thought back on it, she couldn't believe the things Ma had let them do at so young an age.

Looking at her family crowded beside her in the back of the buckboard, Beth was struck by how much they'd changed. Buck had been tiny when she'd gone to Boston to study. She'd missed so much. She was never going to be so far away from them again.

Which reminded her of Mandy—which made her want to cry. So she looked away from all the blond-headed little brothers and sisters and noticed Alex riding along to church.

He cleaned up well. And he noticed her noticing him. Their eyes connected in that same weird way, and Beth looked quickly away before she could get drawn in.

When they got to Mosqueros, she saw Alex head for a nearby stand of trees instead of coming inside to services. As he leaned against a shady oak, Beth ached for him and all his emotional scars. Finding a faith in God would be the best first step in healing those scars, but Alex would never know if he kept leaning. She was tempted to go have a talk with him, but there was no time.

Parson Radcliff, who'd just taken over for Parson Roscoe, called them inside. Beth thought the skinny, energetic young man and his pretty wife, who expected a baby—their second—any time, were going to be a letdown after Parson Roscoe's years of support and kindness.

Beth noticed the Reeveses sitting in the back on the right as they'd always done. Except now they took up two pews. The older twins were missing—grown and gone just like Mandy most likely. But the triplets remained. At fifteen, Mark, Luke, and John were tall as adult men but gangly still. Then there was a second row of squirming, whispering blond boys. Beth counted five, but they were stair steps, thank heavens. No more Reeves babies born in bunches.

Beth sat in the front pew beside her family through the service, and it pulled on her just like her family and Texas and being a caretaker. This church was part of her, part of home. Beth noticed her little brothers were more wiggly than usual. Although what did she know about usual anymore?

Ma whispered to Sally and she took fidgety Buck's hand and

led her youngest brother outside as the congregation rose to sing a closing hymn.

They were just finishing "Shall We Gather at the River" when Sally screamed in what sounded like agony. "Buck, run!" Sally screamed again. Beth had never heard her tough little sister make such a horrible sound.

Pa was down the aisle and out the door like a shot, Ma half a step behind.

Laura yelled at Beth, "I'll take care of the young'uns."

Beth raced after her parents. When she stepped outside, she saw Sally screaming at Buck to run faster.

Buck cried out in pain.

"Go, Buck. Run to Pa!" Sally was behind Buck. She looked up and her eyes locked on Pa, then she veered off, waving her arms wildly.

Buck slammed into Pa's legs. Beth took one look at the welts on Buck's face and knew they'd wrangled with a beehive.

Sally raced, doing more shouting than screaming, her arms flailing. She headed straight toward a water trough standing on Mosqueros' Main Street.

Beth knew, whatever stings Buck had gotten, Sally's had to be worse. She'd shoved her little brother out of the way and led the bees after her. Beth raced toward Sally.

Sally hurled herself into the water. A swarm of bees lifted into the air above the trough and buzzed away in a dark cloud, back toward open country.

Beth reached Sally and caught her arm. Ma was a step behind her on the other side of the trough. Together they lifted Sally until her head was above water.

"Buck! Where's Buck?" Sally's face and neck were already lumpy and swollen from the stings. She had on long sleeves, but Beth saw that her hands were swelling. Bees floated to the surface, drowned, but too late to stop many of them from stinging.

More churchgoers crowded out, everyone rushing toward Sally, talking wildly.

"Buck's okay, Sally. You saved him. He's crying, stung a little, but he's fine." Beth slid her arm behind Sally's shoulders and, with Ma's help, lifted her from the water trough.

Pa came up beside them and took Sally into his arms. Buck clung to Pa's leg sobbing.

Beth took a second to inspect her little brother. He was stung, too, but nothing like Sally. She'd pushed him away and taken the brunt of the enraged bees on herself.

"Laurie!" Beth made eye contact with Laurie, who had the other little brothers with her. "Take care of him!"

"Got him, Beth." Laurie scooped Buck into her arms and began soothing him. She took him to the trough and bathed his welts with the tepid water.

Beth scanned the area. The bees, wherever they'd come from, were long gone.

"Pa, I hurt!" Sally began crying.

Beth nearly froze from the shock. Sally knew hard work. She knew broken fingers and bitter heat and bruised muscles. She knew how to keep going and she never complained—except when Ma insisted she wear a dress to town. And they all knew how much Pa hated tears. All of them tried to avoid crying for their pa's sake, and all of them failed on occasion.

Except Sally. Sally never, ever cried.

Pa took Sally to a grassy spot, one of the few in this rugged land around Mosqueros. He lowered Sally to the ground. Beth saw more and more little white welts rising on her sister's face and hands. The rest of her body was protected by her clothes, unless they'd gotten under her skirts, but she had hundreds of stings on her exposed skin.

Sally's uncharacteristic tears scared Beth right to her gut.

Pa knelt on one side of Sally, talking quietly, for once in his life not letting tears send him running.

Beth eased Sally's skirts up a bit and found drowned bees and ugly welts all over her legs. She also found a knife stuck into Sally's boot and wasn't a bit surprised. The McClellens, whether girl or boy, were a tough bunch. Pa and Ma had taught them well. And Sally was the toughest of them all.

Ice. Cold compresses, that's what helped bee stings. And ice in Texas in midsummer was not even possible. She thought of the tepid water in the trough and doubted it would do any good.

"We need water! The cooler the better," Beth shouted.

"I'll get it from the town well." Vivian Radcliff, young and dark haired with kind eyes, looked to be ten months along toward birthing a baby, but the parson's wife could move.

Beth knelt opposite of Pa and studied Sally's condition. Her face continued to swell. One eye was nearly closed. She'd be in terrible pain for days.

A sudden high-pitched wheeze came from Sally's puffy lips. Her eyes went wide to the extent possible. She lurched into a sitting position, her mouth open. The noise came again, as sharp as the cawing of a crow. Sally's throat was swelling shut.

Beth had heard of this when so much poison entered someone's system she couldn't help but react. She even knew of a tiny surgery that could help, but she'd never done it. To cut at Sally's throat, if her incision was misplaced, would kill instantly. Her hands shook as she prayed Sally's throat didn't swell completely shut.

A high whistling gasp for breath came again. Then it stopped. Sally's nearly closed eyes gaped open. Her mouth moved silently. She reached for her neck as if to pull someone's strangling hands away.

At that second Beth's eyes landed on Alex, hanging to the back of the gathering crowd. Terror had bled the color from Alex's face. His eyes riveted on Sally.

Beth knew. Without asking, she knew that Alex could help. "Get over here!"

Alex's eyes went from Sally to Beth. He took a step backward, shaking his head.

She erupted from the ground and ran around her dying sister. Shoving her way through the crowd, she caught Alex's arm in a vise. "You have to help me, Alex."

Their eyes locked again. She remembered well the way he'd drawn strength from her before. She didn't have time for him to work up his nerve. This wasn't a dislocated shoulder. Her sister would be dead in minutes without Alex's immediate assistance. Even now, this second, her body was being starved of oxygen and she might have brain damage.

She gave him ten seconds then she sank her fingers into his arms, digging in with her nails. "Now! Right now!"

Her orders had a visible effect on Alex. His eyes focused. He nodded and charged to Sally's side and shouted, "Clay, let me in. Now!"

Pa jerked his head up then moved quickly aside.

Alex fell to his knees.

Beth rounded Sally's body, knelt across from Alex, and prayed.

Give him strength, Lord God. Give him courage. Give him speed and a steady hand.

"Who has a knife?" she shouted.

Pa drew a knife out of his boot. Beth knew Pa kept his knife razor sharp. It would work, but she shuddered to think of how dirty the blade might be. She thought of the knife in Sally's boot, but it wouldn't be even close to clean either.

At the same instant Laurie, breathing hard from a fast run, shoved Beth's beloved doctor bag into her hands. "I got it from the wagon. I thought you might need it."

With a shout of relief, Beth tore open the black leather satchel and dug inside, extracting her scalpel. Her mentor in Boston had given her this bag and the supplies in it after she'd been working with him a year. She kept it with her at all times, even on a buckboard ride to church.

"Hang on to this, Laurie." She gave her precious bag into her sister's keeping and extended the scalpel to Alex.

Beth saw the moment the doctor in Alex took over. Color returned to his face. Alex took the knife with confident fingers.

Beth caught hold of Sally, holding her still as she jerked and battled for any tiny breath of air. "We can sterilize the knife." Beth grabbed her bag back from Laurie and pulled the top wide open.

"Have you got carbolic acid?" Alex glanced at Beth's precious supplies.

"Yes, a good supply." She looked at Laurie, standing close, desperate to help. "Can you get the bottle of carbolic acid out of my bag?" Beth quickly described it.

Laurie produced a small container.

"No, not that. Dover's Powder is an emetic."

"What's that?"

"Well, it is a painkiller but Sally doesn't need that now. And if you give an overly strong dose, it'll make you sick to your stomach." Beth thought of what an understatement that was. She took the bag from Laurie and pulled out the bottle of carbolic acid, carefully wrapped to prevent breakage.

"Pour some over the knife and my hands then swab some on her neck."

Beth removed the stopper from the glass bottle and the sharp odor of carbolic acid raised her hopes that Sally wouldn't end up with an infection. She obeyed Alex quickly. Beth bent down and looked straight into Sally's eyes.

Terrified. She'd seen the knife. She couldn't breathe.

"Sally, hang on," Beth whispered, trying to get through Sally's pain and fear. Her hand slid to Sally's wrist.

The pulse was strong; her sister was strong.

"We'll save you. I'll save you." Beth had never spoken words that she meant so passionately. And she needed Alex-the-Madman to make them come true.

Alex pressed the razor-sharp scalpel to Sally's throat.

Ten ★

Pa grabbed Alex's arm. "What are you doing?"

Alex pulled the sharp blade back away from Sally's delicate throat.

Beth realized she was witnessing a first. Alex was right and her pa was wrong. Her pa knew everything.

"Let him go, Pa. Alex has to cut into Sally's airway. He has to do it *right now.*"

"You can't cut someone's throat. She'll bleed to death."

"Clay, I know right where to cut. I won't get near the carotid artery. That's the artery that would make her hemorrhage." Alex's voice was deeper than usual, or maybe stronger, more confident. He was no longer the addled man in need of food and clothes.

Beth knew the medical words would help Pa and everyone else trust Alex's abilities. She knew it helped her. Alex had chosen his words deliberately for that purpose.

Pa exchanged a look with Beth.

She nodded her head. "Let him go, Pa. He knows what he's doing."

Sally's body suddenly went into a spasm.

Pa let Alex go.

"Hold her very still." The command in Alex's voice was the same one she'd heard during her apprenticeship from the doctor who trained her. Alex was very much in charge.

Beth gripped Sally's shoulders. Ma was at Sally's head, holding her still so a stranger could slit her throat. Then Pa and Laurie had Sally's legs. Adam, the McClellen's oldest family friend, appeared at Sally's feet and he knelt and held. They all trusted Alex on Beth's say-so.

"Beth, have you got any small tube?" Alex looked up, his gaze hard, almost cruel.

Beth nodded.

"Get it as soon as I've made the incision."

Beth knew all of the people around Sally prayed as hard as they held on. The congregation of Mosqueros's only church stood in a circle around them, praying, too.

Alex made the tiniest possible incision. Blood ran free and nearly everyone in the crowd gasped.

Beth quickly released Sally.

Laurie grabbed Sally's now-free arm, which started reaching for her neck.

Beth found a tiny syringe, part of the standard equipment. Every doctor had a bag and cherished the instruments it contained. What had happened to Alex's?

Alex ripped the syringe apart until all he had left was a slender tube and slid it into Sally's bleeding incision. Then Alex bent over the tube and blew. Sally's chest rose. Alex pulled back and Sally's chest fell, slowly, naturally. The air expelling from the exposed end of the tube ruffled Alex's hair.

After Alex blew life into Sally's lungs a few more breaths, Sally's spasms stopped. Beth felt Sally's terrible tension ease. She no longer needed to be restrained once air flowed in and out of her body. The whole crowd sighed as if they'd been holding their breath, too.

Alex repeated the movements, blowing, pulling away to allow an exhale, blowing. Sally's chest moved naturally as if she were breathing, but it was through the tube, not her mouth. Alex finally stopped, and Beth realized Sally was doing the tube breathing herself.

Beth looked over at Alex. He wiped the sweat off his forehead and smeared blood across his face. Her heart turned over at the unsteady movement. Those calm, knowledgeable hands were now trembling like an oak tree in a windstorm.

He said, in that authoritative voice, "Cloth."

Beth handed him a square of clean white cotton, remembering well how she'd assisted in operations. Alex stemmed the blood that flowed around the tube as Sally breathed.

Speaking to Beth's parents, Alex said, "Sally will be able to breathe through this tube until the swelling goes down in her throat. That could take a while, maybe an hour or so. She'll regain consciousness any time now and we'll have our hands full keeping her still. When her throat clears, I'll suture this incision and she'll be fine. There's the risk of an infection of course, although Beth's carbolic acid will help fight that. Still, it's always a danger."

Alex went on, talking about caring for the wound. Beth knew he was talking more to ease Pa's and Ma's minds than because what he said was important. She knew well the strong effect of a calm presence in times of trouble.

When Alex's instructions were done, he said, "Where can we take her? I don't want her in a buckboard. It's too rough a ride out to the ranch, so she needs a place in town."

"Bring her to my house," Parson Radcliff said.

"No," the banker, Royce Badje, spoke up. "There's an empty building next to the bank. I own it and I'd be glad to see it used for a doctor's office."

"I don't need an office." Alex looked up, his eyes suddenly losing all the confidence and strength that had carried him through until now.

Before he could humiliate himself, which Beth felt sure was inevitable, she reached her hand across Sally's body. "Hush." Anyone within ten feet heard her. But Alex obeyed, and Beth's saying, "Hush," didn't give away much.

"That will be fine, Mr. Badje. Is it empty? We could use a bedroll on the floor for Sally to lie on."

"It's furnished upstairs, so you can live there, Doc. And there are shelves and counters downstairs. It used to be a dry goods store. No hospital beds though. But the town can help get it set up for a doctor."

"I'll run and dust the counters and put down sheets." Royce Badje's wife hurried away, and several women followed her, eager to help.

Alex reacted to the sudden action as if someone had fired the starting pistol of a race. He rose to his feet as if to run.

Beth jumped up and grabbed his wrist across Sally's body. "Not now, Alex. Please. We need you. Sally needs you."

A murmur went through the crowd and Beth knew everyone was wondering what she meant. Ignoring her old friends, she did her best not to shame Alex, but if she had to, she'd hog-tie him before she let him leave. Clutching his wrist with such force it drew him out of whatever nightmare he'd descended into, Beth whispered, "If you hadn't been here, my sister would have died."

Alex came to her again, locking their eyes, that look, the fear, that drawing force, using her strength and courage because he had none. With the same intuition that guided her in caring for patients, Beth knew Alex hated himself for needing her. Judged himself to be a coward and a failure, contemptible. Or at least he held himself in contempt even as he was surrounded by a town full of people praising God for his presence. "I. . .I'm not a—"

"Let's get Sally inside." Beth's voice cut through what was most likely going to be a further denial of what Alex was. Not what he *did* but what he *was*. The man was a born healer, a caretaker all the way to his bludgeoned soul.

As surely as she knew he needed her by his side for strength, she knew there was no way out for Alex. To walk away from this God-given gift was to walk away from his soul. And that is exactly what Alex had done.

And now it was given to Beth as a charge from the Almighty, to help him regain that part of himself. Only then could Alex be healthy and whole again. Beth assured the Lord she would gladly take on that role for the man who had saved her sister.

Pa lifted Sally, with Ma carefully steadying her head. Sally's soaking wet hair streamed down. Blood coated Sally's neck. Her eyes remained swollen and closed. Her face was so covered with welts that her pretty face, so like Beth's, was disfigured. Ma and Pa kept their eyes locked on the cut and the little tube in her neck. They headed—two people who'd learned to work well together as a unit—toward the empty dry goods store.

Beth was able to get Alex moving without his saying anything more. When at last they reached the store, Beth noticed that many folks had trailed along behind. "Please wait outside," she asked politely. "And, Laurie, can you get the rest of the family—"

"I'll take care of them, Beth," Adam cut in. His ebony black skin wrinkled in concern, but his eyes, as always, were calm and competent. "You just see to Sally."

"Thank you." Beth had no idea what she'd been going to say, really. Should the family go home? Should they find a place to stay in town? Whatever were they to do with Ma and Pa and Beth and Sally all unable to take care of them? Laurie could handle it, but she was so young and upset about Sally, too. Adam's taking over was perfect.

Tillie was at his side. She rested one of her gentle, competent hands on Beth's wrist. "For now we'll take them to Parson Radcliff's. They've invited us. We'll be praying for Sally, honey." Adam, Tillie, and their three little ones were close friends to the McClellens.

"Thanks, Tillie." Sighing with relief, Beth kept her tight grip on Alex and dragged him into the store after Ma and Pa. The door swung shut as Pa lay Sally on a counter that looked perfect to hold a cash box and piles of fabric and notions. . .not an injured young woman, but it worked fine. It was about waist high, the perfect height for them to tend Sally. And there was a soft blanket spread on top.

Mrs. Badje fussed, swiping dust away from every surface in the room, to make a cleaner spot for the wounded girl. Several other church ladies bustled about tidying the store up.

"I'll need boiling hot water," Beth said to the kindly Mrs. Badje.

She nodded then vanished out the back as if her only goal in life was to help and be a bother to no one.

Beth turned to her captive—Alex—who, despite his nearly miraculous gift for doctoring, seemed bent on bothering everyone.

He sure as certain bothered Beth something fierce.

E l e v e n

"Let go." Alex jerked his arm away from the claws Beth had sunk into him. "We're alone. You don't have to cover for me anymore."

"We're not alone." Beth jerked her head toward her worried parents who so far only had eyes for Sally. The church ladies had finished their quick cleanup and left, following Mrs. Badje.

"I already told your pa I'm not interested in doctoring and some of the whys." Alex stalked past her to Sally's side, clinging to his anger because it was a strong emotion. He could force the weak cowardice away as long as he was furious. "She's breathing well." Alex ran one finger over Sally's swollen, lumpy face. "Terrible stings. Poor girl." He saw his hand shaking and pulled back. "Beth, bring your kit around here. Do you have tweezers? Let's get these stingers out of her."

Beth extended the tweezers to him.

"You do it." He barked, just like the yellow dog he was.

The kindness and understanding in her eyes near to killed him. She didn't argue; she just did it. Alex became the nurse handing her anything she asked for out of her well-equipped doctor's bag. Alex had thrown his away somewhere in western New Mexico. He'd run from the army's demands. That bag, so much a part of him for so long, seemed to burn his hand every time he touched it...the guilt, the failure at deserting.

But the nightmares! He couldn't face another day of adding to them. One more Indian campaign, always one more. Why couldn't people live side-by-side without taking up arms? What was the matter with the world? Where was God?

Where are You, God?

Alex knew God hadn't moved. It was Alex who had gone to a place beyond salvation. He even believed God would forgive him. He was just too ashamed to ask. He too richly deserved any punishment God chose to give.

The quiet lady who'd brought the blankets returned with rags and water, cool in a basin, blazing hot in a bucket. She slipped out again.

Alex took a second to envy the woman her escape, then dipped a cloth into the cool water and began bathing the pretty young woman's face and hands, hoping the chill would reduce the swelling. "She looks like you," he whispered to Beth.

Beth looked up from where she worked with her tweezers on the dozens of stingers visible on the girl's face.

"My little sister Sally. She's the toughest of the bunch. She drew those bees toward herself to save Buck." Beth looked at him then shifted her eyes to her hovering parents.

They nodded. "Sally'd do that," Pa said.

"The swelling isn't getting worse anymore," Alex reassured Beth's family. All he could see was that welling blood where he'd cut a young woman's throat.

"How long will she need that thing to breathe?" Clay asked.

"A few hours is probably all." Beth was answering the questions.

Good, Alex was afraid of what might come out of his mouth if he started talking.

"She'll be able to breathe on her own real soon." Beth's hands were steady as iron. Alex heard prayers escape her lips as she tended her sister.

Without making a conscious choice, Alex added his own. As he prayed, the thought invaded that he should go back, face his fate for being a deserter, even if it was a firing squad. The frontier fighting with the Indians had finally stopped, except for isolated incidents. He wouldn't have to doctor on a battlefield again.

The fact that he never had turned himself in only deepened his self-contempt. But even if he was beyond God's grace, that didn't mean God wouldn't hear a prayer from Alex for someone else, did it?

They worked for an hour or more. Beth with her tweezers, then bathing the throat wound with blazing hot water. Alex with his cold cloths. Mrs. Badje came in repeatedly keeping the water hot and cold.

As Sally continued breathing steadily, Alex noticed Sophie leave quietly then return much later with the parson at her side. "The children needed to know Sally was doing well." Sophie took up her place at Beth's side. Clay stayed at Alex's left.

The parson shared a quiet prayer with Sophie and Clay. Then the three talked quietly, standing near, ready to help.

Alex heard all of this, but his focus was on the patient and Beth's steadiness. How could a woman be so calm in the eye of a cyclone? And with her own sister riding that cyclone.

Alex wondered how anyone had the nerve to bring children into this dangerous world. Alex's prayers for this girl's healing went up steadily to God.

Beth glanced at him once, which made him aware that he'd been praying audibly. " 'The Lord is my shepherd,'" she began quietly reciting the Twenty-third Psalm.

He knew it well and prayed along. " 'Yea, though I walk through the valley of the shadow of death. . .'" He'd been too long in the valley of the shadow of death.

" 'Thou anointest my head with oil. . .'" Their words became unison as Sophie, Clay, and the parson joined in. " 'And I will dwell in the house of the Lord forever.'"

Just as they finished, Sally's eyes flickered open. It wasn't much because they were so swollen, but Alex felt the young woman's muscles go taut. Leaning close, Alex saw awareness in those barely open eyes.

Alex leaned down and felt a faintest of breaths come easing out from Sally's lips. "She's breathing." Alex looked up at Beth. She smiled and Alex felt as if the sun had come out after a month-long rain. "The swelling has gone down in her throat."

"Can we close the incision then?" She had strength Alex couldn't fathom. And somehow he'd found himself able to use it himself. Borrow it, absorb it. Surely that wasn't possible, but it was the only way Alex could explain what he was capable of, as long as he could look into Beth McClellen's eyes.

Alex nodded. "I made the incision tiny so hopefully one or two stitches, taken from the outside, will close her esophagus. Before I take any stitches, we'll make sure Sally is breathing well."

"Good idea." She smiled then turned to brush Sally's hair back off her forehead. "You're all right, Sally. You're going to be fine. Lie very still."

"Beth?"

"Yes, honey."

"I hurt." Sally's words were more a movement of her lips than audible, but she did manage to breathe out a whisper of sound, which meant air was now passing through her throat.

Beth looked at her parents. "Come over and talk to her and keep her still."

They rushed to stand close to her head and bent so their daughter could make eye contact.

"She'll be vulnerable to infection and hard to keep still." Alex couldn't seem to stop himself from acting like a doctor. Giving instructions and dark warnings. His was the last voice so many had heard, the voice of doom.

"You don't know the half of keeping her still." Beth nodded down at her sister, who managed a twisted smile.

"How's Buck?" The voice, weak and shaky, was further proof Sally was pushing air through her throat.

"Buck's fine, only a few stings. You saved him, little sister." Beth smiled and Sally visibly relaxed.

Alex looked at Sally's concerned but very able parents.

Speaking in a calm, matter-of-fact voice, Alex said, "Sophie, Clay, can you help us hold her?"

Sophie braced Sally's head, but at the same time began talking, distracting her, urging her to be very still. Clay steadied the girl's shoulders. The parson stood by her feet, ready if needed. Everyone in this room, including the patient, was stronger than Alex.

Alex knew that for the next twenty-four to forty-eight hours someone would need to be with Sally every minute. Moving her was out of the question so, for as long as Sally needed help, Alex was the doctor.

Not that Alex hadn't turned his back on a patient in need before. God forgive him, he'd done it in cold blood.

But not this time. With Beth's help, Alex could stay—especially if he didn't sleep. And then once the incision was healing well, without infection—*God, please don't let there be an infection*—Alex would go back to his plans to work for Clay. The man would definitely give him a good chance as a cowhand now. Saving a man's child ought to earn a man some security on his new job.

Just as Alex laid it all out in his mind, the door flew open. Laurie, wild-eyed, burst into the room. "Parson, your wife fell. She's hurt. She says to bring the doctor. The baby's coming."

Alex's gaze latched onto Beth's.

"Go." She gave him a nod of complete confidence. "I can take care of Sally."

"No. Not without you."

The parson grabbed Alex's arm. He hadn't registered Alex's words to Beth. "This way, Doc." He was a slight man, and a man of worship and love, but he had a grip like a mule skinner.

"I—I—Beth, please," Alex implored her.

Beth's lips thinned with temper and Alex well remembered how she'd knocked him to his knees just yesterday. Then she swiftly looked at her mother. "Can you keep her still, Ma? This might take both of us."

"Yes, go if you need to."

"We'll be fine," Pa added.

"Maybe we can bring Mrs. Radcliff back here." Beth grabbed her doctor's bag, rushed around the counter serving as Sally's hospital bed, and was at Alex's side as they ran out.

Parson Radcliff let go of Alex's arm and sprinted toward his house. Alex did his best to keep up. A few heads poked out of upper windows along the street, Mosqueros residents who had heard Laurie hollering as she ran to get help.

Alex couldn't believe it. His second patient in one day. Bitterly, he wondered how he was ever going to convince these people that he wasn't a doctor.

★ Twelve ★

As she ran, Beth thanked God Alex was a doctor.

Standing helplessly beside Sally had brought it home clearly to Beth that she wasn't one. She had the potential and she would be able to help a lot of hurting people, but she didn't really have the training she needed. And Alex did. And he had years of experience after schooling. He'd hated it, but he'd learned what he needed to know.

He had the skill; she had the nerve. Together, they made a great team.

They raced down the Mosqueros street toward their next patient. Beth felt Alex slowing, and, worried that he might duck down an alley and run the wrong way, she caught his hand and hoped he thought she was trying to impart courage when in fact she was taking him prisoner.

Parson Radcliff whipped around a corner. Beth remembered the tidy house the Roscoes had lived in. As they turned the corner, Beth saw Adam outside surrounded by crying children. Tillie must have stayed in with Mrs. Radcliff, leaving Adam to care for the three McClellen boys, Radcliff's toddler, as well as Adam's own three children, two older boys and a little girl nearly school-aged.

Adam looked overwhelmed. Well, he wasn't the only one.

Parson Radcliff slammed through the door and they heard his frantic voice.

Beth followed, still hanging on tight to Alex who, in fairness, had made no escape attempt. Exchanging one worried look with Adam, Beth left him to his fate, kept hold of Alex, and ran inside.

"It happened so fast. Little Andrew knocked his milk over." Tillie referred to the Radcliff's toddler.

Beth was relieved one of her rambunctious little brothers hadn't taken the poor woman out.

"Then Mrs. Radcliff slipped and fell so hard." Tillie shook her head.

That was all the time Beth gave her. The sobbing coming from the back room had her towing Alex along.

Laurie darted up and whispered as if she didn't want to say the words out loud. "I think she broke her leg, the poor woman."

Beth nodded. "Adam looks overwhelmed. Go see if you need to save him."

Laurie rushed out as Beth hurried after Alex to find him hanging back as he listened to the poor woman.

Tillie followed them into the room, and when Beth glanced at Tillie, the older woman's eyes narrowed as she stared at Alex and Beth.

Beth wondered what she saw. Probably the truth. Alex—for all his skill at doctoring—appeared to be the slightest bit insane. Beth caught the sleeve of his blue shirt, thinking she recognized a stain on the back of the shoulder. This was Pa's shirt.

Once she was there, lending support, or rather pushing Alex around, he gathered his nerve and switched from lunatic to doctor. Beth would be able to write a medical textbook based on her dealings with poor, wounded mental patient, Dr. Buchanan.

She set her bag on a table beside the bed. "Tillie, will you get some bandages out of that bag and. . ." Beth listed the things she thought necessary.

Tillie opened the bag. She set a small container beside the

table. "Is this what you needed?"

Beth saw the Dover's Powder and flinched. "No. Good heavens, no, Tillie."

"Then why do you have it in your bag?"

"It's got many uses. It's a good painkiller. But you have to give it very carefully. Even a small overdose will make you cast up everything in your belly and it can last for day and days. Put it away."

A furrow cut through Tillie's brow and she turned back to the bag.

Alex finally entered the fray. He gently but firmly shouldered the parson aside from his place, opposite the bed from Beth. "Mrs.—" Alex gave Beth a wild look.

"Radcliff," Beth supplied.

Alex nodded. "Mrs. Radcliff, please calm down and let's see what's happened."

That voice. It was like a musical instrument. Beth felt her own calm deepening and spreading. Her impatience with Dr. Crazy eased.

Alex asked questions as he ran his hands down the poor woman's leg. He reached her ankle, and Mrs. Radcliff's indrawn breath was nearly a scream. His shoulders sagging, Alex kept examining the area until finally he said, "I hope it's just a bad sprain."

Beth saw the badly swollen ankle. She knew a bad sprain and a break had to be treated very much the same. But a sprain was much less upsetting, and keeping Mrs. Radcliff calm right now was—

The woman lurched up in bed, sitting erect. She clutched her stomach. "The baby. Christopher, the baby is coming. Oh, Christopher, my water broke shortly after I fell. The pains are coming."

—was out of the question, obviously.

The afternoon turned into the longest day of Beth's life.

With no plaster to make a cast, Alex did his best to splint and bind the ankle into immobility. When he had Mrs. Radcliff settled as well as could be expected, he grabbed Beth and rushed back to check on Sally.

Beth insisted he go and leave her to tend Mrs. Radcliff. She was still insisting when he dragged her into the building where Sally lay being coddled and fussed over by Ma and Pa.

Showing no signs of their mad dash except for breathing hard, Alex checked Sally quickly but thoroughly, his words reassuring as he explained the reason for their absence.

Ma gave Beth a significant look, shifting her eyes to Alex, very obviously asking what in the world was going on with the man. Beth shrugged, and Ma shook her head and went back to watching Sally.

When Alex finished his exam, he said, "Things look as if they're going well here. We need to get back to Mrs. Radcliff."

"One of us will come down if she shows any sign of trouble," Pa said. "You stay and tend to the parson's wife now."

"Alex, I could stay and watch—" Beth didn't get to finish. He had her in hand again.

As they hustled down the sidewalk, Alex gave her a frantic look. "Quit trying to get rid of me. I'll never survive this afternoon without you."

"That's a ridiculous thing to say."

"I know. That doesn't mean it's not true."

And since the crazy man was absolutely serious, Beth kept up as they raced back to Mrs. Radcliff's side. Whatever he did— and he did a lot that afternoon—he was professional, skilled, and kind. And through every second of it, he clung to Beth like she was some kind of talisman who was the source of his power. He wouldn't let her step away for even an instant.

Four long years of hard work, long nights, intense training, and massive textbooks, and Beth had been reduced to a lucky charm.

★ Thirteen ★

"His name's Buchanan." Cletus knew he'd put the question wrong. He'd not get a single word out of this bunch. Still, he couldn't stop himself from goading them. "Man claims he's a doctor but he's got blood on his hands, and I'm here to see that he's brought to justice before he kills again."

Stony silence greeted him. These shiftless skunks didn't know Cletus was a lawman. He'd been a no-account himself at one time but no more. He had money and a fine horse and a sharp outfit of clothes and the best gun money could buy. This scum needed to learn how to treat their betters, and Cletus burned with the need to teach them at the end of a shooting iron. But the four men sitting at the table dealing into a card game had watchful eyes and they kept their gun hands loose and ready.

Cletus should've come in and asked if he could join the game. He knew how to play cards and men with equal skill. But he'd been edgy and anxious to track down the doc and he'd gone straight to questioning them. Knowing he'd lost out, Cletus tried to act as if he didn't care. With a shrug, he said, "I heard tell of a man by that name down this'a way matched his description."

"We mind our own business, mister," the closest poker player said, drawing long on his cigar. "Healthy man might wanta do the same."

A little chill climbed Cletus's spine at the measured drawl, clearly a threat. Cletus nodded. There were others in town. He'd handle them better than he had this trash. Probably a bunch of outlaws themselves. Cletus decided then and there he'd start bounty hunting as soon as the last of the deserting cowards were rounded up.

Cletus sidled away from the men, not wanting to turn his back. He stepped out on the wooden sidewalk in the little cow town and stalked away, his feet thudding hard on the boards, grumbling. Seeing a diner ahead, he headed for it.

Gathering the frayed edges of his temper, he walked inside and noticed three long tables, two of them empty. Normal for mid-morning. The third had four men sitting at it. A hefty, grizzled man with a cigar dangling from his lips came through swinging doors carrying a coffeepot.

"Want a cup?"

"Yep. Obliged." Cletus sat at the table with the others.

One looked like he lived in town. Dark pants and a vest over a white shirt. Two others were dusty and sweat soaked, with a Stetson lying on the table beside each. Most likely cowpokes. The third wore a black leather vest, and when he shifted, Cletus noticed a star on his chest. A lawman. Cletus never went directly to the law in any town. Too much chance of the lawman going after the deserter and claiming the reward for himself.

The coffee slapped onto the table in front of him and Cletus was good and trapped. He couldn't ask any questions and he couldn't leave without drawing notice. For now he was thwarted, but not for long. Instead of asking questions, Cletus listened. Sometimes he learned more keeping his mouth shut anyway.

★

Alex had no idea why he hadn't kept his mouth shut.

Not today. It'd already been too late today.

But yesterday, on the stage. *Deltoideus.* He could have helped Beth like an untrained cowboy. But oh no, he had to say the word *deltoideus.* He had to spout off medical words. Now here he was, as good as branded with the name of doctor.

He almost ran screaming when he saw the Armitages. Mrs. Armitage supported her husband. Leo's arm was in a sling, and his face was pasty white. No doubt from exhaustion and pain, but what if he'd reinjured himself?

"Doctor." Mrs. Armitage waved as if he might have missed them coming straight at him on the one and only sidewalk.

He'd just checked Sally for the fourth time and he needed to get back to Vivian Radcliff. Her time was coming close. Beth had promised to look in on Leo and Camilla today. Fine, these were her patients. Except he hadn't let Beth out of his sight.

Beth must have sensed his desire to cut and run because she grabbed his hand in a vise.

"This way, folks. Come on in to Dr. Buchanan's office." Beth waved her arm toward the building Sally was lying in.

Dr. Buchanan's office? Where had that come from? "I am *not* a doctor," Alex growled under his breath.

"Shut up and get in there. I'm going to go get help to move Mrs. Radcliff down here so you can tend everyone at once without running back and forth."

Alex dug his fingers into hers. He could out-vise her any day of the week. "If you leave, I swear I'll make a break for it and you'll never see me again."

The Armitages narrowed the gap between them.

"I should anyway. You can handle this." Alex's gaze met hers. "I'll go. You take over. You needed me for your sister but not for the rest of this."

"Give me strength."

Alex was pretty sure she was praying. Good, let God give her all the strength she needed, and while she was at it, she oughta ask for some strength for him, too. Alex didn't think he had much coming from God. Or more honestly, Alex admitted he was too ashamed to ask.

"I'll get Pa to help the parson move his wife."

"She'll be loud and out of control birthing a baby. We can't have that while we're trying to keep Sally quiet."

"My sister's tougher than you think. I'd wager Mrs. *Radcliff* is tougher than you think. And no matter *how* wimpy they are, it's a sure bet that they're all tougher than *you*."

"Hey, Doc." Leo Armitage was looking straight at Alex. Beth had done more for him yesterday than Alex had. The guy was a jerk to pretend Alex was the doctor.

Alex looked at her, expecting resentment.

She smiled, the picture of competence and calm. . .and strength. "Step right in here to the doctor's office. Dr. Buchanan will have a look at your arm. We've had a busy day already today. Is it all right if we go check on the parson's wife while you wait? She's in labor."

"Of course. We don't mind waiting." Mrs. Armitage acted like she was a bit early for her appointment.

"There aren't any chairs. Won't you get tired standing so long?" Alex focused on the sick one of the group. Let Mr. Armitage decide his own fate.

"I'll be fine. I might settle on the floor though. We'll find a place to get comfortable. I appreciate the help you gave me yesterday, Dr. Buchanan." He let his wife get the door then thanked her so kindly, Alex was humbled. Sure, he'd punched Alex in the nose, but other than that, the guy was a true gentleman.

The couple went in.

Beth went back to dragging Alex.

"I am *not* a doctor," Alex said.

"Give me strength." Beth looked up toward heaven.

The parson's wife, brave pioneer woman that she was, agreed to move to the doctor's office on her injured ankle. Adam and Laurie had vanished with all the children. Tillie was put in charge of moving bedding to the office. As soon as Tillie headed out, and the poor laboring woman was between pains, Alex and the parson carried Mrs. Radcliff down the street with Beth holding the doors.

Alex's doctor's office now had a delivery room, a post-surgical recovery room, and a waiting room. All in the *same* room, granted, but still, it was almost a city hospital.

Tillie left. She said she was determined to find Adam and save all those children. Alex snorted. Adam was probably in more danger than the kids. Pa rode with Tillie, promising to return as soon as Tillie was safe at home.

Leo Armitage was checked over thoroughly and sent on his way.

Mrs. Radcliff was delivered of a squalling son.

Sally went to sleep.

Beth settled in to sit with Sally and her mother for the night.

Parson Radcliff was busy helping his wife get comfortable on a bedroll on the floor, propping her up so she could cradle her baby.

The door swung open and Alex jumped, afraid of what else might happen.

Clay McClellen's spurs clinked as he stepped inside, dragging his Stetson off his head. "I left your son with Adam for the night, Parson. I didn't see any sense bringing him back here. I can ride out and fetch him home in the morning."

"Thanks, Clay. Obliged to you and Adam and Tillie for caring for him. I haven't been a very good father to Andy today."

Clay gave him a good-natured slap on the back. "You're doing fine. That's what a church family is for."

"Clay, why don't you ride on home with Beth now," Ma said.

"She's not going anywhere." Alex found his doctor voice somewhere.

"I'm staying, Ma. Alex has to keep watch over Mrs. Radcliff for a while longer then help Parson carry her home. I'll be needed here with Sally. You go on home and get some rest. Alex and I'll watch Sally. In the morning, ride in with Pa when he picks up Andrew and you can spell me."

"No, you're not staying in here tonight." All Clay's good humor vanished. "It ain't proper."

Alex tensed at the narrow-eyed look on Clay's face.

"Nothing improper will go on here, Clay." Alex wasn't letting Beth go. If she went, he went.

"It's out of the question," Sophie stood next to Beth like a guardian angel in a petticoat.

"No, Alex, she can't spend the night here with you." Clay spoke on top of his wife.

If she left he couldn't do it. He'd look at the poor girl with her throat slit and think of that woman dead over the cliff yesterday. Without Beth he'd start seeing the dead and dying in war. He might fall asleep. He might dream.

"I'll stay," Sophie said. Alex looked at the dark circles of fatigue under Sophie's eyes. The woman needed rest.

"You'll have your hands full with Sally tomorrow, Sophie." Clay clutched his hat brim in both hands, clearly worried. "She'll be feeling better, and you'll be the only one who can keep her quiet. You know I don't have the knack. But I can stay tonight when she's probably going to mostly sleep."

"Isn't that shipment of horses being driven in tomorrow?" Sophie asked. "You have to be home."

Clay paused, his eyes narrow. "I'll manage. Or Eustace can see to caring for the new stock."

Beth snorted as if she was fed up. "If you don't sleep tonight you'll have to sleep tomorrow, Ma. I might as well do my turn now."

"You're just as tired as I am." Sophie didn't budge.

"I worked long shifts at the hospital. I'm used to it. And I can't sleep now anyway. I need to wait until Mrs. Radcliff's ready to go home and Sally is settled for the night. Until then I can't leave anyway. You and Pa go."

"No." Clay stood firm.

"I'm fine." Beth crossed her arms.

"You can't stay here alone with Dr. Buchanan," Parson Radcliff chimed in. "Sally isn't a sufficient chaperone. I assume you've been raised to know what's good and proper." The parson gave Alex a fire-and-brimstone look if ever there was one.

Alex wondered if maybe *his* throat was swelling shut. Beth could *not* leave him. He looked at the traitor pastor. "You've been falling all over yourself thanking me for helping your wife. And now you accuse me of treating Beth with anything but the utmost respect."

"That's not the point." The parson sounded downright starchy.

"Beth leaves or you leave." Clay jabbed his finger at Alex. "Or someone else stays." Clay said it like he was reading it straight off a stone tablet carved by the finger of God.

Alex felt all the old fear, the nightmarish torment, welling up inside him. He took a half step backward. "She can't leave. Don't you want to stay with me, Beth?"

"I do." Beth was at his side in an instant, holding his hand firmly, sounding as if she'd just taken a vow. And Alex supposed she had. She was still trying to protect him. Stop him from making a fool of himself.

"That's the perfect answer." The parson slapped his forehead with the heel of his hands. "I mean it's as if God Himself is shaking us, trying to see what's right before our eyes."

"What?" Alex felt hope.

"Right before our eyes where?" Sophie looked up from watching every breath Sally took.

"Give me strength," Beth whispered her standard prayer.

"Absolutely not." Clay slapped his thigh with his hat.

That must mean Clay at least knew what the crazy parson was talking about. He had a hunch Beth did, too. What else did she need strength for right now?

"I thought of it when Beth said, 'I do.' They can get married." The parson smiled as pleased as if he'd just given birth himself. He had—to a harebrained idea.

"What?" Alex looked down at their joined hands. It made no more sense now that it'd been said out loud.

"That idea isn't before *my* eyes." Sophie's blond brows lowered to a straight, angry line. "They only met yesterday."

"Absolutely not." Clay *had* known what the parson meant.

"And how long did you and Clay know each other before you got hitched?" the parson asked.

"I'm not sure even God can give me that much strength," Beth muttered.

Strength enough to run away from Alex? Or to marry him? Because suddenly, to Alex, it made perfect sense. For some reason the world made sense with Beth at his side. Having, holding, from this day forward. Yes! He found stores of strength and courage inside himself. God himself was shaking Alex for sure. He might even be able to go back to doctoring. . .not that he was a doctor.

"Beth, will you marry me?"

Fourteen

Beth's eyes locked on Alex's and she couldn't get free. That same weird, deep contact that seemed to tap energy from her bones and heart and soul.

She considered herself a levelheaded person. Good in a crisis. Thinking things through, but at the same time acting fast.

Right this minute, her brain seemed to be stuffed with gauze padding. Gauze padding soaked in laudanum. Stupid and numb, pinned by Alex's gaze.

"Uhhh. . ." Beth drew that sound out awhile.

"No. That isn't a possibility." Ma was talking but she wasn't making sense, not through the laudanum and gauze.

"Let's get home, Beth." Pa crossed his arms with that "I've got a revolver and I'm not afraid to use it" look he sometimes got; but that didn't break the connection with Alex.

"One day," Parson Radcliff said so loudly Beth almost understood what that meant. "Parson Roscoe told me the whole story. Clay, you knew Sophie one day and not a full day at that when you married her. And you spent most of that day unconscious."

"That was different." Pa's voice came from far away and nearby at the same time. He'd come to stand next to Beth, Alex clinging to her hand.

Ma had rounded that counter that before had been between

her and the rest of the room. She still kept one hand resting on Sally to make sure she didn't move, but she'd narrowed the gap between herself and Beth.

The parson came close and kept telling the story of Ma and Pa's wedding day, a story Beth had heard many times. Which is why it seemed so easy to ignore the telling now.

"He was family." Sophie kept her hand on Sally.

Beth glanced down at Sally, sleeping. Alive because Alex had known what to do. And Alex would never have come through if Beth hadn't been handy to browbeat him. Not exactly a good basis for a marriage...marriage...marriage. Marriage? Beth's head went numb again. She'd almost pulled out of it there for a minute.

Parson Radcliff's son started crying, underscoring to Beth why she needed to stay. The baby was fine. Mrs. Radcliff's ankle would heal. Mr. Armitage's arm was going to be fine. Beth could have maybe done all of that, though not as well as Dr. Loco here who now spoke.

"We'll be fine. We've made a connection today that will get us through." Alex's gaze took on a desperate edge. His hand tightened on hers until the pain almost seeped through the numbness in her head. The man was afraid she'd leave him.

And she was afraid he'd abandon her little sister. Not because Alex was weak. His behavior was too completely out of control for such a normal word. The man was a lunatic who somehow could tap into sanity when he looked her in the eye. What did that make her? A human straitjacket?

"What do you say, Beth? Will you marry me?"

"Uh. . ." So far that was the only sound Beth was capable of.

"I told you no." They'd formed a tight circle, but Pa pushed in farther so he stood between Beth and Alex, not squarely between, though. Alex still held her gaze, drawing strength, sanity. "I'm Beth's pa and I make a decision like this."

"I saved your daughter's life today, Clay." Alex looked away from Beth and it was like having skin ripped from her body. She almost cried out in pain. Then she watched her crazy would-be fiancé

100

square off against Pa. The madman didn't do half bad standing up to him. That was something that could be said of very few men. Of course Alex was insane. "Why would you deny me Beth's hand in marriage?"

"Don't you put my Sally's life up as if we owe you and Beth is the payment." Sophie left Sally's side.

"Ma, she'll fall off that counter!" With the eye contact broken, Beth found words beyond "uh." Though her head still had that numb, stupid feel. And Ma obeyed quickly, which just showed how upset Ma was by all this. She'd have never left Sally's side otherwise.

The baby started crying louder. "Doctor, are you sure my son is all right?" Mrs. Radcliff sounded fretful, not an uncommon occurrence after a child was born. The woman needed quiet and peace and sleep. Instead she had ringside seats at a circus.

"Dr. Buchanan, you and Beth can't leave my wife so soon after our baby is born, and with a sprained ankle besides." The parson looked scared, and Beth got the impression he thought Alex and Beth getting married boiled down to life and death.

Sally groaned and reached unsteady hands toward her neck, which no doubt hurt terribly. After all, she'd had her throat cut just that morning.

"Settle down, Sally." Sophie abandoned the battlefield.

The parson turned to his wife, went to her side, and knelt by her, where she lay on a pallet on the floor. He reached for his tiny son. "Let me take him, Viv."

Pa turned and looked down at Beth, blocking the whole room from her vision. "Let's go now, Beth. If you have a serious interest in marriage, it'll keep until you know him better."

"Uh. . ." Beth felt some reason returning. She could make sense any minute now.

"Clay, help me." Sophie had Sally's hands, but suddenly Sally was thrashing her head and moaning.

Pa left, and in the midst of the Radcliffs calming the baby and the McClellens calming Sally, Beth and Alex were alone in a little cocoon surrounded by chaos.

And the connection returned. Alex stepped closer. Beth noted that the man was ignoring his patients in order to talk with her. Not admirable behavior. Of course she was ignoring them, too.

"You know how desperately I need you." Alex whispered, stepping even closer so the words were only between them. If there'd been romance between them, those would have been beautiful, loving words.

"I know." It was the simple truth. For whatever reason, Alex needed her nearly as much as he needed air. Oh, he didn't need her if he remained a useless lump sleeping in a stagecoach. But for doctoring, it wasn't about want. It was about need. Maybe after a time he'd be able to function as a doctor on his own, but for now, Beth didn't think he had a chance.

"And you need me, too." Alex's eyes changed, became warm, burning, glittering. . .maybe with madness.

Beth felt her heartbeat speed up, but it wasn't out of fear. "Why do I need you?" The gauze and laudanum must be thinning because she was sure she didn't need Alex for anything.

"Because they won't let you be a doctor here without me." He leaned closer, almost as if he wanted to kiss her. The words held that kind of intimacy. "But with me, you can doctor this whole town. They'll call you my nurse or a midwife, but the label isn't important. Not even the respect. You have a passion to heal."

"How do you know that?" Beth's breathing sped up.

Alex's voice rose from a whisper to something dark and husky and alive. "I know it because I recognize the same thing in you that I have in myself. If you were smart, you'd run. The kind of calling, obsession even, to help people hurts."

"No, it doesn't. It's never hurt me."

"That's because you've never failed."

"I've failed. I've had patients die. I know my place in their lives is to help, but survival, life and death, is up to God."

"You haven't failed like I've failed. You haven't seen butchery. You haven't been surrounded by death and dying, blood and screams, women and children, young men with their whole lives in front of them. . ."

"War. You're talking about a war. What war?" The Civil War was long over. Alex was too young to have been through it.

"The frontier. I was a doctor for the cavalry. I saw the troops, but also the Indian villages. I saw—I saw. . ." Alex's voice faded away. The look of horror in his eyes shook Beth and she wished so terribly she could take that vision from him, that memory.

Alex's hand trembled as it reached to rest against her face. "It's not about love, Beth. It's about something bigger, more important."

Beth wanted to tell Alex there was nothing more important than love. Nothing. "It's about helping these people, using the gift God put in you. A gift that glows and burns like red hot coals and makes you feel like the suffering of others is your own."

Alex nodded his head slowly. His hand settled more firmly against her face and lifted and lowered, gently guiding her to nod along with him.

Somehow that motion of agreement transferred itself inside her, and she knew Alex was right. She did need to heal. And it hurt. And it burned inside her, a flame that never went out.

"You need me as much as I need you." He leaned closer still, his voice only for her. "With me beside you, the work of a doctor is possible for you."

"I'll do it." Beth reached up to rest her hand on his, where it cradled her face. Nodding under her own power now. "I'll marry you."

Alex lowered his head and she thought he'd kiss her. She realized she was intensely curious about how the connection between them would feel if it was expressed in a kiss.

Instead he closed his eyes and rested his forehead on hers. "I'm sorry. I should just go."

"Beth, lend us a hand."

Beth turned at her mother's urgent voice. Sally was half-asleep and only reacting to the pain now, thrashing. Her little sister was going to be fine, but right now she couldn't stand to lie still another second. Sally needed Beth's calming voice.

She felt like she had to tear at something that bound her to Alex, but her mother's need for help wasn't something she could ignore. She rushed to Sally's side and began crooning.

Behind her, she heard Alex go to the Radcliffs and talk with that same soothing tone as she had. A quick glance and she saw he held the fretful baby in his arms.

A miraculous voice. He'd just used it on her to persuade her to commit an act of madness. She was as crazy as Alex. But she was going to do it.

"Sally, honey, listen to me. It's Beth." Her sister's thrashing slowed. Her growing hysteria eased and her eyes focused. She let Beth soothe her. The struggles gradually ceased. While she crooned, Beth considered the madness of what she'd agreed to. But was it madness? Or genius?

As a single woman, she'd never be allowed to use her God-given gift for doctoring. And "God-given" was the key part of that thought. This gift was hers from her earliest memory. The compassion, the gentling voice, the healing touch, the gift for reaching all living creatures.

And now here stood Alex, who had connected to her in a way beyond her understanding. His proposal gave her the chance to fulfill God's call. To Beth it seemed that his very proposal was guided by God.

She needed Alex even more than he needed her.

Yes, she'd marry him.

★ Fifteen ★

I know what you're thinking, Beth."

Beth didn't doubt it. Her ma had always been one step ahead of everyone.

As Sally finally subsided into sleep, Beth smiled at her mother, so tough, so smart, the best woman Beth had ever known. "I told Alex yes. I'm going to marry him, Ma."

"It's true I got married fast, Beth, honey. But my situation was completely different from yours. I had no other prospects, and Clay was your pa's brother. Even though I hadn't known him long—"

"About twenty hours as I recall, and he spent sixteen of those hours either unconscious or in town or riding ahead of you on his horse when we went back to the ranch. I think you probably actually talked to the man for about a half an hour." Beth grinned.

Ma's eyes narrowed. She didn't like not getting her way.

"Alex doesn't seem all that—" Ma's eyes slid to Alex, who was on his knees beside the parson's wife, talking quietly to her. He held the Radcliffs' new son in his arms.

Alex seemed pretty wonderful to Beth right at that second. Sure, she'd thought he was a lunatic at first. But he was coming around. Showing flashes of occasional sanity. At least as long as she was at his side. "There's something between us, Ma. I feel it.

It's meant to be."

"You can't have fallen in love with the man this fast."

"I didn't say love. You're right that it's too soon. But I can—I can *see* into him. He's no good at covering his feelings. I can see he's got a gift for healing like I do. I can see he's wounded from giving too much. And I can see—" Beth looked up at her ma, a woman she respected more than anyone else on earth. "I can see that I will be able to heal him by supporting him and encouraging him." And maybe, occasionally, beating on him with his hat. Beth didn't rule it out.

Ma frowned and shook her head doubtfully. "Beth, honey—"

"He needs me, Ma," Beth cut her off. "And I need him."

"You don't need anyone, Beth."

Pa was there, too. He wasn't ever going to agree to this. Beth knew for a fact that her pa didn't think there was a man alive good enough for any of his daughters. So she wasn't too worried about convincing him. He wouldn't kidnap her to stop the wedding and he wouldn't shoot Alex, unless Alex really provoked him. So Pa wasn't the one who needed convincing—since it was hopeless. But she'd really like her mother's blessing.

"This town—the whole West—will never let me tend to the sick. I thought they would. I did a lot of doctoring when I was back East. But now I know it was because I was at a doctor's side. Alone, I won't be able to do anything."

Alex came up to her side. They exchanged a glance, and Beth knew he'd heard everything. He didn't interfere though. Instead he stood beside Pa, across from Beth, and bent down to examine Sally's throat. "We can't let Sally eat for twenty-four hours. We need to get the esophageal incision to close. I don't want to suture the outer layer of skin because we'll need to take the inner stitches out. She can have a bit of water in about twelve hours. She'll be hungry so it won't be easy to hold her back. She needs careful watching. It's best if she stays here rather than goes home. Jouncing her around could slow down the healing."

Alex looked away from the incision, right at Beth. Then his

eyes cut to Ma. Beth was afraid of what he'd say. Things were balanced on the very edge of disaster. If he said the wrong thing, it could tip the wrong way.

"Sophie"—he looked sideways at Pa—"Clay, I want permission to marry your daughter. I know we haven't known each other long enough. I know that. But we are suited to each other." Alex looked at Beth now.

She nodded. "We are."

"She fills an empty place inside of me. And I think—I hope—I will be a good mate for her, too." Alex looked back at her parents. "We'd like your blessing. We've already decided that we will get married. And we're doing it right now tonight. But to have your support and blessing would mean a lot to Beth, and because her feelings are important to me, they'd mean a lot to me, too." He looked directly at Pa then. "I will treat her with kindness and respect, Clay. I already respect her more than any woman I've ever met."

The two men stared at each other.

Pa had his usual grim, narrow-eyed look, the one he always got when there was a male paying attention to his girls. He looked away first to Ma. "What do you think, Sophie?"

Ma rolled her eyes. "He can't be much worse than your brother, I suppose. And we'll be here to take care of her if he turns out to be worthless, as I firmly believe he will."

A disgusted huff of breath escaped Pa's lips. He looked at Beth. "Marry him then. You can always come on back home."

Beth almost laughed at the depth of her parents' low expectations. She did smile at Alex, who looked offended and hurt and a bit angry. "That's as close to a blessing as you're likely to get from my folks. Maybe if you shape up to be a decent husband they'll give it after a few years. Five or ten."

"Can't say as I blame them." Alex sighed then called over his shoulder, "Can you spare a minute, Parson Radcliff? Beth and I'd like to get married."

"Sure, won't take but a second."

Beth remembered that the parson had been all for this. He

was a man of God. Surely that meant something. What though, she couldn't exactly say.

The parson came to stand by Sally's head carrying his fussing son. Beth and Alex stood facing each other over Sally. Her parents stood in such a way they'd almost work as a best man and matron of honor. Except for her little sister stretched out on a counter, it was a little like a wedding. Not a lot, but a little.

The vows were short and to the point because Parson Radcliff's baby started crying. Beth never knew if Alex would have kissed her because the parson didn't take the time to order it and the counter and wounded young woman between them didn't make it convenient.

"You can go home now, Ma and Pa. We're married now and that makes it proper and legal and safe for you to leave us alone."

"Legal, definitely," Ma said. "Proper—I suppose. But safe?"

Pa shook his head. "No, she's safe. Beth knows how to take care of herself. Alex here looks none too tough. You can handle him if he gets to being trouble. You have your knife, right? Where's your rifle?"

"I don't usually bring it to church." Beth didn't look at Alex for fear of what she'd see while they talked rifles and knifes.

"I'll bring it in tomorrow." Pa patted Sally on the ankle.

"I can turn him into one of my patients in a flicker of an eyelash. Don't worry. I've already proved that one."

"Oh, brother." Alex turned and went to check on Mrs. Radcliff and urged the parson to go home. Alex kept the baby.

Satisfied that her new husband had been reminded of exactly whom he was dealing with, Beth kissed her folks good-bye and went back to tending her now-sleeping little sister.

★ Sixteen ★

The hospital was settled quickly. The parson and the McClellens left. The baby and Mrs. Radcliff slept quietly on the pallet on the floor.

Alex made up another pallet on the floor and gently moved Sally to a spot where she wasn't at risk of falling. "Strange," Alex whispered to himself.

"What's strange?"

Alex jumped. He'd been so focused on Sally he hadn't heard Beth come up behind him. He glanced down, afraid he'd jostled the girl and awakened her, but Sally slept on. Alex rose to his feet and faced Beth. Almost alone with his wife. "I just realized I've got a little sister." Alex smiled. "I kinda like the idea."

Beth's expression lightened. He saw exhaustion on her face, but the serenity and compassion were still there. And the strength, under it all, more strength than he'd ever had.

"Well, once you get to know her, I'm sure you'll find out she and my other brothers and sisters will drive you crazy." Beth grinned. "They're a wild bunch, all right."

"And a wife." Alex almost regretted saying the words, because Beth's smile shrank like wool underwear in boiling water. But there wasn't much point in denying it.

"You've got yourself a wife." Beth nodded but commented no further.

"And you've got a new name. Beth Buchanan. Pretty."

"The name?" Beth's forehead furrowed.

"The name is pretty. . .too." Alex leaned forward and kissed her. He was there and away so fast she didn't have time to use her strength to beat on him. He even took a few steps back.

"Now, Alex." Pink rose in Beth's cheeks. "This marriage isn't going to be—be—about—about k–kissing."

Suddenly Alex was absolutely determined to prove her wrong.

"It's going to be about caring for sick people in Mosqueros," she added.

He'd seen her mad and compassionate. He'd seen her smiling and courageous and tough. He'd seen her thrilled to see her pa and loving with her little sisters and brothers. But he'd never seen her blush. It made his brand spankin' new wife prettier than ever.

"Agreed." Alex didn't agree. He'd break that news to her later. He was watching her so intently he noticed the tiny flinch of hurt when he agreed so quickly. The madness, the haunting seemed a bit further away with every moment he spent in her company. He knew it was just another kind of weakness to think a woman could heal a tormented soul. Alex had to figure out a way to save himself.

And then he thought of Someone else who could save him. God.

He'd believed that fiercely when he was young. But for so long, Alex had believed that his actions put him beyond the pale. Maybe not. Maybe he had reason to hope.

Smiling at his blushing wife, he said, "Our marriage is going to be about caring for sick people."

She squared her shoulders and nodded, as if there'd been no flinch, no hurt. "Good, I'm glad we see it the same way."

"Me, too. We need to get some rest." Alex leaned in and kissed her again.

★

Mandy was awakened with a kiss.

She made a poor princess because she'd have rather stayed

110

asleep. The jerking, huffing train had beaten on her until it felt as if she'd walked into the middle of a fistfight. She'd finally fallen asleep, after trying futilely to sleep sitting up in the uncomfortable seats most of the night.

And now Sidney smiled into her barely open eyes as if waking up a woman half-dead from exhaustion was a romantic idea.

And her Winchester was close enough to grab.

Shocked at that unworthy thought, Mandy forced herself to smile. She also quit breathing because Sidney's breath was foul enough to raise blisters on her skin and his odor was the worse for having ridden all day yesterday in the sweltering heat.

It was still almost completely dark. There was a bit of a cast of gray to the train car so she could see Sidney. . .and smell him.

"Good morning." Her voice sounded as rough and rocky as ten miles of mountain trail.

Sidney pulled her into another kiss. Mandy did her best to hold her breath and kiss at the same time, hoping the kiss ended before her lungs exploded.

"Honey, I found a luggage car near the end of the train." Sidney's eyes were warm, coaxing. His voice was sultry and suggestive. A voice Mandy loved in the normal course of things. "Why don't we go back there and spend some time alone?"

Uh-oh. *Alone* had gotten to be one of Mandy's least favorite words. The man had suggested it many times since they'd met. Propriety had always been a sufficient excuse.

She wanted to be Sidney's wife in all regards. And she would be. As soon as they found some quiet, comfortable, clean spot. With a bathtub.

No luggage car. And she knew all too well that Sidney didn't like the word *no*. She braced herself for the pouting to begin.

"Good morning." An elderly woman moved up beside them. "I've been waiting for you to wake up. Nothing more tedious than a long train ride." She lowered herself onto the bench seat facing Mandy and Sidney as if her joints ached.

Thank You, dear Lord.

Mandy had a moment of pause at that thought. She wasn't sure escaping a time alone with her grimy husband should be such a relief. Certainly she smelled rather—travel worn—herself. But then if she did, why was Sidney so eager to be alone with her?

"We'd be pleased for the company, ma'am." And when Mandy said "we" she meant "I" because Sidney did *not* look pleased. "Have you done a lot of train travel?" Mandy nodded at the seat that faced her.

Sidney was on her left, crowding her up against the window, but he eased away as the woman settled in. A lucky break for Mandy and her assaulted sense of smell.

"Oh my, yes. I'm an old hand. I've got children spread here and there along the rail lines. And I'm always on my way to see one or the other of them."

"Are you riding all the way to Denver?"

"Why yes, dear, I am."

Mandy smiled. "Where are you from?"

The elderly lady, grimy from travel, smiled with the kind eyes of an angel as she began knitting and chattering away.

The woman really had been everywhere and her stories were so interesting Mandy barely minded her sullen, moping husband.

★

Beth had gotten precious little sleep. She was exhausted and groggy. Which is why she remained calm when she noticed a hand on her stomach.

A man's hand.

Not calm after all.

Beth launched herself to sit up straight. The hand remained resting on her belly.

It all came flooding back. . .the hand belonged to her husband. She'd gotten married last night.

Her eyes warily turned to follow that hand up to Alex's eyes, wide open. She caught his hand and returned it to him.

Alex smiled.

Finding a smile curling her own lips, Beth was shocked at the impulse. She'd been out of her mind. What other possible reason could there be for marrying a lunatic? She must be one, too. But at around midnight last night—Beth shifted around in her head and couldn't remember exactly what time it had been—marrying Alex had seemed like a really good idea.

To her surprise she still liked it. She was truly delighted to find herself married to the lunatic. Terrified, too, and the two—delight and terror—were an uncomfortable combination. But still she smiled. She had definitely lost her mind.

"Good morning, Mrs. Buchanan." Alex's voice was gravelly with sleep. His eyes were heavy-lidded. He had a bristly morning set of whiskers.

"Good morning, Alex."

Having him take a bath, shave, and get into clean clothes had made a world of difference in how she reacted to Alex. She hadn't wanted to slug him for hours. Well, there'd been a few mild moments of temptation. Bathing seemed like a really shallow reason to marry a man, but honestly, he'd cleaned up very nicely. Now he had morning whiskers.

An odd thing to be waking up for the first time with a husband.

Alex sat up. He was close enough that it brought up memories of last night's kiss. And then he reminded her of it in an unmistakable way. He kissed her again.

Beth wondered at her willingness to let this near stranger kiss her. It couldn't be a sign of good character on her part. But she let him anyway.

His arms came around her waist and she found her own entwining his neck.

"I'm well, Beth. Let's go home." Sally was awake.

Alex pulled back, grinned down at her, and then turned to her sister.

Beth moved out of Alex's way and went to Sally's other side.

"You had a hard day yesterday, Sally." Alex took Sally's hand.

"I think you're going to be fine, and your ma and pa will be in to see you soon, but for now. . ." He took her hand and guided her fingers to the tiny cut in her neck. Alex was careful not to let Sally touch the actual wound, but he let her touch close enough that it helped her understand the source of her main discomfort. "I had to perform a very small operation. You got stung by bees. Do you remember that?"

Sally's fingers were slow-moving and careful, two words Beth had never used to describe her active little sister. A sure sign she was still feeling poorly. The bee stings had mostly gone down, but there were still tiny traces of each and every one of them.

"Now let me explain exactly what I did. Because I need you to understand why you have to lie very still for the rest of today. And not talk unless you absolutely must. I'm not going to let you eat either. A few sips of water is all. I know that will be hard, but Beth, and soon your parents, and I are here if you need any help. Okay?"

Sally nodded cautiously. "Okay."

As well as possible, Beth concealed a sigh of relief to hear Sally speak clearly.

"Your voice sounds good. You can talk if it feels okay, but no yelling, okay? We're trying to be very gentle with your throat today."

Sally smiled and nodded.

"Good. Now, you had a bad reaction to so many bee stings." Alex went on to explain with his soothing voice in very simple terms what he'd done. It was so clear that Beth suspected that, if it was ever asked of her, she could now perform this procedure herself.

The baby started to cry, and Alex glanced over his shoulder at his other patient. Then with one last pat of Sally's hand, he got up quickly and rushed to the infant.

Beth knew without being told that he was trying to let Mrs. Radcliff sleep awhile longer.

"It's a very good sign that you're wanting to go home, Sally."

Beth took up the task of distracting Sally from her natural inclination, which was to run wild.

As she soothed, Beth took occasional glances at her husband, handling a baby so comfortably, so calmly. She'd helped him find this part of himself. And he still needed her, even more than she needed him.

How strange to be married to a man she'd just met and actually feel good about that. She didn't love him—that would be a bit much—but she felt connected in a way that reminded her of God's words, *"The twain shall be one."* Then she flinched as she thought the verse all the way to the end. *"The twain shall be one flesh."*

Beth had an inkling of what that meant. Well, that wasn't for her. She and Alex were partners, business partners.

Except for that kiss. That had felt like more than partners. And she couldn't say Alex had stolen that kiss, either. He'd given her plenty of time to duck. But there she'd stood, like a brainless sheep, and let him kiss her. In honesty, she had to admit she'd kissed him back and enjoyed every moment.

Not as much as she'd enjoyed whacking him with his hat after the stage wreck, but almost. Very close to as much.

"Doc, come quick!" Mrs. Farley, who'd run the general store by her husband's side for as long as Beth could remember, slammed through the door yelling, "My husband fell. Bart knocked himself insensible. And his head is bleedin' something fierce."

The loud entrance woke up Mrs. Radcliff. She rose to her feet, a pioneer woman after all. Having a baby, even with a sprained ankle, didn't keep her down long. "Give me the boy and go, Dr. Buchanan. Go along with him Beth. I can mind Sally."

"No, your ankle—"

Alex grabbed a chair and sat it with a loud clatter next to Sally. He then swept Mrs. Radcliff into his arms, baby and all. The surprise of it shook a giggle out of the woman. Alex sat his passenger down at Sally's side.

"Thank you, ma'am." Alex grabbed Beth's hand while he rushed for the door. "Appreciate it. Sophie and probably the parson will be along anytime. I can really use Beth's help. Sally, you lie still." They hurried on Mrs. Farley's heels toward the store. The woman was round and her dark hair shot through with gray, but she set a fast pace.

"Alex, I should stay and—"

"There's your ma." Alex jerked his head toward the hitching post outside the doctor's office as they swept past.

"Ma, help keep Sally still," Beth yelled over her shoulder. "Mr. Farley's hurt. We'll be back as soon as possible."

Beth caught a glimpse of Ma's startled face as they rushed across the street, but she left it to Mrs. Radcliff to explain. The town was small and the general store was across the street and only a few doors down from the newly created doctor's office. Alex dragged her inside before she could tell her ma anymore.

Bart Farley was on his hands and knees, groaning. A good sign that the blow hadn't knocked him cold for any longer. A ladder lay toppled over next to the gray-haired man.

Alex was at the man's side instantly, dropping to his knees. "Lie back, sir. Just let me look at you."

Bart resisted Alex's touch, his eyes glazed and unfocused.

His wife knelt beside Alex. "You heard him, Bart. Now you mind the doctor."

"Don't need no doctor, Gina. No sense fussin'." He sounded groggy, his voice faint and unsteady.

Alex got him onto his back despite the resistance and started talking. "You've gone and split your head clean open, Bart. Just stay still. It'll take me but a minute to check you over."

Beth saw at a glance that the man needed stitches. "I'm going for my bag." She whirled for the door.

"Beth, wait!"

Freezing, she looked at Alex and saw his panic. She said, "You go for the bag then."

Alex's throat worked as if he were trying desperately to swallow. His eyes went from Bart, still struggling to sit up, to Beth. "N–no, no, that's fine. You go."

"I'll hurry." Beth wanted to shake the man. But being needed like this had an amazing effect on her heart. She ran.

★

Panic seemed to blow straight out of the top of Alex's head.

Beth was gone. All he saw was blood.

He reached for the man's shoulders and tried to get him to lie back. The blood had flowed down the side of Bart's face. It coated his neck and shoulder, and now Alex's right hand. It was a titanic battle to keep from jumping away.

Light wavered. Bart faded, replaced by another man in another time and place. The man under Alex's hands moaned in agony. An explosion blasted dirt into Alex's back. He reeled forward. Maybe shrapnel instead of dirt. He couldn't feel any pain. The impact blasted him like bullets. The force of the explosion knocked him onto his hands and knees, so he sheltered the man beneath him, covering the horrible wounds from flying debris.

The scene before him widened from the bleeding man. He was outside. Blazing hot, arid, deafening noise, inhospitable sand stretching in all directions. Men, dead men, dying men lay bleeding, limbs severed.

Alex needed to get up, go to them. He looked back at the man he shielded with his body and scrambled back onto his knees. A shredded, blood-soaked United States Cavalry uniform. The soldier's disemboweled stomach gaped open. The man cried out, as if Alex had slit him open with a knife instead of the Comanche Indian who lay dead only feet away, a half dozen bullet holes ripped through the Indian warrior's chest. Blood seeped into the thirsty sand. The earth drinking up life. Feeding on men too foolish to avoid war. The man bleeding and moaning by Alex was dead. He just didn't know it yet. Alex had to fight back vomit as he watched the man try to stuff his guts back into his own belly. Death was imminent, but the man was beyond pain, acting on instinct, mindless.

Like war.

More explosions, bullets whizzed in all directions. Alex's back burned with pain. He'd been hit.

"Stay down!"

Alex hunched low over the man. Ignoring the dead. Protecting himself like a coward while life spilled, crimson and hot, out of Comanche and cavalry alike. Alex couldn't help. He was too terrified, too selfish, too stupid and cowardly. The smell of blood was like a drug, leaving him unable to think of anything but surviving this madness. Weak beyond salvation for letting everyone bleed and scream and die while he cowered and did nothing.

Alex groped for his doctor bag. Lifted it. Gore dripped from it, and entrails and stinking foul blood. He threw the ugly thing aside with a cry of horror. Threw it hard and far as if he could throw away failure and death. But no one could throw that hard. Failure and death were like a stench soaked into his soul. They never left.

"Alex!" The voice cut through the smoke.

The explosions stopped sharply, as if Alex had gone deaf. He looked up into blue eyes. Pretty, living, wise, compassionate eyes. Annoyed eyes.

The room came back into focus. The battlefield left behind.

Beth.

The general store. Bart. Another patient he failed.

Alex's eyes fell shut. He dropped his head in shame as Beth ministered to this man. Not badly hurt at all.

How long had he been gone? How long had it taken Beth to restore him to fragile sanity? To pull him back to the present? How much of a madman had he appeared to be in front of Bart's wife?

Tears burned in Alex's eyes. He hadn't cried in a long time. He'd learned how to cry in war and spent a lot of time fighting that show of weakness. Then finally the tears had dried up and turned to stone in his heart.

Alex's prayers had gone, too. That ugly battle, toward the end of what they called the Red River War, was when Alex knew he couldn't do it anymore. That blood-soaked bag represented everything he'd failed at. It represented the day he'd walked away from his duties as an American, betrayed his country, his fellow soldiers, his wounded patients. He'd walked away to let them all die.

Only days later did he even notice the shrapnel in his back and arms. He was soaked with blood from his neck to his knees. A shocked man in a town with no name cared for Alex. The wounds didn't kill him. But he was dead just the same. Just like that eviscerated soldier, Alex was dead but still moving, too stupid to lie down.

He started to rise to his feet and get away from this single bleeding man. No decent person would want him if he knew the whole ugly truth.

Beth grabbed his hand. "Can we be alone for a few minutes, Mrs. Farley?"

"Well, I suppose. You're sure you don't need me?"

"We will need you in a bit, but for right now, we need things absolutely quiet. Just step outside. I'll call you back in."

"Is. . .is the doctor all right?" Mrs. Farley asked unsteadily. "Is Bart hurt seriously?"

Alex wondered what in heaven's name he'd done. He opened his mouth to ask, but before he could speak, Beth did the talking for them.

"Yes, the doctor's fine. Bart's going to be fine, too. We just need a minute alone." Beth's voice soothed Mrs. Farley and Alex, too.

His senses seemed to heal. He finally had the presence of mind to look at her again.

That's where my strength lies. I have none of my own. I can't find my way back to You, God. Only with Beth can I be a doctor.

A prayer.

Alex had prayed more in the days since he'd met Beth than he had in the years he'd spent wandering the West since he'd run, a broken, cowardly traitor, from that brutal, ugly, senseless war.

The United States Government had allowed the decimation

of the Indians' food source, turned a blind eye to the ruthless near-extermination of the buffalo. Then they'd made promises, food in exchange for the native people going to a reservation. The promises were largely broken and the Indians faced starvation if they stayed within their treaty borders, so they returned to their hunting grounds, more out of desperation than defiance.

Cattlemen came along with their herds of longhorns, and the Indians, hunters for countless generations, considered the cattle fair game. Clashes came, as was bound to happen.

The United States Army had turned its attention to the Civil War, and for a while the native people had been allowed to live their lives, which had included harassment of white settlers. Finally, with peace restored in the East, the government turned to settle the West. The time for treaties and talks was over and the cavalry was given the assignment of ridding the West of Indians. They went to the reservations and died or they left the reservations and died. The devil's own bargain.

Alex had been there to watch them die. His commander had insisted Alex focus on wounded soldiers first, and heaven knew there were plenty of them. Alex stood by during the deaths of so many.

They'd fought Comanche, Arapahoe, Cheyenne, and Kiowa. Alex had come to recognize their arrows and clothing and temperament. And fear them all. That part didn't make him a coward. Only a fool didn't fear a Comanche warrior.

But there were plenty of ways to show a yellow belly. And Alex had found them all. Alex wasn't fit to be near decent folks. He'd lived the last years denying his God-given gift for healing and remaining with those who were as indecent as he could find.

But Beth wouldn't let him go back where he belonged. She'd hate him if she knew all he'd done. Instead she'd married him.

He should never have allowed it. She'd be stained with his filth and failure. He'd kill again with his tenuous hold on reason. At least as a derelict who ran with drinkers and gamblers, though he didn't drink or gamble himself, he hadn't tainted anyone else.

God, forgive me. Protect Beth. Maybe I'll die and set her free.

But Alex had discovered, despite his best efforts, that he didn't die easily.

His nerves calmed. Beth's soothing voice rained her gentle ministrations down on Bart and healed Alex, too. He was able to turn to the wounded man and help. He could survive as long as she was within his grasp.

And from the assurance that he should shove her away to protect her came a soul-deep desire to hold her close forever. He'd married his very own personal savior. He knew that belonged to Jesus Christ, and that was where he should turn for strength. But for now, he needed Beth. Maybe when she'd healed him enough, strengthened him enough, he could turn back to God.

S e v e n t e e n

She'd married a lunatic and that was that.

Beth did her best not to care that she was married to a lunatic, but honestly, it was perturbing. A nice swat to Alex's head with a Stetson would have suited her right now, but there wasn't one handy. She held the idea in reserve for later.

"Here is the thread and needle, Alex." She talked to him in short words, enunciated clearly, to penetrate the fog he seemed to have sunk into. "You sew him up while I get the bandages out." *Ban-da-ges*, three syllable word. She hoped her lunatic husband could handle it.

Reaching for the thread with trembling hands, Beth thought how ridiculous it was that *he* was the doctor. *He* was the one everyone turned to. Worse yet, they might be right to do it. It galled her to admit it, but Alex was a better hand than she with the sutures. At least he was when his hands weren't shaking.

She did a nice job, but she didn't have his skill. She knew the work Alex did would heal faster and leave less of a scar.

The big, dumb jerk.

Beth didn't wander off in case her beloved husband drifted off into whatever asylum he lived in when she stepped away from his side.

Being married was going to be a pure nuisance. She did fetch

122

a washbasin, found fortunately right in the same room. Alex would probably sew his own brains away from his backbone if she left his sight. Blessed, or possibly cursed, with incredible empathy, Beth couldn't help wondering what Alex had gone through to have scarred him so deeply.

The poor, big, dumb jerk.

They soon had Bart Farley sewn up, washed up, and tucked into bed with the help of Mrs. Farley. Bart was already grousing about going to bed when there was work to be done, which Beth took as a good sign. They left him to Mrs. Farley's capable care.

Heading back to the hospital, Beth saw that her ma's and pa's horses were tied up in front of the building where Sally rested. Her folks would have things in hand. Now was as good a time as any. She grabbed Alex's wrist and dragged him into an alley. She needed to figure out the source of his madness before she could fix him. Now was the time to dig into his head. And she intended to do that digging even if she needed to use a pickax. She opened her mouth to start yelling.

"Thank you." Alex pulled her so close she couldn't breathe and kissed every angry thought right out of her head.

★

"I heard you're looking for a man?" A ferretlike man scuttled out of an alley.

Cletus looked the man over. He knew better than to trust this one, but most of his information came from sources like this. Purchased for the price of a pint of whiskey usually. It was Cletus's job to sort the truth from the lies, but he was good at it. "I am."

"C–can we have this—this meeting over there?" The man's hands trembled as he pointed toward a saloon. His lips quivered. He had a thirsty look, a desperate thirsty look.

"Let's go." Cletus led the way.

A half hour later, and a few bits poorer, Cletus smiled down at the notes he'd taken. This was it. The most promising description yet. He stepped out of the bar, missing the smoke and stench of liquor and men enjoying themselves.

A woman gasped and crossed in the middle of the dirt street to get away from him.

Maybe his smile was a little mean. Grunting in satisfaction, he tucked the paper in his pocket. Cletus swung up on his horse and turned it toward the trail. If it was true, Buchanan had been brought low. He'd be easy to catch. Cletus liked things easy.

Of course, in a dead-or-alive situation, Cletus preferred dead. Easier to transport a dead body than a live one. No escape attempts. But if Buchanan was as low-down as it sounded, turning his back on dying men, running like a yellow coward to save himself, it might not be that easy to find an excuse to shoot the man.

Chuckling, Cletus decided not to spend time pondering it. He'd find a way. Or wait until he was alone and make up something.

When it came to dead or alive, Cletus liked to keep things simple.

★

Alex wrapped her up tight and made her part of him. He was a married man. Right in front of God, he'd said his vows to the prettiest woman he'd ever seen, with strength enough for both of them.

"I can be a doctor if you're with me." He eased himself back and saw Beth, her eyes focused on his lips. She wanted this closeness as badly as he did. Well, it was more than Alex had ever hoped for. And he saw no reason not to send all his mending patients home—right now—and close up the doctor's office for the day and just practice being married as the good Lord intended. He lowered his head toward those pretty pink lips.

"Buchanan, get out here."

Alex's eyes dropped shut. His father-in-law. Wonderful, just whom he hoped to see right now.

Alex let loose of Beth with considerable reluctance, slid one arm around her waist to remind Clay the woman belonged to him. He had a moment of such power and pleasure that he was tempted to call Clay "Pa" just to see what would happen. Surely Beth wouldn't let her pa kill him.

Fighting the smile that wanted to spread across his face, Alex said, "What's the problem?" He tried to sound interested, since Clay's daughter was one of the patients back at the doctor's office.

"Luther took some of the men out to bury the bodies in from the stage wreck, and we've got a big problem."

Alex felt his throat begin to swell shut from panic. He glanced at Beth. "How close did you watch yesterday when I did that throat surgery on Sally?"

"Real close." Beth blinked her eyes like a sleepy owl being forced awake in the daylight. "Why?"

"No reason. Just good to know you could perform the surgery should it be called for." Alex turned back to Clay, who'd narrowed his eyes. That look probably came from finding his daughter being kissed in an alley. Wife or not, it was a disrespectful location for such a thing, no denying it. He hoped to find a spare moment, before Clay killed him, to point out that Beth had dragged Alex in there, not the other way around.

"Come on out here. I need to talk to you about the folks who died in that stagecoach wreck." Clay worded it like a request, but Alex saw no choice but to obey, even knowing what his brand-new Pa wanted. Alex was going to be asked to deal with the dead bodies.

Alex walked toward Clay, compelled to move by a will one thousand times stronger than his own—his wife dragged him. "I'm not a mortician, McClellen. I don't get bodies ready for burial."

"You come, too, Beth. I need to ask you some questions. I've sent for the Armitages, too."

Suddenly Alex wasn't quite so scared. This wasn't about laying out a line of corpses. This was about what had happened out on that trail. Alex could handle that. Probably.

Beth came alongside Alex and he slid his arm back around her, this time to hold himself steady.

Coward. Weakling. Failure. Traitor.

The words described him perfectly. He should let go of her, send her back to her pa. Go crawl out in the desert to die. Instead he clung tightly to his wife.

The alley was shaded, and when Beth and Alex stepped out into the sunlight, Alex blinked before he focused on the men standing across the street. No bodies.

Two fully bearded old men and a black man, younger but still with shots of gray through his hair. Alex had seen the old men at McClellen's ranch. Luther and Buff, they'd been called. Adam had been at church yesterday and, with his wife, took the McClellens' children after the accident. He remembered Tillie had been there at the parson's house. Lots of yesterday was a blur.

"They already buried the bodies, Alex." Clay leaned down, nearly whispering into Beth's ear. Alex could hear but no one else was close enough. "But this morning the sheriff rode out to the ranch real early. He went through the papers that didn't belong to any survivors. Figured to find heirs and send word back, along with any money, to whomever would miss those folks. The driver and the man riding with him are known men around here, but the sheriff found papers that had to belong to the woman who died."

Alex remembered that poor woman, lying dead, her eyes begging him to help her. He'd have killed himself trying if Beth hadn't stopped him.

Through the window to Alex's doctor's office, Sophie was visible at Sally's side. Parson Radcliff came pacing down the street, most likely to visit his wife.

The sheriff was talking with Luther, Buff, and Adam, glancing over at Clay every few seconds.

"This young woman has the same name as Mandy's husband. You told me that the other night, Beth."

"Yes, I remember." Beth sounded as if she grieved for a woman she'd never known. She sounded wounded. Alex hated to think of all the wounds that were in store for her as a doctor. "She's the right age. I wondered if she could be Mandy's sister-in-law. Celeste Gray could have been our family."

Clay made a sound so rude it shocked Alex. Why disparage the poor dead woman? "We found her satchel. The paperwork in it is almighty troubling. The only reason I'm telling you two is because you know her name and I don't want you saying anything about her being family to that low-down, yellow coyote of a husband of Mandy's."

Alex, leaning in to listen, jerked his head up at the venom in Clay's voice.

Beth jumped, too, so Alex wasn't wrong in thinking this was a level of anger Beth wasn't used to. "What's wrong, Pa?"

"The sheriff, Buff, Luther, and Adam are the only ones but me who've seen those papers. If we're readin' 'em right, that young woman was *married* to Sidney Gray. The man your sister married just two days ago."

Beth gasped. "What?"

Alex's eyes felt as if they bulged out of his head. A married man, courting Clay McClellen's daughter, and marrying her to boot. The man was a fool.

He glanced at Beth and saw the outrage on her face. She might be a kindly, compassionate woman, but she was a Texas cowgirl at heart. She looked ready to saddle a horse and set out after her sister.

Alex hoped Mandy was as tough, because a man who would tell such lies couldn't be trusted in anything. And right now he had Mandy at his mercy. He'd never even *met* Mandy and Alex was ready to hunt Sidney Gray down.

"I've already wired the town up the trail, hoping to catch Mandy before she gets on the train. I told her it was urgent she come home."

The four men—the sheriff, Buff, Luther, and Adam—approached Alex's little circle as Clay went on. "But I didn't put the truth of what we found in a telegram for the whole world to

127

see, so she might not mind me. I ought to hear right away if she's headed back. If she's not, I know they're heading for Denver. I'll ride out to fetch her home."

"The wire already came, Clay," Luther said. "The telegraph office said the train for Denver went through last night late, and Mandy was on it for sure. She's gone."

Clay's teeth ground together. With a short, hard jerk of his chin, he turned toward his horse. "I'll be going then."

Luther's hand landed hard on Clay's arm. "Nope, you can't ride off to save your daughter and abandon the rest of your family, Clay. You'll be gone for weeks getting to Denver. And it's a big city. Finding her will be hard work."

"Oh—yes—I—can—go get my daughter." Clay's tone made Alex's stomach twist. The man was furious at this dishonor of Mandy.

"Clay, think for a second," Luther said. "You know we'd watch the ranch and your family while you were gone. But you could be all winter hunting Mandy up."

Alex saw Clay's eyes go to the window framing Sophie.

"Your young'uns and Sophie need you. Buff and I have already decided. We're riding out for Mandy as soon as we get the packhorses loaded. We'll bring her back."

Clay's deadly eyes went from Luther to Buff to Sophie. "It don't sit right to let anyone else take care of this business. This is a father's duty."

Those words cut at Alex's heart. A father's duty. His father had used that word many times. *Duty.* But he'd always talked about Alex's duty to the family business. But Alex had no interest in running an industry. He'd wanted to heal. He'd been called to it. A father had a duty, too.

His father hadn't seen that side of things. Clay McClellen did.

Beth spoke up. "You know, Pa, Mandy is legally married to Sidney. That woman was dead for hours before the time you told me Mandy said her wedding vows."

"Sidney didn't know that. He went right ahead and married

her. Then he took off with her, probably knew he had a wife out there looking for him."

"That don't make the wedding less legal." Beth looked at Alex, and Alex saw fear in Beth's eyes. "He's got rights over Mandy now."

Which meant Alex had rights over Beth. He felt a little dizzy just thinking about it.

Clay looked at Beth as if she were a puzzle he'd been trying to solve for years. "You think Mandy'll see it that way?"

"It's the truth. Why would she see it any other way?"

"Then she'll have to divorce him."

Beth shuddered. "That would be a scandal for sure."

Even Alex nodded. He'd barely heard of a divorce. It was a word spoken rarely and then in hushed, horrified tones. To get a divorce was a slap in God's face. A blatant breaking of a vow made straight to heaven. Alex had never known anyone to do such a thing.

"I can solve that problem right quick, Clay. Reckon Sidney'll make it easy for me, too." Luther turned and headed for his horse.

Buff followed silently.

Clay nodded as he watched the old men.

As Luther swung up on his horse, Alex couldn't quite keep his mouth shut. "How can he solve a problem like that?"

Clay turned back to Alex and gave him a look that turned him ice cold in the burning Texas heat. "He can unmarry 'em with his Winchester."

★ Eighteen ★

Mandy had taken a beating.

After days on the rough-riding train, which stopped in every little town along the way, zigzagged east, then back west on its way north, even Sidney had lapsed into a sullen stupor. No more nonsense about sneaking off to luggage cars.

They were rushing to beat winter, but Mandy knew there was more involved than just getting there. They needed to get settled.

Nights were cooler as they headed north, but the late August weather was hot and sunny, turning the train car into an oven. Mandy felt about half-baked.

The train stopped now and again, and Mandy and Sidney got off to eat on Sidney's dwindling money. They'd stretch their legs, but the train paused only long enough to take on water and coal, then they went straight back to chugging along.

With every chuff of smoke, every clack of the wheels, Mandy felt herself moving farther and farther from her beloved family. Although she wept in the dark of night, when Sidney slept, she refused to let the tears fall during the day.

Sidney hated tears even more than Pa. Although Pa was more afraid of tears—the only thing Mandy knew of that her father feared—they made Sidney angry. Sidney said her loyalty belonged to him. And he was right. So the tears hardened in her throat until they felt like stones she carried inside her chest.

Mandy couldn't see why Sidney thought she couldn't love him and her family. Her heart had room for both. Some days those unshed tears seemed to lodge in her heart and focus on Sidney.

Please, God, don't let me be unloving to my husband. Protect me from that. Forgive me for that. Protect me from the heartache I've felt ever since I left my family behind. Protect me.

One morning, after another brutally uncomfortable night of trying to sleep sitting up, Mandy looked out the window in the first light of dawn. She gasped at the view.

Mountains. Majestic, beautiful mountains. They were finally getting to their destination if the mountains were near.

It took the whole day, but they finally saw signs of a big town ahead. Denver. They'd made it.

Mandy watched out the window as the outskirts of town slipped by the ever-slowing train. She reached out and grabbed Sidney's hand. "It's so big!"

Sidney laughed. "This is nothin'. I grew up in Boston. Now *that's* a big town."

A magnificent building loomed ahead of them and above them as they drew nearer. It was built as if it wanted to rival the mountains for grandeur. Mandy saw a crowd gathered near the front of the massive, intimidating building. No doubt the spot the train would stop.

Mandy's heart began pounding.

Oh, Lord, protect me.

She'd never left Mosqueros before. She'd never seen a town like this. She'd read Beth's letters and thought she knew what a city was like, but nothing had prepared her for this reality. She didn't know how a person lived in a town. How did a person hunt for food? Grow a garden? Find lumber to build a log cabin?

A man stood on a box or something to boost him higher than the surrounding mob. He was yelling.

Mandy could hear the anger in his voice but not the actual

words over the locomotive's blasting whistle and screeching brakes. The roiling crowd shoved and grumbled. She saw someone draw a gun and aim it straight up. The sharp crack split the air.

Mandy's hand went to her Winchester, leaning on the seat at her side. Her blood cooled as it did in times of danger. Her senses sharpened until she could swear she smelled that crowd of men and the burn of gunpowder. She rubbed on the callus on her trigger finger while sleet shot through her veins and she waited to fight, protect, defend. It was what she was best at.

As they drew closer, Mandy realized that the only place to leave the train was going to be right into that crowd. Cool, she turned to her new husband, the man who had vowed to love and cherish her. And protect her. Though she probably would be the one doing the protecting.

"I've never been in a city this big before." She kept her eyes flat. Even watching Sidney she was aware of all that went on around her. The growing noise, the anger in the crowd. "If we get separated we might never find each other. I don't think we should step out into that crowd."

Protect me, Lord. Protect us both.

"Don't be childish. You'll be fine." Sidney scowled.

Then the gun fired again and again. A woman screamed.

Sidney flinched. "Maybe you're right. Just looking at that building makes me wonder. Denver isn't the way I heard it was. They might not be so interested in a man with a few lawyer skills." Sidney gave her a weak, nervous smile, then cleared his throat. "I don't know what's going on, but we can't go out into that mess."

Mandy would have gone. She had her hand tight on her rifle and she'd have done it if Sidney insisted, but she was delighted not to step out into that mob scene. "You can be a lawyer anywhere, can't you? Let's find a smaller town. A place where we can homestead. We'll check the land offices in the towns up the trail. I'll help get a place set up for us. I know the land. We'll live close enough to town for you to go in and earn money while I get us settled. I've even helped build a cabin before. Ma and Pa saw to it that all of us learned survival skills. I know how that works in the country but not in the city. I couldn't hunt a deer or find firewood in a city."

Sidney looked between the shoving crowd and Mandy. He finally turned to her and said, "I think you're right. It's. . .it's different from how I thought it'd be. I was going to find us a hotel. Someone gave me the name of a lawyer he heard wanted help."

Sidney's eyes shifted as he said that, and Mandy wondered if Sidney was so sure about that job. "But I'd have to find work fast. We don't have a lot of money to live on until some starts coming in."

"Surely you have enough to pay for another day's fare." Mandy had some, but her ma had recommended not mentioning that, saving it for emergencies. Mandy wondered if that was dishonest, but Ma had talked about hard times and the years they spent living a meager life before Pa—Mandy's second pa, Clay—had come and taken them out of their awful little shack hidden in a thicket.

"Hard times can come on a family." Ma had pressed the paper bills into Mandy's hand during a private moment before the wedding. "My pa sent me off with some money, and now I'll do the same for you. But it's just between you and me, Mandy. It's best to always lay a bit of money up and try your best to live without it. And it might—might hurt Sidney's pride to think I helped you. Best not to tell him, not unless it's absolutely necessary."

Now that rather large roll of bills lay tucked in the bottom of Mandy's shoe. An uncomfortable lump that suddenly seemed to offer security in a world gone mad.

Mandy hadn't counted it and she didn't intend to for a while. Not if she could convince Sidney to leave this awful, dirty, sprawling city. If she could just find a patch of land to homestead, with good hunting nearby. Mandy had heard Pa, Luther, and Buff talk about the mountains. She thought she'd picked up enough details to know what to look for, come hunting time. And maybe she could even do some trapping, have fur pelts to sell. She had her rifle and a Colt revolver in her trunk. Pa had packed in a hunting knife, a whetstone, and a few basic tools, plus enough ammunition to start a war. Mandy and Sidney could live without the money for now.

Sidney turned and looked at her. "You want to homestead? I've heard it's a hard life."

"I'm used to hard work. It doesn't scare me. Maybe we can ride until we find some flat land tucked right up against the mountains. I could grow a garden. The mountains are covered with trees to build a house. And the Rockies are rich hunting land." Mandy felt devious, but she decided to add, "Maybe we could even find a bit of gold if we're lucky. My pa's father found gold and left it to Pa when he died. It helped us buy our ranch back after some bad men took it from us. You're always hearing about gold strikes in the Rockies."

Sidney's eyes took on a strange gleam. She'd finally said the magic word to persuade him to continue on.

The train conductor walked through the half-filled train car. "We can't pull in here, folks. The engineer has decided not to face that mob at the station. Those of you who wanted to get off here, we'll let you off farther down the rails a bit and we'll find wagons to transport you, or if you can, just ride on to the next stop."

All of the passengers stared at the ruckus then stayed firmly in their seats. Because of the irregularity of the train avoiding the mob, the conductor didn't ask for tickets after they'd let the passengers off who were staying in Denver.

Mandy was content to leave the city far behind. She and Sidney went to the land office in each little town. They'd ask questions about homesteading and come away disappointed each time at the distance they'd have to live from town. Mandy wasn't worried about living far out of town. She liked the idea. But Sidney wouldn't hear of it.

Nothing was just right, even as they passed Laramie and headed into Montana. The days began to fade together as Mandy waited for Sidney to find a place to suit him. There was no money to leave the train, even for a day or two, so the wedding night

Sidney had so longed for seemed to be long forgotten.

He did finally decide to leave the train though. Not because it suited him but because the rails ended in Butte, Montana. With a sigh of relief, Mandy saw the beautiful landscape and thought they'd be able to find a nice place near Butte.

And then the land office manager said the exact wrong thing to Sidney about little Helena, Montana, the territorial capital. "Gold."

Sidney decided their journey wasn't yet over. Helena was yet another day's ride by stagecoach. There, Mandy hoped and prayed they'd stop.

Mandy needed to write her family and tell them where she was, except first she needed to know where this journey would finally end.

★ Nineteen ★

"Doctor, where are you?" The voice from downstairs almost sounded like the woman was singing.

Alex cringed. Beth rolled her eyes. They were finishing a quick noon meal in their rooms above the doctor's office.

"That woman is *not* sick." Alex gave Beth a look so comically painful, it was all she could do not to start laughing.

"She just needs the attention." Beth, thanks to Ma and Pa's help, now felt nearly at home. Her family had brought in some furniture and her clothing. Ma had even scrounged up some clothes for Alex and stocked the cupboards. Beth and Alex had been too busy to give it a thought.

Now Beth sat in a white shirtwaist and dark gray riding skirt. Alex had a change of pants and shirt. All of it had been provided by someone else. Not out of financial need, but because in the week they'd been married, the rush hadn't stopped, day or night.

"Well, you go down and pay attention to her," he hissed. They had to whisper because Mrs. Gallup was already coming upstairs. There was no hiding from Nora Gallup. Fastest Whimper in the West.

"Me?" Beth rested her fingertips on her chest with playful grace. "Why, I'd love to, you generous man. But of course—"

"There you are, Dr. Buchanan." Nora barged right into their living quarters.

Beth smirked at Alex. No one would do for Mrs. Gallup but the doctor. The *real* doctor. Beth had never been so happy to be a woman. She let it irritate her a tiny bit that the woman invaded their living space, then shrugged. If they wanted to stop the woman, they were going to have to buy a lock and that was that. Beth looked at the determined woman. Nearly five foot nine, over two hundred pounds, fast moving, and as healthy as a horse.

It would have to be a sturdy lock.

"I'm frantic, Dr. Buchanan. I've had a terrible stabbing pain in my chest all morning. I'm afraid it's my heart again."

Beth doubted it. "Go on down, Doctor. I'll clean up here then join you."

Alex's hand landed on Beth's wrist in its usual vise-like way. But in this case, Beth didn't think Alex was actually turning to her for strength and courage. Well, courage maybe, but only because Nora was seriously scary. By the end of this woman's complaint-filled visit, Beth would be ready to cry for her mama.

"I can use the assistance, Mrs. Buchanan." Alex smiled but his eyes were pathetic. Begging. He did *not* want to be alone with Mrs. Gallup.

Beth knew why, too. The woman seemed bent on being examined from head to foot. Closely examined—*everywhere*.

It wasn't as if the middle-aged woman had designs on Alex. Beth knew that. The woman was just determined to discover an illness. She brought a well-worn medical book along to the exams and gave Alex suggestions.

She didn't insist on the extremely close examination if Beth was around, but Beth had stepped out back to the privy one time and Mrs. Gallup had come in during Beth's absence. Alex had barely lived to tell the tale. Beth came along quietly, to spare all three of them the embarrassment of watching Alex beg.

Mrs. Gallup was cosseted and encouraged and given treatment for stress. Alex suggested soothing baths, chamomile tea, long walks, and he'd even lent her Beth's beloved copy of Jane Austen's *Sense and Sensibility*. For a while, Beth clung to the book desperately. But, being the next thing to a doctor's assigned treatment, Mrs. Gallup was desperate to read it and promised to care for it and bring it back soon. Beth finally acquiesced, quietly gloating because Alex had just ensured yet another visit, which was inevitable in any case. *Sense and Sensibility* was no medical textbook, but Beth didn't underestimate Mrs. Gallup's ability to find something within those pages that she could mangle until it alerted her to a new illness. All told, it took Alex and Beth an hour to convince the woman she wasn't dying.

"You know, Doctor," Beth said sardonically as the woman closed the door behind her, "one of these days that woman really is going to be sick, and you'll miss it because you're so used to ignoring and patronizing her."

Alex groaned out loud and rubbed his face. "You're probably right."

Beth snickered and poked Alex in the ribs.

He grabbed her hand to stop her. "She'll come in with a broken arm and I'll pat her on the head and send her on her way."

"I'm picturing how it will be at her funeral." Beth swept the hand Alex wasn't restraining grandly in front of them.

"In the unlikely event that woman doesn't outlive us both." Alex tugged Beth toward him.

She was spun to face him and gasped in surprise at how close they were and how comfortable being close felt. "The parson will stand there and talk about that poor, poor woman and how nobody listened to her."

Alex clamped his arms around Beth's waist. "Then he'll spend an hour yelling at me for prescribing hot tea for a woman whose heart was failing."

Beth settled her hands on his chest, fighting a smile. "They'll forbid you to ever practice medicine again."

"No chance." Alex shook his head with a mock scowl. "I would never be that lucky."

Beth laughed and a smile bloomed on Alex's lips. He didn't smile much and when he flashed his shining white teeth and lifted the dour expression he so often wore, Beth felt like it was a personal victory. She enjoyed coaxing an upturn out of his lips.

Then those smiling lips leaned close and kissed her. Freezing like a startled animal, Beth drew in her breath until Alex's lips sealed her away from air.

They'd been so busy. Running day and night since they'd gotten married days ago, but Beth had wondered when this might happen. She was her mother's daughter after all. Ma had told her what marriage meant. And how it could be.

Then Alex deepened the kiss and pulled her closer. Beth quit thinking and wound her arms around her husband's neck with a small sound of pleasure. Moments passed and Beth enjoyed the touch of her husband.

"Beth," Alex whispered against her lips, "I feel like I'm alive again."

Beth ran one hand into his dark, closely shorn hair. "You've always been alive, Alex."

Nodding, Alex said, "I just haven't been living. I look back on my life and see that I've wasted so much time. I just couldn't handle all the bad things I'd seen." His eyes darkened.

Beth spoke quickly to keep her husband from sinking into the morose thoughts that plagued him. "I've been praying so hard that you'd find peace."

"Peace. Yeah, maybe that's what this is. I haven't had a nightmare in days."

Beth knew he'd been pulled into some kind of waking nightmare when he'd doctored Mr. Farley. But she slept beside him every night and his sleep hadn't been disturbed. "Peace with your memories and, I hope, peace with God." Beth waited, hoping her husband would really talk to her for once. If he could talk about the emotional scars he carried, maybe they'd lose the power to haunt him.

"God." Alex ran one finger down Beth's cheek while his arm stayed wrapped tight around her waist. "Yes, I started praying again the day I met you. I believe I've found Him again. I started believing that maybe, just maybe, I deserved God's forgiveness for all that I've done."

"None of us deserves forgiveness. None of us is guiltless. 'For all have sinned and come short of the glory of God.'"

"But there's sin and there's sin. Mine were very close to unforgivable. But I've always believed in God's ability to forgive. It's just these last days that I've felt like I even had a right to ask."

"So you've asked at last? You've come back to your faith?" Beth had a hard time imagining softhearted Alex doing something truly awful.

"No, but I've been praying for my patients and for you."

"For me, really?"

"Yes, all prayers of thanksgiving." Alex's eyes caressed her face as gently as that one finger. "If you're willing, maybe you could pray with me now, while I finally dare to ask Him."

"I would love to pray with you, Alex." Beth leaned close and kissed him gently.

They held each other while Alex turned and faced God, for himself and his own sins. Beth felt him stand straight, as if a weight lifted off his shoulders. He didn't speak aloud exactly what burden he carried, and Beth hoped it wasn't because he was still harboring guilt.

When Alex's prayer ended, Beth asked, "Do you want to tell me what you've been through? Would it help?"

"Maybe someday." Alex pulled her closer and lowered his lips to hers, returning the kiss she'd given him. He raised his head. "But right now, I feel like being close to my sweet, new wife. Would you like that, Beth? Do you want a real marriage to me?"

She smiled and curled her arms around his neck.

He surprised her when he swept her up into his arms. She broke the kiss and their eyes met. Their bond was as strong as ever, but it had changed. For the first time what passed between them was laced with something other than Alex's need for her strength. He gave instead of took. He leaned closer, lowering his lips to hers.

The office door slammed open.

Alex as good as dropped her as he turned to face the Armitages. Fortunately, Beth was clinging to his neck and only her feet swung to the floor.

Mr. Armitage. Due to have his arm checked.

Beth gave Alex a quick pat on the back. She said, "Have a seat, Mr. Armitage." His wife came in right behind him.

Beth walked away from Alex quickly to keep herself from grabbing him and abandoning the Armitages to doctor themselves.

As she began removing Mr. Armitage's sling from his perfectly healing arm, the door slammed open again. They were lucky not to have lost a window.

"Doctor, my boy's got a fever and a rash." A young woman rushed in, nearly staggering under the weight of a young child.

Beth saw Alex's shoulder slump, then he got hold of himself and hurried to the woman, relieving her of the burden of her little boy. "Looks like measles."

Highly contagious. They'd soon be overrun.

Beth gave up on stealing away with her husband and rolled up the sleeves of her white shirtwaist to get back to doctoring. With a quiet sigh, Beth reminded herself sternly that this was what she'd always wanted.

★

Mandy stepped off the stagecoach and her legs buckled.

Sidney caught her, but he stumbled back and let the stage catch him.

Mandy looked behind her. "Thank you."

Sidney set her on her feet with a wan smile. "We made it."

She nodded. They hadn't quite made it really, but it was finally close. Sidney had found the place he wanted to be.

Thank You, Jesus.

Mandy squared her shoulders, hooked her Winchester over her shoulder where it belonged, and oversaw the unloading of the things her parents had sent along. Not a lot, but Mandy knew her folks. Even while they were trying to convince Mandy to stay, they'd been planning for if she went. Ma and Pa would have seen to the right supplies.

The town of Helena was much bigger than Mandy had expected, but still only a fraction of the size of Denver. The land office was right next door to the stage station and still open for the day, although the sun was low in the sky. After a quick talk with the station manager, they left their box, trunk, and satchels behind under his watchful eyes and hurried to the land office.

Homesteading wasn't difficult—at least the part where they claimed the land. The closest they could get to town was over twenty miles, but there was water on the claim, or so the land agent said, and trees to build a cabin. More woodland than pasture land, they were told.

Mandy looked at Sidney. "We can't live there. You won't be able to get into town to work." If they pushed hard they could hopefully make it in two days with all their things to carry.

She thought of her few precious dollars from her ma and knew they wouldn't last long if they had to rent a room in Helena.

"This is fine. I can take a twenty-mile ride twice a day on a good horse." Sidney signed the homesteading agreement with a flourish.

Mandy didn't contradict him in front of the agent, thinking to his manly feelings. But once they'd taken the careful directions and stepped outside, Mandy whispered, "Sidney, we don't have a horse."

Sidney smiled at her, that cheerful, confident smile that had first drawn her to him. "We'll get one before long."

"How?" Mandy thought of her money.

"I'm planning to find gold." Sidney smiled then marched to the stage station. He stumbled to a stop when he reached the heavy box and trunk they needed to cart twenty miles. "Why did your parents send all this junk along? Let's just leave it here."

"I can rent a handcart for two bits." Mandy pointed to a sign.

Sidney frowned as if it was just occurring to him how far twenty miles was.

Mandy arranged for the cart and they loaded their belongings into it and headed southwest. Each of them grabbed a handle on the cart, and Mandy enjoyed the sense of their working together. Life could be good if they built a tight cabin and the hunting was easy.

"We'll get out of town and find a sheltered spot to camp for the night," Mandy said as they left Helena behind. "Then we'll get an early start tomorrow."

Sidney turned to her with a light in his eyes. "So we'll finally have us a wedding night."

Trust her husband to focus on the frivolous. Mandy wondered how long it would take Sidney to realize they didn't have any food for supper. It had been a long day on the trail. Her muscles were cramped and battered. Sidney hadn't shaved since they'd left Mosqueros, and neither of them smelled any too good. Mandy felt a headache coming on but didn't mention it.

As they began to put space behind them from bustling Helena, the light left the sky. It was then Mandy saw a fire flickering ahead. She heard the deep lowing of cattle from behind an outcropping of rock on the rugged land and knew what they'd come upon. Someone was holding a herd of cattle just outside of town. No doubt to sell it. Mandy had eaten many a meal around a campfire in her life and her stomach growled at the thought of piping hot coffee and tough, savory beef.

"Hold up, Sidney." She set her side of the cart down. Sidney's forehead was soaked with sweat and he was breathing hard. Mandy was more used to the rugged life, but she was feeling overwhelmed at the thought of the long walk ahead and the brutally hard work they faced to be ready for winter.

Sidney gladly set his side of the cart down. "Time to stop for the night?"

Mandy pointed at the flickering fire. "It's a campsite. Let's go in and see if we can sleep near their fire."

"What about the two of us being alone?" Sidney's impatience was clear.

They heard a voice yell, "Come and get it!"

Sidney's impatience was overridden by hunger. "It's proper for a camp like that to welcome strangers, isn't it? I've heard that."

"I reckon they'll share a meal with us." Mandy smiled and Sidney smiled back. Good, the man had some common sense after all.

"Let's go say howdy." Sidney's smile widened, and Mandy remembered why she loved him.

Which wasn't to say she'd forgotten. She'd just been really tired ever since she'd said, "I do."

They headed for the fire towing their cart. When they were within hailing distance, she put out her hand to stop Sidney.

"What is it?" He sounded eager to be on his way to dinner.

"There's a proper way to approach a cow camp. This close to town I doubt they're apt to suspect us of mischief, but a cattle drive crew is always ready for trouble. We want to make sure they don't think we qualify." Mandy felt her nerves steady and her blood cool, but not overly.

Sidney swallowed and looked lost.

"Let me do it." Mandy waited until Sidney nodded. She shouted, "Hello, the camp."

Her female voice was probably a good idea. A bunch of cowpokes weren't likely to start shooting at a woman. Not unless they were severely provoked. Mandy heard about ten guns being cocked. It didn't scare her. She could see the makings of a well-run cow camp, and she respected the tough life on a cattle drive. Having a fire iron drawn and cocked was just good sense.

"Come on in slow," another woman answered.

The female voice surprised Mandy. She was also surprised by her urge to cry. A woman, out here, with the cattle drive. All of the loneliness for her family hit her like a closed fist. Mandy had her hands full not just breaking straight into tears and howling her head off.

"Let's go." She didn't look at Sidney because she didn't want him to see the tears she felt brimming in her eyes. To stop the nonsense, she hollered as she walked forward, "We're homesteading about twenty miles from town. We're just looking for a place to sleep for the night. Then we'll be on our way." Mandy walked and talked, her cart between her and Sidney.

As she got close in the settling dusk, she saw several women. The one who'd called out stood to the front, her rifle out but pointed to the ground. Even in the dim light, Mandy noticed the woman's deep tan. She looked like she might be Indian. But as Mandy got closer, she saw the woman had hazel eyes and that didn't fit.

The woman wore a fringed buckskin jacket with some of the fringe missing. That meant she was a working cowpoke, because the point of having the fringe was to have a piggin' string handy. And just from the look of the setup, it appeared the woman was in charge.

Mandy's heart pounded harder as she recognized the strength, the command. It was a look Mandy had seen in her own mother's eyes many times.

The woman had on a split riding skirt made of softly tanned doeskin, worn and dirty and obviously the clothes of a rancher.

Mandy was every bit as dirty, but it wasn't the honest dirt of hard work.

"You're welcome at our fire." The woman set her gun aside, but Mandy noticed none of the others did.

"I'm Mandy, and this is my husband, Sidney Gray. We're new to Montana."

"I'm Belle Harden and this is my family and my cowhands. C'mon in and rest yourselves."

Mandy looked around and saw more women. No, not women, girls. The oldest two might be a bit younger than Mandy, but full grown. The older ones had white-blond hair, one was a fiery redhead younger than Laurie, another just a toddler, so dark she really might be Indian.

"These are my girls, Lindsay and Emma." Belle pointed to the blonds. "Sarah's toting my son, Tanner." The redhead had a baby strapped on her back.

"And the little one running around is Betsy." Belle pointed fondly at the three-year-old who waved and yelled, "Hi."

"Betsy?" Mandy felt as if her throat was swelling shut. "As in Elizabeth?"

"Yep." Belle came up close to Mandy, taking note of her rifle.

"I've got a sister named Elizabeth. We call her Beth." Mandy shook her head to fight off a sudden urge to cry. She noticed lots of men. It was a strong crew driving a few hundred head of cattle. Mandy did a quick estimate with her experienced eye and guessed three or four hundred head. This reminded her so much of the times she and her sisters and Ma had horned in on a roundup, Mandy couldn't help herself.

Despite the years of her father's scolding and pleading, despite Sidney's moody way of punishing her, despite her own common sense. . .Mandy burst into tears.

The woman's forehead wrinkled briefly. Then she strode forward and pulled Mandy into her arms.

★ Twenty ★

It's a girl!" Beth lifted the messy, wriggling newborn up so her mother could see.

"My girl. I got my girl. Oh, I wanted her so badly." Mrs. Stoddard burst into tears of joy.

Beth spared the baby her first spanking when the tiny darling started squalling the cry of a healthy, lively infant. Beth couldn't quit smiling as she quickly washed up the baby. It was just the two of them. Oops. Beth grinned as she wrapped the little one in a soft blanket. Three not two.

Alex had gone out of the room to sit with the expectant father. The older children, three active, handsome sons, all school-aged, had long ago gone to bed.

Beth and Mrs. Stoddard had done this peacefully by themselves. Mrs. Stoddard had even protested that her husband had sent for the doctor. She'd given birth to all three of her older boys without help. But her husband went all nervous on her and snuck away for help. Mrs. Stoddard had been a good sport about it, on the condition that only Beth stay with her.

Alex had agreed with the woman's request for privacy. He had left, assuring Mr. Stoddard he'd stay close in the event of need, and he went to rock by the fire with the anxious father.

Beth crooned at the baby as she settled her into her mother's arms then went to invite Mr. Stoddard in to meet his daughter.

The man almost ran over Beth in his haste to reach his wife's side.

Beth could see that Alex's eyes were heavy with sleep. She couldn't keep the smile off her face when she scolded. "You've been napping while I've been hard at work."

Alex didn't deny it. He walked by her side to the buckboard and lent a hand to boost her up. They drove out of the Stoddards' yard on the long trail for Mosqueros.

Slipping his arm around Beth's waist, he said, "Lean on me. Try and sleep."

"I can't. I'm wide awake. I love delivering babies." Beth did lay her head on his strong shoulder. But her blood was coursing through her veins, as it always did after a birth.

"You get all the good jobs." Alex's supporting arm tightened and Beth enjoyed the feeling.

"Can you believe how hectic it's been since we opened the doctor's office?"

"It was bad enough without the measles outbreak." Alex shook his head.

Beth knew he was every bit as tired as she was.

They'd had a steady flow of folks asking for a doctor. They'd delivered three babies, including the parson's wife's that first night. And there'd been someone staying in their makeshift hospital almost every night, thanks to a couple of broken bones and a cowpoke who tangled with a cantankerous longhorn, besides the measles. Everyone recovered well, but Alex and Beth had been running ever since they'd started doctoring.

Until now. Unless some sick or injured person lay in wait for them back in town, their hospital was empty and their town was healthy.

"I guess they really needed us, didn't they?" Alex took his eyes off the trail, which was fine. The way was straight and the horses were placid and calm and interested in going home. "We've helped a lot of people."

Beth saw the hope in Alex's eyes. They prayed together every day, and Alex seemed to bloom during their times of closeness to God. He still insisted she be at his side while he doctored, but Beth hoped he was remembering why he'd loved healing. She prayed that he'd keep getting stronger, steadier, until the day she didn't have to be by his side every minute. Not that she minded being here.

"You're a really good doctor, Alex." Beth hesitated but she went ahead. "I think you're replacing all the bad memories with good ones. Most of doctoring is a blessing. Getting to help people mend, using our God-given talents matched with training to heal. Are you feeling better these days?"

"I still want you by my side."

Beth felt his fingers dig into her waist a bit too hard. She knew she'd trod on dangerous ground by bringing this up. "I plan to be."

The fingers relaxed before they caused pain. Which was lucky for Alex because Beth wouldn't have put up with that graciously.

"But yes, I am feeling better. I'm not ready to test doctoring on my own. And it works, the two of us together, doesn't it?" He turned to look in her eyes.

She felt that connection that they'd had from the very beginning. It was substantial, almost solid, like they were locked together somehow. A team hitched into the same yoke, pulling together. Stronger together than apart.

Alex was obsessed with needing her, but Beth knew that connection went two ways. She needed him, too.

"Yes, it works." There was no reason for her to whisper. There was certainly no one out and about this evening to be disturbed by their voices.

Alex leaned closer, watching her. Supporting her. His eyes flickered to her lips, which suddenly felt dry. She licked them and he noticed.

Then he kissed her and she sure as certain noticed that.

In the silent night, broken by the sound of the horses' hooves and a gentle gusting wind, Beth kissed him back.

He pulled away. Only inches. "We're married, Beth, honey. You know what that means?"

Beth did indeed. Her mother had not shirked.

Alex leaned in again, and this time not even the sound of the horses could find its way into the world where Alex swept her.

★

She was a married woman in every way now.

Beth woke in the first light of dawn feeling perfect peace. They had a home and a doctor's practice and now a true affection. She turned, wanting to study Alex sleeping beside her, holding her close.

He was awake. Watching.

Instantly she felt their connection. Only now it was more solid than ever. Truly there were ties binding them now. A union of the flesh, the possibility of a child.

Those were good things. And she was married to a good man. Beth smiled.

There were no patients knocking at their door, but it was very early. Some would most likely appear. But for now, it was only the two of them.

Alex drew her into his arms. They spent the early hours of the quiet morning deepening those ties.

★

Alex couldn't believe they'd been left alone so long. Late in the afternoon, he bandaged the nasty burn on the little boy's arm while Beth distracted the child with a licorice stick and her sweet voice. When that didn't work, she and the boy's mother held him still and dabbed at his tears.

It gave Alex chills to listen to the hurting child cry. But Beth was here, and he was able to go on.

Doctoring was better. Still awful, but so much better. He finished the bandage and sent mother and child on their way, then pulled Beth close. "Having you near has always been wonderful. But now, after last night, it's even better. Your eyes give me strength, but your arms help even more."

Beth stayed in his arms, holding him close, her head on his shoulder. So generous.

God had given him a miracle when He'd sent this little spitfire into his life.

Finally she pulled away only far enough to smile. "Let's go eat at the diner. The sun is setting, and I haven't had a chance to lay in supplies for the week. Our cupboards are about bare."

Alex shuddered. He'd eaten Esther's food before. "Please, not the diner."

Beth laughed. "I'll tell you a secret that will get you through."

"You know a secret that makes Esther's food better?"

Beth nodded. "No coffee. No dessert. In fact, I recommend just eating her bread. It's pretty good. Her meat is tough, but it doesn't taste that bad. It's not really dangerous."

"I thought I'd broken a tooth." Alex tugged at her waist so she stumbled a bit and he grinned, letting her know he did it deliberately to hold her close.

"I meant dangerous like poisonous." Beth snickered. "You made the mistake of having pie and coffee last time. I tried to warn you."

"Try harder next time."

Beth laughed, and they left the doctor's office arm-in-arm. They'd walked about ten steps down the sidewalk when they saw Esther pulling down the window shade on the diner. Beth turned, her brow furrowed. "How late is it?"

Alex looked at the lowering sun. "Later than I thought. I guess past Esther's closing time. Or she's got somewhere special to go."

Beth shrugged. "Well, we'll make do with yesterday's biscuits and honey, I suppose."

They turned to go home and Alex felt a spring in his step. Home. He had a home and a beautiful wife and he'd remembered how to be a doctor. . .not alone yet, but that didn't matter because he didn't have to do it alone. He had Beth. Life was good.

A tiny flicker of unease broke through his contented haze. He had trouble on his trail, he knew that, but he'd left it far behind.

In the encroaching dusk, a sudden movement to his right made him jump. A man rushing toward them, a dirty, skinny, stump of a man, but healthy looking. Not in need of a doctor.

"I need a doctor. My brother's hurt." The man grabbed Alex's arm and began dragging him.

Alex caught ahold of Beth and brought her.

The frantic man stopped when he saw Beth coming. "No, not her. My brother, he don't want no womenfolk tending to him. He—he won't accept help if she's along."

Alex's stomach plunged. "Then I can't go. I'm sorry, but we work together."

Alex wrenched his arm loose from the fingers that clung to him. He shuddered a bit when the man scowled, revealing broken teeth and an ugliness in his eyes that had nothing to do with physical appearances.

The man took all of five seconds to consider the situation. "She'll have to come then. My brother will put up with it or die. It's a long ride. I've got a horse but—"

Alex exchanged a look with Beth. It was wrong to bring her along, out at night with this unknown man. But—

"We'll hitch up our buckboard and be right behind you." Beth tugged Alex's arm toward the stable where their horses boarded.

Alex fell into step beside her.

"Wait!" Beth stopped so quickly Alex lost his grip on her. Somehow that made the whole unsettling situation worse, no Beth.

Forgive me, Lord, for being so weak, so cowardly.

"What?" Alex turned and went after her as she rushed for their building.

"I...uh...we...uh...you need the doctor's bag." Beth glanced at Alex, silently apologizing for the slip. They both knew that for the public to trust them Alex had to be the doctor, not Beth.

"Hurry." The anxious, unpleasant man seemed to think they were making an escape. He followed right along with them. "I was over an hour on the trail and my brother doesn't have much time."

"Tell me what happened." Alex opened the door.

Beth darted inside and back out so fast Alex didn't even have a chance to join her. She had her doctor's bag in one hand and her rifle strapped on her back, the muzzle showing by her right hand, the butt above her left shoulder. She always wore it this way when they went doctoring out in the country. The two of them turned and rushed toward the stable.

Only as they entered the livery and began, as a team, buckling the traces on their gleaming brown thoroughbreds, the whole outfit given to them as a wedding gift by Beth's parents, did Alex realize the man hadn't answered his questions.

He'd vanished. Now he reappeared at the livery door on horseback.

The man's nervous rush had Alex pushing. "I didn't even hear what was wrong with the brother."

Beth looked across the horses' broad backs, her concerned eyes a match for his. "Okay, done. Let's go. He seems worried to death."

"Do you know him? Is he from around here?" Boosting Beth up onto the high seat of the buckboard, Alex vaulted up behind her as she scooted over.

"Nope. But I've been away a long time. Half the people in town are strangers."

Alex slapped the reins to his horses' backs and they rushed out the open door of the stable.

The man rode ahead, setting a pace to the south that would exhaust the horses before long.

"What's he going this way for?" Beth asked.

"Why not this way?"

"There's nothing out this way. This land is so rugged and rocky, anyone who's trying to carve a living out of this land is in for a bad time of it."

"I can barely keep up with this guy. Does this trail ever branch off?" Alex slapped the horses with the reins. The man rounded a twist in the trail that climbed steadily upward. The trail got steeper and fell away on the left into a deep canyon.

Beth caught at Alex's arm. "I don't know anyone who lives out this way."

Alex looked away from the increasingly narrow trail. "No one?" He carefully skirted a particularly slender section of the trail where the ground had caved away.

The road was shadowed from the setting sun and the notch in the trail seemed to open on an abyss. Who knew how far they'd drop if they went over. To Alex's overactive imagination, it seemed like they'd fall for eternity.

Beth clenched her jaw and remained silent until they passed that spot. Now the trail, still narrow, was less treacherous. "Well, of course someone could be out here I don't know, but look at how rugged it is. Look at the land. No cattle graze out here. This is wasteland. I've heard my folks talk about it plenty of times, that these highlands can't support a ranch. And these woods go on and on for miles. They lead into the desert to the south, and the west is not much better. So where exactly are we going?"

"What do you think?" Alex looked up the trail. The man had vanished. What was going on? Why would he leave them so far behind? What if the trail branched off and Alex chose the wrong branch?

Alex slowed the team. They were losing speed anyway on the steep trail so it was more a matter of not goading the team forward. There was only one way to get the answers they needed.

"Hey!" His voice echoed off the hills and valleys. There was no answer. "Hey, mister." Alex realized they didn't know the man's name. He'd told them nothing about himself.

"Stop the team!" Beth's voice acted like a jammed-on brake.

Alex drew the team to a halt just before a bend in the trail that wound around an outcropping of rock. Gnarled trees blocked their view of the trail ahead so Alex couldn't see the man.

The wind blew, whistling through the hills that rose around them. Alex strained to see the trail better as dusk grew heavier. One of the horses blew a whoosh of breath and shook his head, jingling the traces.

The darkness deepened.

"I don't like this, Alex." Beth surprised him by opening her doctor's bag and producing a Colt revolver. "Something's going on. Why did he lead us out here and abandon us?"

Alex looked from the gun to the bright gleam in Beth's eyes and knew she'd use that weapon to defend herself if she had to. She'd defend him, too. Which sent a wash of failure and shame through him. He was still a coward. He didn't even have the courage to prepare in the event of danger.

"Back the team up. Slowly," Beth ordered.

"There's a nasty cliff back a few yards. Help me watch for it."

Beth was studying the back trail, the rocks overhead. Near as Alex could tell the woman was considering every possible problem before it happened. "Once we're past that, there's a wide enough spot to turn around."

"I could go forward. I think the trail widens near that bend ahead."

"No!" Beth raised her rifle so it was pointing at the sky, her hand on the trigger. "Back up. If he's really in need of a doctor, he'll come back after us. If he's up to something, lying in wait right around that bend would be a real likely idea. Back the team up now!"

Alex obeyed her. Despite his years farther west with the cavalry and the training he'd had in survival, he'd never been in command. He'd taken orders, not given them, unless he was doctoring. Now wasn't the time to start being in charge.

Alex eased the team back, watching the wheels as they neared the sheared-off spot that looked like a mountain-sized cougar had slashed at the trail. The horses seemed more than willing to push downhill instead of pulling up.

Beth watched for about ten seconds then a breath of relief

155

caught Alex's attention. "We're past it. Now let's go back another twenty feet."

"There's a spot where we can turn around." Despite being something of a weakling in his wife's eyes, Alex had driven his share of buckboards so he got the team backed properly and soon had them headed downhill back toward Mosqueros. They came past that treacherously narrow spot and Alex kept the team as close to the uphill side as possible.

"I wonder where he went." Beth twisted to look back.

A bullet whizzed past her face. Missed her only because she'd turned.

"Get down!" Alex threw himself at Beth and the two of them tumbled over the side of the buckboard. . .and right down that cutout in the trail, into the abyss.

★ Twenty-one ★

We'll ride out with you tomorrow and help you get settled." Silas Harden handed Mandy a plate of food.

Beans, beefsteak, biscuits, and blazing hot coffee. The Harden crew had already eaten but their pot wasn't empty, and they all settled in around the campfire, eager to listen to new voices. Mandy had told them their plans, and the Hardens had volunteered to help them get to the homestead. Mandy could barely conceal her almost desperate relief.

"Not necessary." Sidney spoke around a scoop full of beans. He'd been eager to take their food, but Mandy could see his pride was stung by her tears. Sidney wasn't going to accept anything else from the Hardens.

"I didn't ask if we could." Silas settled next to Belle without looking at Sidney. "I told you we were going to. You can ride with us, or trail after us if you prefer."

Belle's cool eyes went to Sidney with a very strange look Mandy couldn't quite understand. Almost like Sidney was everything Belle expected a man to be. As if his behavior was no surprise.

"We're coming." Belle gave Silas a look of such solid support, Mandy could have built a cabin on that foundation. "We've got a while. It's early enough we don't have to worry about beating the weather. Silas and a few hands can run the herd in tomorrow morning and get settled up while we head for your property and get a cabin put together. My Silas is a hand at building."

Silas smiled a private smile at his wife that made Mandy's heart beat harder. She'd seen that smile pass between her parents many times. It was love, a private kind of love.

She and Sidney had never exchanged such a look. Would they ever? It occurred to her that a smile like that might come with time. And with knowing a person inside and out. She didn't know much about Sidney, his childhood, his growing-up years. He'd come from Boston and he was a lawyer. There wasn't much else.

"You'll be glad for the help," Silas said. "Winter comes early up here."

"And stays late." One of the blond girls, Emma, stretched her legs out toward the fire. She had a riding skirt on like Belle, and the same calm, competent look in her eyes. But there the resemblance ended. Mandy knew all these girls plus the baby boy were Belle's children, but none of them looked a bit like their ma or pa except the little boy. Strange.

Mandy had a sudden flash of a wonderful idea. She clamped her mouth shut hard not to beg them to let her and Sidney go home with them. Why couldn't they ask if the Hardens needed help? No shame in working for a ranch. They had some time before they had to put up a cabin. She and Sidney could come back to their homestead in the spring, have the whole summer to get settled. Mandy knew without a doubt, just from the way Belle had hugged her while she cried, that they'd be welcome, whether the Hardens needed hands or not.

It wasn't a comfortable realization to Mandy that she wasn't looking forward to being utterly alone with a gold-mining husband through a long, cold Montana winter. She suddenly felt ridiculously young and wanted her mama.

In Ma's absence, Belle Harden would do.

They made quiet conversation around the fire. Mandy was surprised to learn that an old man among the hands, name of Shorty, recognized her pa's name. He'd known Jarrod McClellen from years back in Colorado. It gave Mandy a strange feeling to get this glimpse of a grandfather she'd never known.

They talked about the life of a fur trapper in the Rockies and Mandy told about her family back in Texas until it was time to sleep. The Hardens provided Sidney and Mandy with bedrolls, but it was immediately obvious that the women slept on one side of the camp and the men on the other, neither Belle nor her married daughter, Lindsay, shared blankets with their men. Proper for a cattle drive, Mandy knew. The best way to preserve a smidgen of propriety when men and women traveled together like this.

Sidney only growled a bit as he went to bed down with the men. Not even he had much energy for nonsense. After the long days being bounced along on the train, stealing sleep in snatches, and the long rough day on the stagecoach, Mandy was falling asleep on her feet. She didn't have a full minute to worry about how Sidney was handling another thwarted "wedding night." Mandy was asleep before her head finished settling on her blanket.

She jerked awake in the pitch-dark and was on her feet and moving, her rifle around her neck and over her shoulder, before she was conscious of what had awakened her. She listened as her hand slid down the muzzle of her Winchester. She could pull that muzzle forward in one jerk, have her right hand on the trigger and her left steadyin' the muzzle in half a heartbeat. She was the best shot in her family, better'n Pa or Ma, better even than Sally, and that was saying something.

It was coming from out in the pasture a ways, beyond the meager light cast by the red coals of the low-burning fire. Before she could step out into the dark, she heard movement and raised her gun, only to see Belle come up beside her, Silas right behind, and the whole camp stirring.

Mandy returned her Winchester to hang on her back and they all stood, frozen, listening.

"Horse." Mandy said. "Have you got one foaling?"

Belle shook her head then said, "Least ways we're not supposed to."

The faint, distressed sound came again, and Belle made a noise of disgust. "It's the blasted stallion of Tom Linscott's." Belle strode into the dark.

Mandy hurried to keep up. "A stallion is out there bothering the horses in your string?"

"Nope," Silas said with a smile in his voice that Mandy couldn't see in the dark, but she knew it was there all the same. "One of our mares ran off from town a few months back, and when we found her, she was running with Linscott's stallion. We're gonna have us a fine little foal. And that Linscott gets a stud fee for his horse. So we got us a bargain."

Mandy and Silas moved after Belle, but slowly. No sense startling a mare busy adding to the horse population. As Mandy's eyes adjusted to the dark away from the fire, she saw Belle kneeling beside a dark, wriggling lump on the ground. The mother licked and nudged at her baby.

"It's a little colt," Belle said, looking up from the baby. "I might just see if I can't earn a few dollars on stud fees, like Linscott does."

"We're not raising that thing up as a stallion, Belle. That horse of Linscott's is a brute. No one is safe within a country mile of the critter, and you know it." Silas crossed his arms. "We have to geld him."

Mandy noted that Silas's order wasn't given with an over supply of hope.

"We'll see, Silas. We don't have to decide tonight. I just didn't think the horse'd been run off long enough to settle." Belle laughed. "I can't wait to tell Linscott. He's *loco* on the subject of that horse of his. He'll probably try and make me pay."

Belle and Silas both laughed at that, and Mandy almost felt sorry for Tom Linscott.

★

The next morning they were up, fed a hearty breakfast, and heading for the homestead just as the sun began to lighten the sky.

One of the hands made a fast trip to town and came back with some building tools. So, they could commence putting up a cabin right away.

Silas stayed with the cattle but promised to catch up with them as soon as he'd dealt with the cattle buyers and laid in supplies.

"Look at the colt, Sidney." Mandy rode alongside her husband in the cool morning breeze.

The colt was pure black. Mandy recognized his regal lines, even in his skinny, uncoordinated movements. Mandy was tempted to agree with Belle that he ought to be held back for breeding.

Sidney glanced at the colt and shrugged. "A baby horse. So what?"

"He was born just last night." Mandy knew Sidney hadn't awakened. He was the only one in camp who hadn't, save Tanner. "He's a beauty."

Mandy rode slowly, making sure the foal stayed ahead of her as it gamboled along behind its mother. With some trepidation, she leaned closer to Sidney. "What would you think about asking the Hardens if we could hire on for the winter? We could work for them and come back to put up the cabin in the spring."

"No." Sidney scowled at her in an expression Mandy was already fully tired of. "I'm not a ranch hand. I'm a lawyer. And besides, I'm going to dig for gold."

"Being a miner isn't any easier than being a cowhand, and a cowhand usually makes more money." Mandy should have never brought the idea up.

Belle dropped back beside them just as Sidney mentioned gold. "Best to use the land for wild game and a garden and lumber. You can live rich on the plants and on the animals that roam wild here and raise a good herd of beef with the sweat of your brow. It's a rich land in ways other than gold. Gold is worth so much because it's mighty scarce. Hard to find, harder yet to hold on to if you do find it. Helena started as a mining town and it only turned civilized when the gold played out. Finding gold is a purely uncivilized business."

Sidney gave Belle the benefit of his scowl.

Belle held his gaze for far too long, as if she were studying him, looking inside his head, probably searching for a lick of sense.

Sidney turned away first and spurred his horse to ride with the men.

"I told Silas to send a telegram to your people in Texas, telling them you made it here safe and sound."

Mandy gasped. "I meant to write a letter. I was so tired last night it never crossed my mind."

"Well, just tell me what you'd like said. I don't have any paper with me, but I can contrive a letter and get it to your folks. Maybe I'll have Lindsay write it. She doesn't get snowed in so early."

Mandy reached out and caught Belle's hand. "Thank you. That would mean so much to me." For a second, Mandy was afraid she might cry again. "I never cry. What is wrong with me?"

Mandy looked away and her eyes settled on the foal. She tried to focus on the little guy to distract herself from the nonsense of tears. His mother, working today as a pack animal, was at the end of a string of horses. Because Mandy had dropped back to follow the colt, now she and Belle were bringing up the rear.

The shining black colt kicked up his heels and ran away from its mother. Mandy smiled to see his vigor.

Nodding, Belle said quietly, her eyes on Sidney, "Silas is my fourth husband and the first one who's amounted to much."

A squeak escaped from Mandy's lips. "Four husbands?" She'd never heard of such a thing.

"The Rockies are a brutally hard land, Mandy."

"So's West Texas."

Nodding, Belle added, "Weaklings and idlers don't last long out here. None of 'em." Belle's eyes never left Sidney. "So how much do you like that husband of yours?"

"L–like him? I *love* him."

Belle made a little sound deep in her throat. "Reckon that's usually the way, at least at first."

Looking away from Sidney, Belle said, "You ever need any

help, you get yourself back to Helena and ask for Roy and Lindsay Adams. My place gets cut off in the winter, but my girl, Lindsay, lives not that far from Helena, south and west of town, up in the high-up hills. And they're known in town. Someone can ride out for them. She and Roy will come a'runnin' to help or take you in with them. I promise you."

"A–alright." The offer made Mandy jumpy. She didn't need to be taken in by anyone.

"Lindsay!" Belle called. "Girls! All of you come on back here."

As Belle's girls fell back beside them, Mandy tried to ignore the niggling of worry in her stomach. It was almost as if Belle *knew* there was going to be trouble. Not so much a warning as it was a *plan* for when the inevitable happened.

Just as the three older girls, with Betsy riding double with Emma and Tanner strapped on Lindsay's back, came into line with Mandy and Belle, a sharp snarl turned them toward where the foal had pranced.

Wolves sprang out of a copse of trees toward the wobbly baby.

Mandy jerked her rifle up and fired one-handed while she slung the strap off her shoulder with the other. She jacked the next bullet into the gun with a whirl of her hand and fired again, whirled and fired, whirled and fired. She had four wolves down, all within a foot or two of the colt before anyone else got off a shot. The foal stumbled back and tripped over the body of a still quivering wolf.

Cold, the way she always felt when she was shooting, iced over her nerves as she saw a shadowy movement in the woods. Her Winchester came around.

Belle fired before Mandy could, then Emma followed. Two more wolves fell forward and revealed themselves from where they'd crouched, lying in wait for an easy meal.

The foal's mother whinnied frantically, pulling against the lead string. Their whole party stopped in its tracks to stare at the dead wolves.

"Done?" Emma asked.

"One ran off before I could get him." Belle stuck her fire iron into its spot in the boot of her saddle.

Mandy slung her rifle back into place as she noticed Belle's gun. It was a Spencer like Ma preferred. It made Mandy homesick.

"I'll get the colt and calm the mare." Emma rode toward the foal and herded it back to its mother's side. The nervous mama licked her baby then nudged it toward her udder. The foal found comfort in warm milk.

Belle turned hazel eyes on Mandy, and those eyes glittered as gold as Sidney's dreams. "Where'd you learn to shoot like that?"

Mandy felt the ice recede from her veins and she looked down at the barely visible muzzle of her gun. She'd already returned the fire iron to its proper position angled across her back, butt high on the left, muzzle low on the right. She'd honed her skill, worked hard to give herself every edge. She'd tried a dozen different grips and made the strap herself to suit her. All to get it into action fast. It was the only way she'd found to best Sally and Ma, and then they'd copied her and taken to wearing their own strapped guns, so she'd practiced even more.

Though honesty forced her to admit she'd found a gift for shooting from an early age.

"My ma taught me, I reckon."

A smile quirked on Belle's face. "Your ma? Not your pa, Clay, the man Shorty said he knew as a boy?"

"Pa helped, too. All my sisters are hands around the ranch and shooting is part of it. You oughta see Sally. I can beat her for speed and accuracy, but when there's trouble, running, fighting, then it's a mighty close thing. I reckon I win out, but Sally's steady when there's trouble."

"Like wolves jumping out of the woods aren't trouble." Belle smiled.

"And my sister Beth, she's not so fast as any of the rest of us. Pretty fast, but we can beat her. But she's a hand at ghosting around in the woods. She's so quiet she can slip up on a deer in

the woods and slap it on the rump before it sees her comin'."
Mandy thought that might be a bit of an exaggeration, but Beth
was a hand at sneakin' and no one could deny it.

Belle studied her. Then Mandy looked past Belle and saw all
her girls staring straight at the strap she'd created just to suit her.

"Can I see it?" Belle asked. "Up close? I might rig something
like that for my Spencer."

"Ma has always favored a Spencer. I prefer a Winchester like
my pa." Mandy handed the gun over with a grin. "You and Emma
are crack shots, too."

Belle was focused on the gun. "We've run afoul of our share of
wolves in these mountains, I reckon."

Then Mandy looked past Belle and her girls and saw Sidney
staring at her, clearly appalled. He knew she was a fast, accurate
shot, because she'd told him and because she took her Winchester
with her everywhere, wore it as faithfully as a bonnet. But she'd
never really demonstrated it before. She'd thought he'd be
impressed, respectful, proud. Instead he was disgusted.

Mandy's smile shrank like a Texas morning glory in the
noonday sun. Belle looked up, saw the direction of Mandy's gaze,
and followed it. Mandy immediately schooled her expression,
sorry she'd let it show that Sidney had hurt her feelings. Judging
by the frown on Belle's face, Mandy had gotten control of herself
too late.

Poor Sidney, Belle was not impressed. Well, he wasn't at his
best. Mandy made allowances for that, but Belle could only know
what was in front of her eyes. Mandy knew she and Sidney would
be fine. Whatever needed done, Mandy could do it herself, so
having Sidney around to help, even if he was just digging for gold,
would be better than being alone. They'd survive.

Having the girls studying her gun and talking with her made
Mandy so homesick she could barely talk.

"We're going to have a time of it getting that foal home. It's a
long walk. It'll be hard on the mare, too." Belle studied her mare
with a furrowed brow. "She's older and she's one of our best. I'd

have liked to get a few more years out of her, but that trail ride home might be too much for a new mother. I had no idea she was so close to foaling." Belle shook her head and kicked her horse back into motion. They all made their way toward Mandy's homestead, talking guns and wolves and foals.

Mandy worried about Sidney but couldn't help enjoying the female companionship. It made her think of her sisters. Especially Beth. What she'd give to have seen Beth again before she left. Sweet Beth with the healing touch. Beth had such dreams of helping others. Mandy knew her little sister would find a way to make those dreams come true.

By now Beth was settled into the ranch, surrounded by the family, doing what doctoring Pa would allow and wrangling with him to do more. Mandy smiled to think of her sweet sister living the safe, quiet, nurturing life of healing, just as she'd always dreamed.

★

Alex lost hold of Beth as they plunged over the cliff. He bounced off rock outcroppings, rolling along with stone and scraping mesquite. Alex's head cracked on something solid and he was only aware of sliding until he rammed to a stop. Alex heard the crack of a rifle and a rock spattered his face, slitting his skin.

He forced his dirt-gritted eyes open and saw Beth, her expression dazed, skidding to a stop beside him. He forced himself to move, urged on by another whining bullet even closer than the last. Grabbing Beth by the back of her collar, he took a fast look around and saw they'd landed on a ledge about twenty feet below the trail.

A bullet cut his arm and he had no choice—he pulled Beth with him over the edge. Again they fell. Then Alex hit something and rolled. His hand was ripped loose from Beth and he lost track of her until he landed hard again.

Bullets roared overhead, but from where they lay none came close.

Alex searched and found Beth flat on her back about ten feet down the still steep rock face. He slipped and slid down to her just as she tried to get to her knees. He dropped dizzily to the ground beside her. Blood soaked the hand he reached out to her.

"We're out of range." Alex's voice drew Beth's eyes around and he saw her face burned raw by the rocks. "Honey." He hated knowing she was hurt.

She shook her head hard. "We've got to move. He'll come down to check that we're dead."

"No one's crazy enough to follow us over that cliff."

Rock's rained down off to their side and they both looked up. They couldn't see to the top, but someone was definitely coming down.

Beth shoved herself to her feet. Alex noticed she had her doctor's bag hanging from her shoulder and the Winchester on her back.

"You held on to the gun?"

Beth gave him a wild look. "Of course I held on to the gun."

"You had time to think of grabbing the doctor's bag while we were diving away from gunfire and going over a cliff?"

Beth arched a blood-soaked brow. "Of course."

"In the half second before we jumped, I was praying, figuring we were going to die."

Beth shrugged and managed a grin. "In the half second before we jumped I jammed the handle of my doctor's bag hard onto my wrist and took a firm hold of the strap on the Winchester, figuring we were going to live." Then Beth's smile widened. "But I prayed while I did it."

"You are the perfect woman." Alex smiled back.

The rocks tumbled down from overhead again. Beth and Alex glanced up. Then their eyes locked. They staggered to their feet and ran.

★

A bullet tore through the air as Beth dragged Alex over yet another steep slope.

Beth did her best to keep them well ahead of the man pursuing them, but he kept coming. He was on high ground so he had a shot at them every so often and the bullets were so close it was terrifying. Their pursuer was a top hand with a gun. He'd been after them for over an hour. The night had settled into full dark, but bright stars overhead made too much visible. That was just a pure shame.

"You've never seen that man before?" Alex asked.

"Why, you think he's after me?" Beth skidded down the rocky incline, stones clattering away under her feet, her rugged riding skirt protecting her as much as possible.

"Well, I've never seen him before." Alex lost his footing and slid along on his belly for a while. Downward, always downward out of this high country.

Beth knew with a sickening certainty that they were being driven toward the desert. Their only possible path was directly away from her parents' ranch and Mosqueros, the places that offered safety. No one she knew of lived this way. Once they entered the driest part of this land, they'd be trapped, either dying of thirst or facing their assailant with his sharp eye and endless supply of bullets.

Thinking out loud, Beth said, "We could try and dig in, make a stand. Even hide and hope he goes past us in the dark. We're going to have to lose this guy or fight him. He's not giving up." Beth touched her rifle, slung down her back, to make sure it was in place while she tried to think of a way to do either.

"Can we get back up that cliff we came over?"

"I don't know. That man came down by choice. He didn't jump, so maybe, but I'd hate to go back and find out we were stuck."

"We'd be trapped back there, him in front of us, our backs to that rock wall."

She'd married a lunatic, but he was a smart, logical lunatic. "I've thought of another way, but it's a long, hard run and a long, long chance, and it will carry us even farther from safety."

"But we'll be alive, right?" Alex was breathing hard, but he was keeping up, even pulling her along.

"And Pa will come. It shouldn't take long for someone to miss us and Pa knows tracking."

"And we left the team and wagon behind. Hopefully they'll head for the livery. Your pa can back trail it."

"Yep, he can read sign like the written word. He'll come with the whole of his ranch hands backing him and save us."

"So we just need to stay alive until he gets here." Alex glanced at her. "You're sure we can't stand and fight on our own? We've got two guns and plenty of bullets."

Beth puffed as she ran. How long could they keep going? "He's a dead shot, Alex. He missed me by inches through pure luck and he was a long way up that trail. We're up against a tough man." Beth got to the bottom of this latest rugged gully and scrambled to her feet, pulling Alex up, grimacing at his bleeding arm with its slipshod bandage.

"Then I guess, at least for now, we'd better keep running." Alex had never uttered a single note of protest or pain, she'd give him that. For a semi-crazy man who thought himself a coward, Alex was holding up really well.

"What do you think he wants? It's not to rob us, because we left the team behind and they're the most valuable thing we have."

"He may think we've got money."

"No low-down thief works this hard for money." Beth thought of what lay ahead of them if she followed the only plan she could think of—at least ten miles over country more apt to sit on end than lay flat.

There was a creek that wound this way, that had at one time run past a little shack she'd lived in, when her ma was between husbands. That creek was fast moving by the thicket where they'd used to live, but this far out it faded into an arroyo that only ran during the rainy season. It would be flat and smooth.

They'd make good time and hunt for the right place to leave the arroyo and circle around to head back north. They couldn't stay on it long though, because it ended in the Pecos and she wanted no part of that wild runaway river. Beth had heard the stories many times. The Pecos had killed nearly as many people as the desert.

It was late summer though. The arroyo would be easy to traverse and just as easy to abandon. They'd leave these treacherous hills behind and gain some space between them and their pursuer. . .if they couldn't shake him.

A sharp crack overhead had Beth looking back and expecting to see the gunman gaining. Instead she saw lightning. Rain. Coming from the north. Beth shuddered at the thought of floodwaters. "Alex, do you know how to swim?" Beth breathed hard as they ran hand-in-hand on the broken ground.

"That's a strange question to ask right now." Alex puffed the words out. He was right. They shouldn't be wasting a single breath. Only it wasn't wasted breath, Beth knew that.

"Just answer the question." A mesquite bush slapped her arm and nearly snatched the rifle away. She didn't dare lose that.

"Can't say that I do. I've never tried it. Why would you ask that?"

Alex was right, it was a strange question. Even more, it wasn't a question that required an answer. Because whatever Alex said, they were going for a swim.

"Never mind." Beth groaned and tightened her grip even more securely on the rifle.

★ Twenty-two ★

For a girl who never cried, Mandy had been at. . .or over. . .the brink about ten times in the days since she'd gotten married. She hoped it wasn't some new affliction.

But watching Belle and her family and cowhands prepare to ride away brought tears to her eyes. Silas and his drovers had arrived a few hours after the rest of them had gotten there—land was already cleared for a cabin and a stack of trees had been felled, using the ax and other tools Silas and Belle had provided plus a few things in the crate Pa had packed for them.

Once he'd arrived, Silas took over. The man could build a house so well, Mandy nearly heard music playing while everybody followed his orders.

Pausing with one hand on the saddle horn, ready to mount up, Silas said, "You know we could take another day or two." He looked at a couple of his hands. "And some of these men are riding to Divide, not taking the high trail back to the Harden ranch. They could stay even longer. Help you split the kindling and mud the cabin."

Mandy looked at the solid cabin behind her. True, it needed the cracks chinked but Silas had told her and Sidney how. "Thanks, but we're fine."

Belle, already mounted, said, "We've left a lot of work for

two people alone. There's no shame in accepting help from your neighbors."

The whole crew had been here for three long, hard days. Belle and Silas were leaving behind a good, tight log house, with a solidly built barn close to hand and a well-built corral. That was so much more than Mandy had ever dreamed of having done so quickly. Her hopes and prayers for protection had been to just survive the coming winter. She'd expected to spend it in a cabin the size of a line shack—if she was lucky.

But the Hardens had done even more. They'd also chopped wood for the winter, stocked the cupboards, and left behind two riding horses, leather for those horses, and a milk cow, a brood of chickens in a little henhouse, and a buckboard. They'd also built a few rustic pieces of furniture. And, the most wondrous thing of all, they'd left the little newborn foal and its mama.

Belle nodded then spotted the stupid, brimming tears, Mandy assumed, and rode up close. "I'm mighty grateful for you watchin' after my horse. We'd have lost the foal for sure if he'd taken that long trip home. It'd be mighty hard on the mare, too. She's an old one. I'll be back for the pair in the spring." Belle's warm, yellow-gold eyes said far more than her words.

Mandy knew Belle was worried about leaving. And she knew Belle and Silas would have gotten that foal and mare home somehow. But it would have been hard on the pair. That was the truth. So it was best to leave them behind for now. Of course Belle's daughter, Lindsay, lived a short day's ride in the direction of home, but even that was a long, steep trek.

The Hardens had come up with the only real thing Mandy could do for them and asked for it—and then acted as if the Hardens owed the Grays.

"I'm so glad there was something we could do to help." Mandy fought back the tears, not proud of this new inclination. "It doesn't begin to make up for all you've done for Sidney and me."

Sidney was hanging back by the steps. Every thank-you had been grudging. It was all Mandy could do not to rap him on the head with the butt of her Winchester.

Mandy neither yelled at her husband nor cried, knowing either would delay the Hardens, and they needed to get on the trail. Mandy had done everything she could to convince them she could finish their winter preparations on her own. And she could.

They could have survived with no help. But God had sent people in her path. Mandy prayed for protection steadily. It was the longing of her heart to feel close to God and protected from the often rugged life in the West. Both here and back in Texas.

God had certainly provided beyond any hope Mandy had dared. She and Sidney would live comfortably through the winter because of Belle and Silas Harden.

"I found the straightest trees I could"—Silas studied the cabin—"but there are plenty of gaps. You remember how to mix up the mud and daub it in, right?"

Silas had done one whole side already, most of the higher logs on the cabin, and he'd given the barn a first coating of mud, keeping his men working late into the night. But the plaster of mud needed to dry before more could be added, and where knots in the trees had forced them to leave good-sized gaps, the cabin was going to need several days worth of patching.

Now the Hardens were riding out, leaving behind supplies and the riding horses—which Mandy hadn't realized were a gift until a few minutes ago, and the foal, which meant the Hardens would return in the spring—and it was more than Mandy could stand without tears.

Sidney stood behind her glowering. Mandy expected taking the charity—Belle had called them housewarming gifts and payment for sheltering the mare and foal—had pinched him.

"They're rich people," Sidney grumbled as soon as the Harden company was out of earshot. "They don't know what it's like starting out. They could have given me better advice about where to hunt gold. All Harden would do was talk about caring for the horses and how to lay in wait for a deer. And how to mix the stupid mud up to patch holes in the cabin."

173

Mandy caught herself rubbing the little callus on her trigger finger and stopped that telling action. "We'll look around, Sidney. We'll find a place for you to dig your gold mine. But winter's coming down on us. We need to add a new layer of mud right away and jerk that venison."

Mandy looked out the door at the two big bucks hanging from a tree just outside the door. Emma had gone hunting and brought them in.

Mandy looked at Sidney and gave him an encouraging smile. "We're going to be happy here. If you don't find gold soon enough, you can ride to town and work until the winter settles in. We're going to make a good life."

She looked at the trees and scrub brush surrounding their home, cutting the wind. "It's a likely place we picked for a home." The Hardens had picked the exact site and done it well, but Sidney had picked Montana.

Sidney looked away from the hanging deer. "You really know how to butcher those deer?"

Mandy nodded, proud she'd be able to help make them comfortable.

He shared his most charming smile, and Mandy remembered fully why she'd agreed to marry him. "Will it hurt anything if you wait an hour or two to get started?"

"No, they can hang a while. But it's best to get a job tackled if it needs doing." Mandy took one step away from their little cabin.

Sidney slid an arm around Mandy's waist and pulled her back hard against him. Then he leaned in and kissed her. "I know something else that needs doing."

Mandy let the kiss drive every other thought straight out of her mind.

Sidney was right. The deer would still be there. It was far past time to give the man his wedding night.

★

They hadn't seen their pursuer in a while, but who needed a

gunman when Beth was determined to kill them both?

Alex thought his legs were giving out. His arm burned like fire where it'd been creased by a bullet. They'd run all night through pouring, soaking rain. When he'd suggested they seek shelter, Beth had bullied him into moving on. The storm had cleared off about the time the sun came up.

The one good thing was they hadn't been fired on in hours. Maybe they'd lost that madman in the storm.

Alex had never been a lucky man so he wasn't optimistic. They ran on. Alex had long ago given up on doing anything but keeping pace with his wife.

"There it is!" Beth yelled.

"There what is?" Alex looked at the little slave driver he'd married.

"The arroyo I was looking for." She pointed and Alex caught a glimpse of shimmering water curving far below them. They'd been coming down out of high country all day, but from the look of the cut the arroyo ran through, they were still pretty high. She'd never said a word about an arroyo. Except, she had said—

"Wait a minute. About the time it started raining, you asked me if I could swim. I said I can't." They reached the edge of the cliff that fell thirty or more feet into what looked like raging floodwaters.

"I remember." Beth looked downstream. "Maybe we can run alongside it. We don't necessarily need to jump in."

A sharp report of a gun cut the air and a rock exploded. The ricochet slit Alex's face.

Beth gave Alex one wild look. "Sorry."

She grabbed his hand and, swim or not, he knew that while the fast moving water was only *apt* to kill them both, the bullets were for sure deadly. He clutched her hand and they jumped.

When Alex fought his way to the surface, his first thought was that he'd lost hold of Beth. As the water swept him along, he looked frantically for her. His eyes landed on that madman who'd lured them out into the mountains last night. The man was a long way away. Out of rifle range. At least Alex sure hoped so.

The man was so focused that Alex knew this hunter was staring straight at him, not Beth. The man yelled, and the canyons and water echoed the words until Alex couldn't possibly miss what he said, even over the roar of the rushing water. "Dead or alive, Buchanan! Dead or alive!"

And suddenly it all made sense. Alex knew exactly what this man was after. And he knew that unless they were very lucky—and Alex had never been lucky—Beth was going to die to pay for Alex's sins.

Alex caught sight of Beth being swept along by the current a few feet behind him. Their eyes locked. He knew she'd heard that awful shout. As they were rushed along by the raging floodwater, and since luck was unlikely, Alex started to pray.

Then the flood waters sucked him under.

★

"Dead or alive, Buchanan!" Cletus might as well have been howling at the moon. Buchanan and his woman couldn't hear him. Didn't matter. It suited Cletus to blow off some steam by yelling, so he did. No one around to care, so why not?

Cletus's druthers were to get a man before that man knew he was being hunted. Made life easier. Now Buchanan was warned. But Cletus had been hunting men for a long time and he knew the main trick was to just keep coming. Always coming. Like a hungry wolf on the trail of blood.

Cletus had left his horse behind. His gun wouldn't fire if he jumped in the water, and he wasn't going up against Buchanan without a gun. So he'd come along slow. No harm in slow as long as it was sure and steady. These waters flowed fast, and the walls of this washed-out arroyo were steep most of the way to the Pecos. There'd be little chance for Buchanan to climb out of that water for long, brutal miles.

Chances were Cletus would just scout downstream and pick up Buchanan's body. Smiling, he turned back. In the daylight he could cut his time in half and he could get his horse and ride around this mess of mountains instead of through them. If he didn't get there in time to cut Buchanan off, he'd get there later and track the man down. Buchanan was wanted. No law would protect him.

If the yellow-bellied doctor heard nothing else, Cletus hoped the deserter heard laughter echoing off the walls of the wild mountain canyon.

★

"Montana?" Sophie looked at the telegraph and was stunned. "What in the world is Mandy doing in Montana?" And who in the world was Silas Harden, the man who'd sent the wire?

She marched out of the telegraph office. Sophie had heard everything about that skunk Mandy had hitched herself to. She'd never liked the man. Too smooth to suit Sophie from the first day. Didn't have a callus on a single finger. Bad sign.

Clay would have to find Luther and Buff and send them in the right direction. Sophie had no doubt he'd do it. Her husband was a good man. A man to count on. Not like Sidney Gray.

But if Clay didn't fix this, Sophie vowed to the good Lord she'd saddle a horse and go herself. And yes, she'd take all the young'uns with her. That skunk who'd stolen her Mandy was not going to get away with marrying Mandy when he was already married. Yes, Sophie determined with grim resolve, she really did want to go herself.

"Clay!" Sophie saw Clay coming out of the doctor's office with Sally at his side. Sally, her girl. She'd almost died.

Sophie couldn't find it in herself to hate the strange Alex Buchanan even if it galled her that Beth had married the man. Even if the man stacked up to be some kind of lunatic. Still, she'd be grateful to him forever.

She had two daughters married. Both married to men Sophie thought were mighty strange picks.

"Sophie!" Clay marched toward her, Sally nearly running to keep up.

Sophie hurried just as fast toward him. They met in the middle of the mud-soaked main street in Mosqueros.

"Beth's gone!" Clay raged.

"Mandy's in Montana," Sophie said at the same moment.

"What?" they spoke the word in unison.

"Beth has disappeared." Clay talked faster and his words distracted Sophie from her disturbing news about Mandy. "Her horses came in last night, pulling the doctor's wagon. No one's see her all day."

Since it was nearly noon, something had definitely happened to Beth. All thoughts of Mandy and her plight were put aside. For now.

Sophie and Clay turned and walked side-by-side. Sally fell in line with them. All three of them jerked on their buckskin gloves as they headed for their horses, tied three in a row in front of the general store.

Sophie looked at Sally and could see the still-raw scar on her throat. A tiny scar that saved her life. "Is Alex gone, too?" She'd forgotten about her son-in-law.

"Yep." Clay jerked his reins loose from the hitching post and swung up onto his black gelding. "No one saw 'em leave town, but the wagon came in from the south. Rain washed out all the tracks from last night, but the wagon must have come down after the rain passed." Clay wheeled his horse to the south. "The horses stood, still in their traces, out front of the stable this morning. There's wagon tracks heading south."

He paused and turned back to Sophie. "Mandy's in Montana?" Clay's voice almost screeched. "What in the world is Mandy doing in Montana?"

"Who can say? Let's go save Beth. Then you'll need to wire Luther." Sophie spurred her horse south, Sally one step behind.

The tracks just kept on going south out of town, the one direction Beth would never go.

Sally was the first to notice a second set of tracks. "Someone rode out after them."

Clay swung down to study the sign. "The wagon came down the mountain empty. You can tell by the way the trail left by the buckboard wanders that there was no driver on the way back. That means—" Clay looked up.

Sophie read his fear as if he'd shouted it. Beth had been led up this lonely trail by someone and that someone had come back alone.

They were at a full gallop in seconds.

★

"Grab the log, Alex!" Beth saw their chance. Not to get out of here—there didn't seem to be a spot where the banks weren't straight up and high above their heads—but a log would help them stay afloat.

Alex heard her over the roar of the surging floodwaters. He must have because he obeyed. He grabbed for one of the dozens of branches of the stout trunk and, glory be to God, he held on.

Beth was behind him. For the first time, instead of fighting the current, she kicked hard to speed herself up. The Winchester was still wrapped around her head and one shoulder. The doctor's bag, with its medical supplies and the trusty Colt revolver, was slid hard up her arm until the handles were stuck tight. They'd been awkward to hang on to, but she'd done it, clung to them like they meant life or death.

They very well might.

She dragged herself forward, thinking of her sharpshooting sister, Mandy. It was Mandy who'd started using a strap so she could get her gun into play faster. Beth might well owe Mandy her life, if things came down to life and death, and the gun made the difference.

Fighting the water an inch at a time, she was battered and bruised and half-drowned from this wild ride. But at last she got to the tree and clung to the gnarled roots. The tree looked like it had been torn whole right out of the ground.

She was on the off side of the tree from Alex so she hoisted herself up to lie on her belly across the trunk. And there he was, doing the same thing with a frantic expression on his face—looking upstream.

When she appeared, he saw her and smiled. That frantic look had been his worrying about her. "Beth. Thank God you made it." He breathed hard twice, changing his grip so his body was more fully supported by the tree. "I'm so glad you're all right."

Beth squirmed around, too, trying to get a firmer grasp on the tree. She felt like she was using her last ounce of energy to pull herself up. She set her now soaked Winchester and her waterlogged doctor's bag on her lap. Maybe everything was ruined. Maybe the rifle and the Colt wouldn't fire. But she'd held on all this way down the flooded creek.

The branches spread out to the sides in a way that kept the tree from rolling. Alex and Beth raced along on their clumsy raft at a sickening speed, and every second swept them farther from the safety of Beth's family. But for this one second, they were alive. They were even sort of safe. At least safe from that back shooter. The river might still get them.

"We both made it." Alex panted as if he were storing up air for the future. As if he were planning to be underwater again soon.

The creek roared. No gunfire split the air. No human voices. A bird cawed in the early morning sun as the water splashed and rumbled along. Beth smiled. "Even you. Even I-can't-swim-Alex made it."

"I'm not sure what I did once I hit the water qualifies as swimming, but if it does, then, yes, I can swim." Alex sighed.

Beth leaned back and found the roots of the tree made a fair backrest. "We'll keep going downstream until we find a place with low banks where we can climb out. Then we'll circle around, give the arroyo a wide berth in case that man's coming downstream, and head back for Mosqueros."

"No!" Alex shook his head—dead serious. The day was breaking and Beth could see it clearly in his face that, for the first time, Alex wasn't going to obey her.

Well, that was annoying.

"We're not going back north to Mosqueros. We're going west to Fort Union."

Beth patted the flat of her hand on one ear, hoping to dislodge water so she could hear what the man was saying. Maybe the water in her ears had kept it from making sense.

"I've heard of Fort Union. It's in New Mexico. It's a long, hard ride over some mean country." Beth didn't bother to mention that they didn't have a horse. "Why would we go there for safety when we can just go back to Mosqueros?"

Alex sighed.

Beth saw something so kind and wise and gentle in his eyes that she wanted to crawl along this swirling, splashing log to his side and give him a hug.

"We're going there because we've been swept so far west that we may actually be closer to it than we are to Mosqueros."

Beth doubted it. They'd definitely come a long way in the right direction. But still—

"And we're also going there because I figured out who that man is."

"You know him?" Beth felt some meager satisfaction to know the man had been gunning for someone other than her. It was very meager.

"I don't know his name, but I know his type. He's a bounty hunter."

"And he's after you because—" Beth waited.

"Because I'm a wanted man, Beth. There's a price on my head. I should have told you. I should never have married you."

Beth gasped then sucked in some of the water still streaming off her face. She started choking. At last she managed to say, "Alex, what did you do?"

"I'm a deserter from the cavalry. As that man so cruelly reminded me, I'm wanted dead or alive. Only it's pretty clear to me that he's only interested in dead and he's going to make sure you're dead right along with me. I'm not going to stand for that.

We'll make a run for Fort Union and I'll turn myself in."

"What do they do to deserters, Alex?"

Alex's eyes finally fell. He'd been pretty brave when he announced he was turning himself in to the cavalry. Now he wasn't quite so courageous.

"What, Alex? Tell me." Dread came in waves just from looking at Alex's expression.

"The punishment for desertion"—Alex swallowed hard but he raised his head to look her square in the eye—"is a firing squad."

★ Twenty-three ★

Mandy skinned the buck with a smile on her face. She was truly Sidney's wife now.

She wondered how long it would be until she had a little one to raise. She'd mothered her little brothers and sisters all her life, of course with her ma in charge, but Mandy knew the way of mothering, and all the fun and love and hard work. She couldn't wait.

God, protect me and Sidney and our children.

Her married life had finally, truly begun.

She made quick work of skinning the bucks then set the hides aside to tan, a process that would give them thick, comfortable blankets for the winter—or she could use them to make shoes or coats or gloves. She knew how to do all those things.

She hoped Sidney would show some interest in learning, because it was a big job. But she enjoyed the labor of her hands and took great satisfaction in knowing she could make a good life for herself with the strength of her back. Sidney liked to say he was working with his head not his back. But Mandy figured God had given her a strong back for a reason so she didn't mind using it.

She cut the meat of both bucks into strips, setting aside a haunch to hang in a cool cave Silas Harden had scouted out. They'd eat venison steaks and roasts, and Mandy could contrive a good stew with the supplies the Hardens had brought for them. The rest of the meat would be smoked and stockpiled for the winter that she'd been grimly warned would come early and stay late.

"Mandy, I'm going to hike around, see if there are any likely spots for mining." Sidney came out of the house tugging his suspenders over his shoulders. Broad shoulders that had cradled Mandy last night.

She was truly in love with her husband. She knew he wasn't perfect. He was a city boy, not used to frontier living. But he'd learn, and if he took a notion to hunt for gold for a while, she'd let him. A man needed a dream.

Sidney had the shovel that Pa had packed with him. He slung it over his shoulder and whistled as he headed into the woods.

"Sidney, there's a cave just a bit up this trail that way." Mandy pointed to the west. "I don't know much about gold mining, but a cave might be a likely place to look." She'd heard of mines and she'd heard of panning for gold. They had no pan, so the cave sounded good.

Sidney turned away from his own direction and walked over to Mandy, who was covered neck to ankle in a huge apron, her hands bloody from butchering, her hair a bit flyaway, because when it had escaped in bits from its knot she'd been careful not to tuck it back in, considering the mess.

Sidney leaned down and kissed her gently, then pulled back to smile. "We're going to be happy here, Mandy. If I find a vein of gold, we'll be so rich we can buy and sell that Harden clan and we'll eat roast beef every day and not have to hunt."

Mandy knew she'd married a dreamer, but his dream seemed to have shifted. What about being a lawyer? Well, he could always be one of those, too; and in the meantime, she'd keep venison on the table.

"Can you leave that and show me this cave?" Sidney looked uneasily at the deer, as if worried that he'd be remembering this mess when he was eating later.

Mandy fought a smile. "I'd love to walk over there with you." She set aside her heavy knife, then wiped her hands as best she could on the apron and took it off. She was still untidy and she suspected she smelled none too good, but she left the worst of the mess behind.

They strolled through the woods until Mandy came upon the cave mouth, nearly concealed by a clump of quaking aspen that was just showing the first signs of fall color. Mandy had listened closely while Belle and her whole family talked yesterday, educating her in the way of mountain living. What woods burned and carved well, which were best for building, what plants had medicinal uses. What wildlife was about, some dangerous, some not. Some tasty, some not.

Emma Harden had found a good spring, which is why they'd built where they had. A steady water source made a well unnecessary.

The whole group had talked and taught and been so kind. Mandy had sensed their quiet worry about leaving Mandy and Sidney here alone, but Mandy had convinced them she was a frontier woman, same as them. In the end they'd left her and Sidney to saddle their own broncos, which was the way of the West, be it in Texas or Montana.

Mandy slipped through the nearly solid wall of aspens. The Hardens had stacked rocks and rigged a gate in front of the cave entrance so it was a trick to get inside.

"Couldn't they find a cave around here that was easier to get in and out of?" Sidney asked. It was his first querulous comment of the day. Of course he'd only been out of bed about ten minutes.

"They picked this and blocked it off to keep out wild animals. I'm going to hang my jerked meat in here. We don't want to be feeding the local grizzly bears and mountain lions and wolves, now do we?" Mandy grinned at him as they entered the cave. It wasn't huge but once they'd passed the entrance, they could stand upright in it and it went back nearly twenty feet. The light was dim but Mandy saw that someone had rigged a sturdy branch in one corner to use as a hanger for meat. That was going to save her a lot of time.

She sure didn't see any gold, but that wasn't her project. "I've got a deer to cut up and a hide to tan. Then I'm going to chink the cabin and barn. Two people would make it go a lot faster." A hint she wished he'd take.

"Maybe later, honey." Sidney came near and tossed the shovel on the ground. He wrapped his arms around her waist and kissed her. When he finished he said, "I'm so proud of all you know how to do. You can really tan a deer hide?"

"Sure. It'll be great, strong leather when I'm done. I'll use the deer's brain to tan the hide then smoke it to keep it soft."

"The brain?" Sidney flinched.

Patting him on the chest, Mandy smiled at her city-boy husband. "We can use the hide all winter as a blanket. I even know how to make moccasins and pants for you. You might want them if you're doing hard work. They're a lot sturdier than broadcloth."

Sidney kissed her again. "I have married myself a fine woman." The next kiss lasted longer.

"Now I want you to quit distracting me and let me get to work." His smile told her he was teasing.

She smiled back. "Good luck. I hope you find a wagonload of gold." She almost added, "But don't get your hopes up," but why discourage him? She'd leave that task to the Rocky Mountains.

"I'll be back here in a while to hang the haunch of venison so I'll see you soon."

"Bye." Sidney turned to the very barren walls of the cave with a bit of a bewildered look on his face.

Mandy couldn't help him. She had no idea how to go about finding gold.

Slipping out the narrow opening of the cave, she started thinking of what they'd have for a noon meal. Something encouraging.

Mandy needed to keep her husband happy.

Beth needed to keep her husband alive.

"We are not going to some fort hundreds of miles over rugged desert and mountains to turn you over to a firing squad."

"It's the only way to keep you alive, Beth."

"No, it isn't." Their tree trunk rounded a curve in the flooded arroyo and Beth yelled, "Hang on."

She could have skipped yelling. Alex was watching the banks as carefully as she was. He'd already seen the curve ahead and gotten his arms wrapped tight around the branches he balanced between.

But she felt like yelling so it suited her to do it. They'd been floating along all morning, half the time squabbling, half the time sitting in grudge-soaked silence, all the time clinging to their tree. It had a tendency to slam into the bank like it was going to right now.

Beth sat leaning against the roots. Alex was on the other end of the tree. He'd slid closer to Beth slowly, inch by inch, until they were almost within arm's length of each other. But that last gap between them had no branches so there was nothing for him to hold on to. So they'd stayed apart, when Beth would have dearly loved him to hold her in his arms through this wretched ride.

They clung to their handholds as the tree jammed straight into the sheer wall that lined this arroyo. It hit so hard Beth lost her grip for a second, but she scrambled to regain it and stayed atop the God-supplied raft. The top ten feet of the tree snapped off with a sharp crack. Beth wondered how long before their boat was battered down to firewood. There were no low banks to climb out on.

The collision sent the tree spinning. Beth ended up downstream of Alex, but it wouldn't last. The tree would swivel again soon though. Many branches had been stripped away, leaving the top of the tree slender, but the roots were tough and still showed some green in places scraped raw. So the current tended to catch them and hold them back, letting the top of the tree get ahead again. They finally settled in again, with the rushing waters.

Beth's legs dangled into the flood. It helped her keep her balance to straddle the tree. She was exhausted, starved, and battered from the events of the last twenty-four hours. She wanted her ma so badly she felt like, inside, she'd reverted to a three-year-old. But outside, where it counted, she was a lawfully wedded woman trying to talk some sense into the half-wit she'd married. "It isn't the only way to keep me alive. We'll just make our way back to Mosqueros. I'll be safe there."

"But that man will keep coming. He'll be after me, and from the underhanded way he went about trying to take me in, I'd say he was definitely more interested in the 'dead' than the 'alive' on that wanted poster. And if he's gunning for me, you could get caught in the crossfire."

"I'll be careful. Pa was a major in the army during the Civil War. He might know someone who could give you advice."

Alex shook his head. "I'm going in, Beth. And you're coming with me. I'll face my punishment like a man and y–you'll be set free. I've been half out of my head for a long time. I should have gone back and faced this years ago. But I was too much of a coward."

"What happened, Alex? Why did you run? Is that why you were acting so crazy on the stagecoach? Is that why you can't do any doctoring unless you keep me at your side?"

Alex kept his eye on the bank.

Beth was always looking, too, hoping to find a lower spot where they had a chance of climbing out. But there'd been nothing.

"Ever hear of the Red River War?" Alex sounded so tense Beth almost stopped him. If he sank into that awful place he'd gone when she left him alone with Mr. Farley at the general store, Alex might not remember to hang on to the tree.

"That's not familiar. I've heard of a Red River in Texas." Beth adjusted her grip, wondering if she was going to have to shimmy along this tree at the risk of her own life to drag her husband out of his dark thoughts. "We don't have to talk about this now, Alex. It might be best to wait until we've reached the shore."

As if he hadn't heard her, Alex said, "I was in the cavalry when it broke out. I'd defied my father's wish to go into business with him. He was part owner of a railroad back East and very wealthy. But I was always drawn to doctoring." Alex raised his eyes to meet hers and she felt that deep connect. "You understand that, don't you?"

"Yes, I do." It was a tie almost as binding as their wedding vows and the ties of the flesh.

"I fought with my father for years, and when I went off to college, I was so rude, so defiant. When I was finally ready to practice medicine, I deliberately chose the West, the military because I felt led to the great need I believed was out here in the frontier. And I got here and the campaign started they called the Red River War."

Beth sat silently and prayed for strength for her and Alex. Her eyes still locked on Alex's, letting him draw strength.

"The Indians had a choice. Register and go peacefully to a reservation or be taken there by force. Only trouble was too many of the Indians were starving on the reservations. They'd go in, surrender, and then stay put until they realized none of the promised food was coming. Then they'd run away. Die on the reservation, die off the reservation. Some choice, huh?" Alex gave her a bitter smile.

"So, I was helping the cavalry round up the ones who'd refused to surrender." Alex shook his head. "It was so awful. It was nothing like I thought it would be when I set out to be a doctor. I had to go right onto the battlefield with the soldiers—guns firing, sometimes cannons. Knifes, bows and arrows. Hate, so much fighting and killing and hate. My job in that carnage was to save the wounded. It was so stupid. Why not just fight to begin with, instead of having the battles then trying to tend to those ugly wounds? Severed limbs, gut shots, men slashed by knives. And it wasn't just men. There were women and children in some of the Indian villages, and I had to tend to them, too. Little children savaged. Women dead or dying. Both soldiers and Indians lay side by side, bleeding. And I had to save the soldiers first. Even if one of the cavalry men was clearly beyond saving, I had to tend him while a less badly wounded warrior or even a woman or child lay close at hand. I could've saved them if I'd been allowed to give up on the soldiers."

"So you deserted when you couldn't take that anymore?" Beth wanted to hold him. She was afraid she'd send them all into the water if she scooted forward, but he needed her. Right now his pain was almost as bad as that of the bleeding, dying soldiers. She moved forward, carefully, an inch at a time, knowing she shouldn't—but her heart wouldn't allow her to stay away from someone who needed her so badly.

"I was kneeling beside a dying man who was soaked in blood. He'd been slashed across the belly and his insides were spilling out. He was—was—" Alex flinched, swallowed hard, and went on. "He was trying to put himself back together, out of his head, just driven by some freakish instinct. I picked up my doctor's bag and it was soaked in blood. My hands, my clothes, the ground, the whole world was soaked in blood."

Alex rubbed his head. "There were horses, too. Someone was shooting horses. I can't remember exactly what I saw, but I can hear those horses screaming. The gunfire. My bag swimming with blood."

Shaking his head, looking into the past, he said, "I just threw the bag and ran. A coward. I couldn't do it anymore. I betrayed my country when I ran, and the punishment for that is a firing squad. I've been so out of my head. I have dreams about that dying man, my doctor's bag, those dying horses. I haven't slept in years because of the nightmares. I tried drinking to shut down the madness, but the drinking made it worse. I had the dreams when I was wide awake then. I haven't done anything but move, as if I could run away from the horror when it's stuck inside my head."

Beth finally reached him and pulled him into her arms. He jumped a bit, as if he'd been so far gone inside his memories that he hadn't noticed she was close. Their eyes met. It was the same powerful connection they'd had from the very first.

"Until you, Beth. Until you dragged me out of the madness that's been plaguing me and forced me to help Mr. Armitage. And even as terrified as I was of doctoring again, the strength I stole from you gave me the first moments of peace I've had in years. I wanted it so badly that I just took it, took you, took everything you offered."

Alex slid his hands deep into her bedraggled hair. "And now I could get you killed. I won't do it." He shouted the words, his fists clutched her wind-dried tresses. His jaw set into a tight, hard line. "I'll die myself before I hurt you. I'll die gladly."

He pulled her tight and kissed her as if he was desperate for her touch. Desperate to feel her and hold her.

Beth fought back the tears until she heard the tight choking sound coming from Alex's throat. Then a sob broke free and Alex gave in to tears. Beth couldn't hold hers a moment longer, despite years of training to the contrary.

Together, they held each other and cried.

★

"They went over that cliff?" Sophie couldn't keep the horror out of her voice.

"Yep. I've looked hard. It's a long way down, but I see clear sign at the bottom that they got up and moved, so they survived the fall. And one rider led them up here then went back down the trail."

Sophie and Clay's eyes met as they stood silently adding things up.

"If they went down this cliff and he went back to town, then the way to find them is to find him." Clay arched his brows as if daring Sophie to deny the obvious.

"I'll go over the side here, Pa." Sally studied the steep slope and walked along the edge, looking for a better place to go down. "I'll trail Beth and see where she got to from this direction."

"Nope, you're not going down there alone."

"Where does this end up?" Sophie searched through her memory. This was a barren, forbidding stretch of land, and she was only slightly familiar with it.

Clay stared down the twisted and gullied terrain. Then his head lifted and he had a shine in his eyes that lifted Sophie's dread. "The arroyo. That's where Beth would go if she had to run this way. She'd head for that dried-up streambed."

"Except it's not dried up after last night's rain," Sophie reminded him.

"Which means they might be getting swept down, maybe all the way to the river," Clay added.

"If they don't drown first," Sally added somberly. "Remember those floodwaters that almost swept Pa away that first night he came to us?" Sally looked at Sophie.

Only years of practicing being brave kept Sophie from visibly shuddering. "I remember. A flood is a fearsome thing. Where do we go, Clay? Where do we ride to fetch Beth home? Alex and Beth." Sophie kept forgetting about him. But she glanced at Sally's scar and knew she'd never really forget. And she'd never be able to repay him. Yes, they'd definitely ride to save both Alex and Beth.

"If she makes it to the water and gets herself a ride on it, I know right where she'll be able to climb out. And that arroyo twists and turns so much we might even be able to get there ahead of her. If not, we'll be able to pick up sign."

"Or meet her heading for home," Sophie added hopefully as she swung up on her roan. "We can send word to the ranch and have Adam and Tillie look after the young'uns along with Laurie. And maybe Adam can send that wire to Luther, too."

"You know," Sally said as she spurred her horse after Clay and Sophie, bringing up the rear, "that man who came down this trail might well be riding to intercept her just like we are. And he's hours ahead of us."

No one said more. They were too busy riding for all they were worth without breaking their necks on the steep, muddy trail back to Mosqueros.

★ Twenty-four ★

Sidney came in from the woods, his shoulders slumped, the light waning. He'd been gone all day.

She'd even taken his dinner out to the cave because he didn't come in. Besides, she'd hauled the deer haunch to the cave. That had been the real point of the cave after all—cool storage for meat.

She'd finished the deer, started tanning the hide, put another layer of mud on the cabin, fed the animals, started dinner, and even found time to play with the little black colt. And still her husband didn't come. Now, just as she was starting to worry that the venison roast would dry out, here he came. With a sigh of relief, she stepped outside to wave hello.

When he caught sight of her, he straightened and began walking faster, a determined, if slightly forced smile on his dirty face.

Mandy didn't think she'd ever seen Sidney dirty before. Not from work at least. "Dinner is ready as soon as you wash up."

Nodding, Sidney came up onto the three steps that made a stoop on the back of the house. "I had a good day. It takes some practice to get the shovel to work and I kept hitting stone. I might ride to Helena tomorrow and buy a pickax."

Mandy didn't mention that they had almost no money left.

And she certainly didn't mention her ma's money. Sidney probably had enough for a pick. And though it came in very handy, she didn't really need money to survive.

A pickax—one tool her folks hadn't included in the supplies they'd sent, nor had the Hardens included one in their housewarming gifts, even though they knew Sidney wanted to dig for gold. Mandy was sorely afraid that omission showed their dim view of gold mining.

"Do you want me to ride along?" Mandy wasn't sure Sidney knew the way to Helena. It was a long and poorly marked trail through broken ground and heavy woods. She worried that he'd ride off and not find his way back to her.

"No need. You'll be alright here alone, won't you?" Sidney was suddenly very attentive, despite the lines of exhaustion on his face. "Are you afraid to stay here without me?"

"I'll be fine. I just thought the two of us together might scout the trail better. Are you considering asking around about a lawyerin' job?"

Shaking his head, Sidney said, "Of course not. Why work as a lawyer when there's gold to be carved out of these mountains?"

Mandy was careful not to let him see her sigh. Why work indeed—as if Sidney hadn't worked himself to the bone today. For no money.

Sidney ate heartily of the roast but didn't talk much. He kept yawning and rubbing his eyes.

Mandy noticed ugly blisters on his hands and knew the man would harden up if he kept mining. That might not be a bad thing.

He went directly to bed after he ate, and Mandy felt a twinge of hurt that he hadn't stayed to talk with her while she cleaned up after the meal or invited her to turn in along with him for the night. After all, there was no one else to talk to around here. If they didn't talk to each other, then they talked to no one at all. That would be a lonely life indeed.

Mandy had grown up surrounded by people. Lots of brothers

and sisters on a thriving cattle ranch. There was always plenty of company. Now she washed the dishes alone, to the sound of her husband snoring in the little bedroom the Hardens had included on this tightly built cabin. The aloneness almost echoed in her ears.

She said a long, heartfelt prayer for her family, and things she needed protection from: homesickness, loneliness, resentment.

She missed her family terribly. It was all she could do to keep from crying when she thought that she might never see them again.

Afraid she could slip into a life seeded with envy, she turned her thoughts to praise, fighting off feelings of jealousy that Beth was now living at home, soaking in that peaceful, settled life.

★

Their log hurled toward the bank. The canyon narrowed.

"Brace yourself, Alex!" Beth swallowed a mouthful of dirty water, choking as she clung to the log.

She saw Alex jerk awake. He'd nodded off for a minute when the water had calmed briefly. He grabbed for the log and held on tight.

The current picked up. The water churned white and rough, a sudden dip of their tree splashed water high.

Beth was heartily sick of this ride. They'd been careening along for a good chunk of the day. The sheer canyon walls lining this arroyo had prevented them from climbing out.

Alex blinked his eyes and tightened his hold on the nearest branch. The tree was now about six feet long. The narrow end had been battered and snapped off repeatedly.

Then Beth saw what she'd been looking for all day. "There's a break in the canyon wall, Alex." She pointed to the arroyo wall, just past this narrow spot.

They had to survive the narrows first, but past the white, churning water breaking over protruding stones was their first chance to get out of here. They'd be very lucky to get through the rapids, but once through, they could finally get out of here and go. . .where?

Alex said Fort Union.

Beth said home.

He was too big to knock senseless and drag along back to her parents' ranch. If she'd had a horse she could manage it.

The log rammed into one of the bigger stones.

Beth flew forward, clinging to her handhold, the rifle and doctor's bag securely hitched to her body. She stayed with the bouncing, twisting log for a few seconds, remembering a particularly feisty bronco she'd busted when she'd been growing up. Then a second jolt tore her loose from the tree and sent her tumbling head over heels into the water.

She went under and resisted gasping for breath—barely. She rammed into a stone with her shoulder and flipped onto her stomach. Slashing at the water with her arms, she surfaced, dragged her lungs full of air, and then was plunged beneath the water again. Battling the rushing current, she emerged from the torrent once again and sighted that low spot in the arroyo bank. She struck out for the shore using strength born of desperation. She wanted out of this place, and who knew when she and Alex would get another chance.

The low spot was a tumbled-down pile of rocks, looking as if the bank had caved in. It wasn't a long stretch, and the water seemed to be taunting her by sweeping her away from that chance for escape.

Submerged again, she collided with something soft. Her head cleared the water and she was face-to-face with Alex. His eyes looked glazed and a rivulet of blood trickled down from his temple.

Beth slung one arm around him and continued kicking toward the shore. They looked to be going past when a sudden eddy swirled them around and kicked them out so hard they landed with a thud on the scattered rocks.

"Hang on, Alex. We made it, but you have to hang on." Beth's legs were still in the water, and it was as if there was a gripping hand on her feet, determined to drag her into the depths. But she was a tough Texas cowgirl and she hadn't gotten to her ripe old age of twenty without facing trouble head-on. Her grip on the rocks held as if God Himself gave her strength, which she suspected He did.

Alex's movements were clumsy, but he dragged himself forward, inch by inch. Slightly ahead of her, he turned back. Some of the daze was gone from his eyes and he caught hold of her wrist and tugged her up beside him.

The streaming water gave one last yank, like a spoiled child denied its toy, then she surged forward and landed like a beleaguered catfish, *splat*, beside Alex.

They were truly on dry land.

Beth used every ounce of strength she had to turn her head, now resting on the forbidding scratchy rocks, and open her eyes to see Alex.

He stared at her, bleeding but with a weary smile. "We made it, Beth. We're safe."

Beth closed her eyes and dragged in more precious air. "We are." Then her head cleared enough for her to add, "Except for that bounty hunter behind us and a firing squad ahead of us."

"Just give me this moment, okay?" Alex asked.

Beth lay there breathing until she had the energy to do more than breathe. With a groan, she pushed herself to her hands and knees and looked at the mess in front of her. Yes, they'd found a break in the arroyo wall, but they still had about a hundred yards of jagged rock to climb before they could really say they'd made it.

"Let's go, Alex." She looked at him, to goad him into moving. The whole left side of his face was soaked with blood. Beth reared up on her knees as Alex tried to rise. "Stop. Don't move." She wrenched her doctor's bag off her arm and saw that she'd left a deep welt from having the bag so tightly wedged. Opening the bag, water spilled out and Beth poured the soggy stream onto the rocks, careful to protect her precious, and possibly destroyed, contents.

"I'm fine, Beth. Let's get up this rubble of rock before we worry about a little scratch."

"Hush, you've lost a lot of blood. It will only take a minute for me to get the bleeding stopped."

Alex shook his head, but Beth suspected he felt terrible because instead of arguing more, he rested the unwounded side of his face on a warm, mostly flat stone and let her work on him.

She found a roll of cotton bandages and quickly formed a tidy, if soggy, pad to press on the small cut.

"Ouch!" Alex lifted his head. "Be careful. My head's taken all the abuse it can for one day."

With a gentle laugh, Beth started crooning to him. "I'm sorry you're hurt. Just be still. Let me help you. Let me—"

"Don't use that voice on me like I'm a scared little girl," Alex grumbled, but he lay his head back down and quit scolding.

Stifling another laugh, Beth kept up her soothing talk as she tended Alex, pressing on the wound until she was satisfied the bleeding had stopped. Then using another length of the bandage, she wrapped it tight around Alex's head. She bathed away the blood that made him look so terribly injured and decided he'd live after all.

By the time she was done, Alex had seemed to fully rouse from the daze left by the head bashing. "Thanks, honey. You're a good doctor."

"Only good?" Beth arched a brow.

"Great." Alex got to his knees, leaned forward, and kissed her. "The best." His eyes met hers and he kissed her again, slowly, deeply, beautifully.

Beth had never felt anything like that kiss. It was "thank you" and "I'm glad I'm alive," and, to her wary heart, it was "I love you."

She kissed him back just as fervently as he kissed her. When the kiss ended, their eyes met and Beth knew. He'd said it with a kiss. Now it was time for her to be just as brave with her words. "I love you."

Alex's eyes showed shock then deep abiding gratitude. "I love you, too." He pulled her hard against him and this time the kiss was pure passion.

And that's when reality finally, fully returned. Beth jerked away from him and grabbed his wrist. She felt his pulse beating strong and alive and vital. "I love you too much to stand by while you turn yourself over to a firing squad."

The pleasure in Alex's eyes faded, replaced by grim determination. "And I love you too much to stand by while a heartless man kills you because you happen to be sitting next to me on a wagon seat. I won't do it, Beth. I won't save my own life at the cost of yours."

"We can move." Beth grabbed his hand. "We can leave the area, go back East. That man wouldn't follow us to Boston. We could go where your father lives."

"Lived. My father's dead. He died ashamed of me because his son had turned deserter and run rather than face danger. I disgraced him and failed him in the lowest way possible, and I never had a chance to make it right. I'm not doing it again, disgracing you and myself the way I did him. I'm going to stand up to what I've done and take the punishment.

"I'd do it for you, to protect you, and no other reason. But there *is* another reason. A good one. It's the right thing to do. I turned my back on God and honor and country when I ran. And I won't live with that on my conscience anymore. I can't be a husband to you with that stain on my soul. I've made my peace with God. Now I'm going to face my punishment from my country and do it with honor. I can't call myself a man unless I do."

The fear of losing a man she now knew she loved was agonizing. Beth wanted to scream at him. She wanted to knock him over the head and drag him far from danger. But what she saw in his eyes stopped her. It was sanity. He was more fully lucid than he'd ever been. He wasn't drawing strength by being near her. He was finding strength of his own. She hated it. But she couldn't deny him.

God, give me the strength to do what's right.

Tears burned at her eyes and she had to force the words through her tightened throat. "All right, Alex. We'll go back, together. We'll make it right. And maybe the cavalry will punish you in some way less than a death penalty. Whatever they decide, I'm yours now. I love you and I'll stand beside you."

"I should go alone. I should have faced this first. I should never have married you and dragged you into my mess." Alex shook his head and those tears threatened again. "But I'm so glad I did." Alex's tears spilled over and he swiped quickly at his eyes with his wrist.

Beth had never seen a man cry before Alex. Her pa would die before he'd do such a thing, and she'd always considered that strength. But Alex's tears had their own kind of strength. He had the courage to let her see deep in his heart. To know his fear. To share his sense of honor. To respect his courage—more courage than she suspected she had—she'd have definitely run from this.

Or maybe not.

Alex pulled her into his arms and held her as if he were drowning again, with no floodwaters involved. Then at last he straightened. "Let's go. Let's find that fort."

They clambered up the treacherous rocks, and after some discussion and Beth's careful study of where the sun stood in the sky and Alex's vague memory of where Fort Union stood in the world, they set out, knowing Alex might never come home.

★

Sidney had set out for town midmorning. It wasn't that long of a ride but he didn't return all day. Mandy waited up long past bedtime and slept fitfully until first light.

Frantic, she saddled the remaining horse the Hardens had left her; strapped her rifle on her back with firm, determined movements; and headed to town at sunup to track him down. "He's lost or dead. I should have never let him go alone, Lord. Help me find him. Protect him."

Her prayers were continuous as she raced toward the city. She followed Sidney's tracks easily. She tried to be furious, thinking he'd been delayed in town and had just stayed over, unmindful of her worry. But she knew better. Deep in her heart, she knew Sidney would have come home.

But maybe he was just lost. That could have happened. She prayed that *had* happened. She should have started searching last night, but she hadn't truly begun to fear the worst until after sunset. By then, if his trail led in an unexpected direction, she might have missed it in the dark and wandered all night.

She prayed fervently as she rode.

Protect him, Lord. Protect him. Protect us both.

She found him facedown on the ground about halfway to Helena. His horse stood nearby. Its reins hung down, ground hitching the well-trained animal. Mandy noticed a pickax strapped to the saddle.

"Sidney!" Mandy threw herself off her horse's back and dropped to her knees. She gently tried to roll her husband over, and as she did, he groaned, deeply, quietly, but he was alive.

"Thank You, God," Mandy said through her tears as she leaned close to see where he'd been hurt. "Sidney, speak to me."

Her husband's eyes flickered open, heavy lidded. He grinned at her and hiccupped.

Mandy smelled liquor on his breath and sat back on her heels. All her terror twisted into fury. "You're drunk!"

Sidney's smile faded, and he rubbed his forehead then winced. Mandy saw a welt just below his hairline. He probably was injured, from falling off his horse on his ride home. Then either knocked senseless or too unsteady to get up, he'd slept here, flat out on this cold, stony trail all night. While she'd been beside herself with worry.

Sidney had never had a drink in his life. He'd told her that clearly when they'd talked of marriage and Mandy had expressed her dislike of hard spirits.

"Get up, Sidney Gray. Get on your horse and let's get home!" Mandy realized she was using the same voice on Sidney that her ma used on the little boys. Not a good sign.

Moaning, Sidney said, "Don't yell. It hurts my head."

Clenching her jaw tight, Mandy stood and stepped back as Sidney clumsily got to his feet. Without speaking another word to him, she swung up on her horse and headed home. She didn't even look back. He didn't want her to yell? Fine, she just might not ever speak to him again. Because honestly, she just didn't know what to say.

When she reached home, she hung her rifle on its pegs over the door, thinking it might be best to step far from her fire iron in her current mood. Not that she'd shoot her husband, but a rifle made a likely club and she wasn't sure of her self-control.

She set about making lunch. The time for breakfast had long passed.

Sidney didn't show up for over an hour, and when he came in, he was walking, leading his horse. Mandy wondered if he'd been unable to mount or if he had fallen off again. She was too angry to ask.

He put his horse away, came into the house, shoved his hands deep into his pockets, and spoke directly to his toes. "I'm sorry, Mandy. That never should have happened. I was tricked into it. I told you I've never had a drink before, and it's true. But I wanted to ask some questions about gold mining and the only place I could find men gathered was in a saloon. I sat down with a group and they offered me some whiskey. I could barely keep it down, but I wanted them to think I was one of them." Sidney shrugged. His voice was heavy with regret. "It will never happen again. You've got my word."

"Do you know how worried I was when you didn't come home last night?" Mandy slammed a plate laden with venison stew on the table. "I almost set out for you then, but I kept waiting and hoping you'd come home. I should have gone hunting, but the night falls early. I'm still not really used to it. Then I was afraid I'd miss you. You riding home, me riding to Helena. I kept making excuses and waiting and waiting and waiting. I've spent the night believing you were dead, Sidney!" Mandy's voice rose to a screech and she turned away from him, shocked at the tears that tore loose. Marriage to Sidney was, she was sorely afraid, going to be a tearful business.

"I'm sorry. I promise you, before God, it will never happen again." Her wayward husband came up behind her and slipped his arms around her waist, pulling her snug into his arms. "I should have taken you with me. Then no man would have expected me to go in that filthy saloon. I will never put you through anything like that again. Please, Mandy. Please, can you forgive me for hurting you and failing myself?"

The words flowed from Sidney like poetry, soothing Mandy's anguish. She gradually, prayerfully released her anger and fear. He continued with promises and vows of love, interspersed with quiet kisses on her neck. Finally she leaned back against him, letting her head fall back onto his shoulder.

"Do you forgive me, Mandy love? Please tell me you still love me. If your heart hardened toward me I wouldn't want to live." He turned her slowly around. His words fell like sweet breaths on her face, and she realized he'd washed and cleaned his breath before he came in. That was thoughtful of him.

She allowed his kisses, praying for God to release her from the anger she still harbored. At last she was able to return his affection fully. And when that moment came, Sidney pulled back, his eyes glittering with something that looked far too satisfied for Mandy's taste. But he poured out on her vows both lavish and contrite. His kisses were generous and passionate. The combination lulled her into trust.

At last she could not deny him the words he begged for. "I forgive you, Sidney. I love you. You know I do."

He swept her into his arms and carried her away to their bedroom to rebuild their bonds of love. If she, for one instant, considered denying him, she recognized it as an unworthy part of herself.

★ Twenty-five ★

Sophie nearly screamed with the tension of waiting. Clay was running as fast as he could. So was she. Sally was hard at work, too. They were all doing what had to be done before the two of them set out on a journey that could last days.

She and Sally took care of procuring spare horses and packing for a journey.

Sally squabbled with Sophie the entire time. "I can help, Ma. Let me come along." Sally tied the string of horses together. A spare for Clay and Sophie, so they could ride fast, switching saddles to let their animals rest. Plus a packhorse loaded with food and supplies, everything Beth and Alex might need if they were in dire straits.

Watching Sally's competent handling of the animals, Sophie knew that indeed her daughter could help. "You're not full strength yet. Alex told you to take it easy or you could end up with a relapse. Your throat could even possibly swell again. Taking a long, hard ride to save your sister doesn't qualify as easy."

"But Ma—"

"And the young'uns need you. It's going to be you and Laurie caring for them. We might be gone for days, even weeks." Sophie didn't have time but she couldn't stop herself from dragging Sally into her arms.

"Let me go instead of you." Sally's arms wrapped tight. "I can stick by Pa better'n you. And you know it."

"I do know it." Sophie pulled back and ran her hand through Sally's long white-blond hair, so like Sophie's. All her daughters took after her with their slenderness and strength and grit. "I'd let you go if you weren't still healing from those bee stings. You know you're not at full strength. Now don't get so set on going that you end up slowing us down and risking yourself and Beth with your stubbornness."

Sally's mouth formed a mutinous line, but she was an honest girl, and she couldn't deny that she still tired easily and that wound on her throat was still tender.

Sophie knew her daughter. And this wasn't something Sophie was doing on a whim. Sally had to stay. Sophie had to go.

Muttering dire-sounding but unintelligible words, Sally finished loading a packhorse just as Clay rushed out of the telegraph office. Clay mounted his horse, rapping orders and worries at Sally that ought to make the girl feel badly needed at the ranch. Sophie was glad her tomboy daughter was staying with the family. She was a young woman to count on in an emergency.

"I sent word to Adam so he and Tilly'll likely come over and check on you. Maybe even stay for the duration. Until he gets there, you'll have to care for the children and fill everybody in on what's happened with Beth. I wired Luther about Mandy being in Montana, and there might be an answer, so send someone in every day to check at the telegraph office."

Sally jerked her chin in agreement while shooting Sophie rebellious glances.

Clay grabbed the string of horses and turned for the trail. Sophie was after him instantly.

They set a blistering pace and didn't speak as they rode hard through the afternoon and evening.

It was long after the sun had set that they finally had to admit they couldn't go on in the dark. They made a cold camp and ate jerky and biscuits. As they collapsed on their bedrolls, Clay pulled

Sophie close to him. She wanted to pour out her fear for Beth but she kept her lips tightly closed. Talk solved nothing and she'd learned Clay wasn't inclined toward unnecessary words.

But some were necessary. "Where are we headed?" Asking that earlier would have been a waste of time. Clay obviously had a direction in mind. Sophie was content to trust him and follow. But now there was time.

"There's a break in the arroyo wall. I've seen it once or twice. Beth will likely climb out there."

If she hasn't drowned in the floodwaters. If the fast-moving water doesn't sweep her on downstream. If whoever was after them hadn't found a perch and shot them dead as they floated past. Sophie didn't utter her black thoughts. They qualified as unnecessary words.

"It's on the western side of that canyon. The man trailing her went down the eastern side. He doesn't know the lay of the land. We'll beat him to Beth and Alex and be there to protect them if that coyote does turn up."

Sophie had ten more questions and she asked none of them. They had a long day tomorrow and they needed sleep to get through it. Sophie was a woman used to doing what needed doing. Right now, what she needed to do was sleep. She closed her eyes, but her unspoken fears proved stronger than all her years of self-control. She tucked up tight against Clay and held him. She noticed he held on right back.

That was enough communication from her husband to let her fall asleep.

★

The land was still mighty rugged, but Beth found a trail straightaway that led in the direction her stubborn husband wanted to go. Since the only other choice was to head back to Mosqueros and maybe face down that dry-gulching bounty hunter, Beth chose to head on west.

They set a blistering pace for two people on foot, and walked far into the night. Their clothing dried on their backs and the squishing of their boots finally was silent.

Beth knew they'd intersect with people somewhere along this way. And she had enough money tucked in her shoe to buy a horse and some dry bullets. She might get some food, too, although if she could get the bullets, she could take care of the food on her own.

They finally had to give up for the night, and Beth searched for a likely place to sleep. They'd had nothing to eat all day, though they'd swallowed their share of water. She was too tired to think of food now, and it was too dark for her to even search for greens or berries.

She found a felled ponderosa pine that had fallen down a steep slope and brought an avalanche of rock with it, creating a decent cave. The tree looked as if it had been lying there for years, its needles shed until they made a fair bed. Beth decided to hope the tree would stay wedged over their heads for one more night.

With nothing to use as a cover, they snuggled together in the dark. Beth rested her head on Alex's strong shoulder, but her mind was in such a turmoil that sleep wouldn't come, despite her exhaustion. "Alex, is there nothing I can do to convince you to come back to Mosqueros with me? We can talk to someone. Get advice. Maybe there's a way you can—can serve out your time. Maybe we could talk with a lawyer, or maybe the sheriff would know the right way to turn yourself in."

Alex's lips stopped her talk. He didn't reply to her suggestions, which was a reply in itself. His kiss, first just one of comfort, became more. It was as if he was desperate to be close to her. But though they'd been together as man and wife fully, he didn't urge her to that closeness. Instead, he kissed her for long moments then finally pulled back.

"I love you, Beth. I want you to be safe. While we tried to find a trick to get me out of the punishment I deserve, you might be killed. If one man is after me, there may be ten."

"But I caused this, Alex." Beth reached up a hand to rest on Alex's mouth. She could barely see him in the shadow of their little cave. "He'd have never endangered you if I'd let you go on

207

with the life you were living. You told no one your name. You stayed to yourself. He'd have searched in vain for years. It's my fault that you're being hunted."

"No, it's not." She felt more than saw him shake his head. "It's my own fault. This all happened because of my actions."

"You said you weren't a doctor, and this man was probably looking for a doctor."

She felt Alex kiss each of her fingertips. "I was a pathetic wretch of a man. You brought me back to life, and now I have to clean up the mess created by my cowardice."

"It sounds to me as if you were pushed beyond what any man could bear, Alex." Beth pulled away and tried to see his eyes in the night. "Surely the cavalry will have something short of execution for a man who served long and honorably until that one horrible day."

Silence stretched between them. Alex's hand stroked her hair. She could see the darkness of his tanned skin against her white hair.

"If they do, then I'll serve my time, be it in the cavalry or in prison. But I don't want you to wait for me, Beth. It could be years, and even if I serve my time, I'll be a marked man. A disgrace."

"Not a marked man, Alex. A fallen, broken man. Disgraced is the opposite of graced and God is gracious. He can wash it all away. I don't care what kind of past you have or what kind of punishment you have to face. I know you to be a decent, honorable man. I will wait for you forever."

"No!" Alex shook his head almost violently. "You can't waste your life on me."

"I can't do anything else, Alex. I love you." Beth kissed him and felt his kindness and his love and his regret. "Don't ask me to abandon you because I can't. I won't."

"I love you, too, Beth. It's another act of cowardice and selfishness to let you stay with me. I'm so sorry I'm not strong enough to turn you away." Alex pulled her close again. He whispered against her lips, "I have no right to be so blessed."

★

"You're going to town again?" Mandy felt a chill of pure fear.

"If you want to come along, you're welcome to." Sidney smiled that charming smile, and Mandy remembered his promises of just a few days ago. He'd never make such a mistake again as going into that saloon. "I should have bought a gold pan so I can work that spring."

"I've already got a rising of bread started."

Sidney had slept late and Mandy had let him. He'd worked hard with the pickax every day since his wretched visit to Helena.

"And I've got the willow lathes soaking to make the bedstead. I thought you'd help me with it." Mandy knew how to stretch those lathes to make a foundation for the straw tick mattress she planned to build. But once they started soaking, she couldn't take them out of the water unless she planned to use them. They'd harden. Worse yet, once they hardened they'd not soften and be pliable again. She spent hours yesterday hunting these tough, flexible branches. But if it meant not letting Sidney go to town alone again, maybe she should just abandon the work. There were more willows to be stripped.

"I forgot to buy what I need to pan for gold." Sidney was so earnest in his quest. "I'd never heard of that before. They said it's a lot easier than a pickax."

Mandy didn't know all that much about gold, there being a distinct lack of it in her part of Texas. But her pa had money from a gold strike her grandfather made in the Rockies, so it stood to reason that there was gold around here somewhere. All Mandy really knew about gold was one wild tale after another passed on from campfires. Most of it wasn't for the delicate ears of women, but Mandy knew how to listen when it was thought she was rolled up in a blanket asleep by a campfire.

"You know there'll be no more saloons for me, don't you, honey? I've given you my word and I intend to keep it. Come along if you're doubtful. I'd prefer to have you along with me."

Sidney pulled her into his arms and proved himself to be very persuasive.

The air was colder today. Mandy was positive she smelled snow. She'd faced snow often enough in Texas to know the signs. A heavy snow might prevent her from searching out new willows. If she didn't get this bed made today, they'd spend the winter on the dirt floor. The Hardens had offered to stay longer and build more furniture and put down a wooden floor, but Mandy was capable of both.

Mandy knew she wasn't treating her husband like she trusted him, and that was a wifely sin to her way of thinking. "I'd best stay home. You go on in and buy your gold pan. I trust you, Sidney."

"Thank you." Sidney kissed her and distracted her from even her mildest worry. Then he saddled up and rode away while she went to work on their bedstead.

Mandy prayed steadily for her untrusting heart as she worked on weaving the lathe around a frame the Hardens had built for her. This would get them up off the floor. She had the bedstead done and just needed to wait for the lathe to dry so she could drag the mattress inside. She heard a horse trotting into the yard. It was long enough since Sidney left, if he pushed hard into Helena and back. She hurried outside, hoping to welcome her husband.

A strange man was dismounting from the most magnificent black stallion Mandy had ever seen. She ducked back inside, jerked her rifle off the pegs over her front door, and stood with the weapon cocked and pointed before the man had his stallion lashed to the hitching post.

"Move along, stranger." Mandy held the gun dead-level and didn't so much as blink. The man was less than ten feet away from her, but she felt her blood cool and her hands steady. She had the nerve to pull the trigger if he made any sudden moves. It worried her sometimes this chill that over came her when she needed to shoot. And she hated the thought of killing a man. But she knew she could do it.

"Howdy, ma'am." The man smiled but stayed at a respectful

distance. He had golden yellow hair that dangled down to his shoulders. He was tall and broad, his shoulders wrapped in a coat tanned nearly white, with long fringe and slightly darker brown chaps. He looked to be young, under thirty, but he had eyes that understood the business end of a Winchester and enough sense to refrain from startling her.

Mandy didn't shift her focus, but only a blind woman could fail to notice the midnight black horse standing tied to her hitching post. The horse fairly vibrated with indignation at being restrained. It stood, its head high, its legs braced as if it was one wrong move from attack.

"Recognize the horse, Mrs. Gray?" The man's eyes were so blue Mandy felt as if she could see right through them to the sky behind. For a young man, he had a fair supply of wrinkles at the corners of his eyes, like many a man who'd spent long hours in the hot summer sun and bitter winter wind.

"No, I've never seen this horse before. I'd remember." She dared a glance at the horse.

The man made no move toward her or toward his gun. He seemed satisfied to stand, his hand raised just a bit, a look in his eyes that said he understood and even respected the gun aimed straight at his belly. "You've never seen him, but I was hoping you'd say you'd met his son."

The foal. Yes, the little black fireball could be a miniature of this fierce steed.

"You're Linscott." Mandy thought hard, searching for a first name. "Tom Linscott."

"That's right. The Tanners sent word that their mare had put a foal on the ground out of my black." Linscott reached a hand very cautiously out and patted his stallion on his massive, well-muscled shoulder.

"Tanners?" All Mandy's suspicions roared back to life and she raised the gun an inch, taking a bead.

Linscott recognized her doubts and smiled. "Oh yes, I mean Harden. They call it the Harden ranch now, I reckon. Hard to keep track, Belle and all her husbands."

Four, Mandy remembered that well enough.

"We've gotten so we don't pay no attention to the name of a new husband and just keep on calling it the Tanner ranch, although Silas is shaping up to be less worthless than the earlier men she married. They named their boy Tanner so that makes it even harder to forget the ranch's real name. . .or I guess I should say its former name."

Mandy didn't lower the fire iron. "I don't know you, Mr. Linscott. And the Hardens said they were running for home, expecting to be snowed into their high mountain valley for the winter, so they couldn't have told you about the foal."

"I didn't talk to the Hardens." Linscott's eyes narrowed as if he was growing tired of explaining himself.

Well, too bad for him.

"The cowhands I talked to said you were a pretty little thing and fast with your rifle. Said you shot four wolves in the time it takes most people to draw and aim. Said you even beat Belle to the draw, and that's sayin' somethin'. I'd have to admit they got it right."

Got what right? Her shooting or that she was pretty? Sidney always told her how pretty she was. She'd heard it from her pa, too, but Pa always said it was a nuisance being pretty in the West. Made more men for him to run off.

Linscott's eyes were warm as he studied her, paying particular attention to the long gun she had braced against her shoulder. She thought that's what he was looking at. She hoped it was.

"The Hardens get snowed in, but the hands that helped with the drive don't live at their ranch. Silas and Belle handle the ranch themselves except at branding and when they run cattle to market. A good share of the drovers who were with them spend the winter in Divide, and a few of them hired on to my outfit at the Double L. I was interested in the little guy. I always go visit foals of my black sires."

Linscott heard the soft whinny of a horse and turned to look

over his stallion's tall shoulders toward the corral. "There he is."
He spoke like a prayer. He had eyes for nothing but the baby
frolicking at its mama's side. Then suddenly, as if he couldn't hold
himself back, he strode toward the barn without another word.

Mandy felt like a fool standing there with her rifle aimed at
nothing. "Mr. Linscott, I insist that you ride on. I don't want. . ."

The man wasn't even close enough to hear what she was
saying anymore.

Mandy lowered the rifle. With a quick motion that she'd made
a thousand times before, she slung it over her shoulder by its strap
and hung it angled across her back, muzzle hanging down on her
right, gun butt up on her left. Then she followed after her visitor,
pausing to pat the cranky stallion on the nose as she passed him.

The horse tried to bite her hand off. She laughed and rounded
him, giving his iron-shod heels their due respect.

As she tagged along after Mr. Linscott, it crossed her mind to
threaten him with her husband. It might be wise to cloud the issue
of how alone she was here. She could say her man would come
a'runnin' if she gave a shout, but Tom Linscott had a solid look to
him. Trail wise and straightforward, she doubted he'd bluff easy.
And since Sidney was in town, all it'd be was a bluff. She kept
herself away from Linscott but went up to the fence to watch the
beautiful little colt.

Whistling softly, Mr. Linscott said, "He's perfect. A pure
imitation of his papa." Linscott pulled off a worn glove, tucked
it behind his belt buckle, and fished around in the pocket of his
fringed, buckskin jacket. He crouched low and reached a hand
through the split-rail fence. He opened his hand to reveal a chunk
of carrot.

The colt noticed and froze, staring at that hand. The more
civilized mare wandered slowly toward the offered treat.

"C'mon, good girl. You got yourself a prize of a baby, didn't
you, lucky lady? Good girl. Good girl."

Mandy almost went for the carrot herself. She was amazed at
Mr. Linscott's voice. It was familiar. She'd heard those soothing

tones from cattlemen all her life as they gentled a nervous horse and fractious cattle that needed doctoring.

A lot of ranching was done with pure muscle and a sturdy rope, containing the animals for whatever purpose. But when a body needed to handle the critter, to break a horse or to doctor one, most good cowpokes could croon to them, ease their fears. No one was better at it than Beth. She had as much of a gift with animals as she did with people. This man wasn't in her league but he was good, very good.

The mare was obviously an old, well-trained cowpony. Belle had said she was too old to make the long trek home so soon after foaling. The mare didn't hesitate to approach a human hand attached to Linscott's gentle voice.

The foal danced and skittered, his wide black eyes showed white around his pupils as he watched his mother approach that dangerous hand. He pranced forward, then turned and ran a few paces away, then wheeled and rushed toward the security of his mama again. The baby pawed the dirt and shook its short mane.

Mandy crouched so she could look through the railing on eye level with the colt. She used her own animal soothing tones. "You are your father's son, sure enough."

The foal heard her voice and calmed and gamboled forward. She'd talked with him every day since his birth, while she'd tended his mother and the other two horses.

The mare nipped at the carrot, and Tom reached through and ruffled her ears. He looked sideways at Mandy. "The little guy knows you."

"I've been introducing myself to him every day when I feed the mare and brush her coat. He's a long way from tame, but he's not too afraid."

The foal came as far as his mother's hindquarters and ducked low to steal a comforting sip of milk.

Mr. Linscott's low chuckle deepened Mandy's enjoyment of the little colt. He slowly rose from where he crouched and the mare stayed close, letting him pet her, a reward for the carrot.

Mandy stood, too, realizing just how tall Mr. Linscott was—as oversized as his stallion.

Mr. Linscott turned to look at her while he caressed the mare.

Mandy recognized his type, right down to the ground. A cowboy. A man who fought nature every day and won, or at least survived to fight again the next day. A man like her pa.

Her eyes traveled from where he touched the mare up his long, strong arm to his square shoulders, and she looked straight into his eyes.

And he looked back.

Their gazes held for a second as she looked into those eyes. Blue eyes. As blue as hers. As blue as the heart of a flame.

Why had she thought she wanted a city man like Sidney? The moment that thought fully formed, she turned away and gripped the fence, riveting her gaze on the little colt.

Think of something to say. Think. Think.

Suddenly what had been pleasant and familiar was awkward and the silence, before companionable, was uncomfortable. "So, uh—B–Belle, um. . .said you'd try and get her to pay stud fees. Is that right?" There, a safe subject.

"Oh, I'll try." His voice called to her. She almost glanced over to see if he was offering her a carrot. "I got a reputation for guardin' that stallion like he was made of pure gold. But I know Belle Tanner, uh, Harden, I mean. Gotta learn that woman's new name, I reckon." Mr. Linscott chuckled again.

"I won't get anywhere with Belle. She's a tough one. And truth be told, my stallion probably lured this little lady into breakin' her reins and runnin' off with him. Belle don't owe me nothin'. But I won't admit that right up front. I'll be surprised if that confounded woman don't try and charge me money for the lost use of her mare over the winter." Mr. Linscott laughed harder. "But that woman sure got herself a rare little foal. My stallion breeds true, but I don't know as I've seen a prettier little baby born from him."

Mandy made a point not to turn and smile at the invitation

Mr. Linscott gave her with his good-natured talk.

A touch on her shoulder brought her around and backed her about five feet down the corral fence. She fumbled again to speak. "Well, I—I need to get on with—with my—"

"Let me split that firewood there." Mr. Linscott still had his hand raised where he'd touched her, to draw her attention to where he was looking. He nodded toward the mountain of firewood the Harden clan had left behind. A little of it split but plenty left that wasn't.

Mandy glanced up and saw those eyes again. She looked quickly away. "There's no need of that. Thanks for offering. But no, I have a busy day laid out, so I'll say good-bye now and—"

"And I heard you needed to daub your house again. When I rode in, I saw a patch of clay soil, not far from here. That works faster and better than mud. I'll go dig up a supply and do some chinking. I need to thank you for takin' care of this little guy."

Mr. Linscott leaned his elbow on the fence. "Belle owes you, but my hands said they helped you. . .uh, you and—and your man get settled." Mr. Linscott straightened, and out of the corner of her eye, Mandy saw him adjust his hat. "They said your. . .uh. . . h–husband. . ."There was a few seconds of silence then Tom went on. "He isn't used to ranch life and maybe he'd be willing to accept some neighborly help. I like knowing my black's offspring are well cared for, and I can see that this one is. To my way of thinking, I owe you for that, and I pay what I owe."

Mr. Linscott turned away from her, and finally she felt free to turn and watch him. He headed straight for the woodpile. "Splittin' wood is heavy work for a woman. I can take some of that weight off your shoulders."

It was the honest truth that of all the chores that needed doing before winter landed hard on Mandy's head, splitting that mountain of cord wood was the most daunting. She could do it, but it would be long hours of hard labor just to keep even with what they needed to burn, and she needed to do more than keep even. She needed to get ahead and store up the wood before winter made that work impossible. And the chance of Sidney splitting all that wood was slim. "There's no need for that, Mr. Linscott."

"Call me Tom." He grabbed the ax, checked the edge with his thumb, then pulled the glove he'd shed back on. "And I'm doing it. Even a sharpshootin' cowgirl like you can't stop me."

He caught a length of wood, about three feet long, and up and settled it on the log used for a cutting block. He hefted the ax, testing the weight of it in his hands. Then taking a firm grip, he swung the ax with a single, smooth motion, and the log split in half. He set one of the three-foot-long halves back on the block and split it again.

Mandy watched his well-oiled movements, envying him his strength. She wasn't really thinking about much except the hard work Tom made look so easy, until he stopped in midswing and looked up at her, glaring. "Did you need something?"

Mandy realized she was staring. "No, no, I'm sorry. I—I have chores." She turned and almost ran to the cabin. Slipping inside, she hesitated to remove her gun from her back. Then knowing Linscott was no danger—not only was he no danger, he'd protect her—she hung her gun on its pegs and went back to building her bedstead. She was fully conscious of the steady music of the swinging ax and the presence of a man who was not her husband doing a husband's job.

She remembered the way Tom had assumed that the job was hers. It struck her like a blow that somehow he knew Sidney wasn't going to help. What had the cowpokes he'd talked to said that gave him that impression?

She didn't have to wonder though. She knew exactly what they'd said, nothing she didn't already know. Sidney was a city boy with no skills necessary to survive in the West.

Dismayed, Mandy forced herself to stay inside and work, alone, on the bed she shared with Sidney. It damaged something fragile, deep in her heart, to admit that she was ashamed of her husband.

★ Twenty-six ★

Beth was so proud of Alex she could hardly speak.

She also was sorely tempted to bash him over the head.

She suspected that made theirs a marriage like most.

They'd pushed hard all day up a trail and down. Beth kept a lookout for signs of a ranch or a larger trail—one that led them away from Fort Union.

Beth had found a skinny stream and they'd had plenty to drink. She'd gathered pinecones and carried them in her skirt. They could get nuts out of them if nothing easier and tastier showed itself. The nuts needed to be baked to crack out of their shells so that meant a fire and too much time. It had to wait until they camped for the night.

So they'd had no food all day and the front of Beth's stomach was rubbing against her backbone. They needed energy to keep up a good pace, so meager though the nuts were, they'd eat them.

Beth had done her best to dry out the firearms and she thought the bullets looked useable. They'd never really know until she fired the gun, but she wondered if they were being pursued, and gunshots sounded for miles. So she hoped for the best and decided to set a rabbit snare and hope they snagged something bigger for breakfast.

The sun was dropping in the sky and Beth had begun scouting

for a place to sleep when she heard a twig snap. Beth grabbed Alex's arm, jerked him off the trail, and dove behind a bank of mesquite trees.

"What—"

"Shh!" Beth cut him off as she looked back and saw nothing. Someone was coming. She had no doubt. If it looked like the someone was friendly, she'd go out and ask for help. If it was the bounty hunter—

Beth lifted the Winchester off Alex's shoulder. He'd carried the heavy gun and her loaded doctor's bag all day. She quickly and as silently as possible loaded the rifle then did the same with the Colt. She'd left the chambers empty so they'd dry thoroughly. Hopefully one of them would fire. To be prepared in case one didn't, she eased her knife out of her boot and set it close to hand. She didn't offer one of the weapons to Alex, and he didn't ask.

Minutes ticked by and the rider or riders didn't come along. A thrill of fear climbed Beth's neck. Someone was riding carefully. Maybe even hunting.

Catching Alex's arm, she dropped back farther off the trail, not wanting to let anyone get behind them. The trail sloped upward into a wooded area and Beth saw some heavy boulders that would give them protection while affording her a good field of fire. She did her best to not make a sound, no twigs snapping for Beth. Alex was trying, too. And Beth appreciated it. She finally reached the rocks and ducked behind them.

"Beth, honey, it's Pa."

"Pa?" Beth shot to her feet. Pa and Ma came out from behind a bank of scrub pines. Both had their pistols drawn. Ma had her trusty Spencer repeating rifle hanging from her back. Pa toted his Winchester 73 the same way. They'd left their horses hidden somewhere.

"Ma!" Beth rushed around the boulders, barely aware of Alex rising to his feet as she dashed away. She flung herself into her mother's arms, and Ma holstered her gun and hugged her so tight it hurt. Beth had never felt anything better.

"Howdy, Clay. We're glad to see you two." Beth glanced sideways to see Alex shaking hands with her pa. Pa clapped her husband on the back and smiled.

"How'd you find us?" Beth liked thinking her pa had some affection for her husband.

"We've been following your trail all day. We knew you'd have to climb out of that arroyo to the west side. It's the only low spot. We crossed the arroyo north of where you jumped in and headed south to meet up with you heading home. But we went south a far piece before we crossed your trail. You're heading northwest instead of northeast toward Mosqueros."

Beth grinned at Ma, then turned and threw herself into her father's arms.

"I'm happy to see you're both alive and well." Ma gave Alex a quick hug. "Mostly well."

Alex pointed to the bedraggled bandage on his head. "I had a run-in with some rocks, but Beth took care of me. She's a fine doctor."

Beth heard Alex's generous words and turned to smile at him. She really did love this man.

"So'd you get lost? What are you headed this way for?" Pa lifted his hat and scratched his head.

All the excitement went out of the reunion.

Beth went into Alex's arms and wondered how hard it'd be to kidnap the stubborn man.

"Clay, Sophie, we were heading to—"

The sharp crack of rifle fire split the air.

Pa staggered forward. "Get down." Vivid red bloomed on his shirt. "Everyone! Get behind those rocks."

He fell against Beth, reaching out his arm to grab Ma, then slammed into Alex as he fell, taking them all to the ground. As they landed, another shot ricocheted off the boulder nearest at hand. Pa was conscious and the four of them crawled and dragged themselves to shelter.

The rifle fired again. Bits of stone exploded into the air but the rocks were a solid shield.

"How many?" Pa gasped and pulled his Colt from his holster.

Beth knelt beside Pa, tearing his shirt open to see where he'd been hit. High on the shoulder. Maybe a broken collarbone.

Ma had her Spencer out, her head down but listening for movement. There were no more shots fired. "What's going on, Beth?"

"There's one man out there. A man came to us last night. No, two nights ago now, I guess."

"It was just last night." Ma said quietly, her attention riveted on any noise from beyond their shelter.

Beth shook her head and didn't bother trying to sort it out. The sickening wound pouring blood from her father's chest was too much to deal with and count back days, too. "He told us he had a sick brother. We followed him, then he started shooting and we've been on the run ever since."

"We saw signs of him. Only one man?" Ma asked.

"Yep."

"Why didn't you just shoot him like a hydrophobic skunk?"

Beth dragged her doctor's bag off her arm and jerked it open. *Please, God, give me enough of the healing gift to save Pa.*

"Thought of it, but he was a crack shot, and once he got above us on that cliff we had no place to lie in wait for him. We just headed out as fast as we could. Then we reached that arroyo and it was flooded. The shooter was still on our trail so we jumped in."

Ma glanced over. "Let Alex take care of your pa. You get over here and help me keep an eye out. If we pinpoint him, I can slip around and get a drop on him."

"Don't you dare, Sophie," Pa gasped as Alex pressed on the gushing wound.

"Lie still, Clay." Alex moved up to the side opposite Beth. "You're losing too much blood. You'll be passed out in a few minute if I don't get the bleeding stopped, and then you won't be able to give orders to anyone." Alex pushed hard, his arms straight, as much weight as he could muster on the wound. "Beth, stay right here. I need two hands."

"No, Alex. You'll have to do this one on your own." Beth leaned over and jerked Pa's Colt from its holster and scooted to the far end of the boulders. They were unprotected on both ends but had a rock wall behind them, which curved around and made it impossible for someone to sneak up or come at them from above.

Beth nearly fell backward when Alex grabbed her arm and pulled. "I'm not asking because I need you to encourage me. I'm asking because I need two hands to save your Pa's life. Get over here."

Beth exchanged a look with Ma.

"Help him, girl. I won't go slipping out. I'll just keep us covered."

With a jerk of her chin, Beth went back to Alex's side. Together they fought a short, brutal fight for her Pa's life.

"Forceps," Alex ordered. "Bullet's still in there."

"That's good, Pa." Beth slapped the instrument into Alex's hand.

"Beth, I've got to keep pressure on his back while I take the bullet out from the front. Get on this side with me. He's losing too much blood."

Beth nearly threw herself around to the other side of her poor pa.

Alex, his hand soaked in raging scarlet, took her hands and guided them beneath Pa's shoulder. "Press up hard. Plug that hole. As soon as the bullet's out, I can sew him up." Alex dug.

Pa lay still, silent, his face twisted in pain, his teeth gritted, his face sallow, letting Alex jab at his wound.

At last a dull scratch of metal on metal told Beth Alex had found the bullet. With a sickening scrape, he got hold of it and dragged the ugly bit of lead free.

Beth pressed on Pa's back, the entrance wound, with all of her might. She'd have lifted him if Pa hadn't worked with her to keep his shoulder firmly against her fingers. She nearly cried out in grief to think of how badly she was hurting him.

A sudden burst of rifle fire startled her. Then Ma returned fire—slow and steady she shredded an area directly in front of the boulder, without exposing herself. Ma lay down a field of fire, to the left and right of where the shots had come.

The bounty hunter's rifle fire ended.

"I've got to get over there," Pa spoke between his teeth, a deep groan escaping as he struggled to sit up. Beth noticed Pa pushed with his left hand but not his right. It wasn't working since he'd been hit.

"Sophie," Alex's voice was all doctor now. All authority.

Sophie quit shooting. "What?"

"Tell your husband to lie still if he wants to live."

"Clay!" Ma's voice must have penetrated Pa's fierce determination to protect his family. "I'm all right. I'll tell you if I need help. Now let Alex patch you up."

Pa's eyes met Ma's, and they communicated so much in that one look. Love and respect and fear and rage. All mixed up with deadly determination not to let this man do them any more harm.

Beth had never loved her parents more than she did at this very instant.

Pa subsided.

Alex worked so fast Beth could hardly follow his movements. He poured carbolic acid on Pa's wound and began sewing, cutting off the flow of blood. "I don't think he got a lung or an artery. It looks like his collarbone is broken."

Alex finished with motions so swift and sure that Beth could imagine him on a battlefield, racing from one wounded soldier to the next. Dispensing life in the midst of death.

"Clay, we need to roll you over and close the hole in your back." Alex spoke slowly, his voice low so as not to give information to their enemy, but clear to get past the agony.

"Beth, now, help me." Alex's voice was rock solid but his face was utterly colorless, and after he spoke, he clenched his jaw so tightly she was afraid he might break his teeth.

Beth hated every second of treating her pa. She thanked God fervently that Alex was here for this because causing Pa pain, even if she knew it was absolutely necessary, nearly sent her into fits.

They got Pa onto his belly and Alex dosed the wound with the sterilizing liquid then attacked it as if he had a hundred patients waiting, all screaming for help.

Beth had a clear view of how it was for Alex during war. The relentless pressure. The bleeding and dying. The cries of pain. The stench of death. All surrounded him as he fought for life in the midst of it.

She'd have run away, too. Now she knew she would never have stood it. She loved Alex more fiercely than ever and she vowed to God that she'd do everything in her power to protect him from whatever punishment the cavalry had in store, even if she had to write to the president of the United States.

The rifle fire began again, higher this time, so shattered fragments of rock blasted down on them. The gunman thought he'd found a way to force them out of their hiding place.

"Cover his wound, Beth. Don't let anything fall into it." Alex took the last few stitches, and quickly, as if he was working under threat of his own death, he pulled bandages from the doctor's bag.

Beth had hung them over her shoulders to dry during the day and she prayed now they hadn't become so dirty during the time they were in the air that they'd poison Pa's wound and bring on an infection.

Alex surprised her by soaking a pad of the bandage with the carbolic acid. Then he pressed it against Pa's injury and used more bandage, this time left dry, to fasten the bandage in place.

The rifle fire continued, deafening. The shards of rock rained down.

Ma returned fire with her Colt. The smoke and smell of the fired rounds made Beth wonder how much ammunition they had with them. She hoped it didn't come down to the stuff she'd hauled through floodwater today.

Splintering rock and shredded leaves, cut from overhead by their assailant's bullets, rained down on them.

"Get him on his back again. I didn't bandage the exit wound yet." He'd been in too big a hurry to close the back wound.

Beth helped, feeling her hands tremble as she shoved her father around like a. . .like a. . .a *patient*. She'd helped with Sally, but Alex hadn't needed her this desperately. He'd only needed her presence to give him strength. Now they had four medical hands working as hard and fast as they knew how, fighting for Pa's life.

The gunfire stopped. A heavy grunt sounded from beyond their fortressed position.

"I think I got him." Ma sounded grim and angry. There was no pleasure for her in shooting a person, no matter how evil that man.

Alex poured on more of the sterilizing carbolic acid.

Beth silently thanked God for Dr. Lister's brilliant invention. A wound could turn septic so easily. She asked for divine help in the healing of her beloved pa.

Alex quickly finished the bandaging then looked up at her, his stern doctor demeanor only for show. She saw beneath it to something so fragile that Beth was afraid he might splinter into pieces right in front of Beth's eyes. With a hard jerk of his chin that didn't reach his eyes, he said, "Okay, go help your ma. I just need to watch and make sure the bleeding has stopped."

Alex's hands were coated in blood. It had gotten on his disheveled white shirt, and his pants were sticky and crimson.

Beth saw those hands start to shake.

Alex wiped sweat off his forehead and smeared blood across his face without realizing it.

Beth was afraid if he knew he'd fall apart. She said, "Alex!"

He looked at her. She let her eyes connect with his. She saw the awareness in him that he hadn't clung to her, not for strength. They hadn't had that sharing Alex had relied on at first. He'd done this on his own. But now he drew from her. She felt him calm as their eyes held.

His voice sounded steady when he finally spoke. "We're done

here. Your ma needs you more. Doesn't she, Clay?" Alex looked down at his patient.

"Yes." Clay's voice was barely a whisper. "Go, honey. Alex and I will be fine."

Beth's eyes went back to Alex's and he gave her an encouraging nod. "Go. I'm all right."

She felt as if her flesh tore when she turned away from Alex. It was possible she needed him as much as he needed her. She crawled to Ma's side.

Ma shoved Pa's rifle in Beth's hands. There was an ammunition belt on the ground in front of them. Ma looked at her and gave her a little smile. "We've fought bad men before together, Beth honey. Fought 'em and won."

Beth returned the smile, looked down at her father's blood all over her own hands and clothes, and felt her heart harden for the task ahead. "And we'll win again this time, won't we, Ma?"

There was a loud groan from about a hundred feet away.

One blond brow arched on her ma's confident face. "Maybe I've already finished the job."

Beth took a quick glance in the direction of that sound, then leaned close to her mother and whispered quiet, so no man would hear. "I'm glad you're my ma."

With a quick jerk of her chin, Ma whispered, "I'm glad you're my daughter, Beth. Now let's snake out of here. I'll go right, you go left."

"Pa ordered us to stay under cover." But that was before the dry-gulcher was down.

"Your pa always was one for giving orders." Ma smiled.

Beth smiled back.

"That coyote is hurt, but he's not dead," Ma added. "So we've got to go careful. You're the best there is at ghostin' around, girl."

Beth eased down on her belly. She took one quick look at Alex and Pa.

Alex had moved around so he had his back to them. Pa had let his eyes fall closed, which wasn't like him.

She braced herself to move out of the sheltering rock. Hoping she was up to the task ahead, she prayed, "Give me strength, Lord. Give me strength."

As she moved forward, she saw her ma vanish around the other side of the rock whispering, "Help me. Help me. Help me."

Beth scooted along quiet as a sliding snake. She rounded the sheltering boulders and headed in the direction of the shrubs where the man lay groaning in pain. She headed for the man's feet.

Her ma would be coming from where it sounded as if his head rested. They both slipped along, using every bit of cover in case the man was up to caring that they were coming for him.

Beth got to the edge of the bushes and saw the man's boots twitching. He was making plenty of noise now so he must be beyond caution. Beth got her gun leveled in front of her, mindful of where Ma would emerge from the bushes. She inched in until she could see the man's legs, then his belly. Her gun held steady and she saw up to the bounty hunter's arms, which were holding a gun aimed straight at Ma.

"Hey!" Beth shouted, drawing the man's attention.

His gun swung around. Ma slid out of the bushes and swung her gun hard at the man's head. It hit with a thud. The bounty hunter dropped back unconscious, but a spasm made his gun go off.

"Look out!" Ma yelled.

Beth heard a crack from overhead, where the bullet had hit. She threw herself sideways, hoping to pick right. She had no idea which way to dive. She rolled onto her back and saw a heavy branch plunging toward her like a spear.

The impact was the last thing she saw before the world went black.

★ Twenty-seven ★

Alex, get over here!"

Alex heard the shot and was moving before Sophie shouted at him. And why was Sophie's the only voice he heard? He had time to die a thousand deaths in the seconds it took to reach Beth, who lay crushed under a huge, dead tree limb.

Sophie was already at Beth's side. "Grab the other end. This fell when the gun went off."

Alex lifted on his end and he and Sophie staggered under the weight, edging it away from Beth then throwing it to the side.

"What's going on!" Clay's voice was furious.

It sounded to Alex like he was getting up. "You've got to go to him." He used his doctor voice on Sophie and even she minded him. "Keep him still. If he starts bleeding again we could lose him."

"I'll be right back." Sophie rushed away.

Alex turned to Beth and saw blood. Crimson rushing blood. Then there were two of her, then one, then three. Alex sank to his knees beside her.

Stay here. Stay here. Keep me here, God.

Alex knew where else he was likely to go. Where he went every time he doctored, unless Beth was at his side. His mind went to war.

God, keep me here. Give me the strength to help her.

His vision faded and widened but Alex fought it. Brought himself back to Beth. He fumbled at her neck until he found a heartbeat. Strong, steady. Her neck was already soaked in blood but Alex found no injuries to her neck's arteries that would drain the life out of her in seconds, with nothing he could do to stop it.

Alex heard distant explosions. Cannon fire. Thundering horses' hooves on a battlefield. His hands were coated in blood, blood that had left the soldier's body, taking his life along with it.

Fighting the madness, he dragged himself back to Beth, ripped his shirt off and wadded it up and found the worst source of the bleeding. "Head wound." The sound of his own voice steadied him a bit. Maybe if he kept speaking aloud. "Head wounds bleed. That doesn't always mean they're serious."

Where was Beth's doctor's bag? The wounds needed to be sutured. If only all he needed to do was put in stitches, maybe he could stand it. But what else was hurt? Her spine? Her brain? Were there broken bones? Was she busted up inside? Alex tried to check while he staunched the blood.

He needed help. He needed his faithful nurse and assistant and fellow doctor. He needed his wife.

"Beth, honey, please stay with me." Alex pressed on two freely bleeding wounds, one on her jawline, one on her temple, and worried about an injury to her backbone. If she woke up, if she could talk to him while he cared for her. . .

Please, God, please. Let her be all right. Give me the strength to care for her. Give me strength. Give me strength.

For a moment he heard Beth's voice praying that prayer. Almost like God had sent her to be with him, even when she was asleep. The blood lived and grew. He put the pressure on the wounds again. Still the blood seemed to gush and grow and fight. It soaked into Alex's bunched-up shirt, then crawled up his arms and leapt at his body.

Shaking his head to keep it clear, Alex held fast on the mean gash on Beth's temple and the other on her chin. An awful, scarring cut on her beautiful face. Alex used both hands, trying to attend both wounds at once. He noticed blood trickle down from the corner of her mouth. From that cut on her chin? Or was she bleeding in her mouth or had she been crushed inside, her lungs or her heart? If that had happened she'd die. There was nothing he knew that would save her.

Seconds ticked past. Alex raised his crimson shirt away from the gash on her chin, hoping the bleeding had stopped. Blood trickled still.

His vision blurred and focused on a cavalryman. He reached for the wounded man. A horse screamed in pain. A cannon blasted. Dirt and shrapnel pummeled Alex's body, knocking him forward over the wounded, dying soldier's form as the man fumbled at the wound in his stomach, pushing to get his intestines back inside his belly. Alex reached for his doctor's bag and saw it covered in gore.

A sudden blow snapped Alex's head around and he stared into the furious face of his mother-in-law.

"Help her." Sophie nearly peeled his eardrums away with her harsh order. She raised her hand and slapped him hard across the face. "Get busy and help her."

Alex suddenly realized where his wife had learned her bedside manner. Staring at Sophie, he braced himself to get slugged again and realized that the strength he'd drawn from Beth was in this woman, too. She seemed to know. Rather than draw back her hand she let him look, let him steady himself by using her courage when he had none of his own. It was enough for the world to come fully back.

"Y–yes, ma'am." Alex turned back to Beth. He'd stopped working on her head wounds, let the shirt slip from his hands. She was coated in blood.

"Don't you have something else to do to my daughter besides try to stop a bleeding cut?"

Alex felt like a mother mountain lion had just roared in his face.

Sophie snatched the shirt from Alex and pressed on the

wounds herself. "Is that all that's wrong with her?"

"I don't s–see any other injuries. Nothing external." Alex shook his head almost violently. "She needs stitches to stop this bleeding. M–my bag."

"Go get it yourself. I'll stay with her. And tell Clay to lay still or I'll hog-tie him."

Alex knew well that he faced a will far stronger than his own. If possible, a will even stronger than Beth's. He scrambled to his feet and stumbled forward, then lurched toward the boulder that hid his wounded father-in-law.

Cold blue eyes waited for him around that boulder. "How's Beth?"

"I need to put some stitches in. I think. . .I hope she's just knocked out from a tree branch falling on her." Alex remembered that trickle of blood coming from the corner of Beth's mouth. "Stay here. I can't doctor two people at once so don't do anything to tear those stitches. Your wife is helping me."

Clay seemed willing to drill holes in Alex's brain with his fiery blue gaze. That spurred Alex to hurry just so he could get back to yet another McClellen who was willing to do him damage if he didn't stay clearheaded. Alex decided being terrorized worked surprisingly well in this case to keep him focused.

Grabbing Beth's doctor's bag, which they'd been struggling to dry out all day, he rushed back to his wife, lying soaked in blood, her skin pure white against the sticky crimson flow.

Alex had a needle ready in seconds. Trying to detach from what lay ahead, piercing his wife's lovely skin to put in the barbaric sutures, he pushed, rushed along, letting his hands work and trying to keep his addled brain out of it. Going for the worse of her wounds first, Alex snapped, "Move the rag and hold the edges of this wound closed."

He barely heard the dictatorial tone of his voice but knew it for the take-charge doctor voice he was fully capable of using. Being knocked on his backside was one possible reaction to his dictatorial voice.

It didn't happen. Instead she obeyed all his instructions and proved to be an able assistant. She lacked Beth's finesse, but the woman had steady hands. Alex wasn't much surprised.

It took ten stitches to close up the gash on Beth's forehead. It ran along her hairline. There'd be a scar, but her hair would cover it.

Sophie had kept steady pressure on Beth's chin while she minded Alex's orders about the cut he was suturing.

Alex glanced up at Sophie. "We'll do her chin now."

"Ready." She nodded and smiled. That strength was still there; Alex didn't even have to look in Sophie's eyes to feel it steady him.

"You're a good doctor, Alex. I hope the day will come when you can trust yourself again."

"So do I." Alex turned back to his patient. When Beth's other cut was closed, Alex hoped that scar would fall just beneath the curve of her chin. Maybe that wouldn't harm her pretty face much either. But Alex knew without a doubt he wanted his wife alive and well, however scarred. And he knew Beth and her clear, level head well enough to know she'd agree. It occurred to Alex that Beth's scars would be visible while Alex's were invisible, but they were both scarred nonetheless.

"Look at this." Sophie ran her hand, smeared red with mostly dried blood, over Beth's head. "There's a big bump on this side, as well as the cut. Hopefully she just took a bad whack and got knocked cold. If we give her time, she'll come out of it."

A low groan turned Alex and Sophie toward the outlaw. Though he didn't move, Sophie dived at the man and had him hog-tied and gagged so fast Alex could barely see Sophie's hands move. There was violence in Sophie's expression, but it didn't pass to the man overly much, though he was securely and tightly bound.

Turning her back on the bounty hunter, Sophie went back to caressing Beth's head. Part gentle mother, part grizzly—Sophie McClellen.

"I'm glad you're my wife's mother. I'm glad I got to know your whole brood."

Sophie looked away from Beth, her eyes narrow, her gaze sharp. "You say that like it's in the past. Like we're not going to be part of your life anymore."

Swallowing hard, Alex couldn't do other than tell the truth. "That man chasing us is after me to arrest me and turn me in to the cavalry at Fort Union. I'm a deserter. I told Beth we needed to get to the fort so I could turn myself in. That way she'd be safe. I'm wanted dead or alive, like all deserters, and this man is a bounty hunter. He didn't seem overly concerned about the 'alive' part of 'dead or alive,' and he didn't seem too worried about Beth getting caught in his crossfire."

Sophie held his gaze.

Alex waited, giving her plenty of time to realize that it was that act of cowardice, deserting from the cavalry, that had led to Beth's injuries. Clay's, too. This was all on Alex's head.

"You look at my daughter with eyes shining with love, Alex. Do you love her?"

Alex turned to stare at Beth, ashen white, completely unmoving. He felt as if his love had nearly killed her. "Yes." His words were barely audible. He said them to Beth rather than to Sophie. "Yes, I love her. And I almost got her killed." Alex felt tears burn at his eyes and felt them spill over.

Sophie gasped and Alex looked away from his silent, fragile wife. Sophie looked at what must be obvious signs of crying on Alex's face as if he'd suddenly sprouted a second nose.

Dashing the tears away, Alex said, "Stay with Beth. I need to go check on Clay again."

One hard hand snaked out and grabbed Alex by the wrist. "No, don't let him see you"—Sophie's voice fell to a breath of a whisper—"crying. It'll kill him faster'n a bullet."

That made no sense. "Okay, you go. Tell him she's going to be fine."

"Is she going to be fine?"

"Yes, everyone's going to be fine." Alex felt confident of that. Everyone but him. He was facing a noose.

"I'll stay here with you until they're well enough to travel, then I'll go on to the fort alone. No sense taking Beth with me any farther."

"I've heard some of what they do to deserters. Lots of room for a decision to go hard against a man or go easy. I think it'd be best if your family rode along with you to that fort."

His family. Alex's eyes fell shut from the sweetness of those words. Sophie was counting him as family. It had been a long, long time since anyone had.

Sophie released Alex's arm and went to check on her husband.

Seconds after Alex heard Sophie speaking quietly to Clay, he saw Beth's eyes flutter open.

He bent down and angled himself so he was right in her line of vision, so she wouldn't move an inch. "Hey, you're awake."

There was a glazed look in Beth's eyes, but he saw her fighting it, trying to make sense of the world around her. At last her head cleared enough that she saw him. "What happened?"

"A tree fell on your head." Alex smiled, ignoring the terror he'd felt.

"That would explain the pain."

"I can get you some laudanum."

"Not right now. I've had it before. It makes me feel so stupid and groggy. Let's give the headache a chance to ease without it."

"Okay." He didn't mention the stitches. It was a lot more than just a headache.

A loud grunt from a few paces beyond Beth's wounded head drew Alex's attention and he saw Beth react. "Lie still. We're fine, honey. That's the polecat who was after us." Alex suddenly straightened. "You know, I think your ma shot him. I oughta go have a look, huh?"

Beth managed a smile. "It'd be the right thing to do."

"Even if I'm more inclined to shoot him again?"

"Even then."

"I'll do it then." Alex studied the man.

His piggish eyes blinked open and the man glared at Alex, but

234

thanks to Sophie's skillful hands, the man would neither move nor speak a word.

"Okay, it looks like your ma's bullet creased his skull. Knocked him cold and cut him good, but nothing that won't heal, unless he gets infected." Alex turned back to Beth. "I'm done checking him."

Beth nodded. "Sounds good to me. Maybe a little later you could dose him with the carbolic acid."

"Why waste that on a man I want to see get a fever and die?"

Beth shrugged, then winced, but managed to pat Alex on his arm. "Well, it burns like the very dickens. So pouring it on his open wound would be worth something."

"True." Alex nodded as he imagined tossing a little salt in on top of the carbolic acid. He liked the image. "Okay, I'll do it. Later. When I'm done doctoring you."

Alarm flared in Beth's eyes. "You're not done yet?"

"I'm done, but I want to closely observe my patient for a while yet." Alex said, "Lie still now. I'm going to wash some of the blood away."

"Blood?" Beth started to sit up.

Alex restrained her. "Just be still. You've got a cut on your head and a few stitches where you bled. But you're fine. No sense joggling your head around and causing yourself pain just because you're so vain you want a mirror to pretty up in."

She narrowed her eyes and he'd have kissed her if she hadn't been such a gory, bloody mess.

He found a canteen among Sophie and Clay's supplies and had Beth looking much less horrifying very soon. Then he kissed her as a reward for her taking his ministrations so well, just as Sophie returned from fussing over Clay. "How's Clay?" he asked her.

"As growly as a grizzly bear because I told him he had to lie still. If it was up to him, he'd get up and ride right now. How's Beth?"

"She's awake."

Sophie's eyes went to Beth and a smile bloomed on her face. Alex noted the resemblance between his wife and Sophie and decided Beth would only get more beautiful.

"I think"—Alex looked up at Sophie and smiled—"both our patients are going to make it."

Then Alex thought of Fort Union and what he had coming there. Beth would get more beautiful, no doubt about it, but her beauty would be for her second husband...after the United States Cavalry disposed of her first one.

★

A hard knock at the door had Mandy scampering out of the bedroom to answer it. She didn't even want to meet Tom's eyes, but she had to thank him.

He was covered with wood chips and he'd taken off his coat and hung it over the hitching post. Mandy saw that his stallion was now in the corral with the mare and foal.

She frowned at Tom. "Is it safe to put your stallion in with the little colt? Sometimes a stallion can attack."

"The black's not like that. He's next thing to a killer in the normal course of things. No one rides him but me and he barely tolerates me. But he's gentle with his brood mares and the babies."

Mandy saw the regal horse sniff the baby, then lift his head and look around, as if scouting for danger.

"I put him in there a while ago. I hated to leave him hitched for hours. Hope that's okay. I had a bait of corn with me so he's not eating your feed."

"It's fine. I should have thought of it myself." She would have if she hadn't been strictly avoiding this man ever since she'd come inside.

"I'm just back with a load of clay." Tom nodded at a bucket full of red mud sitting on the ground beside him. "I didn't finish splitting the wood because I decided it'd be a better idea to work on the cabin a while. There's a patch of red ground about a hundred yards that way." Tom nodded toward the west. "I'm just letting you know that I'll be working close around the house for a while now. Thought you might hear me working and think I was prowling around." Tom reached down for the bucket.

Simple human decency for Mandy to speak. "I'll help. I want to see how the clay works patching the cabin. And I want to know where you found it."

Tom nodded and headed around the corner of the house.

"Wait!"

Pausing, Tom turned back, a brow arched.

"I'll make you something to eat. I've got biscuits and some roast venison. I could bring you out a sandwich."

Tom nodded. "I'm hungry enough to eat the deer with the fur still on, ma'am. I'd be obliged for a sandwich." He looked down at his hands, coated in red clay. "I'll wash a layer or two of this off first." He set the bucket down and went to the watering trough.

By the time he was done washing, Mandy was back with the food. She'd made two thick sandwiches with the salty meat and brought along a cup of steaming hot coffee for him and one for herself. "I'm sorry I didn't think of it earlier. All your hard work and I didn't even offer to feed you." She didn't feel quite right inviting him inside, so instead she came down the two little steps from her cabin and gestured to them. "Have a seat."

When Tom was settled, Mandy handed him the tin plate.

With a generous smile, Tom said, "I had jerky in my saddlebags if I'd have gotten too hungry. Never was one to eat by the clock. Not much use for a clock out here." He turned to the house. "I see Silas and his men mudded the north side, but it needs a second coat. The worst of the bitter wind comes howling down from the north."

Mandy followed his gaze.

He turned back to her and smiled. "But cold winds come from all directions out here, and sometimes all at once it seems, so we need to do the whole cabin."

Using the word *we* jolted Mandy into thoughts of Sidney. He should be here. He should put the cold winter winds ahead of his gold mining.

"So tell me about my colt and the wolves you saved him from?"

"*Your* colt?" Mandy laughed and Tom smiled and shrugged.

Then, sipping the savory coffee, talking about taking care of the foal, Mandy stood facing him. The steps were wide enough for two, but she'd have been shoulder-to-shoulder with him and she decided against that. She found it easy to talk while he chewed on the venison she'd roasted slowly to make it tender.

"Thanks, ma'am." When the food was gone, Tom stood and Mandy backed up too many steps but couldn't stop herself. "Mighty tasty. A sight better than jerky, and that's the honest truth." He went back to his bucket of clay. Hoisting it, he rounded the cabin, set it down, reached in, and picked up the thick, sticky mud.

"Tell me how the clay works. Did you add water to get it like this?" Mandy reached in and got a handful for herself, forgetting awkwardness as she played with the pliable soil.

"Nope, dug it out of the ground that way. It's not far from the spring and it's already well soaked. I didn't bring more because it'll dry out fast. You'll be hauling heavy buckets for days if you use this stuff. You'll wear yourself out toting it home. So I'll do as much of that for you as I can today."

"Mr. Linscott, I—"

"Call me Tom, ma'am. Seems strange to be called mister out here. Makes me feel like I'm the new schoolteacher or somethin'."

Mandy laughed. She couldn't imagine Tom Linscott standing in front of a classroom with a ruler. "All right, it's Mandy then, not ma'am."

They worked over the heavy clay for hours in near silence, only talking when Tom said he was running for more clay. He did the highest parts of the walls, where Mandy couldn't have reached without a ladder, and he was fast enough he did most of the lower walls, too. That required being on his knees. Mandy did the middle and would have done more, but she could barely keep up with him as it was. She sighed with gratitude to think of all the work she'd been spared by not having to carry those heavy buckets.

As they neared the end of the task, Mandy looked down at

Tom, working on his knees about five paces to her right. "This is way faster than mixing the mud, and it's not as runny."

"Yes, it packs in tighter, too, and lasts longer." Tom had rolled up his sleeves and had clay nearly to his elbows. He scratched at his nose and left three stripes of red clay on his cheek.

"You look like you're wearing war paint," Mandy laughed.

Tom finished filling the last crack between two logs on the foundation of the cabin. He turned his head sideways and smiled up at her.

"Thank you for thinking of the clay and helping me mud these walls." As she said it she realized the day had worn down. "Will you need a place to stay tonight?" Her light heart gained some weight.

"Um. . .I suppose I didn't figure on it. I could stay and finish splitting the wood, and I could put another coat of mud on a few spots tomorrow. Is—that is, I'd like to"—Tom's brow furrowed and a look of distaste turned his lips downward—"meet your husband. I'm surprised he left you here alone. And with all this work needing doing. Where is he?"

He quickly glanced at the pile of kindling he'd split. Mandy realized she'd forgotten all about her husband for the last few hours, and Tom knew full well that the work he was doing was work she'd have had to do, not Sidney. Which meant he was doing this out of pity.

Mandy carefully added the last patch on the cabin. It might need a few places filled in tomorrow, after the clay had thoroughly dried, but for now it was done. She couldn't decide how to respond to Tom's question. The simple truth was, "Sidney knows I can take care of myself. He had errands in Helena."

"My wranglers told me the Hardens left you pretty well supplied."

Tom knew far too much about her business and Mandy burned with the shame of it. She couldn't bring herself to admit Sidney was on his second trip to town, and both times for supplies for his gold mining. "I don't know when he'll be home. Soon, I'm sure. The Hardens were very helpful to us. There were just a few things we needed before winter set in."

Tom rose, to tower over her, and she looked up into blue eyes, kind but worried, too, and maybe just a bit too interested.

She turned and strode toward the water trough where she could rid her hands of the sticky red clay.

He came up beside her and washed vigorously in the wooden water trough.

The Hardens had found this rotted log and brought it in and set it up to hold water. Someone had done nearly everything for her, all the things that should have fallen to her husband. It stung.

"I'm sorry, Mandy. I didn't mean to speak out of turn."

Nodding, Mandy paid far too much attention to the red under her fingernails. "That's quite all right, but I think you need to go now, Mr. Linscott."

"I think you're right." Tom turned and headed for the corral. Mandy watched him catch his rogue stallion with quiet competence that she couldn't help but admire. As he rode out of the yard, he came close to where she'd mindlessly stood watching him. "Thanks for your help with the foal. He's in good hands; that's a comfort to me. I thank you for letting me repay you in this little way." He touched the brim of his Stetson and rode away without waiting for her to respond.

Which was good, because she was speechless. He was just the latest in a line of people who had helped so much and somehow made it seem like they were indebted.

God, when I asked for protection, You responded beyond my dreams. Thank You, Lord. Thank You.

★

Sidney got home at a decent hour with his gold pan. No whiskey on his breath, though Mandy felt as if it was outside the bounds of honor to check closely, and to ask would be to accuse him of lying.

Sidney made no mention of the split wood, even though Tom had stacked a neat pile of it by the front door and the rest was lying in a jumble by the chopping block. And he didn't comment on the fact that their house had turned a dull shade of brick red from all the clay.

Mandy couldn't decide if he thought she'd done all that work today and accepted it as her doing her rightful chores, or did the man really not even notice. How did he think a house got heated and a meal got cooked anyway? Maybe he had no idea how much work was involved in mudding a cabin.

Though she wasn't sure why, Mandy didn't tell Sidney that they'd had company.

They sat at the rustic table Silas Harden had built out of split saplings. They ate deer meat shot by Emma Harden and butchered by Mandy. And they sat in a house much warmer because of Linscott's hard work, and cooked that deer over a fire fueled by kindling Tom had split.

There was a dry sink made from a hollowed-out, split log. That and the bedstead, which she'd finished, was all the furniture they had. But it was a good start.

They enjoyed the stew, cooked in a pot that was among the things stowed in the crate from her parents. The Hardens had left some of their camping gear in the form of tin plates, knives, and forks. They claimed it made a lighter trip home, but Mandy wondered what they'd be short of next year for their drive.

Mandy was so relieved to have a solid roof over her head she didn't think of wanting more. Anything else, she'd build through the winter. Sadly, she now knew she'd have to do all of this herself. Sidney didn't have the skill to do it—there was no shame in that. But that he didn't have any interest in learning was shameful indeed.

As they sat surrounded by comfort, provided by others, all Sidney could talk about was his gold pan.

Mandy nearly squirmed with her own shame for comparing her beloved husband to another man. She needed to bridge the gap she felt between them. "Tell me about your childhood, Sidney. Did you have brothers and sisters?"

Sidney straightened a bit. He'd been slumped in his seat, looking exhausted. "Not much to tell really. I was an only child. My father died in the Civil War when I was a youngster. Don't even remember him."

"Really?" Mandy found this glimpse of her husband's young life fascinating, which made her realize how little Sidney talked about himself. "My pa was in the War, too. Where'd your pa fight?"

Shaking his head, Sidney said, "We didn't ever hear many stories about Father. He died a hero, my mother used to say. Died in the Battle of Shiloh."

Mandy gasped. "My pa fought in the Battle of Shiloh. What's your father's name? Maybe they knew each other."

"It's. . .uh. . .J–John Gray." Sidney's eyes flickered to Mandy's and away. "Mother and I ended up living over a—a store. She took in. . .washing and such. I left—that is, I *didn't* leave school although I *wanted* to. I wanted to help support us, but Mother always lamented her lack of a good education. She believed things would have been easier for us after Father died if she could have been a schoolteacher. So, she pushed me to stay in, and I worked as best I could after school to help out. She died the year I started studying at Yale Law School in Boston."

"I'm so sorry you lost your parents so young. My pa, the one you know, isn't my real father. Ma was married to my pa's twin brother and she was widowed. So, I know how sad it is to lose a father. And you lost your mother, too. . ." Mandy shook her head. No wonder he didn't talk about himself much. "So much sadness."

"Really?" Sidney asked. "You've never said that before. I figured Clay McClellen was your real pa."

"He is. I mean he's *real*. He's a wonderful father. And all my little brothers came after Ma married him. It's too bad your ma didn't remarry. Times were real hard for us after Ma's first husband died. Having a father makes such a difference, and I'd think for a boy it would be even more so."

"She knew a man or two." Something dark passed across Sidney's expression that Mandy found frightening. She'd never seen even a glimpse of the cruelty his expression clearly said he was capable of. Then he closed his eyes and took a deep breath, and when he opened them, he was her Sidney again. "I was always glad to see them go."

"You said your parents were gone, but you never talk about them." Mandy wished she could say the right thing to make up for all Sidney's losses.

Then she remembered something else. "Beth lived in the East for a few years and she wrote home often. She spoke of Yale. Isn't it in Connecticut?" Mandy had never gone to college. She'd finished high school and gone home to the ranch and lived with her family and helped run the household. But that didn't make her stupid.

"Oh, sorry." Sidney gave her a sheepish smile. Charming, sweet. "I meant Connecticut. Slip of the tongue. New Haven, Connecticut. Harvard is in Boston and I considered going there, almost chose it. Well"—Sidney stood quickly and his chair slid back hard and almost fell over—"it's been a long day. I'll turn in now."

It had been a long day for her, too, and it wasn't over yet. "So tomorrow you'll try panning for gold then?"

"Yes, I'm hopeful that the spring might show some color." Sidney suddenly looked very young and nervous.

Mandy's heart turned over to think how far this life was from the big cities back East. He'd have been rich and comfortable if he'd stayed in Connecticut to be a lawyer. But he'd chosen Texas. He'd never really explained why. And now he'd come to yet another wilderness. It had been his idea to come, but he hadn't really known what he was getting into.

She lifted the plates off the table and carried them to the sink. A door shut and she turned to see that Sidney had gone on to bed. Mandy finished clearing the table then decided to go see how

Sidney liked the new bedstead.

She swung the door open and decided he must like it. He was already asleep. Then she stared at his back and decided maybe he was just a bit *too* still. She doubted he could have lain down more than two minutes ago, so how could he be asleep?

She thought of Tom Linscott chopping her wood and sealing her cabin. She should have mentioned the visit. No reason not to. She could say something even now. Then she decided if Sidney wanted to play possum, she'd embarrass him by speaking, acknowledging he was faking it. It suited her not to tell him about her day anyway. Maybe tomorrow she'd bring it up. Or maybe he'd notice all the work and that would start them in talking.

She slipped back out to finish cleaning the kitchen.

Alone.

★ Twenty-eight ★

What had looked like a long hard trek over rugged dry ground was easy with Pa's horses.

Beth didn't mind that it wasn't hard, but she wished desperately it was still long. "I think it's time to camp for the night." Beth lifted her hand to her head, feigning weakness. The act was completely beneath her—playing dainty, fragile woman. But at this rate, they'd make the fort by nightfall.

"You're fine." Alex arched his brows and refused to take her seriously.

She should have taken some class in the theater when she was back East. She had minimal skills as an actress. She was fine. She'd whined around until they'd stretched their time out resting from their wounds for about three days too long. She'd healed so thoroughly, her stitches were nearly ready to come out for heaven's sake.

She'd have stayed longer if they hadn't gotten weary of that whining pig, Cletus Slaughter. Of course they couldn't let him go, but it wasn't in Ma's makeup to just shoot him like a rabid skunk, so they were hauling him along back to the fort, too, draped over his saddle for the most part, since he was given to escape attempts.

That had gotten old by the middle of the second day. Now

they just put him on his horse and hauled him along like he was part of their supplies.

Pa had picked up sign and led them to the Santa Fe Trail and they were making good time. Too good.

Alex had fallen silent for more than a day now. Beth couldn't get him to say more than a rare word. He looked ashen but determined. He was riding to face a firing squad. And he was doing it to protect her.

The trail grew wider and more obviously well traveled. Fort Union couldn't be far ahead.

Beth and Alex rode side-by-side in the lead. Pa and Ma brought up the rear, with Cletus draped over his saddle on a horse being led by Pa and a pack animal tied to Cletus's horse.

The sun was low in the sky, but there was plenty of daylight left. It was way too early to camp and Beth knew it. She guided her horse so she was within whispering distance of Alex. "There must be another way."

Turning as if his neck was rusty, Alex looked her in the eye and was silent for a long time. "God bless you, Beth honey, for wanting to save me and protect me. But it's settled. I'm going to do the right thing."

"Even if it kills you?"

"*Especially* if it kills me." Alex's voice rose. "I got myself messed up in a killing business by being a coward. Slaughter proved that to be a plain fact." Alex jerked his thumb in the direction of the bounty hunter dangling over Pa's saddle. "If I have to die to save your life, then I'll do it willingly."

"I'll still collect the reward on you, Buchanan." Cletus had been riding with a kerchief tied over his mouth, but he must have slipped it off. "You're hauling me in as a captive, but I'm on the side of the law."

"Shooting at my wife and daughter puts you on the wrong side, Slaughter." Pa spoke in a voice that would have made Beth quake in her boots if it'd been aimed at her. "I'll make sure they understand that when you try and collect your bounty."

Slaughter wasn't so smart. "That's *my* money. You're all thieves. You're all as bad as the man you protect. I'll see to it the lot of you gets locked up—"

A dull thud ended his tirade. Beth looked back and saw Cletus now hanging limp. Ma spun her pistol in her hand, having obviously just used the butt end of it on Slaughter's hard head.

She looked a little embarrassed. "Sorry. I should have just put the gag back in his mouth, but I am worn clear beyond my last bit of patience with this fool." She holstered her gun with a quiet shush of iron on leather.

Pa grunted and it sounded like satisfaction. Beth wouldn't have minded using the butt end of a pistol on Slaughter herself, so she knew how her parents felt.

Beth wanted to continue pleading with Alex but instead turned to face forward. She let her eyes fall shut, trusting her horse to carry her along with the others. She couldn't bear to think of what lay ahead.

A rider coming fast from behind caught up. It was a cavalry officer.

"How far to the fort?" Pa asked as the man slowed up alongside.

"I'm hoping to make it in time for supper. But unless you push it, it'll be full dark when you get there." The officer jerked his head at their prisoner. "He dead?"

"Nope," Pa said, "we're bringing him in for shooting me and my daughter." Pa lifted his arm to draw attention to the sling Alex had fashioned to make the trip more comfortable. "We bested him and now need a place to lock him up."

"You want me to take him on in? He'll be uncomfortable moving at a gallop, but I'll do it."

"Nope, go along. We'll make the fort when we make it." Pa touched the brim of his Stetson, and the officer nodded, clearly delighted not to have the man on his hands, and rode off.

Pa maneuvered his horse until he'd ridden up between Alex and Beth. He turned to Alex. "If you want out of this mess, we'll help you. You can ride off, start over somewhere."

Alex and Pa exchanged a long look. "There's more to that offer, isn't there, Clay?" Alex's words were husky and raw, as if Pa hurt him somehow.

Beth wasn't sure how. She held her breath hoping Alex would say yes and she and her husband could cut off from this trail and make a run for California.

"You know there is. I'll help you, but I won't let Beth go along. Not while there are varmints like Slaughter gunning for you."

"Pa!" Beth grabbed his arm. "My place is with my husband." The fear Beth felt was yet a new kind of worry. Fear of being separated from Alex. Because she loved him. She had already figured out that she cared about Alex. She was committed to him and respected him and even loved him, but not until this moment did she realize how deep it went. She had fallen completely and deeply and forever in love with Alex Buchanan.

Pa didn't answer Beth. Instead he kept his attention on Alex.

Beth was terrified Alex would ride off into the sunset, leaving her behind.

"You know I can't do that, Clay. I can't ride away from this. I've tried that before and it's only brought harm to the people around me." Alex gave Pa's arm a significant look then studied the bandage on Beth's head.

"I'll go with you, Alex. We can head anywhere you want. Maybe we could go north and find Mandy and her husband. Leave this behind." A firing squad, that's what Beth had pictured, though maybe they'd hang him instead. Beth wondered if the condemned got to choose.

"You did bring this trouble on us, Alex. But you saved Sally. Nothing about your past brought on those bee stings. Pure and simple, if you hadn't been there, one of my daughters would be dead. You cared for Beth when she was so badly hurt. You bandaged me up when I got shot. All those things put me in your debt and I pay my debts. I'll tell 'em you made a break for it, got away clean. You're a good man and a gifted doctor. The War broke a lot of men, and broken men don't deserve to die."

Beth looked from Pa to Alex, knowing that if Alex rode off, she'd go with him. Pa could grab her and hold her back, but he couldn't hold on to her forever. She was tempted to shout that right out loud, but if she did, Alex wouldn't go. Protecting her was more important to him than living. She felt the same way.

"I appreciate that, Clay. I sincerely do. But I won't let you dishonor yourself, nor Sophie and Beth, to protect me. And letting a guilty man go free isn't honorable. If I die at the end of this, knowing I did some good for your family and the others I doctored in Mosqueros will make it easier to bear. I'll always be grateful for the time I spent being part of your family."

That was the end of it, and the only reason Beth didn't scream and cry and punch Alex in the face to make him go was because she knew it wouldn't work.

They rode on as the dusk settled on the land. Her folks dropped back to ride side-by-side again. They were silent, increasingly grim. All of them knew full well what they rode toward.

In the waning light, Beth caught her first look at the American flag waving proudly over the fort, still at a distance but closing fast. Her time with her husband was nearly up.

Pa and Ma rode up so they were four abreast on the well-worn trail as the sun dropped over the horizon.

Only a lifetime of discipline kept Beth from using her own gun butt on Alex's mulish head, throwing him over his saddle, and running off with him.

"I was a major in the army during the War Between the States, Alex. I still know a few people from those days. When we get there, I'll send a wire or two, insist that you be given a fair hearing."

Alex shook his head. "I want to face this, sir. I want to take my due punishment."

"You will." Pa kicked his horse so he moved ahead and Ma went along.

Just as the stars came out, they rode through the gates of Fort Union.

★

"Luther!" Mandy lost every bit of decorum she'd ever possessed, and being raised in a wild land, she'd never had all that much. Laughing, she threw her arms wide and ran down her steps toward her old friend as he dismounted. She flung herself into Luther's waiting arms.

He lifted her clean off her feet with a familiar chuckle. "Good to see you, girl. Good to see you're doing well." Luther nearly hugged the stuffing out of her.

"Buff, you came, too." Mandy welcomed Buff just as enthusiastically.

Buff's cheeks turned pink behind his full beard and he had a mile-wide smile and a sturdy hug, but he didn't say a word. Buff wasn't one for much chitchat.

"Come on inside and I'll get you some coffee."

Luther and Buff followed Mandy into the house.

She wondered if she could get ten words out of the two of them.

"Where's Sidney?" Luther asked.

Mandy was struck by the strangeness of the question. Luther wasn't one for small talk, so why would he say such a thing? Luther's way was to look around, see that someone wasn't there, and figure it all out for himself.

"Panning for gold." Mandy wasn't sure why that made her feel warm, like maybe she was blushing.

As Luther and Buff sat down, Mandy nearly laughed aloud with delight that there was a chair for each of them. Thanks to the split wood and only needing to touch up the cabin with a bit of clay, she'd had the time to contrive two more chairs. She'd also tanned both deer hides, hunted up another buck and smoked that meat, and gone a long way to gentling the foal. There'd been a light snow in the night after Tom's visit, and she felt the winter pressing on her harder every day.

"So, tell me why you're here, Luther. You're not leaving Pa's ranch for good, are you?" Mandy noticed she'd twisted her fingers together until it maybe looked just the least little bit like she was begging Luther to say he'd moved up here and planned to stay. Near her. The bitter homesickness was such a weakness Mandy felt shame.

Luther didn't answer. He'd hung his fur hat up and now he seemed fixated on smoothing his hair. Not likely since he didn't have much. But his hands ran over the top of his head and the silence stretched.

"Best to just out with it," Buff said.

That was a lot of talking for Buff. And it didn't miss Mandy's notice that the talking was to make someone else do the talking.

Luther nodded then leaned back a bit in his chair to straighten his leg and extract a battered-looking, overly fat letter from his pocket. He extended it to Mandy.

She reached eagerly for it. "A letter from home? From Ma?" She felt like singing. When she grabbed the bulging envelope, Luther didn't let go. Mandy looked up smiling, thinking he meant to tease her. She saw something in Luther's eyes she'd never seen before—a look of fear and regret and maybe even pity. The smile melted off Mandy's face and she braced herself for bad news.

"There's such in that letter that's gonna upset you, Mandy girl. It's from your pa and it explains everything. There's even proof. I'm sorry for it."

Mandy tugged, less eagerly but more deliberately.

Still, Luther held the letter.

"Is someone sick?" Mandy felt her heart beat faster. She nearly choked on the only question she could think of. "Is it Beth? Was she hurt on the trip—"

"Nope, she wasn't hurt. No one of your kin is hurt. But—but there was an accident all right. A stagecoach overturned. Beth came upon the wreck and—and—"

"And she had to go to doctoring. That's why she missed my wedding." Mandy well knew her little sister's healing ways and

251

compassionate heart. She could never walk away from someone in need.

"It's gotta be said." Luther sat up, squared his shoulders, and faced her head-on. "I'm sorry to be the one saying it."

"What, Luther? Tell me."

"There was a young woman about your age on that stagecoach. Name'a Gray. Celeste Gray."

Mandy frowned, and her hand on the envelope turned white at the knuckles from fear. "Some family of Sidney's? A sister? No, that can't be. Sidney said he doesn't have any sisters, or brothers either. He's never mentioned any family. Maybe a cousin coming to the wed—"

"Not a sister, Mandy girl." Luther looked sideways at Buff. "Not a girl cousin."

Buff shook his head.

"Tell me what's going on right now!" Mandy was ready to explode from the tension.

Luther rubbed one big rough hand over his face, still doggedly hanging on to the letter. "It was his wife."

Mandy shook her head and almost smiled. What he said made no sense. "*I'm* his wife."

Mandy saw Luther swallow so hard his whole beard quivered. "Sidney was—girl, he was married already."

"B–but she's dead?" Mandy heard her voice, but it sounded like it was a long distance away. "Sidney is a widower? When did his wife die?"

"Near as we can figure, a few hours before he married you."

"A few hours?" Mandy shook her head, thinking that she must be addled.

Luther held her gaze.

She'd known Luther all her life and he'd never been one to joke around. So why was he doing it now?

"B–but he'd been sparking me since he came to Mosqueros. He proposed to me. He couldn't have—"

The cabin door swung open and a very beleaguered Sidney

stepped inside, his gold pan hanging dejectedly from his fingertips. "Is dinner ready?" His eyes focused on Luther and Buff, and his eyes widened in recognition. He narrowed his eyes and turned to Mandy and scowled. "We've got company from Mosqueros? Already?"

Mandy's eyes went to the letter she still shared with Luther. With sudden strength she jerked it out of her old friend's hand.

★ Twenty-nine ★

Fort Union wasn't like Alex expected. It had no stockade surrounding it. No intimidating row of logs standing shoulder-to-shoulder, sharpened to points on top.

Instead, the fort looked, in the moonlight, like a frontier village with broad streets meeting at squared-off intersections. The line of buildings visible were adobe. They looked well-built and well cared for.

There were no apparent bristling weapons, no alert guards. It was a quiet village. Even this late at night, it seemed that there should be some activity.

Clay led the way into this placid military outpost and went up to a man strolling along the front of a row of buildings. "We want to see the officer in charge."

Alex thought of the battles, the death, the danger, the blood. And here he stood in the midst of almost complete peace. A coyote howled in the dark night. A breeze blew quietly as the heat of the day eased until it was nearly too cold, as the desert was apt to do. His stomach twisted as he wondered if he'd end up dying in this peaceful place.

He'd lost the best part of himself in service to his country. But that lost part, the caretaker, the healer, had recently been resurrected. Alex almost regretted that. If they'd have locked him up and shot him at dawn before he met Beth, a part of him would have welcomed it. The end of his living nightmare. But now he had so much to lose.

But resurrecting himself included his faith. If he entered into eternity, he'd spend it with God.

God, forgive me if I don't welcome that closeness to You. I so wanted to have a life here with Beth. Thank You, though, for giving me a chance to heal my relationship with You.

The sentry straightened and saluted Clay. "The colonel ain't here, sir. Rode all the way back East to meet face-to-face with President Arthur." The sentry made that announcement wide-eyed, as if stunned by knowing his commander could speak to someone so lofty.

Alex had to admit that this dusty outpost seemed a world away from the president of the United States.

"The lieutenant handles things while the colonel is away, sir."

Beth swung down off her horse.

Alex hesitated, as if once he touched this military ground his fate would be sealed. Reluctantly, he dismounted, too.

Beth came to his side and clutched his hand. Her strength propped him up again, like always.

Sophie went to stand by her husband.

The guard's respectful reaction to Clay made Alex aware of his father-in-law's military bearing and former rank.

"No need saluting me, son. I took off the uniform years ago." Despite his words, Clay fell into the authority without trying and made it known he was an officer to be obeyed. "We'll see the lieutenant then." Clay slipped his gloves off as he spoke and touched the brim of his Stetson in a casual salute.

The man shook his head frantically. "Lieutenant Deuel's gone to his quarters for the night. I can't wake him." Alex saw fear in the soldier's wide-eyed refusal to get his commanding officer.

"Where are the sentries?" Clay asked. "Does the whole fort just go to sleep at night? Are things that secure?"

"I've seen no danger in the year I've been posted here," the young soldier said. "We don't even have many men stationed here anymore. We're always hearing rumors that they'll close the fort up and move us somewhere else. I guess I'm the closest we've got to a night watch. I take a shift then hand it off to someone else. It's pretty peaceful."

Sophie came up and smiled at the young guard.

The man forgot Clay and looked first at Sophie, then Beth. From his fascinated reaction, Alex wondered how long it had been since the young man had seen a pretty woman.

"Go get the lieutenant," Clay ordered. Alex suspected Clay didn't mean to start giving orders to a soldier. He just couldn't quite control himself.

The young soldier tore his eyes away from Sophie. "The l–lieutenant, he won't see no one now 'til mornin', sir."

"We don't want to put this off." Despite his assurance that he wasn't an officer, Clay made that sound like another direct order.

The guard was sunburned and looked about fifteen years old. Alex wondered if he'd looked that young when he'd first joined the cavalry. Now the barely grown boy shook his head, looking genuinely sorry. "Lieutenant Deuel don't do nothin' he don't hafta do. He won't come out for you. Not even to see to a prisoner." The young man gave a significant look at Slaughter then went back to fixing his fearful eyes on Clay, as if he expected to be court-martialed for disobeying. "In fact, were I you, I'd ride right on out of here and come back when you hear the colonel's returned."

Clay sighed. "We're not going to ride into the hills and wait for the colonel."

The sentry came right up to Clay and whispered. Alex leaned in to catch the words. "Lieutenant Deuel's got a—a streak of—of—" The young man looked over his shoulder as if he might be observed. "Sometimes he's of a mind to make rulings just because someone bothered him. They don't make a whole lotta sense."

The man glanced around again and stood straight and spoke loud. "He's a fine man, the lieutenant."

Furrowing his forehead, Alex tried to figure out what the

soldier was talking about. He'd said two almost exactly opposite things. Then Alex noticed another soldier just rounding the end of the building row. So what this soldier whispered when he was alone was different from what he'd say for all the world to hear. Apprehension tightened Alex's gut. What kind of fort was this? And what kind of decision could he hope for from this temporarily in-charge officer, Lieutenant Deuel?

"Have you got a place we can sleep for the night? And a place to lock this varmint up?" Clay jerked his head at the bounty hunter. He either didn't catch the undercurrent of the soldier's words or, more likely because Clay didn't miss much, he thought he could handle what lay ahead.

"The prisoner is named Cletus Slaughter. He shot me and my daughter. He claims he's a bounty hunter and attacked us all because he was after my son here." Clay jabbed his thumb at Alex.

A place warmed in Alex's heart that he hadn't known was cold. When he'd broken with his father, even though Alex still believed he'd done the right thing, the hurt had gone deep and never healed. Now, to have Clay McClellen call him his son. . . Alex was shocked at the urge to cry.

Alex wasn't sure what had caused this strange compulsion toward tears, but he desperately wanted it to stop.

The sentry shook his head. "Yes, sir. I'll have him locked up, sir. But seriously, you should just ride out. Go to Santa Fe and turn this guy in. Or go to Santa Fe and hide. I mean. . .uh. . .wait until the colonel comes back."

"We're staying," Clay glared at the man.

The nervous soldier nodded and hollered.

Three more recruits came out of a nearby building with the leisurely movements of men who had never been in battle and didn't fear that one might be starting up.

Alex envied them.

"Lock this prisoner up."

Two of the newcomers lowered Cletus from his horse and untied him.

Slaughter grabbed immediately for the kerchief that had kept him mercifully silent. "I'm not the one who should be arrested here." Slaughter's eyes were bloodshot and the corners of his mouth were foaming white. He looked for all the world as if he had rabies. "I'm a bounty hunter and I've worked with the colonel a lotta times over the years, bringing in the cowards that desert the army." Slaughter jabbed a finger straight at Alex's chest. "That man is wanted. Arrest him."

The sentry looked between Slaughter, Alex, and Clay. "Your son, you said?"

Clay nodded. "And we're here to straighten this out. We rode in, didn't we? And we had that would-be bounty hunter tied down. We'll answer all these questions when we talk to the lieutenant."

The soldier swallowed visibly, even in the dim moonlight, at the mention of the lieutenant.

"If you want me locked up, I'll go quietly." Alex stepped forward. He needed to take his punishment right from the first.

"Nope, I'll trust you folks. You rode in and you didn't hafta." The sentry ordered Slaughter taken away, still fuming and raving. The other soldier took the horses to bed down for the night.

"Do you folks need to see a doctor? If you've been shot, maybe you oughta have him look at you." The sentry gave the sling on Clay's arm a long look. "The doc'll get outa bed in the night for you." An obvious commentary on the lieutenant refusing to work after hours.

Clay looked at Beth, then Alex. Both shook their heads. "I think we're good. We've been doctored up enough. A place to sleep sounds good, though. I don't suppose there's a meal to be had here?"

"I think I can find some stew left from supper, still simmering. The cook makes enough to last a couple'a days usually and it tastes like slop from the first day to the last. It's filling though, keeps the front of your belly from rubbin' against the back. I'll bring some over." The guard pointed to another man approaching them. "He can show you to your quarters."

As they were guided to a long slender building, Clay asked, "Isn't this a barracks? Our womenfolk aren't going to bunk down with a bunch of soldiers."

The man escorting them shook his head rapidly. "Oh no, sir. We'd never do that. We have plenty of empty beds. No need to share. We've been a warehouse for supplies for all the Western forts and a place to watch over the Santa Fe Trail. But the trail don't need no watchin' over since the trains went through. And that goes for supplies, too. They're all sent by train these days. And there's no warrin'. It's plumb peaceful. Since the Indians lost the last war, they've all gone to the reservation. We barely even think of fighting."

"The Red River War," Alex said quietly. The Indians had indeed gone to the reservation. But not without a lot of killing first.

"Yep, I didn't sign on here until that was ended. Now they've cut back on the number of soldiers housed here at Fort Union until we're almost empty."

"All right, soldier. Sounds fine." Clay reached for the door, but the escort beat him to it. Alex noted the obedient tone of all the enlisted men to Clay.

The line of buildings had a porch stretching the length of them.

"Your food ought to be here shortly." The soldier grimaced and Alex wondered just how bad the food was going to be. "You can eat together in this room, and I'll unlock the door to the next room so you can have private sleeping quarters. Both are cleaned and set up for visitors. We never have many, though."

The soldier's glum claims of a boring military life sounded blissful to Alex. Why couldn't he have been the company doctor of this place?

They entered the long thin building and there was a main room, with doors leading off to the side.

"This room used to be set up for visiting officers so there's an actual bedroom. Same next door," the young recruit told them.

"Thanks." Clay pulled his Stetson off.

Alex hadn't heard so much as a word of complaint from Clay or Beth all through this long ride to the fort, but they had to be hurting. Clay had lost a lot of blood and had a bullet wound that was a long way from healed. Beth's injury hadn't been as serious, but she'd taken a hard blow to the head and she had to be suffering from it after these long days in the saddle. Alex thought he saw lines of fatigue and pain on Clay's face, but maybe it was just lines burned by living in Texas. He had a few of those himself.

The soldier lit two lanterns that sat near the door then left just as the other soldier came in with a pot of stew and some tin plates and forks. "I scared up some biscuits, too."

"Obliged." Clay took the food.

Sophie relieved him of it and had the table set and the stew on by the time the young soldier had said good night.

The stew was rank; a brown paste that showed no sign of beef or vegetables. The biscuits had the appeal of chewing on a piece of adobe that'd been drying in the sun for a hundred years.

Alex choked down enough food to stave off starvation, fearing for his teeth the whole time.

The four of them ate silently, too hungry and tired for talk. At last, the meal could be called to a halt, leaving them longing for the days on the trail when they'd lived on hard tack and beef jerky.

Alex stood to escort his wife next door. He rested his hand on Beth's back to guide her. "You need some rest."

"Hold up." Clay's voice stopped them cold.

It occurred to Alex that he was obeying Clay's orders, just like everyone else.

"Beth, you oughta stay with your ma and me."

Alex turned, surprised. "No." Alex squared off against Clay. "Why don't you want her to stay with me?"

"Pa!" Beth protested and wrapped two arms tight around Alex's waist. She clung to him now, when so recently she'd been holding him up. She really did care about him. She was truly his wife in every sense of the word.

Alex didn't want her upset. She was walking wounded, too. But after he faced the charges against him tomorrow, he might never have his wife in his arms again. He wasn't giving her up tonight. His chest tightened until he could barely breathe. He was surprised how hurt he was by Clay's effort to separate him from Beth. "Not an hour ago you called me your son."

Clay held Alex's eyes. What passed between them was beyond words, but Alex saw it all. Clay's gratitude for saving Sally's life, the respect Alex held for Clay's strength of will, the fear Clay held for his daughter, the regret for all Alex would put Beth through in the near future. It wasn't even the future. He'd already begun slowly, surely, breaking her heart.

Sophie's hand came up and rested on Clay's. "Let it go. Let them be together for the night."

Clay looked down at his wife's hand then back up at his daughter, also hanging on to a man—but not him anymore. Clay shook his head. "Fine. I'm sorry. I just—" He shook his head again, harder. "You're going to hurt my girl. I'd do anything to stop one of my daughters from suffering a moment's sadness. And every minute you're together, the hurt's just going to get deeper. I think you should—make your break from each other now. Get on with it."

Alex knew Clay was right.

"You're wrong, Pa. It doesn't work that way." Beth let go of Alex and stepped toward her father. For a terrible, grief-stricken moment, Alex was afraid she was leaving him, even though he knew she probably should.

"No, he's not." Alex felt his hands slip from around Beth as she stepped toward her parents. "No matter what punishment they hand out tomorrow, you're going to have to leave me behind here. They'll lock me up for sure."

Beth turned to him and placed both hands on his chest. "He's wrong because it's already too late. If they take you away from me, I'm going to be as sad as I know how to be. One more night won't make it any worse."

Alex looked into those strong, wise, beautiful blue eyes, and though he found strength there as always, he didn't find the strength to let her go. He kissed her, right in front of her parents. "Come on then."

Sophie took one of the lanterns and, still holding on to Clay, left the room without looking back.

The other lantern lit Alex's way as he pulled Beth outside and into the next room. It was clean and had the same front living area as the room where they'd eaten. They passed through it into the officer's bedroom on the north.

Once the door was closed and Alex had her with him, he could breathe again. How was he going to manage when they locked him away? With grim amusement he knew it wouldn't be for long. The firing squad would limit his time for suffering.

"You're sure you don't want to go with them, Beth honey? I'm sorry. I want you with me, but that's not fair to you."

"I'm staying, Alex. And I'm exhausted. I just want to lie down." Beth's blue eyes met his in the dimly lit room. The lantern flickered and it seemed to Alex that the light went deep into Beth, until her soul was visible. Her beautiful, gracious soul.

When they lay next to each other, Beth's head resting on Alex's shoulder, he couldn't hold back the words, though he felt like laying them on Beth only added to her burden. "I love you, Beth."

"I love you, too, Alex." She nestled closer.

Rising up on one elbow so he could look down at his precious wife, Alex leaned down to kiss her gently. "I almost wish you didn't. If you love me, then what happens to me tomorrow is going to hurt you terribly. It's a scar on my soul that I've brought this pain to you. One more thing I need forgiveness for."

"Okay, I forgive you." Beth lifted one of her strong, healing hands and rested it on the rough stubble of Alex's face.

He hadn't bathed in days, unless he counted muddy floodwater—and he didn't. "I shouldn't be near you. I've got no right to touch someone as wonderful as you. I shouldn't let you touch me. Your pa was right."

The room was dark with the lantern extinguished, but the moon washed the room in silver. Alex saw Beth, her skin cast midnight blue. Her eyes sparkling like stars.

"It'll be settled tomorrow, Beth. And I will face whatever punishment they have for me. I am so thankful for the short time I've had as your husband."

"Hush." Beth rested her delicate, healing fingers on his lips. "We'll figure it out, Alex. Don't talk like it's settled. Don't give up hope."

"I wish I could give up hope. It might hurt less if I didn't have any."

"Well, don't ask me to give up. Because I will never give up on you, Alex. Not as long as there is a chance." Beth pulled his head closer.

Alex resisted, feeling like he sullied her even by holding her close.

But Beth had been stronger than him from the beginning. She got her wish for closeness.

Alex didn't get his wish to give up, because having Beth in his arms gave him a hope that would not die.

★

"Mandy, I'd like to talk to you outside, right now." Sidney glared between Mandy and their guests belligerently.

"Care to tell me who Celeste Gray is?" She met his eyes.

His arms came uncrossed and the look on his face changed. Mandy wasn't sure what she looked like exactly but it must have been fearsome because Sidney backed up a step. "C–Celeste?" Sidney's stuttering told Mandy all she needed to know.

"Yes, she's dead by the way. But then, I bet you're not going to mourn your *wife's death*, are you?" Mandy rubbed her thumb over that little callus on her trigger finger.

"Celeste's dead?" Sidney had the wide-eyed look of a deer who knew he was shortly going to be venison.

"Yes. In fact it sounds like she died in time."

"In time for what?"

"In time for our marriage to be legal."

"Who told you about Celeste?" Sidney's eyes went from Luther to Buff. He tried for a scowl, but it wouldn't stick on his face when he confronted the two extremely serious men who now sat at Mandy's table.

"What kind of a sidewinder courts and marries a woman when he's already married?" Mandy couldn't believe she'd said those words aloud. "It was all lies, wasn't it? The chance for a job in Denver. You must have known we were leaving Mosqueros long before you announced it to me."

"No. Mandy, I don't know what you've heard, but Celeste and I were never married. I knew her. But she. . . If she claimed we were married she was lying."

Mandy held the letter up to show Sidney. "I wonder what my pa wrote in this letter he sent along with Buff and Luther." She waved the letter. "It's fat. Room for lots of details. Maybe even proof. My pa has never lied to me. Luther and Buff have never lied to me." Mandy stood so suddenly that her chair toppled over backward with a loud clatter. "In fact, I've really never been lied to much in my life. That's why I didn't recognize it when lies started pouring from your dishonest lips." Mandy ripped the letter open with a vicious wrench of her hands. The envelope split with a loud sizzling hiss.

"No, Mandy. Don't read that. You've got to give me a chance to prove I'm telling the truth."

Mandy pulled a heavy sheet of folded paper from the envelope, along with a thin letter. She unfolded the heavy document first and read it. "A marriage license." She looked at the next thing contained in the envelope. A picture of Sidney sitting, dressed formally. Behind him stood a pretty, dark-haired woman in a gown that looked white. Both of them looked terribly serious.

"Those were found among her things." Luther had such regret in his voice that Mandy felt bad for Luther. He understood how badly this made Mandy feel, and in his whole life, Luther had never caused anyone in her family a moment's pain. "Your pa wrote a letter explaining everything. We're here to take Mandy home."

Raising her chin, she stared at Sidney.

Letting him see her anger.

Her sense of betrayal.

The—she faltered over it—the pain. It was as if her heart broke in half. She physically felt the agony in her chest.

"Mandy, please, you've got to listen to me." Sidney was across the room in two long strides.

Scraping chairs drew Mandy's attention, and she saw Buff and Luther standing, wary, ready to step between her and Sidney.

The humiliation.

Everyone knew about this. She looked back at Sidney. "You have disgraced me. Made a fool out of me." Her eyes fell shut under the weight of it. "I can't believe anyone is possessed of such a lack of honor."

Sidney took the marriage license from her hands and she didn't fight it. Why bother?

Mandy forced her eyes open to watch her husband squirm.

Sidney studied the parchment for far too long, and Mandy knew he was spinning his lies, testing them in his head before he spouted them at her. "This is a forgery." He glanced up then away. Then he looked back, his gaze strong, his shoulders square. The man had learned how to lie very well, which spoke of much practice at the sin. "I'm telling you, this isn't true. We had this tintype made. I can't deny I knew this woman. But I never married her. You and I are married, legally married. I love you and I thought you loved me." Temper flashed in his eyes. "I expect you to trust me."

"Over my father? Over Luther and Buff, whom I've known and trusted all my life? Over my own perfectly good two eyes?" Mandy hated Sidney's sincere tone, that injured anger. It broke Mandy's heart yet again to know she couldn't tell if this was the truth or another lie.

"No, I'm not saying they're lying. They got this and they believed it. I don't blame them. And your friends rushed up here to protect you. I respect all of that. I'd have done the same for my own daughter." Sidney reached out and grasped Mandy's wrist. His words were a stark reminder that they could indeed have a daughter on the way. Or a son. That was the way of married life.

"But they were fooled by this woman. Just like I was. I knew her, and for a while I thought we might be in love. But I found out she was a dishonest schemer and left her. She's followed me before and caused trouble for me. Nothing like this, but it's true that part of the reason I came West was because of her—her obsession with me. That's the only word I can use to describe it."

Mandy just didn't know.

"That's an official marriage license." Luther spoke from his spot on the table.

Sidney gave Luther a single furious glance. "She's very good at what she does. And she has enough money to pay dishonest men to do fine work for her."

"A judge has signed it and it bears his seal." Mandy could see that Luther still didn't trust Sidney a whit.

Well, now neither did Mandy. How could she be sure of anything he told her, ever again?

Shaking her head, Mandy stood and stared at her husband, trying to see inside Sidney's head.

The corners of his mouth turned down, his eyes shown with hurt. Yes, hurt. She'd hurt him by not trusting him. Or else he was a very good liar.

"There's a way to find out." Luther pulled Mandy's attention again and she could see that Luther knew her mind. Knew her doubts. Knew her hurt and love and betrayal and wasn't going to stand for her taking Sidney's word for anything.

"How?"

"You stay out of this." Sidney turned a grim face to Luther. "You come in here with your lies and—"

"How!" Mandy spoke loud enough to shut Sidney's mouth.

He turned back to her, forbidding and annoyed.

Mandy felt a strange kind of power in no longer worrying about making Sidney happy. He'd been prone to sullenness, and she'd worked hard trying to please him. Well, no more. It was now his turn to do some hard work.

"There's a judge's name affixed to that license and it's from Boston," Luther said. "We wire him and ask if he really signed this document. This looks mighty official to me—"

"Celeste is a skilled forger," Sidney interjected.

Luther talked right over him. "And it's not some small wedding in a church in the middle of West Texas, where the parson might be a circuit rider and have moved on and the witnesses might be few. Wire the city and have 'em check the records."

Mandy turned to Sidney. "That sounds fair."

"No, it's not fair." Sidney stepped so close he was nearly plastered against her. He loomed over her, bending down to glare until their noses almost touched. "You should take my word for this. You should *trust* me. We took vows, love, honor, and obey. You are *not* honoring me, Mandy Gray."

Mandy almost laughed in his face. "I'm not honoring *you*? Even if you're telling me the truth, Sidney, you should have told me about this woman. You've never told me *anything* about your life. You know what? That's the reason I doubt you now. Because I know nothing about you. Why is that, I wonder?"

"I haven't had an easy life. I don't like to talk about it." Sidney sounded pouty. Well, his pouting days were over if he wanted to clear up this mess.

"Maybe your life was hard." Mandy didn't bother to point out that she'd lived with her mother and sisters in a thicket for a few years after her first pa died. They'd had a tiny, rickety shelter and they'd lived on rabbit and fish and greens. Her life had been hard, too. And she'd told Sidney all about herself. "Maybe you don't like talking about it and maybe you've kept quiet partly because of this woman, but what it adds up to is I don't really know you. I spent the last two months listening to you be charming and sweet and flattering, but I didn't hear a word about who you are. If you'd talked with me about your growing-up years, including the trouble you've had with some obsessed woman, we wouldn't be in this spot right now, would we? To my mind that makes you a liar. Whether a liar about being married or a liar about who you really are, I'll decide for myself after the judge writes back. For now, you're going to have to sleep in the barn."

So many things flickered across Sidney's face Mandy could barely keep up. Anger, hurt, disdain, contempt. Love. He might really love her. And he was really married to her. But what kind of tragic excuse for a marriage did they have with all this unknown between them?

"I'll do it, Mandy. I'll move out of the house and we'll send your wire and wait for your answer. I'll do it all because I love you. But when the truth comes out, I'm going to make you *beg* me for forgiveness." Contempt won over all Sidney's warring emotions. He stormed out of the house.

Mandy realized he'd always looked down on her. He'd done it in subtle ways, but she knew now he'd made her grateful that he loved her. While he'd been charming her, he'd let her know in a hundred little ways she was lucky he'd chosen her.

Pa had known that. He'd never forbidden Mandy to see Sidney, but he'd pressured them to take more time before they married. And when Mandy wouldn't listen, he'd pressured them to stay in Mosqueros, probably knowing it would fall to him to take care of his daughter once Sidney's true nature was revealed.

But Mandy hadn't listened to the wisest man she'd ever known, a man who loved her with all his heart.

And once she realized that, Mandy held herself in contempt.

★ Thirty ★

The four of them had plenty of time for breakfast—more dreadful stew. Then they had time to sit. Alex wound up tighter and tighter.

Clay had gone early to find the lieutenant and returned to say he wasn't in his office yet and no one would dare bother him at his residence. He'd also sent a wire to someone back East he'd known during the War.

At Sophie's urging, Alex cleaned himself up after breakfast. He shaved and washed up good. Clay even found a store on the base and, with Sophie along to advise, got clean clothes for Alex and himself.

Alex felt like a fool getting gussied up to go face a hanging, but the hours were creeping by so slowly, Alex agreed more to keep moving than for any other reason. Back in his room, Alex poured water from the ewer into the painted china bowl then removed his shirt.

Beth gasped. "What happened to you?" She came up behind him, where he stood in his undershirt with his hands cupped in the water of the water basin.

Alex let the water flow back into the basin as he looked over his shoulder.

Beth touched his upper arm, beside the strap of his sleeveless undershirt.

"A scar from the war." He wished he'd never let her see it. He forgot about those scars for the most part. It was the scars inside his head he couldn't forget.

Beth pulled the shoulder of his shirt aside then pulled down on his neck. Another gasp followed as she looked at his back. It was ugly. He'd neglected his wounds until they'd festered. He'd nearly died from them. They were rough and they covered his back and his neck, and there were more above his hairline and below his belt.

He turned to face her. "Forget the scars, Beth. They're nasty but they're all healed up, have been for years."

Beth's brow furrowed. "You told me you'd been wounded, hit by shrapnel, but I had no idea it was this bad."

Shrugging, Alex said, "I didn't know it either. Never have given it much thought. The wounds were long healed up without much attention from me. It's the nightmares that came with the war that are my real scars."

Beth pulled him close.

He wrapped his arms around her waist. "I'm so sorry I got you into—"

Beth silenced him with her lips. He felt her arms around him, touching his back and the deep ridges and gouges of his wounds. One more burden he'd laid on his precious wife.

When he pulled away, he hated to turn his back, knowing the scars would bother her.

She seemed to know it, with the sensitivity she showed in everything. "I'll go wait with Ma and Pa."

He nodded and she left the room, then he got back to cleaning up.

The noon meal had come, stew again, this time with the added bonus of being cold. There was coffee that tasted—crunchy.

Alex did his best to cover his nerves, to put on a good front for Beth.

"I've sent a telegraph home to Mosqueros tellin' the family where we got to." Clay grimaced at the coffee but kept drinking. "And I've asked the telegraph office there to forward any wires that came from Luther."

"I wonder if he's found Mandy," Sophie said.

Alex had heard just enough about the man Beth's sister had married to wonder what was wrong with these McClellen girls to use such poor judgment picking husbands, himself being the prime example. The fact that Beth loved him only made him wonder the more.

Clay shook his head. "I reckon he'll let us know as soon as he catches up to her."

A sharp rap at the door drew their attention, and Clay went to answer it.

An older soldier waited there, his hair gray where it showed beneath his cap. "The lieutenant will see you folks now."

"It's about time," Clay snapped.

Alex knew he was wound up like a fifty-cent pocket watch, but Clay had acted pretty calm until now. Maybe it was the same act Alex was putting on for Beth. Most likely all four of them were putting on acts.

"Didn't see no sense in hurryin' you along." The soldier, his face clean shaven and his uniform clean and sharply pressed, looked worried. "You're not gonna like the lieutenant. In fact, were I you, I might just forget this whole thing and head for the hills. You rode in, you know. No reason you couldn't just ride right back out. Wait a while 'til the colonel comes back."

"Let's get going," Clay ordered. "We're not running."

The soldier shook his head with what looked like genuine regret and escorted them across the yard to the commander's office. They walked past a man sitting at a secretary's desk and heard a loud voice ranting in the next room—Cletus already spewing his lies.

As they entered, Cletus glared at them without taking a break in his complaints. "I was attacked by the doctor and his cohorts. I had a right to bring him in, and by fightin' me, they threw in with him and committed their own crimes. I want the lot of them locked up."

The lieutenant's eyes shifted from Cletus to them. He had eyes so light blue they looked gray. His uniform was so posy fresh Alex wondered if he changed it several times during the day, not a bit of this desert dust anywhere. He had a white plate in front of him, half-full of the mess they'd had for dinner. He was chewing as if every bite nearly killed him. The lieutenant ate his on thin fine china, with a long-stemmed goblet that looked like crystal to Alex. The silverware was placed in almost painful precision above the plate.

The lieutenant quit eating, leaving most of the food behind, then lifted a napkin from his lap and dabbed at his mouth as if he wished he could wipe the whole meal away. "Take the table service away, sergeant. And when I'm done with these folks, bring me that cook. She's fired."

"Yes, sir. I'll have the cook brought in as soon as this meeting is over." The older man moved quickly to lift the dishes. "But, sir, I don't think you can fire the colonel's wife. I mean the colonel's gonna come back sometime and he might not like it."

"Bring her in here!" Lieutenant Deuel roared.

Alex and Beth exchanged glances.

The soldier toted the dishes out, and two other uniformed men stood stiffly at attention. They were positioned on either side of the lieutenant behind him, posed so rigidly they matched the flagpoles standing proudly beside them.

Lieutenant Deuel shifted his solemn gaze from Cletus to Alex. "Sit down. I'm Lieutenant Deuel. Mr. Slaughter has made some serious charges against all of you."

Clay introduced himself and the rest of them then said, "We've got charges of our own, sir." Clay saluted as was proper, officer to officer, even if one of those officers was long separated from the service. "I'm Clay McClellen, formerly a major in the Union Army. We came in to get this cleared up."

Alex should have saluted, too, maybe. He was afraid the lieutenant would take it as an offense considering he was a deserter. Except maybe if he *didn't* salute the lieutenant would take it as an offense. Unable to decide, Alex remained still. He'd never been very good at military things.

"You speak as if deserting one's post is something easily resolved, Mr. McClellen. I assure you it's not."

Someone had lined up five chairs in a painfully neat row across the desk from the lieutenant. Cletus sat down hard on the one farthest to the left and scooted it back a few inches.

The lieutenant flinched like the misaligned chair created a disorder he found unbearable. Slaughter didn't notice, but Alex did and resolved not to scoot under any circumstances. He'd known men like the lieutenant and the oddest things could set them off.

Cletus leaned back in his chair, dirty and grizzled with his sparse beard.

Alex's efforts to clean up, hoping to look like a respectable citizen, seemed dishonest next to Cletus's grime. He'd hoped that would make the lieutenant trust him, but somehow now, to Alex, it seemed like he'd put on a false front while Cletus was presenting himself as a hardworking, decent man. The lieutenant might be partial to cleanliness, but surely no one would pronounce a sentence higher or lower based on a man's clothing.

Clay caught Alex's eye and jerked his thumb at the chair farthest to the right. Beth, with a bandage still on her head, sat next to Alex. Sophie sat by Beth. Clay, with his arm in a sling, took the chair beside Cletus.

The lieutenant was young. Younger than Alex in fact. He had a baby face that didn't look capable of growing whiskers. How did such a young man come to be in charge of a fort? But then, despite its size, Fort Union wasn't much of a fort these days.

"Now"—Lieutenant Deuel folded his arms on the desk in front of him and nearly stabbed Alex to death with those gray eyes—"Mr. Slaughter accuses you of shooting him, taking him prisoner, and assisting an army deserter."

Clay stood. "We defended—"

"Sit back down." Deuel talked over top of Clay and raised his hand to ask for silence. "I didn't ask you. And I know some of that is a lie. It is obvious to me that you've been injured."

Clay sat back down.

"Mr. Slaughter would have me believe he was just defending himself when he shot you and your daughter, Mr. McClellen, but no woman would shoot at a man, so seeing a bullet wound on you, Mrs. Buchanan"—Deuel looked at Beth—"puts a lie to at least part of his charges."

"That woman—" Cletus stood and stormed toward the young officer.

Both soldiers behind Deuel stepped forward.

"Stop or I'll have you removed and locked up, Mr. Slaughter." For his youth, the lieutenant had considerable power in his voice.

Though he was fuming, fists clenched tight as his jaw, Cletus sat back down. He made Alex think of a snapping, snarling wolf.

"Now, what I see here is a deserter." The lieutenant turned those cold eyes on Alex and the little bits of hope he'd nurtured faded. "What was your rank, Dr. Buchanan?"

"I was a captain."

The lieutenant arched his brows.

Alex felt his collar tighten, wondering if the man would feel some satisfaction in ruling against a man who'd outranked him.

"Well, Captain Buchanan, as you know, the punishment for desertion can be execution."

Lieutenant Deuel watched him with sharp eyes.

Alex couldn't quite control a gulp. "Yes, I'm aware of that. I've come in to face whatever punishment you deem necessary."

One of the men behind Deuel caught Alex's eye and gave his head a tiny, frantic shake. Alex ignored the man.

Deuel nodded. "I will take the fact that you came in on your own into consideration. But that doesn't change the fact that you've confessed and it won't require any trial to find you guilty."

Alex wanted to protest but he fought the impulse. "I *am* guilty, Lieutenant Deuel."

The soldiers standing at attention exchanged looks. One of

them rolled his eyes.

"However, there's more than that. If what Mr. Slaughter is telling me is true, then the group with you has committed crimes."

The lieutenant's eyes skimmed down the row, running past Beth, Sophie, and Clay.

Alex's stomach twisted at what he saw in those eyes. Then he looked closer at the lieutenant. There was something—

"I'd like to respond to that, lieutenant." Clay spoke politely but with that same authority that seemed to be part of him, but more apparent here in military surrounding.

"I'm sure you would, Major McClellen. But right now it's *my* turn, and the only speaking *you'll* be doing is to answer my questions."

Clay's jaw tensed but he nodded. "Yes, sir."

Lieutenant Deuel definitely had a hostile attitude toward Alex and he was extending that to the McClellens. But then based on the soldiers behind the lieutenant and the way the man was treating Slaughter, it was possible the guy was hostile to everyone.

"Now, how long ago did you desert, *captain*?" Deuel laced the military rank with venom.

"I served with Colonel Miles out of Fort Dodge. I—let's see—" Alex had done his best to forget the details, which left him only with vague haunting memories of blood and death. "It was the summer, or autumn maybe, of 1874. I—I rode with the supply wagons Colonel Miles sent under the command of Captain Lyman to Camp Supply in Indian Territory. I was supposed to restock bandages and make sure Colonel Miles's new camp on the Red River had whatever I thought necessary. We fought a battle with the Kiowas and Comanches on that trip that lasted—I can't remember how long—days. We were surrounded." Alex rubbed his head wishing he could wipe away the nightmare.

He felt his vision widening as the room faded and the rifle fire cut through day and night.

"There was a terrible rainstorm." He could feel the mud everywhere, hear the report of guns. Horses wounded and screaming in pain. Men dead and dying. He smelled the blood, even in the downpour. "There were around a hundred men and only ten or so armed. Captain Lyman had us dig in, but the Indians had us under siege and they meant to keep after us until we were all dead."

Fingernails sunk into his arm and he pulled himself back to see Beth leaning toward him. He looked in her eyes and they steadied him.

"Give us strength." He heard her whispering, her lips barely moving. Strength. She asked God for enough strength for both of them.

He asked for strength, too, as he tried to remember what happened after that siege.

"We—we got out. Someone came. Then I had to tend the men hurt in the Battle of Buffalo Wallow. They'd just been brought in when we were rescued. Those men had barely been given a week to heal, and we had wounded from the battle near Camp Supply. Some of them were still terribly wounded when a new battle broke out in Palo Duro Canyon. The colonel ordered me to the site. I told him—" Alex looked up into the lieutenant's eyes. "I—I couldn't do it. I couldn't face more death. I had men still trying to decide which side of the Pearly Gates they were going to end up on right there in camp and I was shaky. My hands wouldn't quit shaking and I—I hadn't slept since the siege. I had nightmares if I even dozed off. I was barely able to keep up with the job I had there. But the colonel said they needed me and I had to go."

Alex remembered refusing, maybe begging. It was all a blur. "In Palo Duro, it was Colonel MacKenzie's Fourth Cavalry that took on Iron Shirt and his Cheyenne, and there were Comanches and Kiowas there, too. The cavalry captured a whole village. There were a thousand or more people in that village. Most of the women and children were fine, but a few were hurt. I tried to see to them, but I was ordered to tend the cavalry first. Women and children suffered and died while I bandaged scratches."

Alex ran a shaking hand deep into his hair. "And there were

a thousand horses. We slaughtered them to keep them from the Indians. I heard the shots where they were killed and the screaming of the horses. And the wounded kept coming. I saw them fall on the battlefield and I went to them, trying to bring them back behind infantry lines. Then I—I was hit. Shrapnel from somewhere. It wasn't a bullet wound, I don't think. The scars on my back don't look like bullets. I didn't even know I'd been hit until later. But I was tending a man. . ." Alex's voice faded as he saw that man dying under his hands, trying to put himself back together, and the blood and entrails dangling from Alex's doctor's bag.

Alex dragged himself back to the quiet room. "Death everywhere."

Give me strength, Lord. Give me strength.

"I ran. Or I suppose I ran. I don't remember it very well. Someone told me later I'd been shot and that man did what doctoring he could. I don't know where I was. Far from the battlefield by then. I don't know if it was hours or days or weeks later." Alex looked up. "I did it, sir. I cracked under pressure and ran like a coward and never went back. I couldn't do it anymore. I couldn't be a doctor. I couldn't have any more blood on my hands. And the army wouldn't let me stop."

"So you were shot in the back while you were running away?" The lieutenant sounded as merciless as that battle.

"No, sir, I don't think so. I think it was from our own side. Maybe a ricochet. Like I said, I didn't even know I'd been wounded until later. I had to wade out into that battlefield to help the men who were down. I was ahead of our troops. It was our own cavalry weapons. It happens in war. It's madness."

Trying to bring himself fully back to the room, Alex found Beth, holding his hand in a viselike grip that hurt now that he was aware of it. He reached with his free hand and caught hold of her, two of his hands entwined with one of hers. "Beth honey, I'm so sorry. I'm sorry you found yourself bound to a coward."

Her grip eased. She'd been using the pain of her grip to drag him back to the present.

Alex wondered how much of his cowardice had shown in this room.

"You were with Colonel MacKenzie at Palo Duro?" Deuel asked, his voice sounding tight, strained. His face flushed red.

"Yes, sir, I was." Alex's heart sped up at the rage boiling out of the lieutenant.

"My brother was with the company on that supply train. He'd been mending, but after Palo Duro, he had no medical care. He died a few days after Palo Duro." Deuel's words landed like stones on Alex's already battered conscience.

Another person died because of him. How many had he failed *before* he'd run away? How many *after*?

Beth's grip on his hand tightened.

Alex swallowed, but it felt like something hard and unmovable had lodged in his throat.

"My brother died for want of your medical attention."

Silence held firm in the room. If Alex had a chance when he'd entered the room, that chance had just died as surely as the lieutenant's brother.

"I find you guilty, Captain Buchanan." The lieutenant's fist slammed on the desk with the force of final judgment. Without taking his burning eyes off Alex, Deuel said, "I'll decide your punishment by the end of the day. If I have my way, you'll be facing a firing squad with the sunrise, doctor."

Lieutenant Deuel's words hit as hard as the shrapnel that had been the final blow to Alex on that long ago day.

"No." Beth threw her arms around Alex. "You can't do this."

Alex pulled her tight against him and felt her hot tears brush against his face as he held her.

"Lock him up," the lieutenant shouted.

Someone grabbed Alex's arm and he let go of Beth.

She clung to his neck, crying.

"It's all right, Beth. Don't cry. Don't waste your heart on me."

"And lock the rest of them up, too." The lieutenant snapped his fingers as if he held the power of life and death over all of them and delighted in using his power—and abusing it. "All of them. Slaughter and all three of the McClellens."

"Th–the women, too, Lieutendant Deuel—sir?" The man holding Alex's arm stuttered, and Alex saw a surprising amount of fear in the young man's face. Not the respect and obedience expected toward a superior officer, but cold, trembling fear.

"Yes, the women, too. And you carry out those orders without further question, private, or I might just throw you in with them when I line the lot of them up in the morning."

"What?" Alex erupted.

Beth gasped.

"Calm," the private whispered to Alex. "Obey him."

The private pulled Alex so they were headed for the door. With their backs turned to the lieutenant, he whispered, "He won't do it. At least he don't mean it about the McClellens being shot."

Both men holding Alex nearly dragged him out of the office. He looked and caught Beth's eye.

She'd risen to her feet and now looked anxiously after him.

He needed Beth. In the second their eyes held, he realized that, yes, Beth had stayed by his side during his doctoring, but she'd been close every moment.

He thought of that first night in Clay's bunkhouse. The first time he'd tried to sleep after Beth stormed into his life and forced him to use his healing skills. The nightmares had come when Beth was gone.

He'd never spent another night alone. Nor another day. It wasn't just during medical treatment that he was one wrong thought away from sinking into his nightmares. It was all the time.

Knowing he was going to be locked away from her twisted inside of him, unlocking his nightmares. Blood, horses screaming. "No! Beth!" He heard himself shout but wasn't sure if he spoke the words aloud or if the cry came only on the inside.

He wrenched away, but the soldiers had too firm of a grip on him. They dragged Alex out, and the door slapped shut behind him.

They were in a small outer office, with a soldier sitting with his hands clutched together at a secretary's desk. "What'd he do now?" the lieutenant's aide asked.

"He ordered this man executed," the private said.

Alex fought to listen, fought to understand the words being spoken.

"Get a wire off to the nearest fort with a commanding officer who outranks him," the private said. "Do it quick before he can stop you."

That made no sense. Alex shook his head and heard the bullets whizzing past.

The man behind the desk dashed out of the room. Alex's two escorts followed.

"My wife. I need Beth." Alex hated the sound of his voice. Desperate, cowardly, broken.

God, I'm broken. You heal the brokenhearted. Help me, Lord Jesus Christ. Give me strength.

Once they were outside, the men said, "He's crazy."

Jerking his head up, Alex hated it that they knew. "I'm crazy?" He needed to beg them to forgive him, beg the men he'd killed to forgive him. Beg Beth. Beg her parents. Beg everyone to forgive him.

"Not you, Doc. We mean the lieutenant. He's crazy on the subject of his brother. And it's gone straight to his head bein' in charge of this fort. He's been throwing around any orders he can think of since afore the dust settled on the colonel's trail. We'll do somethin', Doc. We can stop this."

"Stop this?" Alex only barely understood what they were saying, but he struggled to keep his nightmares at bay.

"And that Cletus Slaughter, the colonel hates him. He's brought in more deserters draped over his saddle than any other man in the West. Decent men who'd just had enough or had trouble at home. War can break a man, Doc. You're not the first. I ain't seen much fightin'."

The man escorting Alex was younger, but he had the weathered skin of a frontier soldier. Kind eyes, but smart, like he'd seen a lot of hard living. But he'd let it make him wise instead of broken.

"But I've seen a bit of it. And I think—I think. . ." The man fell silent and the silence drew Alex, helped him get a better grip on the here and now and pull him out of the past. "I think many's the man who—to break—to reach a breakin' point and walk away—well, sir, I think that might be a kind of courage some of us never find."

Shaking his head, Alex said, "No. I ran. I was a coward. Men died."

"A lot of men ran. They don't deserve to be shot in the back by the likes of Slaughter. He's been makin' good money with the army's rewards. If the colonel was here, I'm not sayin' he wouldn't punish you, but this is crazy, crazy. Not even a proper military trial. And to threaten your family, who brought you in. Two of 'em shot. The lieutenant's mad as a cornered he-coon when it comes to his brother. If you'd have been brought in for somethin' else, he might'a just let you walk right out. That ain't justice. Not to my mind."

The men hustled Alex down the long row of buildings until they came to one with bars on the windows. They took him inside and had him inside a cell with the doors clanging shut before he could comprehend all they'd said.

"What about my wife?" He turned, the panic that Beth could be hurt by this insanity making him desperate. Even more desperate than his separation from her.

God, please, please, please, give me strength.

"We'll try to fix it, Doc. If nothing else, we'll break you out tonight and hide you somewhere until the colonel comes back."

Shaking his head, Alex said, "That's insubordination. Maybe even treason to aid an arrested deserter. I can't let you commit a crime to protect me." Alex was now possibly going to *escape* from prison? The only clear thought that came to his muddled head was to wonder what the punishment was for that stacked on top of being a deserter?

"We'll see that your family is treated right, Doc." One of the men opened the door to leave Alex alone in the cell.

The world faded around him. The jail cell, the walls, the hard cot. He heard horses neigh in pain, rifle fire split the air. Clinging to this awful place he asked, "Will my wife and her parents be locked up in here where we can be close?"

If only they'd come, he could hang on. He could stay here, away from his nightmares.

"Doubt it," the soldier who'd done all the talking said. "The lieutenant might see that as being too kindhearted. And this fort is mighty empty. We've got plenty of empty lockups."

Alex's knees gave out as the two men left and he sank down on his hard cot. He saw a man already dead but still too dumb to know it, trying to put his eviscerated body back together. Blood everywhere. Horses screaming and dying. The impact of bullets hitting his back. He fell forward onto the stone floor of the cell.

And now he was alone. He looked down and saw his hands crimson and dripping blood.

God, please give me strength.

And he saw Beth and the crimson faded.

Alex clung to that vision of her, knowing it was given to him by a loving, compassionate God.

★ Thirty-one ★

Mandy, I want to talk to you. . .just you." Sidney threw a scalding look at the men watching them fight.

Protect me, dear God.

Mandy was humiliated by the knowledge that she'd married Sidney and didn't know him at all. But they did have to make a decision. Mandy's first instinct was to simply walk away. She knew Luther would escort her home, back to her parents.

She also knew that she was a married woman. She'd taken those vows before God. She'd meant them with all her heart, a vow to forsake all others and cleave only unto her husband. Until death do them part. She had a sudden, very satisfying fantasy about Sidney being parted from her by death—she was doing the *parting* using her bare hands.

Glaring at him, she pulled herself back to the problem of the moment. "Yes, I think that's wise."

Turning to Luther, she saw the stubbornness that had brought Luther to an old age fighting in Texas and before that in these rugged, beautiful Rocky Mountains. He was a hard man to budge.

"Please, Luther. Sidney and I do need to have this out, and we need to do it in private."

Rebellion shone out of Luther's eyes. For a second, Mandy wondered if he'd take this decision out of her hands and haul her home against her will.

She almost wished he would. Being an adult and making her own decisions was proving to be vexing beyond belief.

If she walked away from Sidney, she could never again marry. After all, she had a husband. And that meant she could never hope for a family of her own. Which brought it fully into mind that she could well have the beginning of that family already. She only resisted resting her hand on her stomach by sheer willpower.

And the next thought followed perfectly after that—if she did have the beginning of a baby, that baby would have a pure weasel for a father. What kind of thing was that to do to a child?

She held Luther's gaze.

Finally, scowling, he rose from his chair. "I'll let you talk." Luther turned those hard eyes on Sidney. The heavy graying brows lowered. "But one thing I won't do, whatever you decide, is leave. You can talk to her all day long, but the way I see it, Mandy is gonna need help until she's ready to head home without you. Or, if you talk her into stayin', she'll need help teaching you how to be a man. And I reckon it falls to me to be that help whatever she chooses."

Luther went to the door and opened it, but he turned back to Sidney. Mandy saw a trace of kindness in Luther's expression. "Instead of mining for gold, Sid, you need to learn hunting. Learn to build furniture and cut firewood. Learn to tan a hide and bust up ground for a garden. Or you need to go into Helena and start up your lawyering, if you really *are* a lawyer. Whether you are or not, there are jobs for a man in a rugged country like this, if he's not afraid to work."

Luther's tone said very clearly he expected Sidney to be afraid. "Either way, you've got some growing up to do, boy."

Sidney flushed and looked away with his usual sullen expression.

Mandy's heart sank to think of just how much growing up her husband had to do. She wasn't sure he had enough time, even if he lived to be ninety.

Buff followed Luther outside and shut the door quietly.

Mandy turned to Sidney, and they just looked for a while, staring into each other's eyes.

Mandy had so much to say she didn't know where to start.

She wished Sidney would do the starting, but she realized he never had. He'd listened and shared his dreams, and he'd poured on the charm, but he'd never done much talking about important, sensible things.

And Mandy was, at the very root of her soul, a sensible woman. "I guess you've got nothing to say to me about this woman? Is that right, Sidney? Is that what I can figure out from your silence?"

"I've told you the truth. That woman is just someone I knew back a few years. I did not marry her. She's crazy. I knew she kept following me around. That's part of the reason I came West—to leave her behind. But I had no idea she was crazy enough to follow me all that way, fake those papers." Sidney glowered at Mandy as if daring her to doubt him.

"So if I do as Luther said and send back East for details on Sidney and Celeste Gray, the names on this marriage license, with dates and the name of the judge and the courthouse where you said your vows, I'll find out there was never any such marriage, is that right?"

"That's right." Sidney's eyes shifted to the side and Mandy knew he was bluffing. A bit nicer word than *lying*, but really no different.

Mandy nodded, silent, as she let the pain flow over her. "Okay, well, that's what I'm going to do. So, until I hear word back from the East, we will not live together as man and wife. We'll stay here and run this homestead and wait for word."

"You owe me your loyalty, *Mrs. Gray*. You swore *vows* to me, standing before *God*, and the first time you have to choose between me and your family, you pick *them*. What kind of vows are those?"

"I owe *you* loyalty?" Mandy would have laughed in his face if the pain hadn't been so great. "What kind of a husband are you? What kind of vows did *you* swear to? You've *never* told me about your childhood. Or what little you've told is vague and probably half falsehood. You know everything about me and I know nothing about you. Was your father really at Shiloh? Did you really go to Yale?"

"I have no idea who my father is." Sidney flung his arms wide and whirled away from her. "My mother was a *dance hall* girl. She didn't work above a *store*. She worked above a *saloon*! My father could have been a dozen men, maybe a hun—" Sidney's voice broke and he sank into a chair. Sobs broke from his throat and his head hung as if it weighed a hundred pounds and his neck couldn't bear the weight.

Mandy was aghast. Her husband was *crying*. She'd never heard of such a thing. Men didn't cry. Compassion for her husband welled up in her. She did love him. Love didn't die in a day. It could be badly wounded, the pleasure could turn to pain, but the love was still there.

But she was a sensible girl—no, woman. All the compassion in the world couldn't make her close her eyes to her husband's treachery. She went up to him and rested her hands on his heaving shoulders.

He was quiet now, a shudder racked his body.

"Know this, Sidney Gray, I am giving you a chance, right now, to tell me the whole truth. I love you and we can start again from this point with honesty between us. But if you've lied to me, I'm not talking about before today, if you lie to me *today* about being married to that woman, our marriage is over. I'm giving you a chance to tell me the plain, flat-out truth and nothing but. But if you persist in your lies until we get word from Boston—"

"I was married to her." Sidney's voice was so low, Mandy could hardly hear it. But she heard. Oh yes, she heard the words that slit her soul deep. "Yes, the truth is I was married to Celeste. She's all the things I said she was and our marriage was a terrible mistake. She was crazy, dangerous. I left her. I ran away nearly three years ago, and I've been wandering ever since." Sidney lifted his head and twisted in his chair to look at Mandy.

"She pursued me in the East until I finally headed to Texas to escape her for good." Sidney took her hands where they now rested on the back of his chair. "It's not fair that I'm bound to her for life. I don't love her. I can't be held to a promise I made without knowing what I was promising."

"Like I was," Mandy said quietly.

Sidney's eyes fell shut. "I love you, Mandy. I never knew what love was until I met you. I love your decency, your kindness, your faith."

"My faith?" Mandy asked.

Sidney had always accompanied her to church. She had assumed he shared her faith. But why would that be the one area where he'd told the truth?

"Yes." Sidney pressed a kiss on her hands, where they were entwined with his, then rose to stand before her. "I learned something from sitting with you in that church. I learned about God in a way I never had before." His eyes met hers dead-on. "I'm a changed man, Mandy. I did a lot of things in my growing-up years I'm not proud of. But I've asked God to forgive me for them. Celeste was so far in my past—"

"You married me knowing you were already married?" Mandy felt dirty and stained.

"And my life was so new. I felt forgiven even for my foolish marriage. Please, Mandy, please give me a chance to be the husband I can be. I've felt so awful with the lies I was holding inside. Now that the truth is known, I can really share my life with you and be closer to you." He slid one arm around her waist. "We truly are married. You can no more deny that than I could honestly deny my own marriage. Please give me a chance. Say you still love me enough to try and go on together."

She felt stained—like a sinner. She needed to forgive Sidney just as God had forgiven her. But how could a woman forgive such a thing?

"Judge not, and ye shall not be judged: condemn not, and ye shall

287

not be condemned: forgive, and ye shall be forgiven."

Mandy knew that verse well. And she knew, to the extent anyone could know, that Sidney was speaking from his heart. But how could they go on? How could she feel any affection for him?

Sidney wrapped his arms around her and she felt a frisson of dread, but she let him pull her close. She tried, with considerable might, to forgive him and find a way to go on with her marriage.

Protect me, Lord. Protect me from all of this, what I feel for him and what I don't feel. Help me know what to do.

At last she got control of the turmoil in her mind and she straightened away from her husband. Looking him square in the eye she said, "If you mean what you say about honesty, then I will stay with you. But we are going to have to *both* be honest."

"Wh–what do you mean? Have you been dishonest, too?" He looked almost eager, as if hoping he wasn't the only sinner in the family.

"Yes, I have been dishonest. I've been very unhappy with you since we've gotten married, and instead of telling you, I've ignored it and acted content. But that's over now. Now I start telling you exactly what I think. And you are going to *listen*."

"What you think?" Sidney's brows arched nearly to his hairline.

"Yes. I know this life is new to you, but there are things a man needs to do on a homestead and you're not doing them. I'm going to teach you how to live in a cabin on the frontier and you're going to learn."

That sulky look crossed Sidney's face.

"No! Stop that right now."

"Stop what? I didn't say anything."

"I can see you being annoyed. I can see you taking offense at my words. Well, too bad. You're going to let me and Luther and Buff teach you the skills you need to survive a Rocky Mountain winter. And I expect you to cooperate and learn. I think we've already proven that you're not doing all that well making your own decisions. Mining for gold is a waste and you're going to have to do it in your spare time. Chores come first."

"What chores?"

He honestly didn't know.

"Didn't you notice all the wood that's been split? Didn't you notice there's no breeze in our cabin anymore?" Mandy swallowed hard, but honesty worked both ways. "A man rode in to look at the foal. His stallion sired the little colt. That man, Tom Linscott, said he appreciated that we were taking care of the little guy and in thanks he chopped a winter's worth of wood."

At that moment the strike of an ax rang out. Mandy knew without looking that either Luther or Buff had gone to work on the remaining cords of wood. The two of them were unable to stand around idling when there was work to be done.

"What do you say, Sidney? Are you going to be a real husband? A good husband? Or are you going to run off on me, like you did Celeste, and go find someone else to marry?"

Sidney stared at her, his lips curled in discontent. But he didn't leave and he didn't sulk. Finally, he said, "Yes, I'll do what you ask. I'll try harder to be a good husband. I know nothing of life out here—hunting, building, caring for animals. But I'll learn. You have my word on that. And right now, my word is worth nothing. But I do love you, Mandy, and I promise you'll never regret giving me this chance."

Mandy nodded and let Sidney pull her back into his arms, though she disliked his touch and was tempted to say so. But she didn't. And well, she realized that not saying so was a kind of lie. But she didn't tell the truth that pressed to escape her lips.

And then another truth made itself known and remained unspoken.

She already regretted agreeing to stay with her husband.

★ Thirty-two ★

Thank you, Lieutenant, for getting him away from me." Beth turned, wearing a smile she hoped looked genuine.

Ma gave a tiny gasp of surprise, but Ma was quick. She suppressed the noise and simply nodded her head. "Terrible mistake to let that troubled man into the family. I can't imagine he was much good to the war effort."

Both of them had been around men all their lives. Beth recognized the lieutenant's type. Well, she'd just see if she could use the man's taste for cruelty to her advantage.

Beth turned calmly back to face forward and lowered herself smoothly into her chair, folding her hands as if she was settling in for a tea party. The truth was just the opposite. She'd seen Alex. Knew he was on the brink. He needed her. And she needed him just as much. "It's true we're married, sir, but I didn't know his nature when we were wed."

The lieutenant's odd, light-colored eyes focused on her with a hungry look, as if he'd found a new repository for his sadism.

"I'm relieved to finally be free of him." Beth shuddered. It wasn't even fake. Lieutenant Deuel's eyes were enough to make a snake shudder. "Thank you. If you're going to lock me up, please, I'm begging you, don't put me anywhere near that awful man."

The door clanged shut with a metallic bang, Beth locked in

with Alex, just as she'd known that sadistic jerk would do. Beth stood pressed against the bars, as far from Alex as she could get, until the soldier left them alone. "Alex, I'm here." She rushed to his side, dropped down, and wrapped her arms around him.

He was on his knees. It took mere moments for him to respond. "Beth honey?"

The gray pallor of his skin and haunted eyes nearly broke her heart. The more she heard about what he'd endured during the war, the more compassion she had. She knew her own backbone. It was pure iron, and she strengthened it with regular prayer. But his tales of blood and death and exhaustion, in a man so tuned to healing, made her wonder if she wouldn't have broken, too.

She noted how quickly he responded to her. He'd not been as lost in the past as other times.

"Alex, they're locking us up together."

"I was praying." Alex's eyes fell shut and he shook his head as if trying to throw away the traces of his thoughts. "I think—I think I'd have been okay. It was pressing against me, the nightmares, but I kept praying and kept thinking of you."

Beth cut off his words by kissing the daylights out of him. She was still kissing him when she heard a throat clear loudly. She lifted her head to see her parents standing in the nearby cell, their arms crossed. Ma's toe tapped impatiently.

"He okay now?" Pa asked.

"Yes." Beth looked at Alex and she saw the strength there. He was still connected to her in that strange and wonderful way. But he wasn't trying to draw on her strength. He had his own.

She stood and helped Alex to his feet. Then the two of them sat on the single cot, and Ma and Pa did the same on their side of the bars.

"Now, you wanted us locked in here with him, isn't that right?" Ma asked.

Beth managed a smile, though she couldn't put much of her heart into it. "Yes, I did."

"How'd you manage that?" Alex asked. "The lieutenant looked

like he'd delight in denying any request."

"I saw that, too. That's why I told him I was thrilled at the thought of your being locked away from me." She smiled.

Alex rolled his eyes and wrapped his arms around her. "Great. So now he thinks I'm so awful my wife hates me."

"Well, admit it, Alex, the man had already decided to stand you up in front of a firing squad at sunrise. His opinion really couldn't have sunk any lower."

"So the extent of your plan was just to get us locked up in here?" Pa asked.

Beth shrugged. "I was pretty sure Alex would need me."

"I thought maybe you'd figured out a way to get us out of this mess."

Shaking her head, Beth said, "Nope."

Then Ma stood from the cot and walked over to grab the bars that separated them. Beth had seen that gleam in her ma's eyes plenty of times before. It was always a good sign.

"Then it's a good thing I've got an idea." Ma smirked.

"I have married myself a wily woman." Pa came up beside her and slid an arm around her. "Tell me how we're gonna set a booby trap for this guy from inside our jail cell."

"First, we need Beth's doctor's bag." Ma looked at Pa.

"I got the feeling the soldiers who are serving under the lieutenant aren't real happy with him." Pa turned toward the door.

"One of them offered to help me escape," Alex said. "Then do a real bad job of hunting for me until the colonel gets back. So, I'd say you're right about that."

"Really, escape?" Beth asked. "But then you'd be a wanted man for something new."

"Yeah, that's all I need." Alex shook his head.

"Besides putting any soldier who helped you at risk," Sophie added.

"I had the same thought, which is why I didn't tell him I'd do it."

"Well, if that disgruntled soldier will help you escape, then he ought to be willing to bring Beth's bag." Ma quirked a smile. "And he'd probably let me and my poor mistreated daughter out of here and allow us to help the colonel's wife cook supper."

Alex saw matching looks of disgust to think of the food they'd been eating. "It sounded like she might be fired before supper."

"No, I met her in the hall, when we were being taken out, and talked to her for a minute. She's an excellent cook. Or so she says. She apologized for the food we've gotten. The man escorting us to the jail agreed. He said we got the wrong meal. Leftovers from a meal she'd prepared strictly for the lieutenant. Since he's the only one who doesn't come in to eat, instead insisting a meal be delivered to him, they dipped ours out of the same pot as his."

"I saw you whispering to her," Clay said. "And the soldier said something about the food. Why's she cooking bad on purpose?"

"Lieutenant Deuel growled at her over a dirty fork the first day after her husband left. She's been torturing him with dreadful food ever since."

Beth smiled. Alex would have, too, if he wasn't facing a firing squad at dawn.

"And now you're going to help her cook for that arrogant little pup to try and cheer him up?" Clay arched a brow at his wife.

"No, I'm thinking of what Beth said when Laurie handed her Dover's Powder, when Alex was ready to cut Sally's throat."

There was an extended silence. Alex could barely remember operating on Sally.

Clay broke the silence. "That is a sneaky thing to do, Sophie McClellen." He didn't sound that upset, and the smile on his face took all the bite out of his words.

"I know, Clay. I'm so ashamed of myself I can barely stand my own company." Sophie sounded like an extremely repentant Southern belle. Beth knew her ma was neither Southern nor a belle, and she didn't have a repentant bone in her body, at least not about this.

Clay smiled. "So, what can I do to help?"

"You can't give him Dover's Powder. That'll make him sick as a dog." Alex shouldn't have bothered to say that out loud, since that was obviously the whole point. But he was a doctor. He'd sworn an oath to do no harm.

Still, it wasn't as if the lieutenant would be sick all that long.

"If we're lucky." Sophie gave Alex a fond—if slightly evil—smile. "Then you, the only doctor for miles around, will jump in and save his worthless hide."

"Hey, I'm a doctor, too," Beth protested.

Sophie glared at Beth.

Who immediately figured out what her ma wanted. "Except tomorrow I'm going to be a helpless little female, one who couldn't hold her own in a pillow fight, let alone a gunfight, and who would faint dead away if asked to tend the tiniest scratch." Beth felt a little Southern belle-ish herself.

Sophie nodded.

"I can't *save* him from Dover's Powder." Alex wondered at his new mother-in-law. "He's just gotta throw it all up."

"When I was growing up, there was a neighbor lady who called herself an old-timey healer. She did a fair job, too. I remember her bringing us a cure every time we got a bad cold."

"There's no cure for a cold." Alex crossed his arms, impatient with quack doctors.

Sophie moved closer to the bars. "It worked every time."

"What did she give you?" Alex felt his pulse speed up. Had someone really found a cure for the common cold? It would soothe the ills of thousands of people. It would—

"She'd leave this nasty-tasting, gluey paste, and we'd take it faithfully three times a day. She also ordered us to rest and stay warm and drink plenty of fluids. And we'd be well in a week or ten days."

Alex coughed then laughed. It felt good considering the dire situation.

Sophie's smile got a bit darker. "No one says your cure will be instantaneous. And while you're *curing* him, he'll be so busy casting up my perfectly tasty dinner, he'll be too busy to issue any execution orders at sunrise."

"He might even decide he owes you his life." Clay ran his hand down Sophie's back.

Alex went to the window of his cell—which he noticed at that moment was standing slightly open. There were bars, but a heavy key was set into the lock.

He caught the eye of the soldier who withdrew his hand from the key quickly and turned to look away as if he hadn't noticed a thing.

"I'm not escaping." Alex pushed the window wider so he could talk with the soldier.

"Didn't say you were, sir." The recruit tried to look innocent.

"You can take the key back now."

"What key?" the man asked, looking straight at the key.

"But if you wanted to save my family a lot of grief, you could let my wife and her ma out of here. They'd be willing to help with the cooking."

The young man furrowed his brow for a minute. Then his expression cleared. "They want to cook for the lieutenant just like the colonel's wife does, huh?"

"I didn't say any such thing."

The soldier grinned, took the key out of the bars, still standing open, and quickly came around to enter the jail. "I think I'd be within my rights to. . .assign these two ladies to a. . .a. . .work detail. Give 'em hard labor to punish them for their crimes."

"Quite right," Sophie said. "And if it's no trouble, we'd appreciate stopping by our rooms. We have need of my son's doctor's bag, too."

"Why, no trouble at all, Miz McClellen." The soldier turned the key in Alex's cell door to let Beth out. He then turned to the cell holding Sophie and Clay. The young man didn't even pretend to relock either door. He hung the key on the wall in plain sight of his prisoners, too.

Alex rolled his eyes.

"I'd be glad to let you pick up that bag, ma'am. Is there anything else you'd like?"

"Well, you could tell us exactly what the lieutenant said to the colonel's wife to inspire the meals we've eaten since we arrived at the fort." Sophie left the room, with the eager soldier at her side.

Beth turned back, looked at the jail doors swung wide, shook her head, and followed after her mother.

★ Thirty-three ★

Not so much, Ma."

She watched her mother pour the Dover's Powder into the stew the colonel's wife had concocted for the lieutenant. Ma mercifully only treated Deuel's food, sparing the rest of the camp.

"Now, lassie, we don't want to give him too little either. I'd be after usin' a heavy hand." Colonel McGarritt's wife had also proved to be an eager co-conspirator. "Why, there's opium in that, you say? He'll need to be ridding his stomach of the vile stuff."

Beth was utterly unsurprised at the woman's opinion. She'd done nothing but rail against Lieutenant Deuel since she and her ma had come in. Plus the whole idea of cooking swill for the lieutenant revealed a cruel streak. Not that Beth didn't agree with the woman.

"I still don't see why we had to waste good food on that'n." Paula McGarritt had proved to be a kindred spirit. "Waste of good meat it is."

"He'll be more likely to eat it. He didn't finish his dinner." Sophie looked up from her witch's brew and smiled. "I reckon your feelings were hurt by that."

Paula started laughing. Beth was very glad the woman wasn't mad at her.

They stirred the powder in, and Paula called out to the waiting soldier, "Take the lieutenant his food."

Beth insisted on carrying the food in to the lieutenant, feeling that, since she was breaking her oath as a doctor, not that she'd been allowed to take it but in her heart she'd embraced her healing vows, then she ought to face up to the bad feelings that might come of this.

Sophie accompanied her.

"What are you two doing out of your cells?"

"We got put on work detail, Lieutenant Deuel." Ma acted put upon, like she'd been chiseling hard rock all day.

"Hmph." Deuel sniffed. "Well done. I'll have to remember to congratulate my jailer."

Then he saw the food and his eyes widened and he smiled. "Well done indeed." He took his first bite with gusto.

Beth's heart beat a little too hard.

"By the way, ladies, I apologize for my actions before." He plowed through the meal as if he hadn't eaten in weeks. Which was very possible.

"Apologize?" Beth quit watching the food go down his gullet. "What for?"

"Why, for losing my temper with your husband of course, Mrs. Buchanan. I was so furious about his possibly neglecting my brother."

Half the plate was empty now, and the lieutenant showed no signs of slowing down. How much of that *had* Ma poured in?

"I, of course, have no intention of having him shot at dawn."

Ma's hand shot out and she stopped the fork before the lieutenant swallowed another bite.

"Beth, I see a...uh...a fly in the lieutenant's plate." Ma grabbed the plate, thrust it at Beth, and said, "Get some fresh food."

"No." The lieutenant made a grab for the plate. "I saw no fly. It's fine. It's delicious. In fact, you can have the job of cooking from now until we sort this business out with the doctor. And naturally none of you will be charged with a crime. You brought the man in. In fact, I suspect you'll be given the reward. Dr. Buchanan will have to sit through a regular military court and we'll need to wait until the colonel comes back."

The lieutenant paused in his efforts to retrieve his plate. His hands went to his stomach. "How strange. I may have—" The man stood from his place at his desk and rounded it.

Beth had a pretty good idea where he was heading.

"Excuse me, ladies. I believe I ate my food a bit too fast." He bolted from the room, holding one hand over his mouth and the other clutching his midsection.

"You follow him," Ma ordered Beth. "I'll go get the doctor."

Ma rushed out, then when Beth followed only steps behind, they heard the sound of retching from around the corner of the building.

"That stuff couldn't kill him, could it?" Ma asked.

A terrible groan of agony rang in the settling dusk.

Beth shook her head. "No. Impossible."

"Help. I'm dying!" Deuel nearly screamed. Then the retching started again.

Ma shouted, "My son is a doctor. He'll save you." She turned to look at Beth and shrugged her shoulders and whispered, "Well, he will."

Ma could have shouted her little comment to Beth since the lieutenant was so loud a herd of rampaging buffalo could storm by and no one would notice over the ruckus Deuel was causing.

"Just go get Alex."

Beth ran in the direction of the lieutenant, but she was careful to round the corner cautiously. No sense getting too close to a vomiting man with a full stomach.

★

Alex spent the next week treating so many small complaints at the fort that he about decided the cavalry was comprised exclusively of a pack of whiners. Either that or the soldiers all wanted a peek at Lieutenant Deuel lying prostrate in bed.

But the lieutenant was up and about finally, and Colonel McGarritt summoned Alex to his office. It was time to face justice. Dreading it, but also glad it was over, Alex washed up from sewing up Mrs. McGarritt's thumb. She'd cut it slicing potatoes.

"Let me help straighten your collar." Beth fussed over him and the colonel's wife did her share of advising, too. She'd taken an immense liking to the whole McClellen/Buchanan clan since they'd pulled her into their Dover's Powder conspiracy.

Mrs. McGarritt went ahead to summon Sophie and Clay. Alex and Beth met them at the door to the colonel's office. The four of them walked in, in time to hear Cletus Slaughter haranguing Colonel McGarritt with his charges against Alex and his family.

"Sit down, Mr. Slaughter. It's best you know that every word out of your mouth makes me more determined to find an excuse to lock you up."

Growling like a whipped dog, Cletus settled into his chair on the far left. The setup was the same as before, but the chairs were simply shoved into a line. If one chair was at an angle or a few inches farther back, no one seemed to notice or care.

"Hello, major." The colonel stood and extended a hand to Clay. The man's full head of white hair surrounded a weathered face with lines that turned up when he smiled. "I was with McCook's Army of Ohio at the Battle of Shiloh. Doubt you remember. I was a sergeant back then."

"I was with Grant. You and Buell's men saved us from a terrible defeat." Clay shook the man's hand with real warmth, and Alex wondered how anyone could come away from war as steady as his father-in-law. Hopefully, McGarritt was just as steady.

Give me strength, Lord.

Alex prayed as he sat down, and he happened to glance at Beth and see her lips move in the same prayer he'd just sent heavenward.

She was thinking the same thing and her eyes flashed with love and encouragement and strength.

"Now, I've been somewhat apprised of the situation, gentlemen, through the report of Lieutenant Deuel. And...uh...well, my wife told me her version. The two stories are quite different." Colonel McGarritt sat down and folded his hands together on papers on his desk. He turned blue, piercing eyes to Alex.

Swallowing hard, Alex knew that from this man he would get fair treatment and justice. But justice might be very harsh.

"You were at the siege by Camp Supply and the Battle of Buffalo Wallow and Palo Duro?"

Alex nodded. "Yes, I ran. In the middle of the fighting at Palo Duro, I—I just snapped. I ran. I deserted, sir. I admit it and will take whatever punishment you deem necessary."

"But Palo Duro was the end of it. There were no more battles after that. And you'd put in your time and then some. Stayed on because of the need, I see from your records."

"You have my military records?" Alex frowned. "I didn't serve here."

"No, but my wife wired Fort Dodge and they sent your records here. They arrived a day or two ago. If you'd have just ridden back to the fort, they'd have probably mustered you out on the spot. Or soon after."

Alex didn't understand what that had to do with it. "I didn't ride back. That's the whole point."

Colonel McGarritt turned to Slaughter. "And you were going to bring him in dead, is that right? Did you even attempt to arrest him? He's obviously shown a willingness to cooperate."

With a snort of disgust, Slaughter said, "Nothin' on that poster that finds any fault with the dead part of 'dead or alive'."

"Well, there's something pure wrong with you shooting two law-abiding citizens from cover. You're going to jail, Mr. Slaughter."

"No!" Slaughter lunged at the colonel.

Clay stopped him in his tracks. Two men standing sentry leapt forward and forced him, howling, back into his chair.

"I have been forced to put up with your cruelty with deserters."

The colonel rose from his seat and jabbed a finger at Slaughter. "But I will not stand by while you shoot a young woman and her father just because they're standing close to a man you want to arrest." The colonel looked at his sentry. "Take him away. We'll decide on a sentence later. But I'd like to see him burn in Yuma for the rest of his life."

Slaughter roared and struggled against the ruthless grip on his arms. They could still hear his shouting as he was dragged away from the building.

"Colonel, I'd like to say something before you go on with your questioning." Beth's voice echoed with strength and kindness and compassion. Even in this situation, Alex felt soothed by her miraculous voice.

"Of course, Mrs. Buchanan." The colonel relaxed back into his desk chair.

"I don't know exactly the rules about desertion, but I know my husband has mentioned being hit by shrapnel. I don't think anyone, including Alex, understands just how badly wounded he was."

"Beth, no." Alex touched her arm. "I won't let you make excuses for me."

Beth patted his hand. "No one in the room, except me, has seen his back. He believes he ran off, deserted. But he also admits he doesn't remember anything for some time after the last battle. His wounds are far more grievous than he lets on. I don't believe he made a thoughtful decision to desert. I think he staggered off the battlefield, shot and bleeding. There are scars on his scalp. He probably had a concussion. I don't think he made a choice to leave. The only crime he's guilty of is, much later, when he came to himself, haunted by what he'd survived, he didn't come back. That may be desertion, but you need to understand he didn't run off, afraid of battle."

"Let's see these scars, doctor." The colonel's eyes narrowed as if he thought Beth was lying.

Reluctantly, but to support his wife, Alex stood, turned his back on the gathering, and unbuttoned his shirt.

Then Beth moved behind him and lifted his undershirt up from the waist.

Alex heard Sophie gasp. Even Clay and the colonel drew their breath in hard. Alex looked over his shoulder and saw horror on the colonel's face and sad resolve on Beth's.

"Are they really that bad?" It was a plain, bald fact that Alex had never spent much time trying to see his back in a mirror.

"They're deep and there are dozens of them." The colonel nodded his head. "It's not even mentioned in the report that you were wounded, not a single word about the shrapnel."

"If he hadn't stumbled off and kept going, he'd have been in the care of a doctor rather than being a doctor. I doubt he'd have been able to treat anyone." Beth's strong, gentle fingers brushed over his hair just above his nape. "If you'll look closer, there are a half dozen more scars on his scalp."

"No, I'll take your word for it, ma'am." Colonel McGarritt leaned back in his chair, rubbing one hand over his clean-shaven chin. "Give me a minute to sort this out."

Alex donned his shirt and did his best to tuck it in and return himself to a tidy state. He sat, holding Beth's hand, feeling as if the Sword of Damocles was dangling over his head by a single, slender horsehair. He watched the perplexed colonel and wondered exactly what his back did look like.

At last the colonel lifted his head, his expression grim. "I think that to let you walk away from this would not be justice, Dr. Buchanan."

Beth exhaled sharply. "Colonel, please—"

The colonel lifted one hand sharply to cut her off. "Let me finish. I can see the weight of the guilt on you, doctor. I think to let you walk away would leave you bearing this guilt. I am going to insist that you spend the next year—"

Alex stiffened his spine as his heart plunged. A year in prison. He could do that. He'd willingly pay the price for his cowardice. But the shame he'd bring on Beth and her family was terrible. He could never ask her to wait. He could—

"—serving as the doctor on this base."

Alex's hopes soared. "Yes, I'd serve you well, sir." Then Alex grimaced. "There. . .uh. . .there are no more wars looming, are there?"

The colonel's stern face lifted into a smile. "No, things have gotten purely peaceful around Fort Union these days. Unless my wife doesn't get the ingredients that she needs to do her baking. Then there's shooting trouble."

Alex smiled. Then he laughed. "Well, I'll be glad to make runs with the supply wagon to prevent that from happening."

They all laughed, more from relief than from the quality of Alex's joke.

A loud rap on the door brought the laughter to an end.

"Come in," the colonel called out.

"I've got a telegraph, sir." A young soldier entered, saluting smartly. "It has to do with this case, so I brought it in."

"Let me see it." McGarritt extended his hand.

The private rushed forward and handed the slip of paper to the fort commander.

Reading quietly for a few seconds, McGarritt raised his eyes and studied first Alex then Clay. At last, focused on Clay, he said, "Well, whom exactly did you send that wire to, Major McClellen?"

"I sent several wires, including—well, I served for a time with Colonel Miles in the Civil War. He's the man who gave me the battlefield promotion to major. I've kept in touch with him over the years."

"And Colonel Miles has kept in touch with many other people. Including the president—the man I was just back East to visit. This is sent directly from President Arthur. Captain Buchanan has been given a full pardon."

Beth gasped and flung her arms around Alex's neck. He couldn't take his eyes off the colonel, waiting for the man to overrule the president.

"It says here that President Buchanan was a distant relative of yours, too, young man. I see no notice of that on your military record."

Alex looked from the colonel to Clay. "I never talk about that. I didn't know him. And I was too young to vote for him. But I know for a fact that my dad didn't vote for my great-uncle James. Father always said it was his uncle's fault we fought the Civil War."

"Your father, who owned a railroad?" The colonel lifted the papers from his desk and waved then at Alex.

Beth jerked in surprise and turned to glare at him. "Your pa owned a railroad? You've never mentioned that."

Alex shrugged. "I defied him to become a doctor. He wanted me in the family business. He made it so hard for me, with all his connections, I couldn't find work. So I joined the army and headed west."

"Well, your family is looking for you, and there's a part of his company waiting for you back East."

"I don't want it, and I don't want to trade on my father's wealth or my great-uncle's political connections or even my wounds to avoid taking responsibility for what I've done. President Buchanan was something of a family embarrassment anyway. My father always called him a muttonhead."

The colonel gasped and Alex winced.

Why had he said that? What if the colonel was friends with Uncle James? What if—

"I was in the military when President Buchanan was in office, young man." The colonel's eyes flashed and Alex's stomach sank. Then the flash turned to a twinkle. "He *was* a muttonhead."

"I asked a few questions in my telegraphs," Clay said. "I found the truth and I didn't see any harm in mentioning that your family had served this country honorably for generations. And that includes you, son."

"I'll take whatever punishment you think is fair, colonel."

"Are you sure you don't want to go back and claim your share of the railroad, Alex?"

Alex smiled at Beth and lifted her fingers to his lips. "I don't want to run a railroad."

"Why not?" Beth looked from his eyes to where his kiss brushed her hand.

"Because I'm a doctor."

★ Thirty-four ★

Luther swung the ax and the cord of wood snapped in half from that single blow.

Mandy watched out her front door and resisted the urge to take the ax, apologize again for her husband, and chop the wood herself.

Sidney had tried over the winter. Never with a very good attitude, but he'd managed his share of bleeding blisters. He still wasn't easy about the job like Luther and Buff, but for a while Mandy had thought he was coming along.

Then spring had arrived and Sidney had gone back to mining.

Too often he wasn't here. He didn't ride into Helena anymore, but he'd taken to leaving for days at a time. Mandy had never seen the hole her husband was digging. Sidney was secretive and hostile if Luther or Buff offered to come along.

Mandy was fed up with his meager efforts to be a homesteader. The life didn't suit him, and it was time he admitted that and admitted there was no gold.

It was time because—Mandy rested her hand on her still-flat belly—because if they left now, they could be back in Texas before she got so big it was uncomfortable to travel.

She looked into the woods, wondering how long he'd be gone

this time. It was already nearly a week.

When he returned, she'd tell him about the baby and then she'd tell him she wanted her ma. The spring had brought several letters including news of Beth's marriage and that Beth was living at a fort with her doctor husband.

Mandy wanted to hear the whole story. And she wanted her sister to deliver her baby.

The little colt, now six months old, galloped around the corral, so black he gleamed, so big and graceful it made Mandy's breath catch to watch him. It made her think of the colt's sire. She could see a perfect copy of that magnificent stallion in the little guy. Except this little one was a friendly cuss. Mandy had gentled him and coaxed him into good behavior.

And it made her think about the stallion's owner. Tom Linscott. He wouldn't come for the baby. Belle Harden would. But the fact that Mandy occasionally caught herself longing for Tom to come, and swamped with guilt at the very idea, was a powerful reason to get far away from this country.

Belle would be here soon to take her baby home. Mandy would wait for Belle, and then she and Sidney would head for Texas. If only Sidney would agree.

Mandy knew that Sidney didn't want to go back. Mainly because he was afraid of Pa. But eventually Sidney would come around. And maybe the baby would be the thing that would finally persuade him. After all, nothing held them here.

Fretting to think of the job she had ahead of her to coax Sidney back toward Texas, Mandy looked away from Luther so he wouldn't see her scowl.

And that's when she saw Sidney racing out of the woods on horseback, a huge grin splitting his face. Sidney swung down from his horse and ran toward Mandy, jumping and yelling while he ran. He looked as happy as a man who'd just found—

"Gold!"

Mandy heaved a sigh of relief, glad to see that beautiful smile on Sidney's face. "Yes, I know you enjoy hunting for gold, but—"

"I found gold, Mandy." Sidney kept sprinting and grabbed her around the waist, hoisted her into the air, and spun her around.

In her whirling vision, Mandy saw Luther watching. Luther knew how badly she dreamed of going back to Texas. Luther wasn't all that fond of the brutal cold either. He'd promised to drop hints to Sidney about Texas. In fact, he'd promised to take Mandy if Sidney wouldn't.

"Y–you're saying you found a gold mine?"

"We're rich, Mandy." Sidney's smile faded and he glanced over his shoulder as if he suspected Luther of overhearing. "I'm not going to take anyone with me. I'll ride out and do the mining on the sly until I've—I've. . .uh. . .dug every ounce of gold out of that mine. Then I'll make one fast trip with it. I'll find a secure bank. Somewhere settled."

Sidney's eyes shifted left and right. He reminded Mandy of a rat she'd cornered in the barn one cold morning. "I don't want to tell anyone until the gold is safe, or others will come for it. Steal my gold."

Swallowing hard, Sidney suddenly looked straight at Mandy. "I probably shouldn't have even told you." His arms dropped from around her waist and he stepped back. "I should have handled the whole thing, gotten the gold somewhere safe, and then told you about it."

"Sidney, I won't tell anyone. Who would I tell?" Mandy thought of Belle Harden. Quite possibly the only person Mandy would see all year. She hadn't even ridden into Helena since the day they'd ridden out here with the Hardens.

"Yeah, yeah sure. And you're my wife. You can't steal my gold. A wife belongs to her husband. So whatever you have is mine anyway."

"So, once you get the gold mined and take it to wherever you decide, I think—" Mandy knew he wasn't going to like this. "I think we should go back to Texas, Sidney. I–I'm going to have a ba—"

"Texas?" Sidney shook his head and sneered. "No. This is my

state. I can be a powerful man in this state. I can *own* this state if I want."

"You mean like buy a ranch? We could buy a ranch back in Texas. I'd like to see my folks. And if you get all the gold, then there's nothing left here for us. Texas—"

"I said no." Sidney glared at her.

"Maybe I could go alone then."

"You're not going anywhere."

"But you're not here anyway, Sidney. You could come when you're ready. You could join me."

"You'll do as you're told." Sidney grabbed her forearm and jerked her against him. "You'll be a decent wife. You'll make me proud for once in your life. Get some clothes that don't shame me."

He'd always been petulant. Even childish. And she saw that expression, one she hated. But there was more now. Arrogance she'd never seen before. Greed. A feverish gleam in his eye.

He'd been so happy when he'd ridden in here. She felt as if his anger now was her fault. But it *wasn't*. That suspicious look, the greed, those had come over him before she'd said a word. This wasn't her fault.

"This is our place." He jabbed a finger toward the ground that separated them.

Suddenly, to Mandy, it was a chasm.

"This is our land." He spread his arms wide, his eyes hungry as he looked around, as if he wanted to own it all. "We're staying." One slash of his hands ended the conversation.

He wheeled around and headed for his horse. As he swung up, the horse sidestepped and Sidney clung to the saddle horn, still not comfortable in the saddle. "I'm the head of this house, Mandy. I expect some obedience from you. Some *respect*. A little *gratitude*. I'll be back, and you'd better be here, wife."

Mandy caught herself rubbing the little callus on her finger. She had her rifle on her back as always. The coldness that came over her in times of trouble, or when she was on the hunt, sleeted through her veins. She hated the cold. Truth was, she was terrified of that cold.

Someday it might freeze solid and never thaw.

"We're rich!" Sidney laughed and spurred his horse in the direction of Helena.

Mandy had no idea where he was going. And only in the most dutiful way did she even care.

Mandy hugged the cold tight to her soul, fearing it and also glad, because she was sure the instant the cold left her, the ice in her chest would melt and she'd be left with a broken, bleeding heart.

★ Thirty-five ★

The driver shouted over the thundering hooves of his four horses. He'd been shouting at the poor horses for days.

Beth was tempted to swing out the door, clamber onto the top of the stage, and beat the man to within an inch of his life for the way he pushed his horses. And it didn't pass unnoticed that Beth was contemplating violence against every man within her reach.

It had been a long trip home.

She glared at Alex, out like a light on the seat across from her. They were alone in the stagecoach, which was a mercy. The man hadn't bathed in days. Neither had she in all honesty. And they both reeked.

They'd planned to take the train all the way to Mosqueros, but there'd been a derailment, and the train was stopped for a time. Riding home on the stage had seemed like a wonderful idea, fresh air, sunshine, horses,

She realized with a sudden start that the stage was picking up speed on the downward slope. Not a good sign. She also realized she hadn't heard that loudmouthed driver holler at the poor horses for a full minute. That was a first for this ill-advised trip.

She looked at her sleeping husband and shook her head. The man was at the end of his rope, and that was a fact. He'd hardly slept for the last month as he'd dealt with all his father's business in Boston and done a fair job of reacquainting himself with his ridiculously large family.

Beth had loved every minute of it. But even more, she loved getting to come home to Texas.

She'd given serious consideration to postponing her arrival in Mosqueros by a long time, with a side trip to see Mandy. Beth had heard that Mandy's baby girl would be all the way grown up by the time Beth got to see her. And Mandy had built a nice new house. Beth didn't know much more than that, but there was an undercurrent of unhappiness in Mandy's letters. They were well disguised, but Beth could read between the lines of the cheerful letters. Mandy was lonely for family. Alex had forbidden the trip and Beth had gone along, being a practical, intelligent woman. She was in no condition to ride all the way around the country.

The stage picked up more speed and there was only silence from the brute of a driver. There must be trouble.

Deciding to let Alex sleep, since she was better equipped to help in the event of stagecoach-related trouble of any kind, she fought with the latches on the stagecoach window and poked her head out the door...to see the lax arm of the driver, hanging over the side.

The man was obviously incapacitated. Which meant, on this long downhill run, along a narrow twisting trail with cliffs at nearly every turn, no one was driving this stage.

She didn't give it a second thought. She slipped out the window, grabbed the roof of the stage, and swung herself up. She landed with a thud on the top, annoyed at how graceless she'd gotten with the passing months. Well, that couldn't be helped. She scooted to the front and, with a scowl at the unconscious driver who lay sprawled across the seat, grabbed him by the neck of his sweat-stained broadcloth shirt and hauled him onto the roof. She slid into the driver's seat, caught the reins, which had mercifully not fallen to the ground, and shouted, "Whoa!"

The horses tried to oblige, but the stage was rolling along at a fast clip.

Beth threw on the brake, putting all her strength into leaning on the long wooden handle. Shouting, calling to the horses to fight the weight of the coach.

They began to make progress slowing the fast, downward motion.

Dead ahead, Beth saw a hairpin turn skirting the bluff, falling away to a sheer cliff on the right while it rose up straight on the left. They'd never make the turn on this narrow road at this speed.

Beth shouted louder at the poor horses. Maybe they were so used to being shouted at they didn't respond to anything else. But she liked to think she had the most soothing shout of anyone in horse-dom.

She twisted the reins around her wrist to take up the length and put her now considerable weight into braking the stage. They weren't going to make it. The trail narrowed. Their chance to throw themselves out before the stage went over the cliff was going to be past. She sucked in a breath to yell at Alex, when suddenly she had the strength of ten.

Alex's arms came around her as he dropped onto the seat from behind her.

"Which one, the brake or the reins?"

She knew exactly what he meant. "The brake."

He took over and had a lot more brute strength to donate to the cause. The stage immediately lost some of its forward momentum.

Beth was able to work the reins better, urging the horses to cooperate until they were nearly sitting back on their heels, fighting the heavy stagecoach.

The stage slowed. . .then slowed again. The curve ahead came nearer and nearer. They were still going too fast.

One of the horses neighed in panic as the sheer cliff had the horse looking straight out over space. The horses and Beth, Alex on the brake, took the corner. They could make it, if only the coach didn't tip.

Beth sawed at the reins, and all four horses, their heads up, took the curve, staying so close to the left side the stage door scraped against the wall of the bluff.

Skidding and sliding, the stage careened, tilted to the right. The wheels on the left lifted up off the ground. The coach canted.

"We're not going to make it." Beth prepared to grab Alex and somehow the driver, too, and jump.

"Throw your weight left!" Alex shouted, pinned to the right side by his need to hang on to the brake.

Beth leaned so hard and fast to the left she nearly lost her seat.

The stage wobbled, yawed upward right, then suddenly snapped down onto all four wheels. The curve straightened and leveled off. With the growl of wooden wheels scraping on rocky soil, they brought the stage to a halt.

Dust swallowed them up. Beth concentrated on breathing for just a second and swallowed a lungful of dirt.

In the blinding cloud of Texas topsoil, Alex rasped into her ear, "Why didn't you wake me up?"

Beth turned and was close enough to look right into her husband's eyes.

He was only inches away, surrounding her, his legs along the length of hers. His arms, now that the stage was stopped and the brake locked, wrapped around her. Although, judging from the fire in his eyes, this might not be a hug so much as a handy chance to throttle her.

"I didn't realize how serious the situation was until I was up here."

"And you got up here how? Exactly?" Alex scowled.

"I just swung myself up. You know I can do that."

Alex's arms slid from where they were wrapped around her shoulders, down to her protruding belly. "I didn't know you could do that now that you're almost ready to have a baby."

"It was a little more trouble than usual, but I managed." Beth realized several things at once, primary among them she wasn't in the mood to be scolded by her husband. She leaned forward and kissed him. "I'm sorry. I should have at least told you the driver was in trouble."

The next thing she realized was that the stage driver needed help. "I wonder what happened to him." Beth studied the man who was stirring. She saw a trickle of blood on his head that looked like... "Is that bruise on his face in the shape of a horseshoe?"

Alex released Beth and clambered up to examine the man.

Beth looked at the team. "I suppose one of the horses threw a shoe and it knocked him insensible."

And the last thing she realized was that she was going to have this baby a little sooner than she'd expected. "Can you handle things up there on the roof, Alex? It's not that far to Mosqueros and I'd like to get on into town." Truth be told, Beth was seriously tempted to turn the stage off the trail and head overland to her ma's house. But it might constitute a crime, what with the mail pouch and all.

"Go ahead. I'll just stop the bleeding and we can ride up here. It's only a couple of more miles and he can lie flat out here better than inside anyway." Alex didn't even look at her, as he was so busy tending the man. And he wasn't looking to Beth for strength either. He had his own these days. Strength of will, the strength of his health, and strength of soul. He'd made his peace with God and man, the past and future and—himself.

Beth loosed the brake and called to the horses, which all four moved out with a good will, considering what they'd been through in the last few minutes.

It was only minutes later that Beth heard stirring behind her and glanced back to see Alex easing the awake but groggy driver through the open door of the stage.

Then Alex came up and sat beside her on the narrow seat. "So how far apart are the contractions?"

Beth smiled. The man was too sensitive for his own good. "I just had the first one a few minutes ago. My water broke, though. I guess it's time."

"It's a little early." Alex didn't sound too worried. The baby wasn't early by much. "I know you're tough, but you really should have sent me up here to do this job. You're going to have to cut back once the baby's here."

"Of course I'll cut back. I've been cutting back since we first found out I was expecting, haven't I? Just like you've told me to?"

Alex snorted in a completely rude way, but Beth didn't take exception, since, if anything, she'd been working harder than ever before.

Then they drove into Mosqueros.

Beth saw the parson first thing. "Hi." She shouted and waved.

Parson Radcliff made a beeline for them, his arms loaded with his now almost two-year-old son, the one Beth and Alex had delivered their first second back in Mosqueros. "Beth, Alex, welcome home. We have missed you."

"Parson, could you find someone to ride out to the ranch and fetch my ma into town?" Beth rested one hand on her currently rigid stomach. "The baby's coming and I'd like Ma to be here for it."

The parson looked momentarily stunned, then nodded. "Can I help you down from there?"

Alex had already jumped down, rounded the stage, and was reaching up to assist her. "I've got her, Parson. But the real stage driver is inside the stage and I need to get him and Beth to our office."

As the parson hurried off the do their bidding, Alex turned suddenly. Since Beth was just ready to let him catch her, she almost fell to the ground. Fortunately, she had kept a firm grip on the seat and was able to scamper down herself with little trouble.

"Is the office still there?" Alex looked at the row of buildings lining the town. Beth's eyes followed in the same direction and she smiled to see that, yes, Mosqueros had saved the doctor's office for them.

Alex turned back, reaching up, looking up to help her, then started and dropped his eyes to where she stood beside him. "You should have waited for me to help you down. You could have fallen."

Beth didn't roll her eyes through sheer practice, born of being married to a man she reckoned. "You get the driver." She patted Alex on the arm. "I'll go see to finding a place to rest him and myself."

Alex nodded and Beth walked on. She realized that while Alex liked to observe the niceties of manners and liked to scold her for overdoing, the truth was he treated her with more respect than Beth had ever known possible. He didn't even hesitate to let her walk off alone. He knew she could handle most anything and, perhaps more importantly, knew that she'd be honest if she couldn't handle it.

She walked toward home, pausing to let another labor pain come and go. Probably not even five minutes between them. This baby would come fast, and Beth had a lot to do before she could lie down.

Alex caught up to her before she reached the office and, with one arm slung around the bleeding stage driver, who leaned heavily, beat Beth to the door and opened it for her, allowing her to proceed.

She smiled as she passed him.

And he smiled back.

She'd never seen one second of regret that Alex had sold his share of his father's railroad and walked away from his chance for a vast amount of power. He'd done it now, just as he'd done it in his youth, to meet the calling God had laid upon his heart.

Her husband had survived torment and nightmares and emerged a strong, wise man of faith.

A man with his own strength, who knew hers, who accepted and loved his wife and worked joyfully beside a doctor in petticoats.

About the Author

Mary Connealy is a Christy Award finalist. She is the author of the Lassoed in Texas series, which includes *Petticoat Ranch, Calico Canyon,* and *Gingham Mountain.* She has also written a romantic cozy mystery trilogy, *Nosy in Nebraska;* and her novel *Golden Days* is part of the *Alaska Brides* anthology. You can find out more about Mary's upcoming books at www.maryconnealy.com and www.mconnealy.blogspot.com.

Mary lives on a Nebraska ranch with her husband, Ivan, and has four grown daughters: Joslyn (married to Matt), Wendy, Shelly (married to Aaron), and Katy. And she is the grandmother of one beautiful granddaughter, Elle.

Mary loves to hear from her readers. You may visit her at these sites: www.mconnealy.blogspot.com, www.seekerville.blogspot.com, and www.petticoatsandpistols.com. Write to her at mary@maryconnealy.com.

Other Books by Mary Connealy

Lassoed in Texas series:

Petticoat Ranch
Calico Canyon
Gingham Mountain

Montana Marriages series:

Montana Rose
The Husband Tree
Wildflower Bride

Cowboy Christmas
Nosy in Nebraska (a cozy mystery collection)